life with friends

THE KALEIDOSCOPE GIRLS

ALSO BY KIMBERLY DIEDE

THE KALEIDOSCOPE GIRLS SERIES
BETTER WITH FRIENDS (BOOK 1)
SUNSHINE AND FRIENDS (BOOK 2)
FIVE GOLDEN FRIENDS (BOOK 3)
GIFT OF FRIENDS (BOOK 4)
LIFE WITH FRIENDS (BOOK 5)

GIFT OF WHISPERING PINES SERIES
WHISPERING PINES (BOOK 1)
TANGLED BEGINNINGS (BOOK 2)
REBUILDING HOME (BOOK 3)
CAPTURING WISHES (BOOK 4)
CHOOSING AGAIN (BOOK 5)
CELIA'S GIFTS (BOOK 6)
CELIA'S LEGACY (BOOK 7)

life with friends

THE KALEIDOSCOPE GIRLS

BOOK FIVE

Kimberly Diede

ENDLESS RIPPLE PRESS

Cover by Carpe Librum Book Design – www.carpelibrumbookdesign.com.

Ebook ISBN 978-1-961305-21-2

Paperback ISBN 978-1-961305-22-9

Large Print ISBN 978-1-961305-23-6

For the friends who help us
put the pieces back together

Chapter One

Fiji Islands

J ACKIE LEANED FORWARD TO stretch the tight muscles of her lower back, trailing her fingertips along the surface of the sea as waves buffeted her shins and knees. The cool salt water felt like heaven to her sore feet after trudging through four airports, three planes, and two hours of deep cleaning inside Matt and Renee's cottage.

She was ready for the relaxing part of this vacation to begin.

How often during recent months had she closed her eyes and imagined the exquisite sensation of ocean waters, swirling around her body to ease the ache in her heart, while the squawking of seagulls drowned out the voices in her head?

She straightened, and stood as still as the ocean's force would allow as she tried to take in the majesty of it all.

A strong breeze carried the tang of brine, evoking the long-forgotten memory of her as a girl, chasing her big brother along the shore of a faraway body of water. They'd hopped over waves crashing against a rock-strewn shoreline. Her parents stood nearby; her dad's left arm was slung casually over her mother's shoulders, while her mother looped her right arm as far around his broad waist as she could. They'd laughed, watching their children's silly antics. Physical displays of affection between her parents had always been uncommon, and it gave the moment weight in Jackie's memories.

A rogue wave knocked against her, pushing her out of her past, and she had to tug a tangled strand of her hair free of the new necklace around her throat. She grimaced when she noticed the way her wind-whipped hair matched the silver chain.

The necklace was a thoughtful Mother's Day gift from her twin daughters.

Aside from that long-ago family vacation to Maine, Jackie couldn't remember any other time her father had visited an ocean. It was sad, because even as a young girl, she'd sensed the way the salt air seemed to put him at ease, as if the white-capped waves had the power to sweep away the tension that normally pulsed out of the man.

Her father had run out of time to do many of the things he'd put off for too long.

Jackie hoped that wouldn't happen to her, too.

"There you are! We wondered where you'd disappeared to."

Jackie glanced over her shoulder at her friend, hopping barefoot across the hot sand toward her, sandals dangling from one hand.

"Hey, Renee. I couldn't wait any longer to put my feet in the water. Imagining this helped keep me going these last few months."

Renee dropped her sandals and wrapped her arm around Jackie's waist, and they faced the horizon together. "You've earned this, Jackie. And no more working. I promise. From here on out, it'll be nothing but relaxing, wine, and catching up."

Jackie laughed. "You're forgetting about the hiking and parasailing we've got planned."

"Shh," Renee hissed, giving Jackie's waist a squeeze before dropping her arm and reaching into the shallows at their feet. She pulled a perfectly round sand dollar out of the water. "Don't let Kit hear you. We need to keep the parasailing excursion a secret from her until it's too late for her to back out. Remember how she hated the idea of ziplining until she tried it?"

Jackie looked around them at the otherwise deserted beach. "She's not even down here."

"Sounds carry a long way on this wind. Can't be too careful."

Both women turned back to the water. Jackie pulled the salty air deep into her lungs and held it there for an extra beat before expelling it in a rush.

"You doing okay?" Renee asked, a hint of concern in her voice. "I know it can feel like the rest of the world has moved on without you, when you're still caught in a web of grief after losing someone you love. At least that's how I felt after Jim died."

Jackie considered Renee's question carefully instead of giving the immediate, almost obligatory response that she was fine. Death was never a comfortable subject, but Renee deserved an honest answer.

She shrugged as she struggled to answer, and her right hand came up to finger the penny-sized locket at the end of her silver chain. "At this very minute, standing in the South Pacific next to you, Renee, I feel at peace. A little melancholy, too, but I can accept that Dad is gone. He didn't want to live like that anymore."

Renee handed her the dripping silver dollar. Jackie let go of the pendant to take the shell and immediately noted the temperature shift in her hand from warm to cold.

"I know it was hard to watch him decline like that," Renee said. She brushed her hand down the leg of her denim shorts. "I didn't know your father well, but it sounds like he was a force, back in the day."

"That he was," Jackie confirmed, her mind conjuring up various memories of her father as he strolled through the halls of the high school, a principal both respected and feared by his students. She chuckled. "I still struggle to picture our sweet Annie filling Dad's shoes at my old senior high. He was such a big man, in both stance and presence. Annie is the opposite."

Renee kicked a tiny splash of water up when a wave hit high on her thigh. "Annie may be short, but I bet she can hold her own with her students. I've seen that woman get mad. She could have intimidated me when I was a kid." She laughed. "She intimidates me *now*."

"You're right," Jackie conceded. "Annie isn't a pushover either. And by the way, she looks great, doesn't she? That exercise plan she's on with Henry must be working. I thought the curves she developed after having three kiddos were cute, but she's complained about her weight for years. She told me she's happy to have lost ten pounds recently."

Another sizable wave barreled toward them, and Renee grabbed Jackie's forearm to pull her farther up onto the sand to avoid getting drenched. Then she touched a fingertip to Jackie's necklace. "That's sure pretty. I didn't notice it before. Is it new?"

Jackie held the pendant away from her décolletage and had to squint down at it as she struggled to find the tiny clasp to open it. "Yes. Hailey and Mack gave it to me last month for Mother's Day. It's quite unique, actually."

The cover of the locket finally popped open, and she angled it so Renee could see inside.

"Oh! I love that tiny picture of your dad."

Jackie's heart skipped a beat as she gazed down at her father's once ruddy complexion. This was the smile she'd worked so hard to earn through the years. She tapped the other half of the locket with her fingernail. "The girls had some of his ashes melted into this side."

Renee straightened in surprise. "His ashes? In your necklace?"

Jackie sighed. "I know. That was my initial reaction, too. I wasn't sure I wanted to have a piece of my father hanging around my neck. But my girls assured me that lots of people find comfort in jewelry like this, so I agreed to wear it to see how it would make me feel. I've grown used to it now. It's a way for me to keep Dad close to my heart."

"I've never heard of ashes-infused jewelry. I'm not sure how I feel about it. But props to your girls for being so creative."

Jackie clicked the locket closed and let it fall back against her skin. "Annie's son, Colton, actually suggested it to Mack at Dad's service. He works at that funeral home, remember?"

A whistle cut through the air, capturing both women's attention. They spun toward the black boulders obscuring the sand pathway that led up to the cottage Renee's husband still owned, despite his moving back stateside to marry her.

"Renee? Jackie? Where are you guys? We're getting hungry!" Annie's voice floated down to them.

"I told you sound carries," Renee said with a wry smile.

Jackie rolled her shoulders to dispel the weighty topic of her father, then motioned toward the path back up to their friends on top of the bluff. "We better go. You know how *hangry* Annie can get. Dipping my toes in the sea was enough for now. The day after tomorrow will be a full-on beach day."

Renee nodded and tipped down for her sandals. Jackie noticed the way her friend's eyes snagged on her locket again, her expression still hesitant. Jackie understood. It had taken her time to get used to the idea of wearing her father's ashes around her neck, too, but now it truly comforted her.

The gifted piece was a constant reminder that those we love never truly leave us.

Behind the cottage, five metal folding chairs circled a fire ring sporting a neat pile of logs. The late-afternoon temperature had Jackie wondering if it ever cooled down enough here to relax around that fire. The chairs had to be blistering hot in the sun.

"How is that metal not burning the back of your legs?" she asked Lynette. The light cotton skirt her friend wore couldn't offer much protection.

Lynette wagged a half-empty bottle of water in her direction. "I splashed it with water, then toweled it off. Made it bearable."

"You wasted some of our bottled water to cool off a chair? I thought we talked about how we're low on water and will have to buy more tomorrow."

Lynette rolled her eyes. "I didn't use *this*." She shook the bottle at Jackie again. "There's a rain barrel on the side of the house. Jeez, I thought *Annie* was the only one who gets crabby when she's hungry."

Annie, who'd looked like she was discussing something of significance with Kit, glanced toward the other three women. "Who says I'm crabby?"

Renee dropped her shoes onto the scraggly tufts of sea grass at her feet and slipped them on, holding her palms up to quiet everyone. "It's been a long day, and aside from the welcome basket Matt's friend left for us, there's no food in the house."

"The wine is tasty, even though it's warm," Kit said, holding up her plastic cup as if making a toast. "We'll have to leave that guy a thank-you note. There's still half a bottle in the fridge if you want some, Renee. Remember, you're supposed to *not* play the role of hostess on this trip, even though we're staying at your cottage."

"I know, but since I'm the only one who knows where things are around here, I need to provide a little guidance. And while wine sounds nice, we should eat before it gets too late. Then we can come back here, enjoy a fire, and finish off the bottle. Does anyone not like lobster rolls? The kids and I found this darling little restaurant down the road from here the first time we came to Fiji. It's really more like a shack, but their food is delicious. It's a favorite of Matt's, too."

Annie stood and donned the pair of flip-flops resting next to her chair. "I've never had a lobster roll, but I'm willing to eat anything but a horse right now."

Lynette and Kit got to their feet, too, and the group made their way back through the small house, grabbing wallets and phones. Jackie watched and listened, enjoying her chatty friends and their happy voices. The lighthearted atmosphere was exactly what she needed after too much time alone, back at her parents' quiet house in Ruby Shores.

Tugging another graying strand of hair loose from her necklace, she vowed to focus on this moment and the banter of her lifelong chosen sisters. She'd pick back up on the business of settling her father's estate when she returned home; she doubted her brother or mother would have magically handled anything in her absence. They hadn't helped up to this point, so why would either start now?

"Which do you prefer, Jackie? Lobster or shrimp?"

Jackie, the last of the group to leave the little house, pulled the door shut. Renee punched a button on the electronic lock and skipped down the three wooden steps to the crushed shell pathway. She led them to a second path covered in gravel that ran alongside the road in front of the house.

"I haven't eaten enough lobster to know which I prefer, but today seems like the perfect day to compare," Jackie said, taking another extra deep breath. This time, the salty air had an oily undercurrent to it, as if a crew had recently repaired the blacktop surface of the road. "How far is it to the restaurant?"

Renee turned to the right. "Remember, I said it's actually more of a shack than a restaurant, but it isn't far," their leader threw back over her shoulder. "Maybe a fifteen-minute stroll."

Annie and Lynette fell into step behind her, followed by Kit and Jackie. A truck rumbled by, not going particularly fast, but the engine belched, cutting off the conversation and spewing exhaust into the air.

Lynette waved a hand in front of her nose. "And here I thought I'd left behind the stench of automobiles and trucks when I escaped New York City for the last time."

Jackie caught Kit's eye. Did Lynette really believe she was done with the city? "How did your consulting gig at your old company go, Lynette?" she asked.

Lynette shrugged. "Fine, I guess. It's funny how fast a person can feel out of touch after leaving a place. At least I did. I think I helped them out of a couple of thorny situations that resulted from the new buyers' lack of experience, but by my last week, I was ready to get out of there. January through the end of May gave me enough time to say goodbye to both the people and the places that meant something to me when I lived in the city. When Donna and I first left, it was the height of the pandemic, and I didn't feel like I had any closure."

Another truck passed, going in the opposite direction.

Jackie preferred the natural beauty down on the beach to this busy stretch, but she supposed Fiji was like any other tourist draw. Not everything could be postcard-perfect scenes and quiet, deserted beaches. People required commerce.

"Do you think you're really and truly done with New York now, Lynette?" she asked, watching her friend's back as the group made its way toward an evening meal alongside the ocean.

Renee must have stopped, because Lynette and Annie pulled up, too.

"I really do. I think I'm just a small-town girl at heart." Lynette sent Jackie a wink over her shoulder.

Both Kit and Jackie laughed.

"Not likely," Jackie countered.

Renee pointed to their right. "Annie, you said you wanted to bring some special seashells home for your little granddaughter. Well, you'll find the best shells on this entire island down that path. At least according to Matt. That's what he told me the first time he walked me from the lobster-roll shack to his cottage. I haven't actually visited the beach at the end of that path yet. I keep thinking I will on one of these trips."

Annie clapped her hands. "Nora would love that! It's hard to believe she's already reached those terrible-twos."

The women continued on their way.

"Remember how excited we all were when you first told us your Ava was pregnant?" Renee said. "We were in Maui, and we all dropped a ridiculous amount of money in that cute little baby shop on Front Street."

"It was a cause for celebration!" Lynette said. "One of the Kaleidoscope Girls was going to be a grandma. *So* fun."

"And I'm *still* the only grandma around here," Annie said, twirling her finger in the air. "The rest of you better get a move on it."

Lynette shook her head. "Don't look at me."

"Me either," Kit was quick to chime in. "If Isaac ever fathers a child, I'll happily wear the title of Grandma, or maybe Nana, even though we aren't blood-related. But he's only eighteen. Let's not push it."

Renee laughed. "How about you, Jackie? Your girls are twenty-four now, right? Do you see either of them having kids soon?"

"Bite your tongue. I hope they both do lots of living before either becomes a mother. And you're one to talk, Renee. Your kids are in their twenties, too. They could be parents."

Either Renee stubbed her toe on something or the idea threw her off balance, because she stumbled a few steps before righting herself. "Let's just say I'm enjoying Annie being our token grandma in the group for now."

As the chitchat continued, Jackie eyed the variety of cottages and small houses alongside their path. Some looked so weather-beaten and worn that she could imagine old, retired sea captains in yellow slickers living inside. Others appeared to be brand-new, with stickers still adhered to windowpanes and dirt yards that lacked any vegetation. All were conservative in size, making her wonder whether building covenants or costs were preventing larger builds. Landscaping, when there was some, also varied. Some homes, like the one they were staying in, sported empty window boxes and scruffy grass, giving them a lonely quality. Others had lush gardens, overflowing with vibrant blooms and greenery, accented with quirky statues and unique shells. The reason for the differences was probably rentals versus family homes. Renee had said Matt rented out his cottage once in a while, too.

"Here we go," Renee said, guiding their small group off the path and onto a small parking area.

As Renee had warned, the tiny, ramshackle building, its red paint peeling, didn't look like a restaurant that served delectable food. But if the length of the lines stretching back from both serving windows was any indication, looks could be deceiving.

Annie moaned in dismay at the additional delay before they could eat.

They joined one line and continued to catch up on each other's lives as they waited. The only time the five of them had gotten together since their trip to Whispering Pines the previous summer had been for Jackie's father's funeral, and that didn't really count.

Jackie hoped there were many more girls' trips in their future—and very few funerals.

Because the eatery only served lobster rolls, coleslaw, and lemonade, the line moved much quicker than expected. She wouldn't have to pick between lobster and shrimp after all. All five women settled at a picnic table within ten minutes with their savory-smelling dinners on trays and a million-dollar view of a wide expanse of beach and ocean.

"When I was here with the kids, they practically inhaled their food and then headed for the beach," Renee said. "Other kids were around, and they both made a few temporary vacation friends. I doubt they've stayed in touch with any of them, but they sure had fun while we were here."

"I hope they didn't miss out on the chance to make lifelong friends like we all did at summer camp," Kit said, flicking a bug away from the rim of Renee's lemonade. "But you kept in touch with the *little friend* you made on that trip, didn't you, Renee?"

Renee laughed around her bite of lobster roll, then wiped her mouth with a crinkly paper napkin. "I guess I did. But I don't think Matt would appreciate being called my 'little friend.' "

"Tell us again how you guys met," Jackie prodded. Although her own love life was dismally bleak, it would be fun to hear about Renee's love story again.

She knew *Renee's* tale, at least, included a happily ever after.

Chapter Two

J ACKIE FASTENED HER SEATBELT and accepted a headset from their grizzled pilot, feeling nervous. She'd only ever flown in larger, commercial planes, so her pulse raced at the prospect of island-hopping in a tiny seaplane. She glanced at her friends to see if any of them were faring better.

Annie, always the adrenaline junkie of the group, kept shifting in her seat as if she couldn't wait to be airborne.

Kit, on the other hand, looked frozen, glued to her seat, eyes wide and fixated on the various controls on the seaplane's instrument panel as though trying to commit them to memory. As a lifelong scientist, her mind automatically evaluated variables and risks. She had likely taken one look at their elderly pilot and calculated a backup plan should the old geezer keel over at a thousand feet above the sea. Jackie hoped the breathtaking scenic views promised on the regional airline's website would whisk Kit out of her terrified thoughts and into their stunning surroundings. As Renee had reminded Jackie, it worked when they'd finally convinced Kit to zipline during their Maui trip. Hopefully she would eventually enjoy this, too.

"Thanks for setting this up, Jackie," Renee said, pulling her attention away from Kit's unease. She seemed more in line with Annie, more excited than nervous. "Matt doesn't love heights, so I could never convince him to do this, but it's something I've always wanted to experience. When we made the trek up to Nanuya Lailai Island the last time we were here, the ferry trip took hours."

The pilot fiddled with a variety of knobs and levers, and the roar of the engine suddenly cut Renee off. He gestured to the headset he wore without even bothering to turn back toward his five passengers. Jackie snapped her headset into place and wondered how many groups he flew between the islands each day. While this excursion promised to be a once-in-a-lifetime experience for her and her friends, it was just another day at the office for their pilot.

As she watched him execute the rest of his preflight routine—a routine that he'd probably completed hundreds, if not thousands, of times before—her mind drifted back to the corporate job that used to make up *her* day at the office. The one she'd walked away from four years earlier. Her actual office hadn't been much larger than the inside of this plane, and although low-lying clouds often scuttled past the window of that Chicago high-rise, there'd been no cockpit capable of granting her soul the freedom it sought.

Had she found that freedom with her next move? At first, her passion to match abandoned senior pets with the elderly had kept her motivated enough to fight through the headaches of building a new business. But lately, the heartaches inherent in the work itself were weighing her down.

Her gaze shifted from the pilot's back to Lynette, her one friend accustomed to building and selling passion projects. Lynette had poured many years and plenty of effort into the business she'd ultimately sold when it, too, became more of a pain than it was worth. Lynette could surely advise her whether she should consider the recent, surprising interest a larger competitor in the Minneapolis area had shown in her pet adoption company.

Jackie's headset crackled to life. Unlike commercial flights, where she often tuned out the safety instructions that she'd heard countless times through the years, she should probably pay attention this time. After all, the man transporting them between the tropical paradises below, and who held their lives in his hands, was just a stranger.

The seaplane's ascent was smooth and quick, unlike any takeoff she'd experienced before. Annie clapped in delight, then pointed toward the small window beyond her right elbow.

"Are those *dolphins*?" she asked, her excited voice sounding too loud through Jackie's headset.

Kit rolled her eyes and pulled the two halves of her headset away from her ears, then relaxed enough to bend toward Annie's window. She could never resist trying to spot animals in their natural habitat.

Jackie scanned the turquoise waters below through her own window, surprised at how low they still flew. "Is this the highest you'll take us?"

The pilot gave a brief nod. "Yup. You pay me for these scenic views. Don't want ya to miss anything. But don't worry. Haven't caught a wing in a wave for at least six weeks."

The way the man's shoulders shook with laughter, he almost had Jackie convinced that he was teasing. Kit, however, was no longer trying to look out Annie's window. She was back to being glued to her seat.

Jackie hoped organizing this day trip, to the island where a Hollywood studio had filmed a movie that was famous during their youth, wouldn't turn out to be a huge mistake.

Jackie bent down to adjust a strap on her hiking sandals. Lynette waited for her while Kit, Annie, and Renee continued on the sand-covered path.

"I still can't believe we're here. I keep expecting to catch the far-off thump of threatening drumbeats, or to stumble into the clearing where that terrifying stone face of my childhood nightmares still lives," Lynette said.

"I knew you'd be excited to visit the island where they filmed *The Blue Lagoon*! I swear you claimed it was your favorite movie for at least a year after we watched Annie's big sister's VHS copy. Patsy would have killed us if she knew we watched it while she and Annie's dad were off playing bridge that night."

"Best sleepover ever! None of us had ever seen nudity in a movie before!" Lynette laughed. "Remember how we used to take turns staying at each other's houses on weekends when we were in junior high? When we stayed at your house, we were always on our best behavior because we were all afraid of your dad."

"And I drank my first beer at *your* house," Jackie said, straightening. "Were we even thirteen?"

The two women resumed walking before their friends got too far ahead of them, but there was no real rush. The seaplane wouldn't be back to get them until four. Passengers from a large cruise ship, anchored offshore, crowded the beach. It was cooler in the shade, and they'd get plenty of beach and sun time tomorrow.

Lynette piled her long, silver curls atop her head and secured the mass with a thick black band from her wrist. "Donna was never much of a beer drinker, so it must have belonged to a boyfriend she'd let into our house. Do you remember how we always woke up to the best homemade caramel rolls when we stayed at Kit's grandparents' house?"

Jackie's stomach growled at the mention of Hazel's baking expertise. "Kit's aunt capitalized on that recipe when she opened the Crystal Café. I ordered a roll when I was back in Ruby Shores for our reunion a few years ago, and my mouth still waters just thinking about it. Hey, do you remember how Annie used to be so afraid that Kit's mom would show up when we stayed there? I never understood why she was so freaked out by the idea. Not much scares Annie. Back then or even now."

"I think Annie's sister came home drunk one too many times. Annie told me once that she hated how different Millie acted after she hooked up with a new group of friends in ninth or tenth grade. I know those two were close when they were young, but they grew apart."

Jackie spied a gorgeous red bloom, just off the path, and stopped to snap a picture with her phone. She had no idea what type of flower it was, but it was pretty enough that she might blow the image up and frame it to hang on a wall back home. "I haven't seen Millie in years. Have you?" she asked, her attention torn between their beautiful surroundings and their trip down memory lane.

Lynette waited patiently on the path. "As a matter of fact, I saw her a couple years ago at Thanksgiving. Remember when Donna and I came back to Ruby Shores? It was the same weekend we celebrated your fiftieth. Owen threw that party for you. Have you talked to him lately?"

"Nope," Jackie said, purposely keeping her answer short and sweet. She didn't want to talk about Owen. Nor did she care much about Millie; she'd never been fond of Annie's big sister, and she regretted asking about her. She'd rather talk about this breathtaking island and how lucky they were to be in Fiji. "Now I wish I'd have watched *The Blue Lagoon* again before coming here. I meant to, after I booked this day trip, but I never got around to it. How much do you remember about the movie?"

Lynette nodded, not seeming to mind the change of topic. "All I could remember about it was the sex and the surprise baby, so I got my hands on an old copy."

Satisfied that she'd captured a decent shot of the flower, Jackie shoved her phone back into the pocket of her shorts. She couldn't see her other three friends in front of them anymore, but as long as they stayed on the path, they'd meet up eventually. "Wait. What do you mean you found a *copy* of it? That movie is more than forty years old! Wouldn't it have been easier to find it streaming somewhere?"

"Maybe, but the marketing director at my old company is a movie buff. When I mentioned to him we planned to head to Fiji in June after I finished my consulting contract, he offered to lend me his DVD."

A mosquito the size of a quarter buzzed Jackie's ear and she swatted it away, thankful again for the bug spray Renee had brought along that seemed to do a decent job of keeping the flying pests at bay. Their hike would have been unbearable without it.

"Was it as good as you remembered? The movie, I mean."

Lynette shrugged beside her. "Honestly, I cringed a lot. We take for granted how much the production quality of shows has advanced through the years. In hindsight, I'm a little surprised that it was as popular as it was back then."

"I'm not. If I remember right, there was lots of nudity, even though Brooke Shields was awfully young at the time. Sex always sells, doesn't it? And hey, speaking of sex and sleepovers, do you remember that other sleepover we had at Annie's house? The night of our senior prom? I always suspected you and Storm had *heavy* sex that night! You guys were all over each other at the dance, and you were really late getting to Annie's house. We were all lucky her folks didn't catch you sneaking in after curfew."

"I suppose Storm did teach me lots more than that movie ever did," Lynette admitted as she kicked a stray palm frond off the path.

While Jackie wasn't interested in talking about Owen, she had no problem digging into Lynette's love life. "This is our second day in Fiji and I've waited this long to ask you about Storm. So spill it. Are things with him still as hot and heavy as they were when we were kids? Well, Storm never really seemed like a kid, even though he was only a year or two older than us, but you know what I mean."

Lynette snapped her fingers, then clapped her hands, as if trying to decide how best to respond. Jackie would understand if her friend felt reluctant to put complicated feelings related to an old flame into words—not that Owen was an "old flame," not in the same way that Storm was for Lynette—but Jackie was dying to know where things stood between the couple.

"Believe it or not," she finally said, "nothing physical has happened with Storm. At least not romantically. Not really. God, it's so hot!"

Jackie laughed. "The temperature or the topic? I saw the sparks ricocheting between you two at Whispering Pines last summer. I know you spent most of your time between then and now in New York City, but do you mean to tell me that the two of you didn't at least attempt to rekindle that old chemistry? He's single, too, isn't he?"

The path was approaching a clearing ahead, and Lynette slowed her steps, as if reluctant to proceed. It took Jackie only a moment to realize why.

"I doubt that stone façade that terrified you when we were kids is going to be around this corner. That ugly thing had to have been a movie prop," Jackie assured her. "Are you really going to tell me *nothing* about you and Storm?"

Lynette resumed their set pace but kept a close eye on what was ahead. "Fine. Renee probably already told you we went out for ice cream after we all returned from Whispering Pines. I know you four always have fun gossiping about me behind my back."

They entered the clearing, and Jackie was relieved that she'd been right in her assumption about the stone-faced creature. It wasn't there. She felt a twinge of guilt at Lynette's accusation. She wasn't wrong, but Jackie refused to acknowledge as much. "We don't gossip. Much. But tell me . . . did ice cream lead to anything else?"

"It gave us a chance to catch up, and eventually to me becoming his landlord. But no sessions of hot sex, I promise."

Lynette's proclamation disappointed Jackie, which surprised her. An independent observer of their conversation might speculate that Jackie had been secretly hoping that if Lynette could start up with Storm again, she wasn't too late with Owen. Then again, did she even want to have any kind of relationship with Owen after the stunt he'd pulled?

"Right," she said, forcing her attention back to Lynette. "You mentioned renting out your house when you asked if you could store some of your things in my garage."

Lynette nodded, then sank onto an outcropping of flat stones with a sigh. "We can afford to take ten, right? I'm surprised the others aren't here."

Jackie took a seat next to her. "Maybe they want to spend a little time near the water before our pilot picks us up. Tell me more about renting out your house."

Lynette extended her right leg and rolled her foot, stretching her ankle. "I'm a little surprised this thing isn't giving me some trouble. I'm hoping I can get through today without it buckling on me again."

Jackie bumped against her with a shoulder. "Quit stalling."

"I'm really not," Lynette said with a laugh. "Storm reached out after we got back from Whispering Pines. Then he swung by the house to pick me up. Donna wanted to talk to him. After that, we jumped in his truck and headed downtown for ice cream. Oh—I almost forgot. He dropped a kiss on the tip of my nose. But that was it. No more kissing after that."

Jackie flicked a tiny red spider off her leg with a shudder. "Disappointing."

"A little," Lynette agreed. "But we had a good visit. We'd both done lots of living between my high school graduation and last summer. He has an ex and a young son. He was more willing to talk about his work than his family, but he shared enough for me to gather that his wife, or I should say *ex*-wife, is younger. Their son—his name is Phoenix—spends most of his time with her. Storm said that was because he's always traveled a lot for his work.

"It sounded like he and Owen have worked on and off with each other through the years. Mostly in the real estate world. I don't think they have any active projects together now, but they seem close. Friends, like us, I suppose."

Jackie wanted to know more about what Storm might have said about Owen, but she knew the moment she asked, Lynette would pounce on her interest, no matter how nonchalant she tried to keep it. All of her friends still seemed to think she belonged with the man.

Too bad Owen had moved on. At least, when he made an obligatory appearance at her dad's funeral, the woman clinging to his arm seemed inclined to convey that notion.

Lynette continued, "And speaking of real estate, Storm mentioned how he'd still love to buy my house from me when I told him about the phone call I'd received from my former business associates, wanting me to come back to New York City. He misunderstood and thought I was thinking about moving back there permanently."

Three men strolled into the clearing, laughing and chatting. When one of them noticed Jackie and Lynette, he gave them a friendly wave, but the trio passed through without speaking to them and continued down the path the women would eventually take to circle back to the beach.

"And you're sure that isn't what you really want? To stay in New York, I mean?"

Lynette shook her head. "I wouldn't have bothered to bring all my things back when I finished with my consulting role if that were the case. Thank you, by the way, for letting me store my boxes in your garage. I promise I'll get them out of there when we get home from Fiji."

"There's no rush," Jackie said. "I only have one car, and the girls can park outside when they're home. But continue with your story before we run out of time and have to hurry after the others. Why would Storm want your house? Didn't you say he lives on Nantucket?"

Lynette inhaled deeply, as if preparing to launch into a long-winded response. "He has a home there, yes. Storm didn't want my house for himself. He has a younger brother, Shane, who needs a caretaker. I guess when they lived in Ruby Shores as kids, they called my house a castle and Sybil a witch. It fascinated Shane when Storm would make up stories about my house. I know the house is too big for just me, now that Donna is traveling the world with her Chester, but I'm not ready to sell. So I agreed to rent it to Storm for Shane."

A thought occurred to Jackie. "If you rent out your house, where will *you* live?"

A flash of movement caught their attention. Both watched a brightly plumed bird settle onto a stunted palm tree. It squawked at them, as if encouraging Lynette to continue.

She waved her right hand to fan herself in the heat of the day, and Jackie noticed the way a clear gemstone—probably a diamond—in a ring with an old-fashioned setting her friend wore reflected the sunlight. Jackie didn't recognize the ring, but she didn't want to cut Lynette off to ask if there was a story behind the vintage piece, either.

"I'll live in the attic. It's a great space up there. There's even room for Donna if she ever comes back home from her travels. Raven, the woman I bought the house from, had set it up as a rental with a full bath and everything. I don't need much space. Remember, I lived in New York for years. I rented out the first and second floors to Storm, but I doubt he'll be around much. Like I said, he rented it for Shane. It seemed like the perfect solution. This way I can still enjoy my she-shed, too. I'm seriously considering setting up some type of consulting practice in Ruby Shores, and the rental income from my house could help me set up shop downtown."

Jackie pursed her lips, thinking back to her earlier idea to ask Lynette for advice regarding her pet adoption business. "So you're really going to hang your shingle out, then?"

Lynette laughed. "I think I will. I haven't heard that saying in years. Honestly, these last six months have shown me I'm still happiest when

I'm working. But starting something new will allow me to craft it in a way that allows me some freedom. Do you think I'll find clients in a town like Ruby Shores?"

Jackie stood and brushed the back of her shorts off, then held a hand out to Lynette. When her friend took it, she yanked her up, but didn't let go. Instead, she gave Lynette's hand a quick shake, in mock business fashion. "I think they'll line up for your help. And I'll be at the front of that line."

Lynette narrowed her eyes at her. "Now I'm officially intrigued."

CHAPTER THREE

L YNETTE PULLED A PLASTIC lounge chair into the shade cast by a white beach umbrella, grimacing at the sting she felt where bright sunlight fell across her shoulders. "I should have reapplied my sunscreen yesterday like you told me to, Renee."

She brushed sand from her hands before reaching for her brand-new zippered beach bag. Now comfortably out of the sun, she grinned at the pink flamingos scattered across the bag's turquoise-colored canvas. Later, her cute bag could be a fun reminder of this tropical getaway with her besties, even amid a future Minnesota winter. Jackie had purchased one for each of them, even going to the trouble of getting their names embroidered on the bags' straps.

Renee, following her lead, also pulled a chair close to find relief from the merciless sun. "I have some sunscreen now if you need it."

Lynette unzipped the bag and pulled out a tube of lotion. "Thanks, but I brought plenty today. I just didn't use enough of it yesterday. I won't make that mistake twice."

Once settled into her chair, Renee tossed her sun hat onto the sand next to them and kicked off her cheap, coral-colored flip-flops. "I never thought I'd be back here, sitting behind this resort again, but I'm so glad I am. Believe it or not, I might have been sitting in this very chair when

I opened the letter from my Aunt Celia about her decision to leave me Whispering Pines."

Lynette slathered the sunscreen over her legs, arms, and shoulders, wincing at the friction against her sunburn, despite the slippery viscosity of the cool lotion. Then she kicked her flip-flops off next to Renee's before settling into her chair. "If I'd visited here before, I'm not sure I could have ever left. In fact, I may just see if the owners might arrange a long-term rental contract with me. I could live in one of those glorious, colorful cottages. Maybe the lavender one. Or the pink. Or the turquoise. They're all so *cute*. Not that Matt's place isn't perfectly acceptable for this trip."

Renee twisted in her plastic recliner to survey the small resort behind them. "I can't believe it's been six and a half years since I brought the kids here. I was happy to hear Lulu's voice again when I called to check on vacancies, but sad to learn that she's a widow now. She used to run Sailor's Cove with her husband, Bill. Their son moved here to help her. It's too much for one person. It's too bad they didn't have room for us this week, but I appreciate her inviting us over to use the pool and their private beach. Are you sorry we all squeezed into Matt's rental? Because we might find a bigger place, now that we're here. There may have been last-minute cancellations."

"Renee, I lived in that tiny apartment in New York for the last six months. Remember how little it was when you came to visit me for the weekend in December? Matt's place is twice the size of that."

Renee snorted. "Yeah, but there are five of us here."

A far-off screech, followed by laughter that Lynette recognized as Annie's, reached them. Lynette smiled, wondering what Annie was finding so funny over at the pool where she was lounging with Jackie and Kit.

Waving Renee's concerns away with one hand, Lynette responded, "We're really only there to sleep. And the beach is nice behind his place, too. There just aren't any chairs down there. Quit stressing about it, Renee! It's fine. And it's *free*. Which, by the way, I'm still not sure I'm comfortable with. Our visit is taking away from his rental income."

Renee scoffed. "No, it isn't. I told you this! He'd already taken it off the vacation rental market because he's decided to sell. He asked me to determine what updates it might need and to meet with a real estate agent before I fly home. The agent he used when he initially bought the cottage isn't around anymore."

"With that ocean frontage, I would think he stands to make a boatload of cash from a sale. If he bought it right, that is."

A man approached who Lynette recognized from their arrival as the son of the owner of Sailor's Cove. He was carrying a tray of frozen cocktails. If those were piña coladas, she could already imagine the enticing combination of coconut and rum melting on her tongue. But the illusion only lasted for a second before her new reality came crashing down on her again. There would be no alcohol on this trip. Or ever again. Not for her. The last time she drank on their girls' trip, not only did she risk her own life, she risked the lives of others.

"What do you have there?" Renee asked the man as he came nearer. "Because it looks delicious."

He nodded. "Virgin piña coladas, compliments of the three lovely ladies relaxing up at our pool. Would you each like one?"

"I would," Renee said, reaching for one of the two hourglass-shaped mocktails.

Lynette hated that her friends now felt like they had to be careful about drinking around her. "Renee, you don't have to have the virgin version. There is no way it'll be as good without the rum."

Their host held the last drink out toward Lynette. "Try it. I think you'll like it. We don't normally allow actual glass on the beach, but I made an exception for you," he said with a wink.

The icy concoction did look refreshing. She accepted the curvy, frost-covered glass and took a sip, allowing the slushy liquid to glide over her taste buds.

The man didn't hide his interest as he watched her. While he was easy on the eyes, she didn't feel an ounce of reciprocal interest. But that didn't mean she couldn't have a little fun. If she didn't exercise her flirting muscles once in a while, she'd get rusty.

She gave a low moan of approval, as if the drink was especially scrumptious. After a second taste, she licked her top lip as she met and held his gaze.

This might be fun . . . Even though she had no intention of letting it go anywhere.

"I'm sorry," she said, her voice descending to a sexy purr. "I didn't catch your name."

"K-K-Kevin," he stuttered. He rubbed the back of his neck, suddenly nervous. That was when she noticed the band on his left ring finger.

Bastard, she thought. *Now you're not getting off easy.*

She straightened one leg and bent the other, draping her wrist over her raised knee and wagging her drink in his direction. Her red cover-up fell open, the gauzy material and sexy black swim suit underneath leaving little to the imagination. She adjusted nothing. " 'Kevin' is my lawyer's name, too," she said, keeping her voice throaty. "I find smart men sexy as hell. Are you as smart as my *lawyer*, Kevin?"

One side of his mouth twitched up in what she suspected was an often practiced grin meant to make the ladies swoon. The twerp even had the nerve to reposition himself with a clumsy step to the left, kicking sand over their flip-flops while giving himself an unobstructed view of her, legs and all.

He nodded, winking again, and Renee made a small choking sound next to her.

Was her friend enjoying this, too?

"I can bring you another of those, and this time I'll add a splash or two of that rum you asked for," he said.

A cell phone rang. Without looking away, he tucked the tray he'd expertly carried the drinks on under one arm, then reached into his back pocket. The ringing stopped.

Lynette took a longer pull from her drink. It was already melting in the heat, and a bead of condensation dripped onto her upper chest. She watched Kevin's gaze follow the droplet until it disappeared into her ample cleavage.

"Are you feeling all right, Kevin? You're looking a little . . . sweaty. Too hot out here for you?"

"It's too *something* out here," Renee mocked, but Lynette kept her eyes on her prey.

She caught another snort of not-so-far-off laughter and picked up Kit's voice, coming toward them. They must have finished up at the pool. The imminent arrival of the rest of their group would spoil her fun anyway. It was time to let the schmuck off the hook.

His cell rang again.

He silenced it again.

Lynette dumped the rest of her drink into the white sand beside her chair, hating to waste it as it actually was tasty, but men like Kevin were only fun for a little while, and he already bored her. As she handed him the empty hurricane glass, her eyes snagged on a single dark cloud, hovering above the Pacific.

A storm cloud.

Ironic.

Storm was the only man she'd never grown tired of. He'd occupied at least a tiny corner of her mind for thirty-five years.

Kevin's phone rang for a third time. Before he could reach for it, Lynette pulled her cover-up closed and shook her head at him. "I don't recall saying I wanted rum. In fact, I've decided I want nothing from you. You may make a habit of flirting with your mother's clientele, but not all women are interested in a vacation fling—especially with a married man. Now, get lost. Better yet, answer your phone. I think your wife might be trying to get ahold of you."

Color flooded his cheeks, staining them a crimson bold enough to rival the color of her cover-up. He opened his mouth as if to protest, but she raised her palm toward him, the silver and gold bangles on her wrist clanging.

Dismissed, he turned on one heel and pulled out his phone, silencing it one last time. "You bitches aren't even paying customers," he shot back over his shoulder before jamming his phone into his pocket yet again and hurrying back toward Sailor's Cove.

In one final effort to have the last word, he held up his middle finger at them before hurrying out of sight.

"Did he just flip you the bird?" Kit asked, dropping into a plastic chair identical to Renee's and Lynette's.

Renee, still holding her hurricane glass, downed the rest of its contents before digging a little hole in the sand to prop it up in. "Remind me to take that glass up with me when we leave," she said. "Yes, Kit, he flipped us off. Well, he flipped Lynette off. She hasn't lost her way with men. She can still eat 'em up and spit 'em out. Nice tattoo, by the way, Lynette. You told us about it last summer, but I just had a bird's-eye view of it when you gave that little prick a peep show."

"Hold that thought," Jackie said, jogging off and grabbing hold of two more plastic chairs situated farther down the beach. She dragged both back through the thick sand and positioned them under a second umbrella. After motioning for Annie to sit, she sank into hers, then jabbed her thumb in the direction they'd just come from. "What did you do, Lynette? You aren't getting us kicked out of here, are you? Because I, for one, need some quiet beach time."

"That jerk only wanted one thing, and I had no intention of taking him up on it. And that was before I noticed his wedding ring. But I had to have a little fun with him before I let him down easy."

Renee sat forward in her chair to pull off the T-shirt she'd worn over her suit. "*That* was 'easy'? Remind me to never get on your bad side. By the way, was that comment a jab at me?" Her words were muffled as her shirt seemed to get stuck when she tried to pull it over her head.

Kit reached over to help, but her fingers got tangled in Renee's hair. Renee yelped in pain. When Kit yanked her hand back, strands of her friend's hair clung to Kit's fingers.

"Eww," she said, shaking the hair loose. "I'm so sorry, Renee. I was just trying to help. Are you all right? Why did so much of your hair come out like that? I didn't think I pulled *that* hard."

Now free of the shirt, Renee tossed it on top of her sun hat and rubbed the back of her head. "Don't worry about it. My hair's practically falling out in clumps these days. Must be a menopause thing."

Lynette wasn't sure hair loss was a symptom of menopause, but she supposed it might be. Getting older sucked. It was better than the alternative, but still. "I just wanted to make sure I've still got it."

"Still got what?" Annie asked. She was fiddling with her phone.

Jackie laughed. "If you have to ask, then maybe she doesn't still have it. Maybe none of us do."

Annie looked up. "Oh. That. We still have it. Don't worry." Her eyes went back to her screen.

Kit cleared her throat. Lynette understood the cue, but Annie's phone didn't disappear.

"Annie," Lynette said, loud enough to capture their distracted friend's attention. "Are we going to have to ban phones? Come on! This is a beautiful beach and prime time to gossip with friends. Put the damn thing away."

A sudden gust buffeted them with sand, and the white canopies on the two umbrellas above snapped in the wind. The one between Lynette and Renee tilted to the left, and Renee jumped up to steady it. Then she dropped to her knees and reached for the base. "I think, if I turn this nut, it'll tighten right up."

Once Renee settled back into her chair, Jackie reached into her flamingo-covered bag—identical to Lynette's except for the name and background color—and pulled out a handful of candy bars. She tossed one to each of them. "Here. Now it's a *real* girls' trip. Chocolate and gossip. And sex talk."

Kit raised both hands. "I think I'm missing something? I was hoping you were going to pull a bottle of wine out of your bag. Or at least a beer. And I definitely heard nothing about sex."

"Well, you did miss Lynette's show," Renee said.

Jackie shook her head as she tore the wrapper off the top of her candy bar. "Sometimes chocolate is better than alcohol. And I'm sorry—I didn't account for how fast these would melt in this heat. But chocolate is chocolate, right? Even if it's messy?"

"Is that your same stance on sex? 'Sometimes it's messy'?" Annie teased, licking at the brown candy smudges on her own fingers. "Kit, the base of the umbrella is stuck in a tube to keep it upright in the sand, and Renee mentioned nuts. Doesn't that imagery bring sex to mind for you? Come on, keep up. Even I got it, while also being *distracted* by my phone."

Kit shrugged. "Oh, I actually do 'get it.' " She emphasized her innuendo by wiggling her fingers in quotation marks. "Remember, I've only been married for a few years. But since poor Jackie here is too stubborn to hook up with Owen—or anyone else, for that matter—all she can do is *talk* about sex."

Jackie snatched Kit's unopened candy bar off the foot of her recliner and shoved it back into her bag. "No candy for you, if you're going to be mean."

The five women continued to laugh and banter for a few more minutes until, one by one, they each spied a trio of surfers out on the water. They fell silent, watching the show with awe. Even from a distance, the surfers' skills were obvious.

Then Lynette remembered Renee's earlier question. "What did you mean, a few minutes ago, about me making a jab at you, Renee?" she asked.

Renee turned from the water. "Oh. What you said about a vacation fling. Because you know that's kind of what I did when I hooked up with Matt on my first trip here."

Their exchange drew everyone's interest away from the surfer dudes.

"You actually 'hooked up' with Matt during that first week?" Jackie asked.

Renee laughed at the expression on Jackie's face. "You really need some time in the bedroom, Jackie. And I don't mean by yourself. You should see your face! Maybe we shouldn't have let Lynette scare Kevin off so fast. He might have been able to help you out."

"Kevin? Who the hell is Kevin?" Kit said. "Isn't that her lawyer's name?"

Lynette shook her head at Kit. "Different guy. Renee, we all know your meeting Matt here in Fiji had a happy ending. Even if it started out as nothing more than a tussle in the sand."

Renee waved her candy wrapper in the air. "I'll have you know an emergency call from work interrupted said tussle, so I don't know if we actually 'hooked up.' I know I said we did, but what does that actually mean, exactly?"

Lynette laughed. "Ask your kids. And I *actually* don't even want to talk about men anymore. It's been too long since I've been with a man, too, and I'd hate to get desperate and go chase Kevin down—for me *or* for Jackie. Speaking of your kids Renee, tell us what they've been up to. It was fun to meet them last summer at Whispering Pines."

Renee's face suddenly glowed. She looked proud at the mention of her kids—as she should. Widowed young, Renee had done most of the raising of those kids alone.

"Let's see," Renee said, her eyes back on the surfers but her mind clearly elsewhere. "Julie is still helping me run Whispering Pines. If not for her, I couldn't have come with on this trip. Summer is our busiest time, obviously, but she's every bit as competent as me at keeping things running smoothly out there. Matt is around, of course, if there's any real trouble, but he works lots of hours. The sheriff's office is still short on staff, even though there hasn't been any noticeable improvement in crime rates in his county."

Renee's voice trailed off and Lynette suspected her friend's mind was swirling with worry over her husband again—something she'd admitted happens too often these days.

"Does Whispering Pines produce enough income to support Julie and you?"

Annie snapped a beach towel open and let it fall onto her white recliner. "Jeez, Lynette, dive right into personal financial information, why don't you?"

Lynette shrugged. "What's the big deal? None of you seemed opposed to discussing sex, and it doesn't get more personal than that. Why is money such a taboo topic?"

"It's all right," Renee interjected. "I don't mind talking about it. To answer your question, no, Whispering Pines isn't big enough to support Julie, too. She knows it. I know it. But it's like the obvious issue that no one wants to acknowledge. She mentions job hunting at neighboring resorts, but I'm not sure if she's actually put her résumé out there. Sometimes I wonder if I should just go get another job and let her run the place. She loves it even more than I do, and I'd never have opened again without her help."

Lynette considered this. "What kind of job would interest you?"

Renee gathered her hair into a stub of a ponytail and fanned her neck. After a moment, she shook her head. "I'm not sure I'm still employable, after working for myself since 2016. I can't imagine working in an office again. In fact, I swore I never would."

Kit reached for Jackie's flamingo bag and retrieved her candy bar, and Jackie didn't stop her. "Julie is young. She has her whole working life ahead of her. She'll need to find something else. Maybe there are other resorts in the area that could benefit from her expertise."

Renee's grimace told Lynette she clearly didn't like that idea.

"I'm sure it's not that simple, Kit," Lynette said. "Sometimes you are a tad too pragmatic. Let me think about it, Renee. There has to be some solution that will make everyone happy. What about Robbie? What's he up to? I know he has fun guiding fishermen around your lake. If he wants to earn a living off of Whispering Pines, too, that might get really tricky."

Another gust of wind rattled the umbrella canopies, but this time they remained securely anchored. Renee pulled sunglasses out of her bag, even though a thin veil of clouds had moved in. Lynette followed suit, hoping it would keep the blowing sand out of her eyes, too.

"Believe it or not, Robbie is making big plans that don't include Minnesota at all."

Lynette rubbed her hands together. "That sounds intriguing. What does he have up his sleeve?"

Renee let her head fall forward with a sigh, as if her son's plans were adding to her heap of worries that her husband's work had created. "He flew out the day after we did."

"Flew out where? He's about my son's age, right?" Annie asked. "Relic's age, I mean. Not Colton. Colton is twenty-six. Relic is almost twenty-one."

Renee lifted her head. "Yeah, he's twenty-one, too. Almost twenty-two. He'll start his senior year of college this fall. He flew to Alaska to work on a fishing boat for the summer until classes start again. If he likes it, his brilliant idea is to take his inheritance from my Aunt Celia and open a guide business of his own up there."

Lynette thought the young man was smart to take his last summer before college graduation to test the waters a little, but his mother didn't appear as sure about that. "We all know your aunt gave you Whispering Pines when she passed. But tell us about the kids' inheritance."

Nodding, Renee brushed sand from her thigh. "When—or should I say *if*—our kids graduate with a four-year degree, they receive fifty thousand dollars from the trust Celia established."

Kit whistled. "I love my Aunt Marge, and even though she eked out a decent living from her Crystal Café, I'm confident we won't be seeing those kinds of bequests when she kicks the bucket."

Jackie tried to slap Kit's foot but couldn't quite reach. "Be nice. Marge is a boss."

"Ladies, hush. We're focused on Renee's family right now. There'll be time to dissect all our families before the week is over," Lynette said, grinning. "Renee, are there any strings attached to how the kids can use the money?"

"Nothing other than the college graduation. Julie hasn't touched hers. I suspect she'd like to invest it in Whispering Pines somehow, but I'm not sure that's a good idea. Don't get me wrong. Both of my kids make me incredibly proud. I'm just terrified that they'll pick the wrong careers, marry the wrong people, or totally ruin their lives somehow. I got them to this point, but they no longer seem as interested in what I think about their choices."

Annie snapped her fingers. "Welcome to parenting young adults, Renee. Trust me. It's *sooo* fun. My kids have minds of their own, too. The nerve of them!" She grinned. "Honestly, I still worry that Ava and her husband over-extended themselves when they bought their expensive house. She doesn't love her bank job, but she better stay so they can keep paying that mortgage. And I certainly wasn't thrilled when Colton chose to work at a funeral home. I suspect Relic will make his share of stupid decisions, too."

Lynette pulled a bottle of water from her bag and wet her sticky fingers, wiping them on her towel. "But don't you see, ladies? Mistakes season us. They toughen us up. No one said life was easy. I know I've made my fair share of stupid mistakes."

Renee frowned at the brown streaks Lynette's fingers had left on the pale beach towel. "I think smearing chocolate on that towel might fill your allotment of stupid mistakes for today. That better come out."

Realizing she'd just stained one of the few towels they'd found in Matt's cottage, Lynette groaned. This girls' trip didn't include a five-star resort with staff to wait on them. "Oops. Guess I'm on laundry duty tonight."

CHAPTER FOUR

J ACKIE FELT A SURGE of relief when she caught sight of a large speedboat pulled up next to the public beach fifteen minutes from Renee's cottage, exactly where the tour company told her they'd be. Booking excursions online didn't give her a great deal of confidence, but so far, so good.

She jogged across the hot sand toward the vessel while the rest of her group got organized. She counted three crew members, their eyes hidden behind sunglasses. They had covered their arms, too, with long-sleeved, highlighter-green tops for protection from the sun.

Salt water and sunshine inevitably damages boats, too, and this craft hadn't escaped nature's wrath. The logo, sporting two-thirds of a jumping dolphin that bore little resemblance to the graceful creatures they'd spied from their seaplane, along with the barely legible name of *Sky Surfer*, was in dire need of a refresh. If their parasailing equipment showed similar wear and tear, it could be disastrous.

Annie ran past her, reaching the boat first. "Hello, gentlemen! What a beautiful day for this! Are you ready for us? I'm so excited. I've always wanted to parasail. But I'll warn you right now"—she lowered her voice a bit, almost conspiratorially—"the chick with the bright orange hair is more than a little nervous. Please make a little extra effort to put her at ease, would you, boys? And maybe keep a bucket handy, in case her stomach revolts? I know she'll love this if we can just convince her to try."

Jackie couldn't help but laugh at Annie's enthusiasm as she reached her friend's side at the water's edge. The cool waves washed away the blazing sand's sting from her feet. She took a closer look at the boat. Between the five of them and the crew, they should fit, but it would be tight. "Hey, guys. I'm Jackie Turner. I made our reservation for today. Are we in the right place?"

"Yes, ma'am," the man at the controls said. She noted the silver streaks in his otherwise dark hair and immediately felt a smidgen of her apprehension ebb away. At least it wasn't a group of inexperienced teens taking them out. "Welcome! I'm Bula, your captain today. If you'll give us ten more minutes, we'll be ready for you."

"Sounds good," she said with a quick tap on the boat. She caught Annie's wrist and tugged her away. "Come on. Let's go see what's holding everybody else up."

Not surprisingly, Kit was the holdup. They found her on the wooden pathway leading to the beach with her arms crossed. Lynette and Renee were arguing with her, but her stubborn expression reignited Jackie's concern about her friend's willingness to parasail.

"What's going on, Kit?" Jackie asked, though she already had a pretty good idea.

"Do you four have any idea what type of injuries we could get, parasailing behind a speeding boat? Not to mention the fact we're in a *foreign country*? We have no idea whether they have adequate health care here. I can't believe any of you are willing to do this!"

Jackie sighed. Anticipating Kit's aversion to any activities that included even a hint of danger, she'd also researched safety concerns about this type of excursion. She'd even made sure they'd have access to medical care in the case of an accident. "Kit, while there is a slight possibility of injury, you're more likely to get hurt walking across a street in downtown Minneapolis than you are parasailing in Fiji."

Kit leveled an irritated glare at her. "That is a terrible comparison, Jackie. I already know how dangerous Minneapolis can be. Remember when my coworker went downtown for a Twins game and got hit by a car? He'll never get out of that wheelchair."

Jackie inhaled sharply. How could she have forgotten about that? She held up her hands as if taming a spooked horse. "Sorry, sorry . . . Look, Kit, I know you aren't a big fan of heights. But you'll have more fun in life if you loosen up a little. You hated the idea of ziplining when we were in Maui, remember? But then you tried it, and you couldn't get enough."

"We were in a forest, no more than a hundred feet off the ground, on that zipline course," Kit countered. "When you told us what you'd planned for today, I did some quick research. You could get as high as five hundred feet in the air behind that boat. That's *five times* higher!" Panic caused her voice to rise.

Lynette crossed her arms, too, mirroring Kit's stance. "Whether you fall a hundred feet onto the top of a tree or five hundred feet onto the water, I'm pretty sure dead is dead."

Jackie slapped her forehead in frustration. "Not helping, Lynette."

Renee placed a hand on Kit's shoulder. "Just come with us in the boat, Kit. If you don't want to actually go up, that's fine. No one is going to force you. Right, Jackie?"

While Jackie thought she knew Kit well enough to *know* she'd enjoy parasailing if she'd just try it, she reluctantly conceded. "Of course we won't force you, Kit. But please, at least come along. If nothing else, you'll enjoy a fun boat ride, and if something happens to one of us out on the water, you can be the first to say 'I told you so.' "

Kit relaxed her stance, and—amazingly—a smile tugged at the corners of her mouth. "I do like to say I told you so . . ."

"That's the spirit, Kit," Annie said, picking up Kit's beach bag and slinging it over her shoulder to rest on top of her own. "Now come on! You might not be excited about this, but parasailing is on my bucket list, and I'm crossing it off today, with or without you."

Annie looped her arm through Kit's and motioned for Jackie to lead the way back to the water's edge and their next adventure.

"Dad would have loved this," Jackie said, letting go of her grip on the strap to touch her necklace. "I can't believe how peaceful this feels. Like we're floating on air. I'd expected it to be so windy that we'd have to shout to hear each other. But we don't. I wish we had a camera or phone up here so we could capture this view."

Renee turned to look at her but kept her own fingers wrapped tightly around the harness they both swayed on. "Hold on, Jackie! If you fall, Kit will have the words 'I told you so' engraved on your headstone."

"Relax, Renee. We aren't going to fall. Although I admit I'm not crazy about the fraying on these straps, even if our captain assured us they'd still hold an elephant up here."

"And I didn't appreciate being compared to an elephant," Renee said with a giggle. "Man, can you believe this view? We are so high above the ocean, the horizon curves. The boat looks so tiny, way down there. Just think. This is the view seagulls get to enjoy all the time."

Jackie grabbed hold of the strap again and swiveled her upper body as far as she could so she could take in the full view. "It's even more breathtaking than I'd imagined. Look, there's something swimming in the water way down there. Can you see it?"

"I think they're dolphins! Oh, man. Thank you Jackie, for booking these excursions for us. Planning this trip was lots more fun with your help."

"Of course. We told you we didn't want you to feel like the host, either last year or this year, even though we stayed at Whispering Pines and now at Matt's old place here. By the way, we haven't figured out where we want to go in 2023. You wouldn't happen to have any other amazing properties you haven't told us about?" Jackie laughed. She swung her feet out of the way and gazed down at the boat, a mere speck far below.

Renee shrugged. "Sorry. I'm all out of properties. And by this time next year, Matt's hoping he won't own the cottage anymore, either. It's too complicated to have rental property on the other side of the world. I'll be sad to never come back here, though. We could stay somewhere else on the islands, of course, but there are other parts of the world I want to see, too."

Jackie knew exactly what Renee meant. She'd always dreamed of visiting castles in Europe or viewing the northern lights from up close in places like Alaska. "Maybe if your son settles down in Alaska, we could visit him. Alaska is on *my* bucket list."

"Please don't even *suggest* that Robbie might move that far away from me. He may be finishing up college this next year, but to me he'll always be my little boy—not some adventure-seeking guide up in the wilderness."

Jackie sensed a tightening in the apparatus holding them aloft. "Shoot,

I think they're reeling us back in," she said, looking between her feet at the undulating surface of the water below. "Just think. If Matt didn't sell his cottage, Robbie could end up working on a boat like this one in Fiji during the part of the year when Alaska descends into twenty-four hours of darkness. Unlike us, when you're that young you have your whole life ahead of you, and the possibilities are endless."

"I'd prefer a job where his feet remained on dry land," Renee said.

The water was drawing closer. Their turn was definitely ending. Jackie could see Annie was already on her feet, excited to go up next.

Renee nodded toward the boat. "Looks like Kit is staying anchored in her seat. I hate for her to miss this. It wasn't nearly as scary as I thought it would be once we got all the way up there."

"I hate for her to miss it, too. But sometimes there is no convincing that woman. Spontaneous adventures have never been high on her bucket list."

A pair of seagulls flew between the two women and the boat.

"How was it?" Annie shouted as they inched closer to the platform.

"Incredible!" Renee yelled back.

Jackie held her breath until her feet were solidly back on the floorboards of the boat, but she knew she'd never forget that delicious feeling of freedom they'd just experienced. The next few minutes involved lots of unfastening and reclipping of life jackets and the sailing apparatus.

"Kit, if you change your mind, I'd go up again with you after Annie and Lynette are done. We paid for three rounds."

Kit slid her sunglasses down the bridge of her nose to make eye contact with Jackie. "I'm good. You talked me into ziplining in Hawaii, but I'm going to trust my gut on this one. If you guys want to risk your lives, that's your prerogative."

Jackie slapped Kit's leg to get her to move over so she could sit next to her. "Do you ever act spontaneously?"

"Not if I can help it," Kit said, pushing her shades back up before scooching over to give her friend room. "Besides, I don't like the looks of that equipment they're using. It looks like it could snap right in two. If that happens, I don't even want to think about where we'll find Annie and Lynette."

Lynette tugged at the straps on each side of her as the crew positioned them for takeoff. "No jinxing us, Kit!"

Kit, Jackie, and Renee fell silent as the crew worked, and Annie and Lynette soon rose high above the water behind them. Jackie felt Kit shudder. She hated to admit it, but it shocked her, too, how far up Annie and Lynette appeared to be going from her new perspective in the boat. "It looks worse from here. I wasn't even very nervous while we were way up there."

The skeptical glance Kit shot her conveyed how much she disapproved of this whole adventure.

"I'm sorry you aren't enjoying this, Kit," Jackie said. "Tomorrow will be better."

Kit snorted. "Can I keep my feet on dry land tomorrow?"

"See, Jackie, that's what I want for Robbie, too. Land," Renee chimed in. "But, Kit, I promise we won't pressure you to climb to any death-defying heights."

Kit cracked her knuckles, as if to dispel the tension that today's events caused her. "What exactly are we doing tomorrow? Can't we have another relaxing beach day?"

"That'll be the day after tomorrow. Tomorrow, we are taking a boat tour. Good food, a few cocktails, and maybe a little dancing are all included. Matt's buddy runs that tour company, and Matt took me out on it. In fact, after we finished up on his friend's tour, he had a romantic fire all set up for us behind his cottage, and that's where he proposed to me."

Kit slumped back against the cushioned seat with a heavy sigh, as if finally relaxed. Annie and Lynette were now high above them, and their crew seemed to have things under control. "I love Matt. I'm so glad you bumped into him here in Fiji when you brought your kids here. Maybe you can teach me to be a little more spontaneous, Renee. I feel like I overthink everything, and I know it causes me to miss out on fun sometimes."

Renee tucked her feet up under her and adjusted the beach towel over her legs. "Some of my supposed spontaneity has actually resulted from hard things. That spur-of-the-moment trip here to Fiji for New Year's at the beginning of 2016 was because I was abruptly let go from my job—after *twenty years*. Zero warning. Same deal with me reopening Whispering Pines. I'd never have considered it if they hadn't forced me into a new career."

Jackie hadn't really thought too much about the heartache that Renee had built her current life on top of. She shivered, both at the thought of her dear friend losing both a husband and a long-term career, and because she felt a sudden chill in the air.

The wind picked up, too.

She noticed that the three-man crew was working feverishly now. Curt orders from the captain had replaced their lighthearted banter.

"That seemed lots shorter than our ride," Jackie said, looking between Renee and the two younger crew members, who were now actively working to bring their friends back in.

Renee nodded, and Jackie felt Kit tense up next to her again.

"Storm's blowing in," the captain said, pointing toward the western horizon. "Wasn't supposed to get here for another hour or two, but see how those birds are heading inland? Better to be safe than sorry."

Jackie looked up, knowing Annie was going to be so disappointed over their abbreviated parasailing adventure. The women were probably wondering why the heck their ride was already ending.

She noticed Kit adjust herself so she was kneeling on the bench seat instead of sitting, keeping a tight grip on the railing while she watched the winch system closely.

A gust of wind pushed at the boat, causing it to rock on the now choppy surface of the water. Jackie glanced around for a bucket, just in case Annie's earlier warning about Kit's stomach came true, either from nerves over their safety or seasickness.

"Should we be concerned?" she hollered to their captain, raising her voice to be heard above the increasing screech of the wind.

The captain shook his head. "It's all in a day's work," he insisted, but she noticed he kept his eyes glued to Annie and Lynette as they inched closer to the boat.

Perhaps he missed the larger swell barreling toward them because his attention was on the two women flying above, but Jackie saw it.

"Hold on!" she shouted.

A split second later the wave hit, sending the boat skittering even harder.

Annie and Lynette were close to the boat now, and one man reached a hand up to help them settle safely on the landing platform on the back of the boat. A collective sigh of relief went up when both women stood on the platform, swaying slightly as they worked to extricate themselves from the harness. They impressed Jackie with their surefooted balance.

"That was amazing," Annie said. Her eyes sparkled with excitement, and Jackie was glad that her friend didn't seem disappointed. "From way up high, we could see the storm rolling in. The lightning bolts looked spectacular! But thanks for pulling us in. Even *I'm* not brave enough to ride out a storm up there."

Jackie looked toward their captain. He tightened the strap of a hat he'd donned, securing it under his chin so it wouldn't fly off in the increasing wind. "Sorry we had to cut that short, ladies!" he said. He looked relieved, too.

"Don't worry about it," Annie replied, smiling up at him as she stepped toward the edge of the platform.

Either it was slippery with water from the waves now splashing up on deck, or she simply didn't see the edge, because suddenly she was in a heap at Jackie's feet, writhing in pain.

One of the crew members jumped from the platform, dropping to a knee next to Annie, while the other secured the equipment and the captain turned the boat toward shore.

"Are you all right?" the man asked.

She nodded and struggled up to a seated position, but Jackie saw the way she was holding her right wrist against her body.

"No, she hurt her arm," Jackie said, pushing the young man out of the way and helping Annie up onto the bench next to Kit. "Here, Annie, take my spot. Do you think it's broken?"

Annie groaned as she raised her butt high enough to collapse onto the bench. "My wrist? Yeah, I'm afraid it might be."

Kit shook her head, and when she opened her mouth, Jackie stretched to cover it with her left hand. "Don't say it, Kit," she warned.

Kit grabbed Jackie's hand and pulled it away from her face. "I was just going to tell Annie to hold her arm as still as she can until we can get her to a doctor."

"And were you going to say that before or after you said 'I told you so'?" Jackie pressed.

Kit shrugged, not denying it. "Would I be wrong?"

"Not wrong, but also not helpful."

"Then I'll keep my mouth shut. This time."

Jackie sighed as she opened her flamingo-covered bag and pulled out a roll of elastic bandage. "I brought this in case Lynette rolled her ankle again. Now help me secure Annie's arm so we can minimize any further damage. Come on, Skipper, get us to shore. Now!"

Chapter Five

"REMIND ME TO ADD new outside chairs to the list of improvements I think Matt should make at this place in order to earn top dollar when he sells it," Renee said. She wriggled her bottom uncomfortably in the metal folding chair. "These things have to go. Ooh! Maybe he should get red Adirondacks like the ones Mom and Dad bought for Whispering Pines last summer! I'm sorry I don't have something more comfortable for you to sit in."

Annie swayed in her chair, a blissed-out expression on her face. "I feel like I'm sitting on a cloud."

Lynette glanced between Annie's face and the new cast on her wrist. Medical staff had wrapped a colored tape around the underlying splint material. Annie had selected the bright orange option, and in this light, it matched the flames in the firepit. "I doubt you'll think that when those painkillers wear off. And"—she hid a sudden smile behind one hand—"you might regret picking such a . . . *vibrant* . . . color for your cast, too."

"Nope." Annie shook her encased wrist like a trophy. "This color will remind me of the Fiji sunshine!" She grimaced, despite the strong narcotics she'd received in the emergency room. "Hey, Kit, is there any of that wine left? Wait, where's Kit?"

With a laugh, Lynette handed their patient a bottle of water. "She's inside. But sorry, girl, you're in *my* camp now. No alcohol. It would be dangerous to mix anything alcoholic with those painkillers you're on. Maybe you can have a cocktail or two on the boat tomorrow if you don't need more of those pills."

"Fine," Annie huffed, accepting the water. "You know, you aren't as fun as you used to be now that you don't drink."

Someone gasped, but Lynette ignored it. Annie was surely right, but being less fun was a price she was willing to pay. Fun was relative. She preferred being sober and *alive*. Not only was it a relief to avoid the drunken stupors and resulting hangovers, she also wanted to live a healthier lifestyle and reverse at least some of the damage that her previous poor choices had caused to her liver and heart.

None of the Kaleidoscope Girls were getting any younger.

Annie's fractured wrist was evidence of that. If she'd fallen like that at twenty, she probably would have bounced right back up, unhurt. As a former gymnast, Annie knew how to fall to lower the threat of injury. But that hadn't saved her today.

Kit rejoined them on the cottage's back patio, balancing three red Solo cups, two of which she handed to Renee and Jackie. Lynette suspected they held wine, and she appreciated Kit's discretion, as Annie wasn't clearheaded at the moment.

"Did you know this was the same wrist I broke when I was a kid?"

This was news to Lynette. She didn't remember Annie having any broken bones. "Really?"

"Yep. And my doctor warned me it would always be a little weaker and at greater risk of injury. Bet the old geezer didn't think I'd make it nearly forty years before I hurt it again. Kit, is there any wine left?"

Kit froze, the red plastic cup poised at her lips. Lynette caught her gaze and gave a discreet shake of her head.

"Sorry, Annie, we're all out," Kit said, lowering her cup. "But I can run inside and grab you a soda if the water isn't doing it for you."

Annie sighed. "No. This is fine. Lynette's right. I need to be careful with the painkillers. But Henry is going to kill me for this."

Jackie grunted. "It was an *accident*. You didn't even get hurt parasailing. You were just walking. Granted, you walked straight off a ledge in the back of a boat, but it was still an accident."

Annie spun on her. "I *slipped*, Jackie. The platform got really slippery with the high waves. I didn't just walk off a ledge."

Lynette tried not to grin at the skeptical look on Jackie's face. But Annie's comment about her husband had her curious, too. "Why would Henry be mad?"

"Because he made me promise I'd join this new pickleball league with him. They're starting one up in Ruby Shores this summer. The man is suddenly obsessed with getting healthy. I don't know what's come over him, but all of this exercising together is taking up my free time. I barely see Nora anymore, and she changes so much every week. You wouldn't believe her vocabulary already." Her eyes widened. "Oh, no!"

"What's wrong?" Renee asked.

Annie held up her broken wrist. "Now I won't be able to take Nora to the pool this summer! Screw Henry. I can't disappoint my granddaughter!"

All four women laughed at Annie's pout. The situation itself wasn't funny, but Annie's overly animated reactions were comical. It was time to talk about something else, before she dissolved into tears over the derailment of her summer plans.

"Annie, tell us how that beagle you adopted from Jackie is doing," Lynette prompted. Pets were usually a safe topic of conversation.

"Little Daisy?" their injured friend asked. A smile replaced her frown. "Nora *loves* Daisy. She's such a sweet beagle. You might remember little Lemon lived with us, but when Relic moved out after the pandemic he took the yorkie, just like I knew he would. So Daisy truly is a blessing. The house would be too quiet if it was just me and Henry there."

Jackie nodded. "I know what you mean. I can't imagine life without Nikki. In fact, adopting her was the first kernel of my idea to open my senior pet adoption agency. Granted, she wasn't a senior at the time, but now she is. What about you cat lovers? Kit? How's Chloe? Lynette, who's watching Ebony? Donna is traveling, right?"

Lynette nodded. "Yes, Donna is gallivanting around the world with her buddy Chester. Ebony is terrorizing Kit's Chloe these days, actually. Hopefully Dean is keeping a close eye on them. I'm told Chloe doesn't have much patience for Ebony."

Kit nodded with a small smile. "And hopefully my hubby refilled his allergy meds, since he's allergic to cats."

Renee laughed. "Dean is allergic to cats, yet you still have one in your home? And he agreed to watch Lynette's, too? The man is a saint."

"That he is," Kit agreed. "But he knew we came as a package deal when he married me. What about you, Renee? You've never mentioned a pet, and I don't recall seeing any dogs or cats at Whispering Pines last summer."

Renee took another sip out of her plastic cup before responding. "Actually, I do have a dog. A cocker spaniel named Molly. I suppose she's more my dad's dog now, but don't tell Robbie I said that. She's nine. She came with us when we moved out to Whispering Pines, but she quickly tangled with a raccoon and then a skunk. That was awful. My folks offered to keep her for a while, and she's still there. It seems to work better for everyone. Dad really enjoys having her around, and I know she's safe. If she was at the resort full time, it would be just one more thing to worry about."

Lynette hated how often Renee mentioned all of her worries. Should she suggest counseling? Maybe not now, in front of everyone else, but later. When it was just the two of them. Perhaps stress, not menopause, was the real reason Renee's hair was falling out.

"Will you be able to bring your cat home to your attic, Lynette?" Jackie asked.

Kit set her cup onto the bricks at her feet. "Jackie, I know you don't like cats, but if Lynette is going to make the poor thing live in her attic, I'll keep her. Chloe will just have to get used to having a second cat around."

Both Lynette and Jackie laughed at Kit's indignation.

"I don't *love* cats, Kit, but I am an animal lover," Jackie said. "I just meant that Lynette told me she rented out her house to Storm, and she's going to live in the attic, and I was wondering if maybe Storm's brother might be allergic to cats or have a dislike of them."

Kit picked her cup back up. "I'm so confused. I think I might need to get more wine from the fridge."

"You said the wine was gone!" Annie complained.

"Shoot. You're right," Kit said, tossing her empty cup down. The plastic made a hollow clattering sound against the bricks. "But wait—you mentioned Storm? And something about his brother? I've been dying to ask if anything came out of your reconnecting with him last summer, but I didn't want to pry. Now that Jackie opened the door, though—spill. I'm tired of talking about dogs and cats. I want to talk about sex again."

Both Renee and Jackie had already heard bits of the story of Storm and her house, so Lynette gave Kit and Annie an abbreviated version.

"Storm is still so sexy," Annie said, swaying again in her chair. The drugs didn't seem to be wearing off yet. "If I wasn't married to Henry, and since you aren't interested in Storm anymore, I'd call him up."

If a woman who wasn't one of her Kaleidoscope Girls mentioned an interest in Storm, Lynette suspected the jealousy dragon would rear its ugly green head over a comment like that. But she knew Annie was only teasing.

"Did I say I wasn't interested?" Lynette said, careful to keep her tone light.

Annie sat up straight, her eyes looking suddenly more focused. "*Are* you? Because the Lynette I grew up with was so hot for that man, she wouldn't have gone almost a whole year without getting her hands on him. The chemistry between you two was off the charts."

Lynette gave her empty water bottle a frustrated squeeze, and the crackling of the plastic mixed with that of the fire. "That was then. Now, I'm just not sure. He was sweet to me when he took me out for ice cream last summer."

" 'Sweet' would never be a term I'd use to describe Storm."

"Annie, if you are going to keep interrupting me, I'll just go to bed," Lynette warned.

Annie giggled. "Now, Storm and 'bed,' *those* two words go together better."

Lynette let her chin drop to her chest. Annie couldn't handle her painkillers any better than she could handle her liquor.

"I'm sorry," Annie said, sobering. "I'll behave. Go on."

She didn't quite trust Annie to hush while in her current state, but Lynette shared more about her conflicted feelings where her old flame was concerned. "As I was saying . . . he was sweet to me. Even dropped a quick peck on the tip of my nose. I kept thinking more might come out of our reconnecting, but aside from his interest in my house, I can't really get a read on how Storm feels about me. Maybe the way we left things when we were kids created too deep of a chasm between us. He mentioned coming to see me in New York in mid-February, but then something came up with his son and he had to cancel."

Renee retrieved another log from a pile of wood nearby and added it to the fire, stirring a flurry of sparks into the air. "Mid-February, as in Valentine's Day?"

Watching the sparks float higher and disappear into the night sky, Lynette thought back to the disappointment she'd felt when Storm's plans to see her fell apart. "Well, yes, but that was probably just a coincidence," she said.

"Or not," Jackie countered. "Did you date anyone while you were working in New York? Because I know you used to go out often, when you lived there before."

"I was there to work," she said, but even to her own ears, it sounded like a weak excuse for her nearly nonexistent social life over the last year. "You guys. Storm broke my heart. Based on my reaction to him last summer, and even when I talk to him on a purely professional basis about the house, I can tell that he still holds the power to break me again. And I'm not sure I want to go through all of that at my age."

Someone groaned.

Renee covered her eyes. "I hate to hear you say that, Lynette. I saw how easily you manipulated that man on the beach behind Sailor's Cove when he tried to hit on you. You have skills, woman. And look at you! Your sense of style runs bone-deep. All you'd have to do is wag a finger at a guy—*any* guy—and I bet he'd come running."

"Not Storm," Lynette whispered.

Jackie got to her feet, picked up Kit's discarded cup and slid it together with hers, then reached for Lynette's crushed water bottle. "Give me that thing. The sound it makes when you keep squeezing it like that is driving me crazy. It wouldn't be any different with Storm if you'd stop pussyfooting around and let him know how you really feel."

Lynette put her bottle into Jackie's outstretched palm but didn't immediately let go. "You're one to talk. It's awfully easy for you to sit here and tell me how I should act, how I should chase Storm if he's what I still want. I don't see you doing the same thing with Owen."

"Ha! New career idea!" Annie interjected. "Lynette could be a *storm* chaser!"

"Be quiet, Annie," Lynette said, frustrated at the interruption. "Jackie, what's *your* excuse? Owen never broke your heart, but I'd venture to guess the indifference you show him has left some scars on his. That man has always had a thing for you, ever since we were kids."

Renee held her empty cup out for Jackie, too. "As Owen's senior prom date, I can vouch for that. There I was, wounded from my breakup, looking as pretty as I knew how to, and the boy would hardly look at me whenever you were nearby. I watched the two of you at Whispering Pines last summer, too. Nothing much has changed. Sure, you two argued, but a person would have to be blind not to see the way you spark off each other. Like Storm and Lynette. I think, deep down, you'd both love to pursue something with those men, but fear is holding you back. Why don't you take a chance, like I did with Matt? You might find genuine happiness. It's not too late."

Lynette didn't appreciate the accuracy of Renee's observations, at least as far as her feelings for Storm were concerned. She felt her hackles raise. "Says the woman whose hair is literally falling out because she's terrified something will happen to her husband in the line of duty," she bit out, unable to hold the hurtful words back. "Renee, I saw Matt in action when he found me last summer, and that man can handle himself just fine. I don't know what you're so afraid of."

Even in the low light of the fire, Lynette could see the color drain from Renee's face. An awkward silence descended over the group, and she knew immediately that she'd gone too far.

Renee got to her feet. "Maybe if any of you ever actually had a husband die on you, you'd possess the empathy to understand why the dangers that Matt faces every damn day terrify me. I thought I could handle it because of how much I love him. Now I'm not sure love is enough. But I'm obviously wasting my breath trying to explain myself to any of you. So I'm going to bed. I think you all should, too, before anyone else says something they can't take back."

Jackie dropped the cups and water bottle to reach for her, but Renee scooted away, too quick for her.

After the cottage door slammed behind her, the remaining four women eyed each other warily. No one seemed sure what to say or do next.

Wearily, Lynette stood. "Renee is right. None of us should judge anyone else's relationships. But my friendship with all of you is priceless, so let's call it a night before any more damage is done. I love you all. Nothing will ever change that. Now, come on, Annie, I'll help you get ready for bed. Kit and Jackie, can you douse the fire before you come in?"

She felt Annie shiver when she slipped an arm around her shoulders to turn the shorter woman toward the cottage. "Are you all right? Is the pain getting worse in your arm again?"

Annie's body shuddered. "It's not my arm. It's my heart. I love all of you, too, and I don't want to fight. Tomorrow will be better, right?"

"Of course. After all, we're the Kaleidoscope Girls. Even our broken bits are beautiful when we stick together."

Chapter Six

"I can't believe you made us leave our phones at the cottage today, Lynette," Kit said. "We're on a boating day trip, touring a bunch of islands in Fiji where we'll see breathtaking, once-in-a-lifetime scenery, and we can't take *pictures*."

Lynette winked and grabbed her beach bag. "Not true. I found a few disposable cameras in a kitchen drawer at the cottage and Renee said to use them. A previous renter must have left them behind."

Kit reached for the camera Lynette had pulled out. "With the quality of phone cameras these days, why would someone bother with these?"

"Because you can use them underwater," Lynette explained. "I know some phones *claim* to be waterproof, but I wouldn't chance dropping mine or getting it wet and ruining it. Especially while traveling. How lost would we be without our phones?"

"Very," Renee cut in. "I lost mine on our Maui trip, remember?"

A light breeze barely ruffled the ocean's surface as their sailing catamaran eased away from the dock, but the wake from a similar-sized vessel, also heading out of port, caused water to spray upward and sprinkle Kit's arm and the single-use camera.

"I forgot about that, Renee! And I think that's Kit's point," Annie said, looking over her shoulder at them from another bench that butted up against the back of theirs. "It feels weird to not at least have it with."

"Annie, you are the worst of all of us. Always on your phone," Lynette pointed out. "Which is why I suggested a 'No Phone Friday.' You can still get some snapshots with these cameras, but we're also more likely to stay present for what promises to be a fun day. We should make the most of this day trip, especially after last night. We're here to enjoy each other's company, not to bicker and argue. How does your wrist feel today, by the way?"

Annie held her arm up. "It was hard to sleep, but I'm able to control the pain with ibuprofen. I left the heavy-duty pain pills back at the cottage. What's a little pain when tropical rum fruit punch is on the docket?"

Lynette would avoid the spiked punch, but it didn't feel like a sacrifice. Too much rum last summer almost ruined their girls' trip at Whispering Pines. She was enjoying her clear head. Phones weren't the only distractions when it came to staying in the moment with her besties while traveling.

"Can I have a camera, Lynette?" Renee asked. She was also behind her, sitting between Annie and Jackie. "I just want a shot of us leaving port. The shoreline looks spectacular with all the bright colored boats, palm trees, and activity."

Kit handed her the one she was holding. "Take this one, Renee. I need to find a bathroom."

Jackie laughed. "Already? We just left shore!"

With a shrug, Kit stood, keeping one hand on the back of the bench as the boat deck lulled back and forth. "I miss the good old days when I didn't have to pee every hour or two. There's a bathroom on the lower deck, right?"

"Yep," Renee confirmed. "When I came on this tour with Matt, the water was much rougher, and quite a few people got seasick. The head was a popular destination."

"Yuck, Renee. That's gross," Kit said, leaving them to find the facilities.

Lynette watched her until she disappeared down the boat's only flight of stairs. "Am I the only one who thinks Kit has lost an awful lot of weight since last summer? I swear she wore that outfit at Whispering Pines, but it wasn't baggy in the butt like it is now."

Jackie spun toward the stairs, but Kit was no longer in view. "Now that you mention it, I wondered about how thin her face looks. And I never noticed smudges under her eyes before. I guess I just attributed it to all of us getting a little older. I'm still not used to this gray hair of mine, but I couldn't stay ahead of it. My hair used to be so dark, but that meant my roots always looked terrible. So I let it go."

"I like your new look, Jackie. As for Kit, maybe Isaac is just eating them out of house and home. Teenage boys can do that. Trust me, I know," Annie said with a wag of her head. "Having Colton, Relic, and Ava's husband all in our house for months during the shutdowns always meant bare cupboards and a nearly empty refrigerator, no matter how often we bought groceries. None of them are teens anymore, but they still have hefty appetites."

Deciding Kit was probably fine, Lynette faced Annie. "You look great, by the way. I know you said the exercise program Henry has you both on takes a lot of your time, but it's paying off. You look healthy." She grinned. "Aside from the cast on your arm, of course."

Annie sighed. "Hopefully this darn wrist won't cause me to gain all the weight back."

Festive music played from small black speakers mounted under the canopy above them. Up here, on the top deck of the boat, open sides allowed for plenty of airflow and unobstructed views, but the shelter above would save them in the event of a sudden downpour or even too much sun.

"Let the party begin!" Jackie said. "I'm so glad you arranged for this today, Renee, but it's too bad Matt's friend isn't working. It would have been fun to meet him. Is this his only boat?"

A young woman came by, carrying a tray of fruity-looking drinks in clear plastic cups. "Would you ladies like a rum punch to kick off today's adventure?"

Annie reached for a cup with her left hand. "Are they guaranteed to take away the sting of a broken wrist?"

The girl grinned, tossing multiple thin braids of her black hair over her shoulder before reaching for a cup and handing it to Annie. "All I can guarantee is that the punch has the potential to help you feel amazing for a while, but pace yourself."

Someone turned the music up another notch, and the young woman swayed to the catchy beat. Her nearly transparent white skirt, hanging loose and low on her dark hips, danced in the ocean breeze, while her vivid orange bikini top created a striking contrast against her skin. She had no trouble balancing her still-full tray of beverages while she shimmied on the softly rocking deck.

Annie sipped her punch and laughed. "Your suit matches my cast," she said, earning a laugh out of the girl as she handed more rum cups out to their party.

Lynette eyed the young woman, unable to squelch the surge of jealousy she felt over her lithe, youthful body and shiny hair. In a way, the girl reminded her a little of herself at that age, though her own dark hair was always a mess of curly ringlets. "You look like you know what you're doing," she said, hoping her smile looked sincere, despite her own internal pity party.

"I'm always happiest when I'm on or in the water," the girl replied, turning to fully face Lynette. "Sometimes I think I'm part mermaid. Who else would like a punch?"

The girl's aqua-blue eyes intrigued Lynette. Perhaps she *was* a mermaid. Laughing, Lynette eyed the tray. "Do you have any without the rum?"

The girl lowered her tray and selected a pink plastic cup. Lynette hadn't noticed them, as they blended in with the vibrant fuchsia of the fruit punch in the colorless cups. "Of course. I love your hair, by the way," the potential mermaid said, handing the drink to Lynette before moving on to another group, one bench over.

A larger swell pushed the boat, rocking it side to side for a moment before it settled again. A dollop of the pulpy liquid ran over the lip of Lynette's cup and flowed over her fingers. She licked at the syrupy mess, then nodded toward the busy girl. "The world needs more of that."

Jackie's eyebrows shot up. "More gorgeous, voluptuous young women making us feel frumpy?"

Lynette wiped her still-sticky fingers on her red cover-up with a laugh. "I admit I felt a little frumpy around her, too. But, no, I meant we need more women supporting women. I was thinking how pretty her hair was when she turned around and complimented me on mine. I know it's a little thing, but still. Besides, I wouldn't want to trade places with her. At almost fifty-two, I know how hard it is to be a young woman in your twenties. She may have youth on her side, but we have wisdom."

Kit rejoined them. She carried a punch of her own in one hand, while her other pressed at her temple. "I hit my damn head on a railing when the boat swayed, just as I was coming up the stairs."

All four of her friends laughed.

"Don't laugh!" Kit shot back. "After Annie's fall yesterday, I think we all need to be extra careful. We don't want any more boating injuries. We need to be smart."

Jackie tugged on one of Lynette's silver ringlets that had escaped from her messy topknot. "Is that the type of wisdom you were talking about?"

Lynette glanced between Annie's bright orange cast and the small red mark blooming on Kit's temple. "Hey, whatever it takes to keep us all alive and thriving!"

The catamaran sailed from one small land mass to another. The grouping was called the Mamanuca Islands. At one point, the catamaran's crew dropped anchor near shore, where the water was shallow enough to stand. They lowered a second, smaller set of stairs into the water and encouraged passengers to climb down to play in the crystal-clear water.

Renee still held one camera. Lynette handed the other two out to Kit and Jackie, then pulled a couple things out of her beach bag. Annie's eyes shifted from the line of other passengers leaving the catamaran to the items Lynette held in her hands: a bread bag and a roll of duct tape.

"I feel like I'm ten again, and my mom is wrapping this wrist up so I don't get it wet in the shower."

Jackie slipped the small camera into a zippered side pocket of her yellow skort she'd donned over her swim bottoms, then pushed all of their bags under the benches to keep things dry and out of sight. "Like Lynette said, women supporting women. You were smart to bring that stuff, Lynette."

After doing their best to protect Annie's cast, all five women headed for the stairs. Other than the crew, they were the last to exit the boat.

Lynette had traveled extensively through the years, but the clear water and pure-white sand below still caused her breath to hitch with the sheer beauty of it all. The cool water lapped against her legs, just above her knees, providing the perfect relief from the tropical sun. Other passengers stood in groups of three or four around them, picking small shells up from the shallows and holding them up for inspection.

"Oh, look," Annie said, bending down as if to pick up something with her casted right wrist and hand.

"Stop!" they all yelled in unison.

Annie straightened, a huge grin on her face. "Got ya!"

The fun continued as the group explored the shallows.

Lynette let her head fall back slightly so she could enjoy the full warmth of the sun on her face, wrinkles be damned. She felt as if the sunlight were flowing down through her neck and chest to flood her extremities with pure gold. It reminded her of the guided meditations she sometimes listened to, but real. "I've always loved the moonlight," she said, keeping her eyes closed. "But you can't beat sunshine to make you feel alive."

A wave pummeled the back of her thighs and she had to open her eyes as her sense of balance shifted. Maybe Kit was right. They should be careful.

"Look at this," Jackie cried. "It's a starfish!"

They admired the tiny red creature as it writhed in Jackie's hand. She released it quickly to avoid harming it.

Renee turned in a slow circle, as if taking in as much of the beauty of this tropical paradise as possible, all at once. Shore was only yards away, and some from their boat had wandered up along the beach and into the palms lining the sand. She paused, squinting toward the land.

"What do you see?" Lynette asked.

With a shrug, Renee raised one hand to block some of the strong sun. "Just a reflection, I think. It's almost like a rainbow, or even a kaleidoscope of colors. Can anyone else see it?"

Lynette moved to stand beside her, but try as she might, she couldn't spy any type of reflection or splash of colors. But she did take the time to commit to memory the sweeping beauty before them. This stretch of sand was likely deserted unless the catamarans swung by.

Scenes from *The Blue Lagoon* floated up from her subconscious.

What would it be like to live in a place like this, unencumbered by society?

A shrill whistle cut through the air as their captain called his passengers back to the catamaran. There were more islands to see, and next on the agenda was lunch.

Lynette grabbed a heavy-weight paper plate from the stack at the end of the buffet table and surveyed the colorful feast before them. "This looks delicious," she said. "We aren't going to go hungry."

"I want to at least try every single dish," Annie said, holding a plate, too. "But this is going to be tricky."

"Here, let me help you," Renee said, taking the plate from her. "We'll fill you up first, then I'll get a plate for myself. Some of the best items go fast, and I don't want you to miss out."

Lynette could read the appreciation on Annie's face, but hated for Renee to miss out, too. "I know you've done this before, Renee. Point out your favorites and I'll take extra. That way, you'll enjoy a delicious meal, too."

Working together, the women were soon all seated at their benches again, ready to fill up after their shore excursion.

Kit, her plate still full, excused herself to grab another bottle of water after asking if she could get anyone anything else.

"I bet men don't do this for each other," Jackie said, making a circular motion with her fork.

"Do what?" Annie asked. She was doing her best to pull the plastic wrap off her utensils with one good hand and her teeth.

Jackie handed her fork to her friend, taking Annie's packet and tearing it open. "Help each other eat," she said.

"Eat?" Lynette repeated.

"Yeah. Just think about it. Would Owen think of helping Storm fill his plate at a buffet table if he had a bum arm? Or when they all went fishing and Henry got that hook in his finger last summer, did anyone offer to take him in for a tetanus shot? Of course not."

Annie nodded. "I probably didn't tell you all about the hook. Those idiots. No one—not even Matt, who is probably the most attentive of them all—suggested Henry get his finger checked. By the time he got home and showed it to me, it was looking infected, and I took him straight to the clinic."

Kit returned with her water. "What did I miss?"

"A little guy bashing," Lynette shared. "And I guarantee not one of them would have thought to bring along plastic and tape if one of them had a broken limb and they were heading out in a boat. Like I said before—women helping women."

"Ah, yes, queens helping queens," Kit added.

Annie—her wrist still wrapped in the bread bag—smoothed an end of the tape that had worked its way loose. "For the record, ladies, I'd never want to do life without you. I hate that we argued last night. No more of that, all right? We stick together, no matter what life throws at us!"

Hours into their day trip, Lynette got drowsy. Everyone looked tired and relaxed. They all had full stomachs. Some sported the beginnings of a sunburn, and the islands were starting to all look the same.

Kit, Jackie, and Annie stretched out on the longer, cushioned benches, enjoying the heat of the sun—made tolerable by the ocean breeze—as the catamaran skipped across the waves.

Lynette and Renee sought the protection of the overhead canopy, enjoying a slushy mixture of crushed ice, fresh coconut milk, and native fruits.

"These remind me of the piña coladas behind Sailor's Cove. I wonder if the married cheat who brought them to us is still hot and bothered by the memory of you," Renee said, tapping the plastic rim of her cup against Lynette's.

"I'm sad our boating adventure is ending." Lynette sighed, staring down into her slush and trying to decide whether she'd just eaten a piece of guava or mango.

"Actually, the fun doesn't have to be over yet," Renee said. She set her nearly empty cup aside. "Remember how I told you to wear your dancing shoes?"

Lynette wriggled her bare toes. She'd need to find her flip-flops again before they docked. "I love to dance."

"I know you do."

Renee got up to go over and talk to the pretty girl who'd served them rum punch at the beginning of their tour. The young woman was pouring drinks at the small open bar near the back of the boat. Lynette watched, curious, and noted that other passengers also looked to be in a near stupor after too much sun, food, and possibly alcohol. She noticed the girl light up and nod vigorously to Renee.

"What is she up to?" Lynette whispered.

Renee sashayed her way back to Lynette's side, and just as she took her seat again, the mellow background music ramped up in both volume and tempo.

Someone grabbed a microphone to announce that it was time for everyone to get up on their feet and learn how to dance, "Fijian style!"

Renee popped back up to her feet, pulling Lynette with her. "Don't you just love reggae?!"

Lynette couldn't have named the music genre, but she laughed over her friend's enthusiasm, and allowed the joyful beat to flow through her. The sensation reminded her of the wash of peaceful feelings the sunshine had spurred in her earlier in the day.

Other passengers also got up to dance, though she did hear a few moans at the effort it took to get up. Renee moved over to their reclining friends, actively encouraging them to get up and dance, too.

Lynette felt a tap on her shoulder and turned to the smiling face of the girl Renee had enlisted to kick off the dancing.

"Can I teach you to dance like a true Fijian?" she said, holding both hands up as an offer to lead.

Why not? Lynette thought. "I didn't know mermaids could dance," she said, placing her hands in the woman's warm palms.

Her dance partner's laughter mixed with the lilting lyrics of the song, and Lynette did her best to keep up with the younger woman's gyrating hips and graceful movements. Any self-consciousness she might have felt evaporated as friends and strangers alike moved onto the makeshift dance floor near the boat's tiny bar. There is a universal joy to be found in dancing, and she could feel the overall mood of everyone on the boat—even those who watched instead of joining in—shift from sleepy relaxation to childlike excitement.

Lynette's dance partner said something about the student surpassing the teacher, and the woman released her hands. Raising her arms high, Lynette gave herself over completely to the music. Others bumped and jostled her, and there wasn't much room, but she didn't care. She couldn't remember the last time she'd danced like this. She didn't want the music to end.

When her four friends made their way to her, they all somehow ended up in a dance line of sorts, shimmying and whooping with laughter, without a care in the world.

Sooner than any of them would have liked, the port they'd left hours earlier came into view, and the volume of the music dropped, but didn't fade away completely.

Lynette felt as if she were coming down from a euphoric height. It reminded her of the gentle return to the parasailing boat after she'd floated hundreds of feet above the ocean. Her heart was full, and her head felt clear and light.

She'd made it almost a year without a drink, proving to herself that she could live a full and fun-filled life without alcohol.

With her friends beside her she felt invincible, as if nothing could ever bring her down again.

She hoped the happy expressions on her friends' faces meant that this day trip had helped to sweep away their worries, too.

She located her sandals and slipped them on, then remembered the cameras. She'd collect them all and send them in to be developed once she got home. That way she could include the best shots from today in the scrapbook she was creating from these girls' trips.

"Renee, can you give me back that camera? I'll get the film developed when we get home."

When she didn't respond, Lynette glanced at her, surprised to see her squinting hard at something on the shore.

"Renee? What is it?"

She finally seemed to hear. "Sorry. I think that's Matt's old friend on the end of the dock. He probably tries to meet his boats as they come in, even when he doesn't actually captain them. What did you ask me?"

Lynette looked toward the shore. There was a man standing on the end of the largest dock, and even from here she thought he looked anxious. *The guy must be a pretty uptight dude to be rattled on a beautiful day like today.*

"I just wanted to gather up the three disposable cameras so they don't get lost," she said.

"Oh, sure. Here. Thanks," Renee said. She still seemed distracted by the man on the dock.

Minutes later, the catamaran brushed up against that same dock, and Lynette watched the man help the crew secure the boat.

Passengers filed off, and Lynette gathered the two remaining cameras from her friends along with her other belongings. By the time she stepped onto the dock, she noticed that Renee had moved aside to talk to the man they'd spied earlier.

It had to be the guy Matt knew, the owner of the boat they'd just spent the day on.

Before Lynette even had time to speculate why the man might have sought them out, Renee spun back around to search the crowd.

One look at her friend's worried expression and Lynette knew something was wrong.

Annie and Jackie laughed about something behind her, but Lynette kept her eyes on Renee.

The woman's face had lost all color. After a day in the sunshine, that in itself was disturbing.

Lynette had a sudden, awful thought. Had someone contacted Matt's old friend because of an emergency back home? Had she made a dreadful mistake that morning by insisting they all leave their phones back at the cottage?

No one could reach them directly all day.

Her thoughts went immediately to her mother's safety. Donna was traveling somewhere in England with Chester this week.

Renee looked to be fighting back tears as she pushed her way through the throng of tourists, her eyes locked on Lynette's.

Or had something happened to Matt? The man who met Renee on the dock was his friend.

What if Renee's worst fears—fears of the dangers Matt faced on the job—had come true?

Chapter Seven

Whispering Pines Resort, three hours earlier. . .

J ULIE PULLED THE TANGLE of wet sheets out of the washer. Experience had taught her that even with the industrial-strength dryer her mother had invested in for the resort, it would take nearly two hours for such a large load to finish. That meant it would be almost ten o'clock before she could make up the three beds in their largest cabin. After another long day of running the resort on her own, she'd hoped to be in *bed* by ten. What she *really* wanted to do was lie down in one of the small bedrooms in the lodge for a nap while she waited for the sheets to dry, but she probably didn't have time. She had a resort to maintain.

As her Grandpa George always said, she could sleep when she was dead.

Doing this all by herself was harder than she'd imagined. She'd looked after Whispering Pines in the past when her mom had taken summer trips, but Robbie was usually around to help whenever she got in a pinch. Until her stupid brother went off and got a summer job on a guide boat—in Alaska, of all places. Would he like it enough to move away from here, where their extended family often hung out, too?

She knew he liked to fish, but . . . *Alaska*?!

A final load of dirty towels was piled on the floor by her feet. If she washed them now, she could dry them in the morning. She'd already stocked the cabin with fresh towels. She scooped up an armload and stuffed the dirty laundry into the washer. Once it began to fill with water, she grabbed the broom and swept the floor. Then she checked their supply of detergent and dryer sheets. Summer meant countless loads of laundry and plenty of cleaning supplies to keep a lake resort running.

She'd need to order dryer sheets. Patting the pockets of her shorts, she searched for her phone so she could add them to her shopping list.

The pockets were empty.

Maybe she'd set her phone on the stainless-steel kitchen island after she'd juggled the over-sized laundry basket and her keys to enter the lodge. Once she confirmed the water level in the washing machine was high enough to clean the towels, she hustled down the shadowed hallway toward the kitchen.

That washer was the next thing Renee should replace. She hadn't replaced it when she purchased the new dryer. Julie knew her mother fretted over every major capital expense she had to make out here, and she wished Renee would let her invest some of her own money in improvements.

Her keys were on the island, right where she thought she'd left them, but her phone wasn't there. She should call it to see if she could hear it ring.

She reached for her pocket again, only to realize how ridiculous she was being. Her phone was missing, and the only way she could call it would be from the landline back at the house. Because when Renee had trouble with the phone line in the lodge's office last fall, she hadn't bothered to fix it since they almost always used their cell phones.

Julie sighed. Her phone would show up. She wasn't really worried about it, but she was exhausted. She'd been on her feet since six that morning, when she heard Matt come back in from a long shift. He'd left again midafternoon, so she was well and truly on her own. The lodge was neat and tidy. All she had left to do was make up the beds in the last cabin, but the sheets weren't dry yet. Maybe she could afford to sneak in a little nap while the dryer did its work after all.

Guests occupied each of the three cabins near the firepit. A bachelorette party would take up both halves of the duplex this weekend, but the group wasn't due in until Saturday morning. A newlywed couple had disappeared into what her mother called the Gray Cabin on Sunday, and she'd barely seen them since. She'd only rented out one other cabin, and that was to a family with four kids, but their Suburban had pulled out around noon and hadn't yet returned.

That left one vacant cabin, and she'd have it polished and ready for the next round of renters by nine the next morning.

No one would miss her if she lay down for an hour while the sheets were drying. Or more like forty-five minutes now that she'd done some extra cleaning and searched unsuccessfully for her phone. And after she made up the bed in the last cabin, she would head back to the house. Maybe she had left her phone there when she'd grabbed a quick sandwich at six.

It felt like she'd just put her head on the pillow when the harsh blare of the dryer alarm sounded, letting her know the sheets should be ready. She stood and smoothed the coverlet she'd mussed despite barely moving in her exhausted state.

In the laundry room, the warmth from the load enveloped her as she pulled a top sheet out of the dryer and fluffed it. The stronger heat of midsummer hadn't yet arrived, so the little extra warmth felt good against her bare legs and arms.

She should have grabbed a sweatshirt for her evening tasks.

Once she'd folded the toasty sheets and placed them back in the laundry basket, she decided it would be best to at least throw the towels in the dryer so they couldn't get moldy in the older washing machine overnight. She'd leave the dryer door open and start them in the morning.

She pulled them out, one at a time, and gave them a little shake before tossing them into the dryer. Shoving the whole tangled wad of them straight into the dryer always resulted in more drying time. As she gave the last wet towel a shake, something clattered to the floor.

Julie froze.

She felt like one did when driving past the scene of a nasty accident: if she didn't look, maybe the carnage wasn't really there. But she looked down, unable to resist. And there was her phone, face up on the tiled floor, nicely spun out, and sporting a shattered screen.

What was she going to do about her phone? She didn't dare try to turn it on yet. Instead, she found a bag of rice in the lodge kitchen, dumped it into a bowl, and buried the phone under the hard, dry kernels. Sometimes that worked to dry it out.

She'd have to tolerate the broken screen, but if she'd ruined the phone, she knew it would mean more than the cost of a new phone. Her mom had told her more than once that the next time Julie needed a new phone, she also needed to get on her own cell plan.

Sometimes "adulting" really sucked.

Feeling a bit lost without a working phone in her pocket, Julie finished making up the last cabin. While she wrestled the three different sheet sets onto the beds and ran a vacuum over all the floors, her mind was busy mulling over the same old questions.

She'd earned a college degree in hospitality management, and she loved working at Whispering Pines. When her great-aunt died, she had passed the resort on to Julie's mother. The inheritance had coincided with Renee losing her corporate job six years ago, so she'd taken on the challenge of reopening the small, historic Minnesota lake resort.

Julie had worked at her mother's side the whole time—when she wasn't off at college—offering both emotional and practical support through it all.

If the resort was larger, with more cabins and associated earning potential, there might be a way to make it profitable enough to support both her mother and herself. Renee and Julie's Aunt Jess also ran women's retreats in the off months, but it still wasn't enough.

For a while, Julie wondered if maybe Renee would tire of running the resort and go back to something related to her old career—and leave her more than competent daughter to run Whispering Pines for her.

But it wasn't looking like that would happen soon.

Which begged the question . . .

Was it time for Julie to leave Whispering Pines and find a job that paid better and had more room for growth?

There were no simple answers, because she loved this place so much.

She locked the cabin door. In the morning, she'd bake their signature chocolate chip cookies and have a plate waiting for their new guests upon arrival. It was tempting to drag the vacuum and cleaning cart over to the house instead of stopping back at the lodge to store them properly, but she followed the process they'd established through the years and took the few extra minutes to put everything back in its rightful place.

No one would be at the house. Maybe she'd heat up that leftover pizza, since the sandwich hadn't filled her up and she was hungry again.

The sound of a vehicle pulling into the resort's parking lot caught her attention. The family in the Suburban had returned. She gave them a quick wave, then headed toward the edge of the resort where Matt and her mom had built their new house.

This was another problem. She was turning twenty-five soon—too old to still live in her mother and stepfather's house. When the world shut down in 2020 and there were no guests at the resort, she and Robbie each claimed half of the duplex, but that wasn't an option now. They needed the rental income; Minnesota summers were too short, and they had to earn all the revenue they could over the abbreviated high season.

She ate the pizza, then tried watching a show, but it didn't hold her interest. Bored, she pulled a pen and pad of paper out of her mother's junk drawer and sat at the kitchen table. It was time to brainstorm about her future career opportunities.

The pad brought back memories of her freshman year in college when her mom went through her job layoff. Renee had handed both her and Robbie pen and paper, along with instructions to help plan a few weeks of unexpected free time over the holidays.

Julie hadn't realized it then, but Renee was trying to figure out how to dream again. Throughout the process, she also taught her daughter the value of thinking differently.

A vehicle pulled up in the drive, and her heart beat faster. It must be Matt, but why would he come home during the middle of his shift?

She dropped the pen onto the still-blank top sheet and went to the back door, pulling it open just as Matt climbed out from behind the wheel of his cruiser.

"I didn't expect to see you tonight," she said.

Matt gave a curt nod. "Julie, why aren't you answering your phone?"

Something was wrong. She could see it in the way he walked. He held his shoulders stiff and fidgeted with his keys as he came up the back stairs into the house. Once he was inside, he tossed the ring onto the kitchen table.

She shut the door. "My phone? It somehow ended up in the washing machine with a load of towels. I'm trying to dry it out in rice now."

Matt, who always looked intimidating to her when he was in uniform as the county's sheriff, strode straight over to the landline phone on the wall and lifted the handset. "It's working. Why didn't you answer it?" The tension in his expression was making her nervous.

Then Julie remembered. "I forwarded it to my cell this morning, since I knew I'd be running around the resort all day and I didn't want to miss any customer calls. But—"

"But now your cell isn't working, which is why I couldn't get ahold of you." Matt pulled a chair back from the table and dropped into it with a heavy sigh. He bent down to remove his boots. "Julie, I need you to go grab that emergency contact list your mom left for us. She's not answering her phone either, so I need to try one of her friends."

Julie looked from her stepfather, through a back window at his squad car in the driveway, and back. A chill passed through her. "Matt, what's wrong? Did something happen to Robbie? It's only his first week on the job. Did the idiot fall overboard up there in Alaska?"

She heard the fear ratchet up her voice, but she didn't care.

Matt kicked one boot off. He glanced up at her before moving on to the other. "It's not your brother. There *is* a family emergency, but not in *our* family. Now, go. Get me that list. We can't afford to waste any more time."

The possible gravity of the situation finally registered. Julie rushed past him and down the hallway to Matt and Renee's bedroom. She flung open the door and couldn't help but smile at the mussed bed and clothes tossed over the back of the recliner her mom had situated just so, giving her the perfect view of the lake beyond while relaxing at the end of a busy day. Matt wasn't as neat as her mother, but Julie knew he'd clean this up before his wife got home.

Unless the emergency was serious enough that she'd come home early, too.

She scanned the room and spotted a pad of yellow paper, much like the one she'd been using in the kitchen. A list of names and numbers, along with other instructions, covered the top sheet in her mom's messy cursive.

The list was long. For such a capable man, Matt sure needed plenty of directions in his wife's absence.

Julie grabbed the list and headed back to the kitchen. "Which friend? What happened? Who knew how to get ahold of you?"

Matt was at the kitchen sink, downing a tall glass of water. He took the offered pad from her and scanned it quickly. The phone on his belt chimed, but he ignored it. "Annie's daughter called. She needs to reach her mom right away. Apparently, Renee wasn't the only one to leave an emergency contact list with her family. Her daughter tried calling Annie and all the other women, too. No one is answering. When she couldn't reach them, she thought to try the resort's phone number, but no one picked up."

"Shoot," Julie said, feeling a wash of guilt for allowing herself to be unreachable. "That's my fault."

Matt's expression softened. "It's no one's fault. Ava—Annie's daughter—told me she was panicking, but then she remembered I was a county sheriff. She tracked me down."

Julie nodded. "Resourceful. Now what?"

Matt dropped Renee's list on the table and sat back down again. "Give me a second to try the girls directly again. Maybe they were just out of range. Do you remember their daily itinerary?" He pulled a cell phone out of the top pocket of his uniform. The one on his belt must be his work phone.

Julie thought her mom might have texted their schedule to her. "I'll try to find it on my phone while you call them."

Matt frowned at her. "Your phone?"

"Shit! Right. That won't work. Knowing Mom, she kept notes if she did any of the planning. Here—"

She took the pad of paper she'd retrieved from the room, tore off the top sheet so Matt could use it, then started thumbing through other pages. Sure enough, Renee had filled pages with more trip-related scribbles. Matt worked his way down the contact list while Julie scanned her mother's nearly indecipherable notes.

"I'm still not able to reach any of the five of them," he said a few minutes later. "Anything useful in there?"

"Still looking. Did Ava say why it was so important for her to reach Annie right away?"

He set his phone down with another sigh, then rubbed his temple as if a headache was forming there. "She did. It's Henry, Annie's husband.

He collapsed at work. They think it's his heart. An ambulance took him to the hospital in Ruby Shores, but then they had to fly him to Minneapolis. Ava was a little hard to understand—she's understandably upset—but I gathered it didn't sound good. *Shit.* Henry was such a great guy."

Julie paused, marking the place she'd left off on Renee's notes with a finger. "Matt . . . you said *was*. Did Annie's husband die?"

He slapped the table. "I meant 'is'—*is* a great guy. As far as I know, he's alive. But we need to get word to Annie immediately so she can come home. Flights from Fiji are long, and his condition must be serious to transport him by helicopter." He jabbed a finger at the pad she was combing through. "What are you finding? Anything useful?"

"Maybe . . . Does the name Lucas Emerson mean anything to you? She listed it, along with a phone number and tomorrow's date. Today is the twenty-third, right?"

He motioned for the pad. "Yeah, but Fiji is ahead of us. It would be midafternoon Friday there already, making it the twenty-fourth. Lucas is an old friend of mine. He owns a touring company that runs these cool catamarans between the islands. We booked one of his tours when I took your mother there before we got married. Come to think of it, I think she mentioned trying to line one up for her friends this week. Damn, I should have paid more attention when she talked about her plans."

Julie almost said not to worry about it, that her mom was used to him being distracted, but thought that would be a cruel thing to say. Matt really was a good guy, and a loving husband. He just had a tough, demanding job. "Why don't you call this number Mom left? Who knows? Maybe they took one of his tours, and that's why no one's phones are working."

Matt picked up his phone again.

Someone knocked at the door. Julie could see a man through the window, and recognized him as the father with the four kids and the Suburban.

Now what?

Torn between Matt's phone call and their renter, she went to the door.

"I'm sorry to bother you, but my youngest locked us out of our cabin. When I tried to call your emergency number, no one picked up, so I took a chance that I'd find you here at the house. I saw you heading this way earlier." Then he glanced nervously at Matt's patrol car. "Is everything all right?"

Julie grinned. "Yes. That's my stepfather's car. Matt Blatso. He's the sheriff. Let me grab my spare keys, and we'll get you back into your cabin. Sorry about the phone. I damaged my cell tonight."

"It's a little scary how reliant we've all become on our cell phones, isn't it?" the renter said. He looked relieved that the patrol car wasn't at the resort on official business.

Matt gave Julie a quick nod as she pulled the door closed, and as she followed the man toward the cabins, she crossed her fingers that Matt could get word to Annie before it was too late.

Chapter Eight

Jackie should have followed Kit's example and used the bathroom on board before debarking. If Annie kept making her laugh with more hilarious stories about her rambunctious granddaughter, she might wet her pants.

It was always fun to see how animated Annie became when talking about little Nora. Jackie wasn't ready to be a grandma yet, but her friend helped her realize how much she looked forward to it someday.

Renee's idea to take the boat tour today had turned out to be the perfect way for everyone to relax and reconnect. The argument around the fire the night before had left Jackie shaken. She didn't even want to think about how lonely life would be without her girlfriends.

"Jackie, we need to find Kit," Renee insisted as she hurried to stand next to them, cutting Annie off mid-sentence.

"She'll be here in a sec," Jackie said with barely a glance toward Renee. "You need to hear about Nora's potty-training escapades. What a funny kid!"

"I'm serious, Jackie. We have to go. Right now."

Renee's tone doused her jovial mood, and she finally turned toward her friend and the man she now saw trailing behind. "What's wrong? And who is *he*?"

"This is Lucas. Lucas Emerson. Matt's old friend from when he lived here in Fiji. This is his boat," Renee said as she jabbed her thumb at the mostly deserted catamaran. "Thank God, there's Kit now. Come on. Lucas will give us a ride back to the cottage. Hurry, Kit!"

Someone must have bumped into Annie on the crowded pier because she lost her balance and fell against Jackie, cast first.

Annie grimaced as she held her injured wrist with her good hand. "What is happening, Renee? It was such a fun afternoon, but now you're acting weird. By the way, it's nice to meet you, Lucas. Your tour might end up being the highlight of this trip for me."

Jackie noticed Lynette step behind Annie, as if to protect her from anyone else bumping into her. Lynette was taller and not as easy to push around.

Then she caught a look pass between Renee and Lynette. Something was definitely up.

"I thought we booked the shuttle bus again for the trip back to the cottage," Jackie said, seeking some kind of clarification.

Lucas Emerson cleared his throat. "I'll explain on the way. Is this everyone?"

Kit had finally reached Renee's side. "What's the rush?"

"No idea," Jackie said. "But come on. He'll tell us on the way."

Renee gave her a nod of appreciation and hurried after the new guy. Lynette grabbed Annie's uninjured forearm and steered her down the path after them.

Kit poked Jackie as they hurried to follow. "Want to clue me in?"

"I would if I could. I wonder if something happened back at Whispering Pines. This guy is Matt's friend. You know, the one who owns the boat we toured on today. He must have approached Renee the minute she stepped off the boat, and she looks upset."

Jackie had to weave around a young mother holding the hands of two toddlers. Once the coast was clear again, she glanced at Kit. "They'll tell us more in a minute. I wish I'd been smart like you and used the bathroom."

Kit shrugged. "I'm learning to be proactive about that. Huh. Nice wheels, Mr. Emerson."

Lucas Emerson slid the door of an ivory-colored van open and motioned for the women to climb in. A large sign next to the curb flagged the prime parking spot as reserved.

"Call me Lucas."

Renee confused Jackie by climbing into the driver's side up front—until she remembered this was Fiji and that was actually the passenger side. Once Lynette and Annie were inside, Lucas ran around the front of the van and started it up. Jackie peeked through the open door, then took the empty seat in the back next to Lynette. Kit, climbing in last, sat opposite Annie.

Lucas jabbed a button on the dash, and the side door slid closed.

The luxurious scent of leather enveloped Jackie, and she spotted a crystal decanter set in the console between them. "I feel underdressed," she joked, hoping to dispel some of the confused tension. This vehicle obviously transported a higher-end clientele than the shuttle bus they'd taken to the pier earlier.

"Everyone buckled in?" their new driver asked. He pulled out of the spot before anyone even answered.

Jackie touched Lynette's arm and gave her a questioning look. Lynette pointed toward the back of Annie's seat.

Annie leaned forward to address Renee. "While I'm sure we all appreciate these extravagant surroundings, something is obviously going on, and whatever it is, it isn't good."

Lucas glanced at Annie in the rearview mirror, but remained quiet.

Renee swiveled to face Annie as best she could with the seatbelt restraining her. "Annie, your kids have been trying to call you. When they couldn't reach you, they called Matt, thinking he might know what to do, since we're staying at his cottage."

Annie's back stiffened.

"My kids?"

Renee nodded. She put a hand on Annie's knee. "Honey, it's Henry. There is something going on with his heart. He's in the hospital. In Minneapolis. Ava wants you to come home. Right away."

Annie slid back in her seat, Renee's hand falling from her knee. "Right away? But how? I don't have a flight home until next Tuesday."

Lucas honked at someone as he weaved in and out of traffic. Jackie had to grab the handle on the side of Kit's headrest in front of her.

"Sorry about that, ladies," he said. "Annie, Matt had some trouble reaching me, but when he did I had my assistant look for a flight home for you right away. She called me back just before your boat landed. She secured three seats on a flight leaving tonight at ten. I'll swing by the cottage so you can grab your things, including your phones, and then we'll head straight for the airport. You'll be early, but you always want to give yourself a time cushion with international flights. It would be a good idea to eat before you board, too."

"Our phones," Annie muttered, as though trying to process everything. "Tonight? But, wait. Three seats? There are five of us."

Renee touched her knee again. "I'll stay here and see if I can't catch a flight tomorrow afternoon or evening. That way I can keep my appointment with that realtor Matt needed me to see about the sale of the cottage."

Annie grabbed her hand. "Renee, you have to be honest with me. Is Henry still alive? If he's not—I can't face that without all of you. But—if it's something more minor . . . the rest of you don't have to leave early."

Jackie hated the way Annie hiccupped her way through everything after the suggestion that her husband might not be alive. Renee's angry face in the firelight from the night before flashed through her mind. She shook her head to dispel the awful thought. Annie wasn't going to lose Henry like Renee had lost her first husband.

Renee unhooked her seatbelt and turned to lay her other hand on top of their clasped ones. "All Matt could tell Lucas was that they had to take Henry from the Ruby Shores hospital to Abbott Northwestern by air ambulance. He's working to find out more and will keep us posted."

Lucas extended his left arm to brace Renee as he braked hard, and everyone slid an inch or two forward. "Renee, please turn around and put your seatbelt back on. Annie, I'm sorry I can't tell you more. I shot Matt a quick text to let him know we are heading back to the cottage now."

Jackie hated the way Annie's shoulders heaved with emotion, but the woman stayed dry-eyed. She reached forward to place one hand on her left shoulder, and Lynette did the same on her right. Kit reached over and entwined her fingers with Annie's as Renee turned to face the front and put her belt back on.

"He's going to be all right, Annie," Jackie said, but even she could hear the question behind her own words. "And we aren't leaving your side until you're back home with him."

They fell silent after that, keeping hands on Annie to show their support, while a kind near-stranger whisked them through a foreign land.

They hadn't even landed yet and already the ten-hour flight from Fiji to Los Angeles had felt like twenty to Jackie. She couldn't imagine how Annie must feel. Their assigned seats were scattered throughout the widebody 787 for this first flight, but Jackie had watched Kit persuade the young woman next to Annie to switch seats with her during boarding. Between Annie's orange wrist cast and the vacant look in her terrified eyes, the other passenger must have taken pity on their friend. The woman might be traveling alone, so it didn't really matter where she sat, but Jackie thought it was kind of her to be so flexible.

Women supporting women, Jackie mused.

She wondered if Lynette and Renee had found flights home yet.

The older gentleman next to Jackie said little throughout the flight, which she was happy about. As their plane began its slow descent, she slid the shade open on her window. A heavy bank of clouds blocked out any sunshine, making it difficult to tell if it was morning or night, though she knew their scheduled landing was at one in the afternoon, LA time. A flicker of lightning on the horizon caused Jackie's already tight nerves to jump in her stomach. Their connection was short, and a delayed landing might mean they wouldn't make it. A delayed connection to Minneapolis could be good, give them some breathing space. But a canceled one? Unimaginable.

The latest word they had on Henry was that they were prepping him for surgery. More than twelve hours had passed since then. Could Henry be sitting up in bed even now, their prayers answered, and be feeling bad about causing Annie to cut her trip short?

Jackie decided that was exactly what had happened. She didn't want to even think about a different outcome.

"I'm sorry, folks, but we're facing a slight delay here."

A collective groan went up throughout the cabin.

The pilot did his best to assure the passengers that the delay would be short, but Jackie wasn't so sure as the plane shuddered in the turbulent air. If this continued, Annie might have to take care of Kit instead of the other way around. Turbulence always ruined flights for Kit.

Jackie put her ear buds back in and tried to allow the meditative music to calm her nerves. Her heart ached for Annie and the terror the woman had to be feeling, stuck in an airplane, thousands of miles from her ailing husband.

The same husband who'd been working hard on his health lately. Had he experienced any early warning signs? Was that why he'd started up on a vigorous exercise program with Annie?

Either way, it reminded Jackie that they weren't getting any younger.

Four years ago, she had taken a leap of faith and walked away from a career that no longer gave her joy. Changing careers in her late-forties hadn't been easy, but she'd done it. She'd thrown herself into her new business venture, relocated to a different city, and worked harder than ever.

But she lived alone. She knew how lucky she was to have the friendships of her old summer camp friends, but was that enough?

The plane bounced again, and lightning flashed outside her window as her eyes popped open. She closed her shade—as if that could keep the storm at bay—and closed her eyes again.

The weather reminded her of the storm that hit Ruby Shores in 2019, sending both her and Kit racing back there to check on her parents and Kit's grandmother, mere days before their scheduled girls' trip to Hawaii. Aside from the damage to Kit's family home and lots of downed trees in the neighborhoods, they'd been lucky.

Scenes from the next day, when the cleanup had begun, came back to her. She couldn't help but smile at the memory of her old friend Owen, wielding a heavy chainsaw, and looking sexy in a way she'd never noticed before.

Was she foolish to ignore this attraction she felt for him?

When they were in grade school together, she'd considered Owen to be her best friend. As the years went by, her girlfriends had become more important to her, and things with Owen drifted.

Despite the way her friends still teased her about Owen having a crush on her, she'd never really thought of him romantically. At least not until she ran into him at their thirty-year class reunion. He'd intrigued her when they grabbed a cup of coffee. She'd wanted to hear all about his life.

How had her former best friend become the owner of the land where her old summer camp used to be held?

Another year had passed before she saw him again, on that stormy night when he and his doctor son rushed to the aid of Kit's grandmother. But since that was right before she'd left on their first big girls' trip, their lives had angled away from each other yet again.

Months later, he had reached out to her mother to plan a surprise party for Jackie's fiftieth birthday. It was an extremely generous gesture, but it was a busy time for her with her new business. It was also the holiday season, and then there was a second girls' trip—that one to sunny

Arizona—just before the world shut down because of the pandemic.

Fate didn't seem inclined to let her explore any kind of romantic relationship with her old friend.

Maybe, if Lynette hadn't almost drowned herself last summer at Whispering Pines, Jackie wouldn't have gotten so mad at Owen for keeping Storm's presence a secret. But with time, she realized fear had caused her to overreact. She'd wanted to reach back out to Owen to apologize for their shouting match the morning after Lynette's rescue. If she was honest with herself, she had to admit she had been the only one yelling. Owen had tried to talk to her calmly about his ongoing friendship and business dealings with Storm, but Lynette's close call had her so freaked out she wouldn't listen.

But then her father's health declined at a more rapid rate, consuming any spare time she had outside of her business.

She reached for the necklace her daughters had given her and rubbed the locket between her fingers.

The only other interaction she'd had with Owen since their shouting match at Whispering Pines was at her father's funeral. It was kind of him to come, but he hadn't come alone. He probably had no idea how much it hurt her to see a woman on his arm. Why would he think twice about it? She'd never been honest with him about her feelings.

Her friends often speculated that Owen had been in love with her for years. If that was indeed true, had she missed any chance she might have had with him?

A flight attendant stopped beside her row and tried to talk to her, but she couldn't hear over the instrumental music playing in her ears.

She pulled out her ear buds and smiled up at the woman. "What was that?"

"I wanted to let you know that we've arranged to have a cart meet you and your two friends at the gate as soon as we land. This is a large plane, and it takes time to get everyone off, but the cart should help you make your connection. I know it's important for the three of you to get to Minneapolis as soon as possible."

While Jackie appreciated the news, how could this woman know anything about Annie's situation? Her expression must have conveyed her confusion.

The attendant gave her a small smile. "One of your friends was feeling a little under the weather, and when I brought her something for her motion sickness, she gave me an update as to why your friend with the broken arm had burst into tears at the news of our delay. We can't control the weather, but we'll do what we can to help make this a smooth connection."

The attendant gave her one last friendly nod, then moved away down the aisle to attend to someone else.

The pilot came back over the loudspeaker and asked the flight attendants to take their seats, as they'd be landing shortly.

Jackie had lost track of time thinking about Owen.

They might make their connection after all.

Over four more hours and two additional time zone changes later, Jackie's head was pounding as she tried to wrestle her slightly over-sized bag out of the overhead compartment.

"You probably should have checked that bag," said the thirty-something-year-old woman who'd sat in the row behind her. She was the same woman who'd ignored the young boy in her care while he'd repeatedly kicked the back of Jackie's seat for the past hour.

Jackie almost replied with a snarky comment of her own, but a second woman from the seat across the aisle reached up and helped free the strap on Jackie's bag that was caught on something.

Turning her back on the impatient woman to thank the helpful one, she hurried down the aisle as best she could. Annie would be impatient to get to the hospital, and Jackie certainly didn't want to cause any more delays.

None of them had dared to check a bag because of the tight connection, so it didn't take long for the trio to reach the pickup zone outside of the terminal.

"Watch for Dean's blue Toyota," Kit said as they exited the revolving door into the fresh air. Dusk wasn't far off, and the air felt lighter with the lower humidity levels than the environment they'd left behind, along with Renee and Lynette, in Fiji.

"He'll take us straight to the hospital, right?" Annie asked.

Jackie suspected the same question had been asked and answered many times already by the way Kit looked, as if fighting to keep her patience.

"Of course," Kit said. She left them and her suitcase to move closer to the curb and check for her husband's vehicle in the mess of traffic.

"Any more updates?" Jackie asked as she rested her spare hand on Kit's roller bag.

Annie shifted from one foot to the other. The poor thing looked positively wilted, her eyes haunted. Jackie suspected there was nothing other than the sight of Annie's husband, still breathing, that could wipe that film away.

"No one is picking up their phones," was all she said.

Jackie's breath hitched. That didn't sound good at all. Annie's three kids had to know she would be beside herself with worry as she fought her way to them all.

"There!" Kit yelled. "He's way up ahead. I must have gotten the door number wrong. He can't come backward, so we're going to have to go to him."

Jackie noticed that Annie looked to be on the verge of tears again. Her wrist must hurt, too, given how she was holding it tight against her body. "I'll pull your bag, Annie."

Annie barely looked at her. She just took off speed-walking behind Kit, who'd grabbed her own bag before leading them toward Dean's car.

Ten minutes later, Dean was the one weaving in and out of the evening traffic toward the hospital where they'd taken Henry. Had it really only been twenty-four hours since Matt's friend had done the same thing, whisking them from one point to another, getting Annie ever closer to whatever destiny had in store for her?

"Have you talked to anyone at the hospital, Dean?"

Jackie hated how hesitant Annie sounded. Had her friend given up all hope in the hours since getting the fateful news about Henry?

He nodded and slowed as he changed lanes, entering a stretch of road construction. "Yes, but only to share your arrival time with Ava. Henry was still in surgery at that point."

Annie, who'd sat up front at Kit's insistence, dropped her face into her palms. "There's no way he's still in surgery," she muttered.

Dean nodded and reached over to give Annie's shoulder a reassuring squeeze. "Keep the faith, Annie. Keep the faith."

Jackie felt her throat tighten and tears prick her eyes at the touching display of support. She didn't understand why Annie seemed so re-signed. The friend she knew never gave up easily on anything. It would be so unfair if she lost Henry, and if anyone deserved a fair shake, it was Annie. The woman had spent her life trying to make the world a fairer place.

CHAPTER NINE

DEAN PULLED UP TO the main entrance at Abbott Northwestern Hospital, near downtown Minneapolis. The row of cars ahead prevented him from getting close, but Jackie knew Annie couldn't wait any longer. She nodded to her desperate friend. "Go. We'll catch up."

Annie jumped out, dashing toward her husband and family.

"You girls go on in, too," Dean said. "I'll park and then call you, Kit, to find out what floor to go to. Unless you'd rather I head home and come back to get you later?"

Two cars in front of them pulled away, so he eased the car ahead.

"No. Please stay, hon," Kit said. She was behind him and slid forward on the bench seat to wrap her arm around his neck. "Since we have no idea what is happening inside, I'd like you there, too."

"Will do. Now go be with Annie."

Jackie and Kit hurried inside. They had to stop at the front desk to check in and get directions. By the time they spied Annie, she was already down the hall, anxiously waiting in front of an elevator. The doors slid open and Jackie channeled the track skills of her youth, sprinting forward. Yelling to catch Annie's attention in a hospital felt inappropriate, otherwise she would have done that.

Annie spied her coming once she'd stepped inside the elevator. Jackie could see her pressing buttons, but to no avail.

The doors slid shut, with Annie inside, just as Jackie slid to a stop in front of the elevator bank.

An amused-looking patient and an orderly pushing his gurney watched.

"Someone's in a hurry," the old guy being transported spat out through a toothless grin. "Wish someone pretty like you was running over here to see me like that."

Jackie ignored him and instead addressed the orderly. "Which floor do they perform heart surgeries on?"

The bearded man in blue scrubs looked confused. "This is my first week on the job."

"Annie's elevator stopped on three. That's our best bet," Kit said, watching the numbers above the closed doors before turning back to the less-than-helpful hospital employee. "Can you at least tell us where we can find the stairs?"

The new orderly pointed down the hallway to their right.

Jackie nodded her thanks and ran for the stairs, Kit close behind. They didn't want Annie to arrive alone, regardless of the news. They should be by her side for support.

Jackie took the stairs two at a time, like she was running hurdles. It had been decades since she'd last done that, though. Would she even be able to get out of bed in the morning?

Kit was lagging. "You're going to give *me* a heart attack, Jackie! Slow down!"

"Can't! We have to be there for Annie."

By the time Jackie yanked open the door on the landing that sported a massive 3 in black paint, Annie was off the elevator and in her daughter's arms. The two women rocked back and forth, no doubt finally finding comfort in each other's presence. Annie's face was buried, tucked right under Ava's chin.

Jackie held back and motioned for Kit to stop as they caught up to their distraught friend.

Ava pulled away from her mother, wearing a surprised expression. "Mom, what did you do to your arm?"

Annie raised her right wrist, looking at the bright wrap around her cast with an identical expression to her daughter's, as if she'd forgotten all about her own injury. "Oh. I fell. It's not a big deal. A small crack."

"That's quite the color," Ava said, smirking at the cast. "Nora will love it."

"Is she here? Nora?" Annie asked, looking around.

Jackie wondered why she hadn't yet asked Ava anything about Henry—unless she'd missed it while climbing the stairs.

Annie shook her head, as if admonishing herself. "I'm stalling. Of course you wouldn't bring Nora up here. She's too young. Tell me. How is Henry?"

Ava glanced over her mother's head and met Jackie's eyes, then spied Kit. She gave them a slight nod of recognition, then captured her mother's left hand in hers. "I'll take you to him. They called me from the reception desk to tell me you were on your way up, and I knew you'd never find us if I didn't meet you by the elevators."

Jackie and Kit hesitated, unsure of their place.

When Ava noticed her mother's friends hanging back, she waved them forward. "You should come, too."

Jackie wondered why she'd said that. Was Henry already well enough for visits from non–family members? She doubted that would be the case—he'd only just had surgery, hadn't he? So, then . . . did that mean whatever news waiting for Annie at the end of this maze that Ava led them through was something dreadful?

Ava didn't seem inclined to share much yet.

Finally, Ava turned into a family waiting room. Jackie scanned the occupants. She recognized almost everyone. Annie's folks were nursing white paper cups of ink black coffee, despite the late hour. Even Michael, Annie's first husband and father to both Ava and Colton, was there. She didn't see Colton, but Relic, Annie's youngest son, stood and walked straight into his mother's arms. Jackie could see he'd been crying.

"Mom, you made it," a deep voice said from behind Jackie and Kit.

Colton strode right past them like he didn't even see them, eyes only for Annie. The last time Jackie had been in the young man's company, he'd worn a suit and helped facilitate her father's funeral. Tonight, he looked younger, more vulnerable, in a hooded sweatshirt and jeans. Relic's T-shirt bore a similar collegiate logo, while Ava wore professional attire, as if she'd rushed straight to the hospital from her job at the bank in Ruby Shores. Everyone looked mussed, as if no one had dared leave the hospital to freshen up. Jackie felt much the same.

"Henry just woke up," Colton was saying. "He's asking for you."

Annie's knees finally gave out on her, and it took both Colton and Relic to hold their mother upright. Tears came again, but this time Annie's expression held a hint of hope.

"He's all right then?"

Jackie saw Colton's gaze swing to Ava, who'd stepped forward to Annie's side again. "Mom . . . you need to be prepared. The doctors say he's very weak, and you'll see that he's hooked up to lots of machines. They told us that the next few hours are critical. They hope the surgery was successful, but there may be permanent damage."

Annie took a deep breath and pulled her shoulders back. "I'm here now. I'll take care of him."

Jackie wanted to cry at the mask of determination that slipped over her friend's tear-streaked face. Annie was lots of things—she was stubborn, loving, a fighter for those she loved—but she wasn't a doctor. If sheer will could keep Henry alive, Annie would do that for him. But Jackie knew it wouldn't be that simple.

"Only one of us can see him at a time," Ava said, "and immediate family only. Colton will show you the way, Mom."

Annie nodded and grasped Colton's arm.

When Colton returned by himself and joined his siblings where they sat, Kit excused herself to find Dean, no doubt lost somewhere in the maze of hallways.

Annie's family greeted Jackie, and then Michael waved her over, catching her up in a bear hug that spoke volumes.

"I'm glad Annie didn't have to travel all the way from Fiji alone," he said, motioning for Jackie to take the seat next to the chair he'd occupied when they first walked in. He dropped into it again with a groan. "They really need to do something about the chairs in hospital waiting rooms. Can I get you something? Coffee? Water? You must have come straight here from the airport. What you probably really need is a pillow and a bed."

Jackie waved this off. If Annie could power through the exhaustion, so could she. "What do you know about Henry?" she asked, keeping her voice low. It wasn't a conversation she wanted to have with the entire room. "What happened?"

Michael leaned forward, elbows on his knees. He put his hands together. "Henry thought he could fix his heart issues with exercise and a healthy diet, instead of getting his ass in here for a procedure. Which his doctors told him he should seriously consider."

"Wait. Annie told us the two of them had started exercising together, but she didn't mention Henry having any specific health concerns."

He rubbed the bridge of his nose. "Yeah, the diagnosis was recent. I doubt Henry told her about what the doctor said. When I talked to him, he tried to make it sound like it was no big deal, but I could tell he was a little worried. Anyhow, I guess he was at work, on the plant floor, and he just collapsed. The Ruby Shores hospital flew him here because they can't treat whatever is going on with his heart."

Jackie nodded. The story matched what Matt had told his Fijian friend. "It's good of you to come, too. I'm sure Annie will appreciate you being here."

Michael spread his hands wide. "I was friends with Henry before I ever met Annie, and I wanted to be here for the kids."

Things were more complicated than Michael made them sound, but Jackie knew Annie had worked hard to smooth things over within their blended family. Not that any of that mattered at the moment. Henry and Annie could use all the support they could get.

Kit returned with Dean, and Jackie introduced him to Michael.

Michael's phone rang, and he excused himself to take the call.

Annie was gone for nearly an hour, and Jackie thought Ava and the boys were looking anxious. She wandered over to visit with Annie's parents, giving them each a hug and accepting their condolences over the death of her dad. While she appreciated their sincerity, she was ready to reach the point where those sentiments stopped coming up, once and for all.

Michael returned and sat down by Dean and Kit. The men hadn't met before, but both were excellent conversationalists, so Kit eventually came over to say hello to Patsy and Lyle, too.

A woman in scrubs came in and asked Ava, Colton, and Relic to please come with her. Jackie thought her expression looked kind but reserved. The rest of the room fell silent as Annie's three kids followed the woman out. Patsy stood and took a step toward the door, but Lyle grabbed her hand and pulled her back to her chair. Jackie suspected the woman wanted to run down the hallway and wrap her daughter and grandchildren in her arms to protect them from this pain.

Jackie exchanged an uneasy look with Kit. She didn't have a good feeling about this.

Her phone vibrated in her pants pocket. She pulled it out and glanced at it, and she couldn't help but smile at the goofy selfie her daughter had just sent. Hailey was hamming it up for the camera beside their border collie, Nikki.

The picture was a bright point of light in what was quickly feeling like a pit of despair. Jackie really hoped she was wrong and that Henry, wherever he was inside the walls of this hospital, was clawing his way back from a life-saving surgery and toward a full recovery.

Annie had told her that during the pandemic, when they all lived together, Henry and Ava and Colton had been able to rebuild their relationships, which had suffered in recent years. The older two kids also reconnected with Relic, Henry and Annie's biological son, during those days of confinement.

They all deserved more time together—under happier circumstances.

The door swung open again, and this time it was Annie.

Jackie could immediately feel the grief radiating out from her dear friend, and she knew in an instant that Annie's family wouldn't get what they deserved.

Annie, whose lifelong quest had always been to make the world a fairer place, was facing one of the greatest injustices of all: the heartbreaking loss of a loved one, gone too soon.

Chapter Ten

LYNETTE FLUNG HERSELF ONTO the bed in Jackie's spare bedroom, buried her face in the pillow, and finally let the tears flow that she'd stubbornly held back. Henry was gone. One of her very best friends was suddenly a widow.

And Lynette hadn't been there for either of them.

Her rational mind knew there was nothing she could have done differently, but that did nothing to ease the ache in her heart. Getting that call from Jackie with the terrible news while waiting for her connection in San Francisco had felt like a punch to the gut, and she still struggled to take a deep breath.

She couldn't stop her tears, but she battled to stay as quiet as possible. The voices of Jackie's daughters reached her from the next room over. These thin walls provided little privacy.

A door slammed somewhere in the townhouse. Lynette jumped at the sound. She must have dozed off.

Angst had filled her last day in Fiji while she'd waited for a seat on a plane home. Renee had kept busy with the potential sale of her husband's cottage, but Lynette had had nothing to do after Annie, Jackie, and Kit left for the airport. She could have gone exploring on her own, but she hadn't been in the mood. Instead, she'd grabbed one of the metal folding chairs and gone down to the water's edge.

She'd probably looked ridiculous, sitting on that awful chair for hours, looking out over the rolling ocean and contemplating life and death and the unpredictability of it all.

She checked her phone on the bedside table and grinned when she found another text from her mother. Life and death might be unpredictable, but Donna was not. The prohibitive cost of a spur-of-the-moment flight from London meant she couldn't make Henry's funeral, but that wouldn't stop her from checking on Lynette multiple times a day.

Donna had enough girlfriends of her own to understand the ripple effects of a tragedy like the one Annie was facing.

Lynette could have used a hug from her mother right now.

She considered calling Donna instead of texting her back, but then realized it was the middle of the night in London.

Someone knocked on her bedroom door.

"Come in," she said, getting off the bed and shoving the phone into her pocket. She groaned when she checked her reflection in the mirror above the room's solitary dresser. Her face was red and blotchy, and her silver curls stuck out in every direction, like a Brillo pad. A quick repair wasn't possible.

Jackie pushed open the door. "You look like hell."

"I feel like it, too," Lynette agreed. She turned her back on her reflection.

"Come to the kitchen and have something to eat. The girls ordered pizza, and I threw together a tray of meat, cheese, and fruit. You must be starving by now."

Lynette's stomach growled at the mention of food—so loud that Jackie, from across the room, smiled knowingly.

"Jackie, I appreciate your hospitality. You drove across the city to pick me up at the airport when I'm sure you'd have preferred to catch up on your sleep. You even kicked one of your daughters out of your spare room, so I'd have a place to rest. But how can we eat at a time like this? After what's happening to Annie's family?"

Jackie entered the room, sat on the edge of the bed, and patted the space next to her. "Sit."

Lynette took a deep breath, readying herself for a lecture. Then she realized what she'd accomplished. "That's the first time I could fully fill my lungs since we found out that something had happened to Henry. How'd you do that?"

"I didn't do anything."

Lynette sank onto the bed next to Jackie and dropped her head onto her friend's shoulder. "Maybe it's just helping to be here with you and your sweet girls. I felt so alone in that airport after I hung up with you. Crowds of people surrounded me, both in the airport and on that last plane, but I felt so isolated. So alone. No one knew me. No one cared about me. I don't know . . . I don't even think this is all about Henry and Annie. I'm not sure what's wrong with me."

Jackie patted Lynette's knee. "I'm glad you came home. To Minnesota, I mean. You don't belong in New York anymore. Your mom isn't there, and I would guess lots of your previous acquaintances moved on without you when you left the city for a while. Work used to be central to your world, but you realized it was demanding too much of you, and you gave it up. I respect that, and I support you, Lynette, I really do. I bet you won't have any trouble breathing at all when you get back to Ruby Shores and the life you built before you took that consulting gig back in the city."

Lynette's breath hitched again, and she lifted her head. "But, Jackie . . . Mom isn't in Ruby Shores either. And now, I've rented out most of my house to Storm for his brother . . . you and Kit are here . . . Renee's settling back in at Whispering Pines . . . and Annie." Her self-pity fell away at the thought of her friend. "Poor Annie. What will she do now?"

Jackie nodded. "That's all true. And to be honest, I've felt some of those same feelings lately, too. Work used to be my escape. When my job no longer fulfilled me, I made the leap and started a new business from scratch. But that's been a struggle, too. I still enjoy parts of what I work on each day, but the bad is outweighing the good—again. Now I find myself in Minneapolis after so many years in Chicago, my girls aren't around nearly enough, my father is dead, and my mother is building a new life for herself all the way down in Arizona."

Lynette's stomach growled again, followed by the doorbell.

"That's the delivery guy. We need to get you fed," Jackie said. "I mean it. Come on. The girls will eat all the pizza if we don't grab some first."

Lynette followed her out of the room toward laughter and the smell of hot cheese and pepperoni. Before they left the hallway, she muttered to Jackie, "How is it that neither of us feels like we're in a good place right now, after all our hard work to build what we thought were our dream lives?"

In response, Jackie squeezed her hand as they entered the main living space.

"Hey, Lynette! I hope you like pizza," Mack, one of Jackie's twins, said as she skipped across the room to catch Lynette up in a bear hug. "It's been forever since I saw you last!"

The knot in Lynette's chest loosened by another notch. She hugged the young woman back. "I swear, Mack, you are all grown up! I think you're even prettier than your momma."

Jackie opened the fridge and brought a tall pitcher of lemonade to the table. "Hey, I thought you were *my* friend! Don't go giving my kid a big head."

Hailey wandered over to hug Lynette, too.

"Hey, sweet girl, I've missed you," Lynette said, giving her an extra squeeze.

Hailey pulled back, leaving her arm wrapped loosely around Lynette's waist. "We missed you, too. It just sucks that it took something like this to bring us together again."

Lynette couldn't have said it better herself.

Jackie handed her a tall glass of ice and lemonade.

"Will this be as good as the fresh lemonade we had with our lobster rolls in Fiji?" Lynette asked, finally feeling herself smile. She enjoyed the camaraderie she always felt when around Jackie and her girls.

"Probably not, but the fancy cheese on this board is fresh from a Wisconsin dairy, only twenty miles from here. Every place has something special to offer."

Lynette snagged a thick slice of cheese off the charcuterie board in the middle of the kitchen island, then moaned as the first bite melted in her mouth.

Easy conversation continued around Jackie's dining table, and Lynette felt the suffocating shroud of fear she'd carried since stepping off the catamaran begin to drift away, lifted by the laughter filling the room.

Good food and even better conversation had eased Lynette's mind enough that she managed a decent night's sleep. After helping herself to coffee in the morning, she went down the short flight of stairs to Jackie's garage. Her friend's car sat in one stall, while boxes filled the other portion of the garage.

Lynette's boxes.

Had she really hauled this much stuff out to New York for her consulting gig?

No, she was moving home with more things than she'd taken out East. She may have gone a little overboard with her shopping in New York, not knowing when she'd get back to the city again. Her wardrobe had needed a refresh, given the limited shops available in Ruby Shores.

The door from Jackie's mudroom opened again and her friend came down, also carrying a steaming mug.

"I thought I heard someone down here and knew there was no way either Hailey or Mack was up yet. What time did you say Renee gets in?"

Lynette checked her sports watch. "In an hour. Flights were such a mess, especially booking them with almost no notice. Her sister Jess is picking her up and taking her back to Whispering Pines. We'll see her again at the funeral."

Jackie grimaced. "I remember standing on the Fiji shore our first day there, staring out at the water and thinking about my dad."

Crouching down, Lynette pulled open one box. "I actually did much the same thing the last day I was in Fiji, when Renee was busy with their realtor. The first part, I mean. I spent hours down by the ocean, lost in my thoughts."

Jackie backed up to the steps and sat on the bottom one, facing Lynette. "I'm glad our girls' trips take us to oceans sometimes. We're so landlocked here. Salt air and ocean water are a treat. One thing I thought about that day was how the only other time we were all together since last year's vacation at Whispering Pines was for my dad's funeral. I specifically hoped we would have lots more girls' trips in our futures and not many funerals. Yet here we are."

"I hate that we have another funeral to attend together already, and that it's Henry's," Lynette said. She dug around in the open box, sure she'd packed what she was looking for in this specific one. It felt good to have a distraction, if only for a little while, from the sad days ahead.

"What are you doing?" Jackie asked, watching her curiously. "Dean and Kit will be here shortly with his truck. You aren't supposed to unpack until you actually get home."

"I know, but I remembered I'd picked up a few pairs of my favorite pajamas from this little shop near the office in New York. Your girls went to bed in ratty old T-shirts and shorts last night, so I thought they might each like to have a pretty matching set, just for fun."

Lynette found what she was looking for and pulled out the short stack of silk and lace. She held up one of the nightgowns.

Jackie stared, her jaw slack.

"What's the matter? Don't you like it?" Lynette asked, worried about Jackie's response.

"Lynette, those aren't pajamas. That is a sexy negligee. You can't give those to my daughters. They literally *scream* 'sex'!"

Lynette closed the box and set the sleepwear on top. "Oh, don't be a prude. Your girls are old enough to wear pretty things like this. And this is what I usually sleep in. What do *you* wear to bed?"

Jackie snorted, eyeing the pile from over her coffee mug. "Nothing like that."

Taking a sip of her cooled coffee, Lynette shrugged. "That explains quite a bit, actually."

"What's that supposed to mean?"

Lynette grinned. "Do you sleep in the same type of ensemble that I saw your girls in last night?"

Jackie stood and walked over to the button on the wall.

"I didn't even hear them pull up," Lynette said, surprised to see a pickup in the driveway when the door rolled open.

"That's because you were too busy implying that my lackluster bedroom attire is to blame for my equally boring love life, weren't you?"

"Maybe," Lynette said. "It's a good thing I have a spare set I can leave for you, too."

Doors on the pickup opened and Kit, her husband, Dean, and their foster son, Isaac, all jumped out and wandered toward Jackie's open garage.

Lynette stashed her gifts for Jackie and her daughters back into the open box. "You guys are early. You remembered to bring Ebony, right? I need to brush my teeth and grab my bags. But first I need a hug."

She kept her hug with Kit brief, not wanting to get choked up again.

Despite Kit's bloodshot eyes, she maintained a soft smile. "Don't worry. We remembered your cat. She is a noisy little thing! You two remember Isaac, right?"

Both Lynette and Jackie greeted the teen, who looked like he'd rather still be in bed.

"Hi, ladies," Dean said. "Good to see you again, Lynette. I just hate that it's under these circumstances." He pushed the sleeves of his shirt up to his elbows as he surveyed the stack of boxes. "All these go? Isaac can help me load them while you grab your things."

Kit gave Dean a quick swat on the butt as she walked past him on the way to Jackie's stairs. Lynette had to smile when she caught Isaac's moan. Some things never changed.

"Thanks, guys. I need coffee," Kit said. "We'll be back in ten."

Jackie and Lynette followed her inside. Lynette had already pulled her gifts for Jackie, Hailey, and Mack back out of the box, careful to keep them out of Dean's and Isaac's sight. She dropped the lingerie on the island.

Kit placed a pod in the coffee maker, started the machine, then spied the colorful items. "Those are so pretty! What are they?"

Jackie smirked. "See? Kit doesn't wear them either, and she hasn't even been married very long."

Kit picked up the deep purple silk number on top. "I didn't say that. In fact, Lynette gave me a nightie very similar to this one before my wedding. I wore it often, until we suddenly had a teenager living under our roof."

Lynette stood near the coffee, waiting for Kit's to finish. She needed one more cup before they hit the road. "Glad you got some use out of it. I'm giving one each to Hailey and Mack, to thank them for letting me use one of the rooms."

Kit whistled. "They'll love that. You are so generous."

"Well, we all know *you* are their favorite aunt, so I needed to score some points with them. I figured those would do the trick," Lynette said, moving Kit's full cup out of the way to refill her own.

"I'm only their favorite because they see me more often. It's not your fault you've always lived so far away," Kit said, picking up her cup.

Jackie set her coffee down so she could look closer at each of the three sets Lynette had brought. "You two realize neither of you is actually their aunt, right?"

Lynette looped an arm through Kit's and turned her so they both faced Jackie head on. "Bite your tongue, woman!" she cried. "Like it or not, we are family. Blood doesn't have to enter the equation."

Jackie pretended to consider this statement, then held up a vivid pink shortie nightgown and matching silk robe. "Fine. You can be their honorary aunties if I can have this one. Those two can battle it out over the purple and green sets. But if I ever find out that either wears theirs for a *boy*, I'll excommunicate you from this little family thing we've got going here."

A whistle from the mudroom cut off their laughter, followed by a series of sneezes.

Dean sashayed into the room, pointing at the sexy sleepwear. "Kit could use a new one of those. I think she lost the one you gave her, Lynette."

He sneezed again.

"Did you forget to take your allergy pill?" Kit asked, ignoring his comment about no longer wearing her pretty nightgown.

"Yeah, and that cat of Lynette's sheds worse than your Chloe. She hates that crate you gave us to use. I swear her hair is falling off her in clumps." He helped himself to a sip of Kit's coffee. "Are you two about ready? Hazel has a long list of things she needs me to fix at her house yet today, so we should get going."

Not wanting to keep Dean and her free ride back to Ruby Shores waiting any longer, Lynette excused herself to grab her luggage. As she walked by the room where the girls were sleeping, she heard a scratching at the door, and opened it to release Nikki. The border collie stood excitedly on her back feet and placed her front paws on Lynette's chest, trying in vain to lick her face.

Lynette gave Jackie's dog a quick hug, then pushed her off, laughing. Ebony wasn't the only pet shedding her winter coat these days. She continued on down the hall, doing her best to brush the black dog hair off her white button-up.

⁂

Poor Dean suffered multiple sneezing attacks between Minneapolis and Ruby Shores. Lynette couldn't help that he'd forgotten to bring his allergy medicine, but she still felt bad for the guy.

She also felt a mix of emotions when they pulled into Ruby Shores. She hadn't been back since last winter when she'd celebrated the holidays with Donna before they each went their separate ways. While she'd worked at her consultant role in New York, Storm had gotten his brother settled into the main two levels of her home. That was the part Storm had rented from Lynette.

What would she find when she arrived back at the house? Had Donna's roses bloomed in their absence? Was the fountain running again? The rental agreement required that Storm maintain both the house and the outside grounds. Lynette and her mother had worked hard to breathe new life into the house. Part of her worried Storm wouldn't be as particular about things as she'd been.

She also dreaded the heartache the next few days would bring. Annie was already back in Ruby Shores, preparing for her husband's funeral.

Dean rolled down the windows and flipped off the air-conditioning as he turned onto her old street. A hot breeze pushed out the cooled, cat-dander-heavy air. Ebony meowed loudly inside the cage between Lynette's feet—something she'd been doing every few minutes since they'd left the city. Lynette suspected the feline was as ready to get out of the truck as the rest of them.

Could Ebony smell home?

"Looks like you have company," Dean said. He pulled into her driveway beside another pickup truck. He whistled. "What a beauty."

"Whose truck is that?" Kit asked, twisting in her seat to look back at Lynette.

Lynette eyed the fancy truck with mixed emotions. It thrilled her to find Storm at her house. But *why* was he here? It couldn't be to see her, because she wasn't even supposed to be back from Fiji yet.

"Lynette?" Kit prodded.

She took off her seatbelt, lifted her right leg high enough to clear the cat carrier on the floor, and opened her door. "Don't you recognize Storm's truck? He had it out at Whispering Pines."

"Oh. Right. I guess I didn't."

Dean glanced at his wife and shook his head. "How could you forget a truck like that?"

Isaac and Dean got out and walked around the larger pickup, pointing at this and that. It looked like the teen had finally found something that interested him more than his phone.

Kit shook her head. "Boys and their toys. Here, give me Ebony, and I'll run her inside. Then we can get you unloaded so Dean can get over to help Grandma."

Lynette started to remove the carrier, but hesitated. This wasn't just *her* house anymore. The garage was still all hers, but it would be too hot in there for Ebony, even for a little while. The attic was probably hot, too, and she'd need to turn on the small air-conditioning unit right away to help make it bearable for both her and her pet.

"Hello!" someone yelled from halfway down the block. "Hi!"

Lynette set the carrier on the bench seat and walked to the street.

From the end of her driveway, she spied two figures walking in their direction. She immediately knew the larger man in back was Storm. The thinner, younger man must be his brother, Shane. Had they been on a walk? Maybe they'd stopped at Owen's. His house was in that direction, though Lynette had no idea if he was in town. She waved when the man walking in front of Storm yelled hello again.

Ebony let out an indignant yowl at being abandoned.

"Hi, I'm Shane. You must be Lynette. My brother said you have curly silver hair and you're real pretty. Thank you for letting us live in your house. I used to think this was a castle. But now that I live here, I know it's just a house."

Kit stepped up to Lynette's side, as if she didn't want to miss one second of this reunion. Dean and Isaac also wandered down the driveway, though they were probably more interested in meeting the owner of the handsome truck.

"It's very nice to meet you, Shane," Lynette said, holding a hand out to Storm's younger brother. He looked at it and then back at Storm, as if he wasn't sure what to do next.

"You can shake her hand," Storm said.

She noticed how he kept his tone patient, and a touch quieter than usual.

Shane nodded excitedly, then shook her hand with vigor. He didn't let go until Storm stepped up and touched his forearm.

Shane's innocent enthusiasm warmed her heart.

"My brother got the fountain working again," Shane informed them. "It was broken. My friend couldn't get it to work, but my brother can fix anything. Want to see?"

Lynette noticed Shane didn't call his brother by name. She glanced over at Storm. It was her turn to feel unsure of what to do next.

Kit saved her. She stepped forward with a little wave. "Hi, Shane. My name is Kit. I'm Lynette's friend. And this is my husband, Dean, and our son, Isaac. Can you show us the fountain? I'd love to see it."

Without hesitation, Shane walked around Lynette and motioned for Kit and the others to follow him. "It's back here. She's pretty, too. The statue. Like Lynette. And you, too, Kit. I like your hair."

Lynette stopped hearing Shane's chatter when Storm took another step closer to her, snagging her attention.

He cleared his throat. "I could pretend to be embarrassed that Shane told you I said you were pretty, but why bother? I am glad to see you, though. Really glad. It's been too long."

She could read the sincerity in his eyes, and she did the most natural thing in the world: she closed the distance between them, wrapped her arms around his waist, and pressed her cheek against his broad chest, ignoring the sunglasses that hung there by a strap.

She felt his surprise, but his arms came around her, too, and he nuzzled her hair.

"You smell like sunshine," he said, inhaling deeply.

He, on the other hand, smelled like a man, sweating in the heat of a June day after a walk with his brother. But she didn't care. She stayed where she was, thankful for the steady sound of his beating heart.

"Owen just told me the news about Henry," he whispered against the top of her head. "That really sucks. He was a great guy. I'm glad I got to fish with him last summer."

An image of a smiling Henry, joking with Renee's son in the parking lot at Whispering Pines, came up for her at Storm's words, and her gut felt the punch all over again.

How can Henry be gone?

The tears came then. She couldn't help it. His warm hand made little circles against her back, offering her comfort. When they were young, tears made Storm uncomfortable. That didn't seem to be the case anymore.

She wasn't sure how long they stood like that on the driveway, mourning the loss of a good man neither of them knew well, but eventually she heard Shane and Kit heading back in their direction. She pulled away and grimaced at the wide wet spot on his gray tank.

"I'm so sorry," she said, touching the mark she'd left with her tears. Now they'd all know she'd bawled like an idiot against his chest.

He squeezed her outstretched fingers, then wiped her cheeks with his thumbs before also taking a step back. "I don't mind, but Shane hates it when anyone cries."

She tried to put on a brave smile. "I'll try to remember that."

Ebony let out another yowl, louder and more pathetic than before.

Storm looked around, confused. "What the hell was that?"

She laughed, relieved that the moment of sadness had passed. "That's Ebony. My cat. Remember her? She's in a pet carrier, inside Dean's truck. She's probably too hot."

"*Remember* her? I damn near broke my neck when I fell off that ladder trying to save her scrawny ass."

Dean sneezed again as he joined them on the driveway. "Yeah, watch that cat. She raises hell on men." He pretended to wipe his nose with his hand to emphasize his warning, before extending it to Storm. "Hello. I'm Dean Adams, Kit's husband. And you're the notorious Storm. Bad boy turned fisherman. Nice to meet you. And nice truck, by the way."

If Storm refused to feel embarrassed about having talked to his brother about her, Lynette wouldn't be uncomfortable about Dean knowing who Storm was, either. Although it must have been Kit that fed Dean most of his information about Storm.

She saw Kit notice the wet spot on Storm's chest, but her friend was kind enough not to mention it. "The yard looks great, Storm. Shane showed me the pretty roses and fountain. And I hate to rush this little reunion, but Dean needs to get over to my grandma's house before she comes over here and drags him home by the ear. She'll have a 'honey-do' list for him the length of her arm. She's getting ready to move into assisted living, but there are things around the house that need attention."

Shane walked over to stand next to Storm. "I'm hungry. What's for lunch?"

Storm nodded at his brother. "We will fix something in a few minutes. First, we need to help Lynette move her things out of the back of this truck and up to her apartment. Remember how we talked about the apartment in the attic?"

Lynette felt a bead of sweat trickle down the back of her neck. She'd dreaded the thought of hauling all her things up the back staircase to her new living quarters, but many hands would make quick work of it.

"I wouldn't argue if everyone wanted to grab a box or two," she said, walking back to Dean's pickup. "And I sure would appreciate the help."

Shane hurried to catch up with her. "I'll help. What should I carry?"

"How do you like cats, Shane?" she asked, swinging the carrier out of Dean's truck.

She glanced at Storm, and he gave her a quick wink. "My brother's more of a cat lover than I am."

She interpreted that to mean Ebony would be safe with Shane.

Fifteen minutes later, they had Lynette's boxes all in the attic apartment. Kit and her family said goodbye until tomorrow, and Shane got busy washing grapes in the kitchen.

"Would you like to join us for lunch?" Storm offered when she turned to go back up to her apartment.

She paused, considering his offer. While more time with him was tempting, what she really needed was a cool shower and to give Annie a call to see how she was doing, now that they were both back in Ruby Shores.

"How about a rain check? I really need to call Annie."

Shane yelled something about the sink not draining like it should, and Storm gave a little laugh.

"Duty calls for both of us. I would like to spend some time with you, though, before I head home. I was going to leave tomorrow morning. Shane's caregiver just needed a long weekend off for something. But now I feel like I should go to Henry's funeral, so I think I'll stick around. Do you want to go together?"

Lynette appreciated his thoughtfulness, but was the funeral something she should attend with her girlfriends, in solidarity for Annie?

Dean would likely be with Kit, and Jackie's girls were also coming in for it. She wasn't sure whether Matt would be able to come with Renee. When she told him as much, he smiled. "I know how much your friends mean to you. They always have. Even when we were kids. I understand. Let me know if you want to ride together. If not, maybe we can steal a little time after."

She almost laughed at his recollection of when they were kids. Even when she was a teen dating Storm, she'd never considered *him* to be a kid.

"You'll know where to find me," she said, and then, before she could talk herself out of it, she leaned forward and kissed him. It wasn't quite the passionate kiss of their younger years, but it was more than the peck he'd dropped on her nose before taking her out for ice cream last summer.

His arm snaked out to pull her close, but she sidestepped him just as Shane yelled his name.

"You better go make sure he doesn't flood my kitchen," she said with a wink, and she skipped up the attic steps, feeling more like a kid again than she had in a very long time.

Chapter Eleven

"I hate this," Renee whispered, leaning close so only Lynette could hear her over the rich timbre of the organ coming from the loft behind them.

Lynette nodded, eyeing their sweet Annie in the front pew. Annie's youngest, Relic, stood to her left, beside the central aisle of the church. Near him, beneath an elaborate funeral arrangement on a small table in front of the sanctuary, rested the urn containing his father's ashes. Lynette could barely bring herself to look at Henry's friendly face, smiling out at everyone from the framed photograph propped alongside his urn.

The heavy scent of flowers and incense permeated the air. Lynette studied the bouquet. It contained not roses, but lilies. Annie had told her once that Henry didn't like roses.

What a strange thing to remember.

Colton flanked Annie on her other side, and when the young man slipped a supportive arm around his mother's shoulders, Lynette succumbed to tears yet again. She couldn't imagine how Annie was finding the strength to maintain her composure, standing in front of her closest family and friends on this awful day.

Maybe Annie was all cried out.

At least the bright orange cast on Annie's wrist added a spot of sunny color to her black funeral attire.

Lynette jumped when fingers skimmed her side. She looked away from Henry's grieving family as the welcome warmth of Storm's arm settled across her lower back, and gladly accepted the white handkerchief he'd pulled from the breast pocket of his black suit coat. She dabbed at her eyes and nose, but when she tried to hand the soiled hankie back—now stained with mascara and possibly snot—he lowered his chin to her ear.

"Keep it."

She twisted the square of stained linen between her fingers, nodding in thanks. She used her free hand to pull a hymnal out and, balancing it on the back of the next pew, searched for the lyrics to "Amazing Grace."

When the mourners raised their voices in unison, singing the ageless hymn, she was reminded of the inevitability of it all. No one escapes the grief of death, but a life lived in community with others can help lessen the pain. And there was no one she'd rather live her life with than the women surrounding her now.

She glanced over her shoulder at Jackie, standing between her twins, and at Kit, holding Dean's hand, with a grateful smile. Renee caught her movement, and when their eyes met, Lynette hoped the woman could see the love for her there as well.

She prayed Annie could feel their support, too, as her husband's funeral neared its conclusion.

Then she heard Storm's deep baritone, softly singing the last words of the hymn.

Was it also inevitable that this man would again become an important part of her life?

She'd given him her heart once before, and losing him had nearly destroyed her. But they'd been so young back then. Too young, with too much living ahead of them.

She spied the brown spots that marred the back of her hand as she closed the hymnal. So many years, filled with both the joys and the sorrows of life, had passed since they'd made those early, bittersweet memories.

They weren't young anymore.

But what if they were too old now and had missed their chance?

Storm gave her a reassuring squeeze when she bent and stowed the hymnal, then let his arm fall away. She immediately missed his warm touch.

They weren't too old. Far from it.

A staff member from the funeral home approached the front and, lifting the copper urn, led Henry's solemn family from the church. As Annie passed by, Lynette gazed upon her friend's stricken expression, and made a vow to herself.

This time around, she'd do her best not to ruin things with Storm.

The aged skin on her hands was proof that she was much nearer the end of her life's journey than when she'd first fallen for Storm. But as they left the pew together and she slipped her hand into his, it still fit perfectly against his work-roughened palm, and when their fingers came together, it felt like the gift of coming home.

Kit let out a low whistle when Storm and a second man, also wearing a tailored black suit, came through Annie's front door following Henry's funeral. "It's like prom night all over again, but Owen ditched the white tux and Storm finally conformed to social norms."

"A funeral is nothing like a high school dance, Kit," Lynette said, but she smiled as the two men moved farther into the house. She remembered everything about how she'd spent her senior prom night with Storm. A woman didn't forget that kind of thing, even after more than thirty-four years. "They're both like a fine wine, aren't they?" she agreed. "Getting better with age."

Jackie joined Kit and Lynette in Annie's dining room, which was situated just off the front entryway, where a wide variety of small sandwiches and other finger foods covered the tabletop from end to end. "What are you two smirking about? And have either of you spied Annie lately? She seems to have disappeared, and I'm worried about her."

Lynette nodded her head toward the front door. "Kit was just ogling Storm and Owen when they walked in the door in black suits."

Kit shrugged. "What can I say? They both cut a handsome figure, and I can't for the life of me explain why my two friends, both also lovely and available, haven't scooped them up."

Jackie froze. "Did you say Owen? He's here? I didn't see him at the funeral. Is he alone?"

Kit stepped over to the table and scanned the offerings. "No, he's not alone. I just said he was with Storm. I was happy to see Storm slide into the pew next to you, Lynette, just before the funeral began. I had to reach around Mack to nudge Jackie when he pulled a hankie out of his pocket for you to use. My brain is having a hard time reconciling this new Storm with the old one. *And* I saw you two holding hands for a minute. Have you given things a try with him again?"

Lynette picked up a hefty ivory plate from the stack of stoneware at the end of the table. The feel of the dish took her back to the Thanksgiving dinner she'd enjoyed here a few years ago, when they'd come home for Jackie's surprise fiftieth birthday party Owen had arranged for the following day. She remembered the teasing Henry endured during the dinner conversation. It had something to do with him and Annie driving into a ditch on a stormy night. Michael, another of the family's dinner guests that day, had apparently ridden to their rescue. Henry remained gracious, but she'd sensed his lack of enthusiasm over his wife's ex saving the day.

"Lynette? Yoo-hoo?! Where did you go?" Kit said as she helped herself to a chocolate-covered eclair and three cream cheese mints.

Kit's prodding pulled Lynette's mind back from that festive holiday dinner. She shook her head. "Sorry. I was just remembering happier times here, in this room. Remind me to tell Annie how sorry Donna is that she couldn't make it back from England in time for Henry's funeral. She really enjoyed visiting with him when we were here for Thanksgiving that time."

Jackie had gotten in line for food, too. "My mom felt terrible for missing the funeral, too, but her feelings are still too raw from losing Dad. Hey, Lynette, are you going to answer Kit? About Storm, I mean?"

Lynette handed Jackie the plate she'd picked up, then took another one for herself. "As a matter of fact, I have decided. I want to try with Storm, and he seems interested, too. We have things to discuss, but I don't want to wait anymore. I'm sure what happened to poor Henry is playing into my thought process. Seeing the family that Annie and Henry—and Michael—built together by taking chances and committing to work through the tough stuff makes me think the risks are worth it."

The front door opened again, and this time Renee entered, along with her husband and daughter.

"Hey, guys!" Kit hurried toward the entryway to welcome the latest arrivals.

Lynette added an assortment of goodies to her plate from the various serving dishes, then walked over to join Kit as she greeted Renee's family.

"Annie's home is so pretty," Renee said, looking around at their friend's house. "And big."

"I suppose you haven't had the chance to come by Annie's place before," Lynette said, before biting a mini carrot in half. "It reminds me of the house she grew up in. Remember that house from our prom weekend? The perfect place to raise a family."

Matt closed the door behind them. "Ladies, if you'll excuse me, I see Owen and Taran. I wanted to give them a fishing report."

Renee watched her husband for a second, then turned back to Kit and Lynette. "You guys remember Julie, don't you?"

"Of course," Kit said. "Here, hold this, will you?" She handed her plate to Renee and, her hands now free, gave Julie a warm hug. "It's great to see you again, Julie. And it's so nice of you to come today."

Julie returned the hug, then gave Lynette a quick wave, too. "Of course! I wanted to come. It was fun to get to know all of you last summer at Whispering Pines. Annie was so nice, and I got to know Henry just a little, too, when we were searching for . . ."

Lynette felt heat rise in her cheeks as Julie's voice trailed off. Renee's daughter looked embarrassed, too, at having brought up the chaos Lynette had created with her drunken behavior the previous summer.

"For me, after I took such an incredibly stupid risk," she finished for Julie to protect the girl from further embarrassment.

Renee took one of Kit's eclairs as she handed the plate back. "Where is Annie?"

Jackie joined them just inside the door. "Hi, Renee. Julie. I was just asking the same thing."

Lynette raised her plate a little. "Why don't the two of you get some food? We can take it out to the back deck, eat quick, then go find Annie to see if she needs anything. There are lots of people here, but I keep seeing her daughter bobbing in and out of the rooms with food. She seems to have things under control. Even Annie's big sister, Millie, is giving Ava a hand, which is a pleasant surprise."

Renee glanced at the food on the dining table. "I can never eat right after a funeral. But I could use some coffee. Or water."

The front door opened yet again, and they had to move out of the way so Jackie's twins could enter.

Jackie introduced her daughters to Julie. The girls were all similar in age.

After another round of hellos, Mack grabbed Julie by the hand and pulled her toward the dining room, Hailey close behind. "I'm starving. Come on, let's let the moms visit, and the three of us can see if Colton and maybe Ava or Relic are around."

Lynette watched as the three daughters of two of her dearest friends became acquainted, and she thought again how quickly time had passed, and how she was the only one of the group with such a small family.

Even Kit had Dean, and now Isaac.

Some things never changed.

Or, just maybe, her new commitment to rebuild a relationship of some kind with Storm could be a fresh start for her, too. Not that kids would ever be a part of anything with him. That was the one thing they were too old for, notwithstanding something like Kit's willingness to foster Isaac. Then she remembered Storm already had a son. She hoped to meet him some day, too.

"Follow us, Renee," Lynette said. "I already had one cup of the punch, and it was delicious. It reminded me of the fruit punch we had on the boat in Fiji. It's back here on the buffet in the dining room. Then we'll go eat and find Annie."

She led her three friends back through the dining room, weaving around other guests as they also helped themselves to food. She spied Kit's aunt by the massive punch bowl she'd sampled from earlier. The empty plastic pitcher told her Marge had just refilled it.

"I should have guessed you were the expert behind this punch, Marge!" she said, setting her half-empty plate on the wooden buffet top so she could fill a fresh crystal cup with the red punch. "Everything you touch is delicious."

Marge snorted, but her smile told Lynette that the woman appreciated the compliment. "I know you ladies had to cut your trip short, so I thought I'd do my best to bring a little of Fiji to you here."

Space was tight in the room, and someone accidentally bumped into Renee, causing her to tilt forward into the buffet. Punch sloshed over the rim of the clear cut-glass bowl, but Marge steadied it before any actual damage was done. Despite the deft save, Renee backed away from the buffet, her face strikingly pale.

"I'm so sorry," she blurted out. "Excuse me."

Lynette, Kit, and Jackie all watched in surprise as Renee spun and hurried from the room, then out the front door, closing it behind her.

"What just happened?" Jackie asked, her eyes shifting between the front entrance and the rivulets of red punch meandering across the buffet top.

Marge whipped the dishtowel off her shoulder and mopped up the liquid before it could drip onto the carpet. "Oh, just a little spill. No harm done. But go check on your friend."

She was right, of course. "We'll get punch later," Lynette said, handing her cup back to Marge. "Good save!"

"Girl, I ran a diner for years. I've still got skills."

Lynette shot Marge a smile, then hurried after Renee.

They found Renee out front, leaning her back against a massive oak tree, breathing deeply.

Lynette reached her first. She took both of Renee's hands in her own. "Are you all right? Don't worry about the punch. Marge didn't let any of it get on the carpet."

When Renee didn't speak, Lynette had to bend her knees slightly to look up into the woman's downcast eyes.

"Renee? What's going on?"

Renee squeezed Lynette's fingers, then pulled her hands away as she straightened and pushed away from the solid tree trunk. She chuckled, but her eyes didn't reflect amusement. "You guys didn't have to rush out here," she said finally. "I just needed a minute to compose myself."

Lynette took a step back, crossed her arms over her stomach, and waited.

Jackie finished the last bite of her ham sandwich, then set her plate on the grass.

Kit just stood there, quietly munching on her last miniature eclair and eyeing Renee.

After three more deep breaths, Renee laughed again. This time, it sounded genuine. "You three look like idiots, standing there, staring at me."

Lynette shrugged. "You said you needed a minute. We're giving you a minute. But we aren't going to leave you. This is what friends do."

Renee shook her head, then bent down to help herself to a strawberry from Jackie's abandoned plate.

"I thought you weren't hungry," Kit pointed out, talking around the food still in her mouth. A chunk of chocolate frosting shot out from between her lips and landed on the bare skin of her chest, just above the neckline of her black dress. She glanced down, picked it off, and plunked it back in her mouth, leaving a brown smudge behind.

"And to think Matt just called you a lady."

Kit shrugged, used her thumb to scrape off the last of the frosting, and licked that, too. "Guess we've got 'em all fooled, don't we? Little do they know, but we'll always be the Kaleidoscope *Girls* at heart."

Lynette gave her dark navy taffeta skirt a swirl. "Dressed in all these dark and dreary clothes does *not* suit us."

"But black *does* suit Storm and Owen," Kit said with a wink.

"And there it is," Lynette said. "Kit brings us back full circle."

Renee dropped the greens from the strawberry's top onto Jackie's plate, then rubbed her fingers against her black slacks. "While I'd love to hear more about that, I'm really more concerned about Annie right now. We need to find her. Check on her. I know how hard this day is for someone who just lost her husband."

Lynette suddenly understood Renee's abrupt exit from the house. "This is hard for you, too, isn't it? You know all too well how Annie is hurting right now, and none of us wants that for our dear friend. Is that why you ran out of the house?"

Renee paused, considering. Then she nodded. "In a way, yes. But it was more than that. When my first husband died, Julie was eight and Robbie was only five. Like today, there was a get-together after Jim's funeral. But between the church service and the luncheon, there was a short graveside ceremony. It seems like people often opt for cremation these days, but it wasn't as common back then. Poor Robbie, he was so confused by the coffin and the whole awful business. By the time we got over to my in-laws'—they wanted to host the luncheon—the kids were running a little wild. I was so devastated at the time that I didn't even try to calm them down like I should have. My folks weren't there yet to help, and one kid ended up knocking a big bowl of red punch onto the carpet. It was everywhere, and my mother-in-law absolutely lost her shit. I know her reaction was about so much more than the mess on her floor, but it was the beginning of an estrangement that would last for years. Even now, my relationship with Marilyn—Jim's mother—is tenuous at best."

Lynette retrieved Jackie's plate as Renee explained why her near-miss with the punch bowl today evoked such a vehement reaction, and her heart hurt over her friend's old pain. With her free hand, she gave Renee a one-armed hug. "And that's why you didn't want any punch on the catamaran, too, isn't it?"

Renee nodded. "Call it PTSD. But, really . . . enough about me. We need to find Annie. She's the one who needs our support today."

Lynette wasn't so sure that only Annie needed help. Renee seemed to be long overdue for help in dealing with the trauma of losing a husband, too. If she still needed to heal from that long-ago loss, it was no wonder she still lived in fear, every day, of losing Matt. The combination of her old trauma, coupled with her current husband's dangerous job, would be enough to make anyone worry.

Chapter Twelve

J ULIE GOT ALL TURNED around when she left the bathroom. She thought the kitchen—where Jackie's daughters were waiting for her—was to the left. But as she walked down the hallway, she soon realized that this part of the house was too quiet.

She was about to turn around and go back when she noticed a floor-to-ceiling shelving unit on the far wall of a deserted living room. The shelves held a collection of sorts. In an instant, Julie realized where she was.

She'd discovered Annie's extensive assortment of kaleidoscopes.

Annie had told her about her collection last summer when, around the fire at Whispering Pines, they'd discussed the nickname her mother and friends called themselves: the Kaleidoscope Girls. Annie hadn't been kidding when she said collecting the scopes had become a lifelong addiction.

Curious, Julie crossed the room and approached the shelves. Most of the kaleidoscopes were the cylindrical shape she'd expected, but they varied in size and materials. There were scopes made of wood, metals, and even glass. It was an impressive assortment of artistic pieces.

But there were also homemade kaleidoscopes. Her kids had probably made them for her over the years, or—wasn't Annie the principal of the local high school?—perhaps students.

While most were tube-shaped, a few resembled eggs, propped on little stands.

"Oh, cute," she said as she carefully picked up one of the egg-shaped scopes from the shelf at eye level.

"They're even prettier when you look through them."

Julie spun around in shock, bobbling the piece but somehow managing to not drop it. She'd thought she was alone.

"I'm sorry, I didn't mean to scare you," Annie said. "I could tell you didn't see me when you walked in."

Julie quickly put the piece back on its stand on the shelf. "*I'm* sorry," she insisted. "I shouldn't have touched this."

Annie pushed out of her high-backed chair with a sigh and crossed the room to stand by Julie. "Nonsense. The purpose of a kaleidoscope is to enjoy the gorgeous shapes and colors when you look through it. Otherwise, they're just 'dust collectors,' as Henry is so fond of calling them."

Up close, Julie could see the tear tracks down Annie's cheeks. Her heart broke for this kind woman she'd only met last summer, but who her mother had known for most of her life.

"*Was* so fond of calling them, I mean," Annie said with a hiccup. "Ugh, that's going to take some getting used to."

Julie hated to see Annie so upset, but she knew how it felt to lose someone. She turned away to give the woman a moment of privacy, then ran a gentle finger across an exceptionally beautiful kaleidoscope. Thin gold bands on each end of the cylinder provided the perfect complement to the dark, polished wood. She wished she could say something meaningful to Annie about her loss, but she struggled to find the right words.

"Both scopes are very special to me," Annie said, nodding toward the kaleidoscopes Julie was admiring. "Lynette gifted me the little egg-shaped number a few years ago. She came across it on her travels somewhere—I can't remember where—and picked it up for me. It wasn't even my birthday or Christmas. I think the best gifts are those that are given for no reason other than love and friendship."

"I'm sure glad I didn't drop it," Julie said with a small laugh, relieved that Annie seemed willing to keep the conversation about kaleidoscopes. Amid so much sadness, maybe this brief reprieve was exactly what Annie needed. "You said 'both' kaleidoscopes are special. Did you mean this pretty one, too?"

Annie stepped closer and picked up the long wooden one with the gold circles on each end—something Julie wouldn't have dared to do; it looked too fancy to touch. "Yes. This one, too. Take a look."

Reluctantly, but with an extra measure of care, Julie accepted the scope. She shifted slightly to face the light streaming through a window. "Wow," she said, slowly turning the scope after raising it to her right eye. "It's like getting lost in a stained-glass Wonderland. This is incredible!"

She could look at the glorious shapes and colors for hours. But was she holding Annie up from returning to her guests?

Lowering the scope, she handed it back. "You know, my uncle works in stained glass. He showed me the big round window he's making for Lynette's house. She'll love it. The pattern reminds me of what you see when you look through that kaleidoscope. Was this one a gift, too, if you don't mind me asking?"

Annie sighed, then returned the kaleidoscope to its place on the shelf. "Michael. My first husband. And the night he gave it to me . . . it was like something out of a romantic Christmas movie." She chuckled.

"But not the squeaky-clean Hallmark kind. In fact, that was the night we conceived our daughter. We weren't even dating. We were roommates—living with Henry, believe it or not. But that night was a turning point in all three of our lives. I used to tease Michael that he used this kaleidoscope to sneak into more than just my heart."

Julie hadn't met Michael, but her mother had pointed him out at Henry's funeral.

"Are you two talking about me?"

Both women spun to face the voice coming from the arched doorway that led to the living room. Julie noticed the color flooding Annie's cheeks.

Michael took a step back, looked down the hallway Julie had taken in error, and waved an arm to someone. "Told you she was probably back here, playing with her kaleidoscopes."

"I should go," Julie said.

Julie couldn't stop thinking about what Annie had said. Being roommates with both her first and second husband when they were all so much younger had to have resulted in complicated relationships later in life. Were things still awkward between this one-time couple?

Annie touched her arm. "No. Stay. Look through as many of these as you like. You must be bored. I could take you around and introduce you to my kids, if you like. Or Jackie's girls."

Michael entered the room, followed by Jackie, Kit, Lynette, and Julie's mom.

"Hey, Annie, you doing all right?" Michael asked.

Julie watched as the man gave Annie a careful hug. Then he scanned the kaleidoscope collection. "I can't believe Henry let you keep that one," he said, jabbing his thumb at the scope Julie had just looked through.

Annie shrugged, her embarrassment gone. "Henry thought it was silly of me to keep such a large collection of kaleidoscopes. He didn't know the story behind every single one."

Probably a good thing, Julie thought.

Renee stepped closer and picked up one of the homemade kaleidoscopes. "Annie, this is the one you made at summer camp, right? I recognize it . . . it was in your bedroom when we were in high school."

"One and the same," she said with a grin. "I couldn't very well get rid of the kaleidoscope that started it all."

Another woman entered the living room. Julie didn't recognize her.

"Did someone say kaleidoscopes?" the woman said. "I sure never guessed my little art project on that blazing hot day at summer camp would have started all this."

"Wendy!" Annie cried, rushing into the woman's outstretched arms. "You came."

The two embraced, both of them close to tears. Moments later, the rest of the Kaleidoscope Girls rushed forward, and they were all in one large group hug. Only Julie and Michael stood on the perimeter.

Julie felt more like an outsider than ever.

When they all came apart, Renee handed the homemade scope to Wendy. "You're the reason we call ourselves the Kaleidoscope Girls."

Wendy, who looked to be about Julie's mom's age, or maybe just a few years older, looked through the scope, just as Julie had done moments ago with the much fancier one. "Oh, I know," the woman said. "I take full credit for your nickname. Actually, I like to think that the five of you have stayed such close friends for so long because of me."

She handed the scope—constructed from a section from a roll of wrapping paper, along with plenty of glitter, plastic beads, and white glue—back to Annie.

"Julie, honey, this is Wendy," Renee said. "She was the world's best camp counselor, and we were the luckiest campers because they assigned her to our cabin. Wendy, this is my daughter, Julie."

Wendy acknowledged Julie with a smile. "I also worked with Annie at the high school. We've been friends for many years, too. I sometimes consider myself an honorary Kaleidoscope Girl. I was lucky to get to know Henry as well." The woman turned back to Annie. "Oh, honey, I am so sorry. I know it doesn't feel like it now, but you will get through this."

Annie tucked her shoulder-length hair behind her ear. "And you know Michael, right? Heavens, I'm not being a very good hostess today, hiding back here when I should be mingling."

Wendy shook her head. "No one expects anything *from* you today, Annie. We're all here *for* you. And for your kids. Speaking of which, where are they? And is little Nora here? I was hoping to see her. I'm sure she's growing like crazy."

Michael cleared his throat. "I saw Colton and Relic head for the basement. If I had to guess, they're gaming. Not to be rude, but just to escape from it all, if only for a little while. Ava is handling the kitchen like a pro. It's how she's choosing to get through the day. Her husband promised to bring Nora over after her nap. I think we could all benefit from having a toddler running around here today. There's nothing quite like the joy a little one can bring."

Julie snorted. "Just keep her away from the punch bowl, right, Mom?"

Renee's aversion to punch at every wedding, baby shower, or graduation through the years had grown into an inside joke for their family.

Michael looked confused at the joke, but Kit nodded. "Your mom was just telling us about the punch bowl at your dad's funeral, Julie. You remember that?"

"Vividly," Julie said. "I'd kind of forgotten about it until we went to my dad's parents' at Christmas that same year Mom met Matt in Fiji. Being there again brought it all back."

She recognized the pity in the eyes of her mother's friends, and it made her uncomfortable. These women seemed to know everything about each other. Did that mean they knew stuff about her, too? She'd bet they talked about it all, including their kids.

That reminded her that Jackie's daughters might still be waiting for her—unless they'd given up when she got lost and then delayed. "I better go find Hailey and Mack," she said, backing toward the archway. "Thanks for showing me your collection, Annie. And I'm really sorry about your husband."

Annie gave her a brief wave. "Thank you, Julie. I'm glad we got to catch up a little. And keep that bit we were talking about when Michael and all first found us to yourself, will you? Grief seems to have loosened my tongue."

"I've already forgotten," Julie said with a wink.

But as she walked back down the hallway, she tried to picture a much younger Annie living with two male roommates. Michael was handsome for an old guy, and Henry had been a nice-looking man, too.

She wouldn't mention any specifics of her conversation with Annie to her mom, but she was going to do a little digging to find out more about what sounded like a love triangle to her.

Then she realized how ridiculous she was being. Just because she couldn't seem to find a man for herself didn't mean she had to live vicariously through one of her mother's oldest friends.

———— ✦ ————

This time, Julie located the kitchen with no trouble. She strode into the room but had to swerve to avoid running into Annie's daughter and the platter of additional sandwiches she held aloft.

"There you are!" Mack said, pushing away from the kitchen island. "We were about to go look for you."

Julie nabbed a bottle of water from the counter on her way to Mack and Hailey. "I'm sorry. I got a little lost, but I found both Annie and her kaleidoscope collection when I took a wrong turn. Have you guys ever seen all of them? She has so many pretty kaleidoscopes. She even has the original one she made when our moms were kids at summer camp."

Hailey set an empty plate in the sink and tossed her napkin in the trash. "She showed us some of them when Mom brought us here once as kids."

"Did you find Annie's sons?" Julie asked. "Ava just took more food out to the dining room."

Mack shook her head. Julie thought she looked impatient, or even anxious, maybe.

"Michael said they're probably downstairs, gaming."

"Michael? I thought you said you were talking to Annie," Hailey said.

Twisting the top off her water bottle, Julie shrugged. "Annie, Michael, my mom, your mom, Kit, Lynette, and another woman who used to work with Annie at the high school."

Mack headed for a door on the opposite side of the kitchen. "Leave it to Colton and Relic to bail on their dad's celebration of life. Let's see if they're down here."

Julie and Hailey followed.

"Annie quit her job?"

Hailey's question confused Julie for a second. Then she realized it stemmed from her comment about the old camp counselor. "Oh, no, not Annie. I think the other woman—Wendy—must have quit. Or retired, maybe? I don't know. Once you get to be the age of our moms, you never know how much longer any of them will keep working."

Mack opened the door and went down a short flight of stairs. "Our mom will probably work until she's ninety. What else would she do? We don't live at home, and she isn't dating Ben anymore."

Once all three were through the door, Hailey pulled it shut behind them. The noise of the upstairs crowd faded away. "Ben has been out of her life for five years or something like that, Mack."

When Mack reached the bottom of the stairs, she glanced back up at them. "Precisely. And as far as I know, she hasn't dated since. All she does is work. I wish she'd find someone new."

Julie looked around the area at the bottom of the stairs. There was a family room off to the left, but no one was in it. "Didn't Jackie start a new business not too long ago?"

"Yeah," Hailey said. "They might be in Colton's old room. Down this way."

Julie heard someone shout, followed by male laughter. "When my mom was trying to reopen Whispering Pines, it was a ton of work. She met Matt, her husband, right before that, but since he was still living in Fiji, they had to settle for the occasional email or phone call for at least a half a year. I'm not sure it would have lasted if Matt lived nearby during those first months."

Hailey knocked on the closed door.

"Yeah!" someone shouted from inside.

Taking that as an invitation, Hailey swung the door open. "We thought you guys might hide out down here."

"Yet you found us," the shorter of the two young men said as he pulled a gaming headset off and tossed it onto the desk beside a large monitor. He hit a button and the animated fight scene flipped to black.

Julie looked around the bedroom. There were no personal items on the walls or shelves. One large painting hung over the headboard, and that was about it. "Kaleidoscopes have even found their way down here," she said with a nod to the painting.

"You found our mom's collection then," the taller of Annie's boys said. She recognized them from the funeral. "I'm Colton, by the way. And this is Relic. My little brother."

Relic snorted, but Julie didn't think he looked like he minded Colton's description too much. She'd guess Colton to be a few years older than she was, and Relic to be around Robbie's age.

"It's nice to meet you. And I'm Julie, Renee's daughter. She's one of the other Kaleidoscope Girls." She jabbed her thumb at the painting with a grin.

A second gaming headset hung around Colton's neck, but he pulled it off and set it beside his brother's. "Did Mom send you down here to tell us we have to come back upstairs? We probably should, I guess. We can only hide out down here for so long, Relic."

Mack sat on the edge of the bed and bounced twice. "Ava is working like a mad woman up there."

Colton smirked. "And we already have dish duty later, after everyone goes home."

"We could help," Mack offered, earning herself a sideways glance from Hailey. "What?!"

"Don't go volunteering me for dishes," her sister shot back.

Julie watched as the two sets of siblings picked at each other. She'd probably miss her brother by the end of the summer, but she didn't miss the bickering. "Our moms are all cloistered in the living room, talking about their good old days. If Annie can hide out a little, you two are probably all right down here."

Colton stood up. "Let's go out to the family room. This bedroom is too small for five people."

"But I had you by fifteen hundred!" Relic moaned.

"Seriously? What are you, twelve?" Colton said.

Julie felt self-conscious. "We didn't mean to interrupt your game."

"It's fine. He needs to practice anyhow," Relic said. He tried to push past his big brother, but Colton grabbed him around the waist, picked him up, and tossed him onto the bed behind Mack. Then he hurried out the door before Relic could fight back.

Once they reached the family room, the three girls sat next to each other on the couch and left the love seat for the boys.

Colton turned to Julie. "You guys have that lake resort then, right? The one Mom went to with her girlfriends last year?"

Julie nodded. "We do. I mean, Whispering Pines is my mom's resort, but it's been in the family for years. Mom inherited it from her Aunt Celia. Celia was a neat lady. Rich. And when she passed away, she even left us kids some money, but we only get it if we graduate from college . . ." She suddenly felt self-conscious again, but Colton and the others looked interested in what she had to say, so she continued. "I'd love to invest my inheritance in Whispering Pines. The place always needs upgrades, but Mom isn't in favor of that. She wants me to save my money for something that will be all mine."

Hailey shrugged. "That probably makes sense. Hey, Mack, why don't *we* have a rich aunt?"

Mack could only shrug.

"I suppose Mom has a point," Julie said. "I have so many fun ideas about how she could expand things out there. But one of these days I'm going to have to accept the fact that the resort isn't big enough to support both of us and go find an outside job. Maybe she'll pass it on to me, sometime down the road. If Robbie wasn't thinking about investing his inheritance in a fishing guide service in Alaska after graduation, he'd probably want to stay involved in the resort, too, but obviously he can't do both."

Relic pulled a pillow out from between his body and the love seat's arm, swinging it at Colton. Colton yanked it from him and tossed it onto the floor. They both vied for more space. Their big bodies didn't fit well.

"Fishing in Alaska sounds pretty cool right now," Relic said. "Actually, fishing anywhere sounds good. Dad loved to fish."

"Robbie's your brother, right?" Mack said.

Julie nodded. "He's working in Alaska this summer to make sure he enjoys guiding up there and to get a better idea of what it would take to start his own business. He may need to work for a while after graduation, but he has more direction than I do these days. But that's enough about me and my family. Colton, what do you do?"

She noticed a smirk on Relic's face, but it dropped away, replaced with an almost blank expression.

"I'm an associate funeral director," Colton said. "And before you make any jokes about it, don't. I enjoy my job."

The lined face of a stout woman in a black skirt, starched white blouse, and sensible shoes came to Julie's mind. She couldn't remember her name, but the woman had kindly taken both her and Robbie to what must have been a daycare room in the church basement when they got anxious before the start of their own father's funeral.

"I wouldn't joke about that. You help families through some of their darkest days," Julie said.

Relic probably used to tease Colton mercilessly about his chosen profession, but she doubted he would harass his big brother after experiencing the gut-wrenching pain of losing his dad.

An uncomfortable silence fell over the group of young adults.

Julie cleared her throat. "I was only eight years old when my dad died. I still remember how nice the people from the funeral home were to both me and Robbie. Mom, too. I admire you for doing such hard work. And I really am sorry about Henry. Today was hard, and it might take a long time, but it will get better. Take it from me."

"I admire you, too, Colton," Mack tossed in. Julie looked over at her, finding Mack's comment strange, and caught the eye roll her twin gave her.

Colton pushed to his feet. "I should get back upstairs and check on Mom and Ava. Relic, can you go let Daisy and Lemon out?"

"Daisy and Lemon?" Julie asked, curious.

Relic sighed. "Our dogs. Lemon is my yorkie, and Daisy is an old beagle that Mom adopted."

Mack's hand shot in the air. "Through our mom's business!"

Relic nodded as he stood up. "They're locked in the garage and probably need to go outside. I'll do it. Hey Colton, go turn off the computer, will you? I only shut down the monitor. Man, I just want this day to be over."

Julie also stood. She gave him what she hoped was a reassuring smile.

"You could go upstairs and clumsily knock over that big punch bowl in the dining room. When Robbie did that after Dad's funeral, we got to leave the shindig right away. Of course, we didn't talk to our grandparents for years after that. They were so upset over Dad, and the spilled red punch tipped them over the edge. But it's an option."

Relic wriggled his eyebrows, but Colton put him in a headlock and rubbed his knuckles against his brother's skull. "Mom would *kill* you," he warned his younger sibling.

Hailey huffed to her feet and brushed past the two brothers, headed for the stairs. "It's moments like this that I understand why Mom prefers to hang out with the rest of her lady friends. Men are so immature."

Julie noticed the way Colton's eyes snapped to Hailey. Then he pushed his brother away. "Knock it off, Relic," he said, his voice deeper than before. He watched Hailey disappear up the stairs.

Mack gave Colton a quick side hug. "It was fun to see you again, Colton," she said. Then color stained her cheeks. "Well, not that a funeral is fun, but . . ."

Flustered, Mack pulled away and headed after her sister.

As Julie hurried after the twins, she couldn't help but wonder if Mack had a little crush on Colton—who seemed like he might be interested in Hailey . . . who had mentioned to Julie that she has a serious boyfriend.

Was Colton following in his parents' footsteps and falling into a messy little love triangle, too?

Julie grinned. Maybe she should write romance novels for a living. Her cousin Nathan could help show her how. He was already living at Whispering Pines for the next year while he wrote a book of his own.

CHAPTER THIRTEEN

A BAND OF TENSION tightened around Jackie's temples. Today's events had brought out plenty of unshed tears and suppressed emotions—important ingredients in a surefire recipe for a migraine. It was time to find the girls and head back to her folks' house for a cool bath and a dark bedroom.

Wait. Do I need to call it Mom's house now?

Henry's funeral had brought up so many painful emotions about her father.

Shouldn't my grief over losing him be subsiding by now?

Her dad's slow slide into dementia and eventual passing were starkly different from Henry's sudden and shocking death. Annie had good reason to feel crushed. But why didn't Jackie feel better by now?

Why do I feel so stuck?

Maybe she'd find the girls in the dining room, looking for more food. But before Jackie could even exit the kitchen, the lower-level door swung open and Hailey appeared.

"Are you girls ready to go?" she asked, relieved to see one of them.

Hailey grabbed the last scotcheroo bar from a silver platter on the island and licked at the chocolate frosting on top. "Sure, Mom. We should get on the road before it gets too late."

Mack and Julie bounced up the stairs behind Hailey.

"You took the last one?!" Mack said, grabbing for the bar in her sister's hand.

Hailey spun away. "Get your own."

"There aren't any more!"

Julie shut the door behind her, smiling at Jackie. "I always thought I missed out, not having a sister, but those two make me think having a younger brother isn't so bad. He'd eat the last bar, too, though. No hesitation."

"I managed just fine with one brother, too," Jackie said. "Less bickering. It was nice to see you again, Julie. I already said goodbye to your mom. Hopefully, we'll see you again before too long, but for a happier reason."

Three people Jackie didn't recognize walked through Annie's kitchen. It had been the same after her dad's funeral—so many strangers in the house.

She'd obviously been gone from Ruby Shores for a very long time.

As Julie said goodbye to Mack and Hailey, someone dropped a heavy metal pan on a countertop, and the thud made Jackie wince with pain.

"Let's sneak out the back," she said, pushing two fingertips against her left temple.

They were almost to the back door when the basement door swung open again, and Annie's oldest son entered the kitchen.

Mack stopped, holding up a finger. "Mind if I run out to the dining room and see if there are any more scotcheroo bars out there?"

Before Jackie could respond, Mack dashed off.

"Sorry, Mom," Hailey said. She opened the back door for Jackie. "She has a thing for Colton and obviously doesn't want to leave yet. But don't tell her I told you that. Here, take this out to the car," she said, handing her a water bottle, "and take your headache medicine. You probably stashed some in the glove compartment. I'll get her out there as quick as I can."

Jackie fumbled in her purse for her key fob as she walked out the door. "Hurry, please, Hailey. My head is killing me."

Too intent on finding her key fob, Jackie wasn't watching where she was going, and she ran right into someone coming up the stairs.

"Whoa, where are you off to in such a hurry?" a male voice said as firm hands gripped her upper arms. "We were just coming in to find all of you and to give Annie our condolences."

Jackie would recognize that voice anywhere. She tried to step back, but the tip of her heel slipped between two wooden boards on a stair tread. She wobbled forward into the snow-white, starched fabric of the man's dress shirt. His hands loosened, but instead of letting her go, he slid them around her back to steady her. She gasped, inhaling the woodsy scent of aftershave.

The scent was a jolt to her system.

She'd hoped to slip out quietly so she could avoid talking to Owen, though she wasn't sure why she didn't want to make the time to catch up with her old friend. But instead of avoiding him, she'd run smack-dab into him.

I am such *a klutz.*

Worse yet, the heel refused to come loose, no matter how hard she pulled.

"Jackie, stop. You'll break it off," Owen said. "If you're feeling steadier, I can get it loose for you. Can you slip your foot out?"

She wriggled out of his arms, but had to place both hands on his chest to balance on one foot. She could feel the rapid beat of his heart through her palms, despite the layers of silky black wool, dress shirt, and, probably, an undershirt.

Their eyes met, and she forgot the part about how she wanted to avoid him.

One corner of his mouth lifted. "Your shoe?"

She dropped her hands from his chest, bracing herself with a hand on the stair railing instead, and slipped her foot from the lodged shoe.

When Owen stooped down to free it, someone chuckled. That was when Jackie noticed Storm and Matt, watching them with amusement from the grass at the base of the deck.

"It's been a hell of a long time since I read a fairy tale, but for some reason, it looks like you two are playing out a scene from 'Little Red Riding Hood,' " Storm said.

Jackie noticed that he also cut a striking figure in his funeral attire, just as Kit had said. The suit fabric puckered at his broad shoulders as he stood with his arms crossed over his chest.

Renee's husband grinned. "I think you mean *Cinderella*, not 'Little Red Riding Hood'! Cinderella lost a shoe running from the ball at midnight. I'm just waiting for the fireworks when he slips that fancy shoe back on her foot, just like in the movie." He half-turned toward the back alley. "I think I hear the horse and carriage coming now."

Jackie had to fight the urge to stick her tongue out at both of them.

"You really wedged this thing in here," Owen grunted from the step below her. He was twisting away at the shoe.

She groaned. "Please be careful. I've only worn these things twice, and they were expensive. I don't want them ruined."

Storm climbed the steps toward them. He had to turn sideways to slip past. Matt shrugged, then stepped over to another knot of people on the back lawn to visit.

"Got it!" Owen said, holding up her shoe like he'd just landed a record-sized walleye. "And look—no damage."

She grabbed for her shoe, but he held it out of reach, seizing hold of her free hand with his.

"Let me help you down to the grass. Then you can put it back on."

The muscles at the base of her skull tightened, and the blood thrummed at her temples. With a sigh of concession, she allowed him to help her down the stairs on one bare foot, the other still wedged in a high-heeled shoe.

"You have a pinched look on your face, like you're in pain," he said. "Are you all right?"

She pulled her hand from his and took her shoe back when they reached the grass. Instead of putting it on, she pulled off her other one.

Relief was immediate—at least to her feet, even if not her head.

"I'm fine. Just a bit of a headache. The girls will be out any minute. I'll grab my car. I need to go take something, maybe find a quiet room. Don't let me keep you. Annie is inside, and she's no longer hiding in the living room. You'll be able to find her."

He nodded, but didn't move away. Instead, he studied her with a concerned expression. "Where's your car?"

Jackie swung one of her shoes toward the street. "Right down there."

Owen glanced up at Annie's house, then back to her. "I'm not in any rush. Why don't I keep you company until your daughters come out? One of them could get your car. I'm not sure you want to walk that far in bare feet."

Jackie peeked down at her toes. The bright orange polish she'd requested when she'd splurged on a pedicure before their Fiji trip winked up at her. The color reminded her of Annie's cast. She gave Owen a quick shake of her head. "You forget. I'm a Kaleidoscope Girl, and we spent our childhood summers at Camp Barefoot. A little gravel isn't going to deter me."

"Believe me, your summer camp days aren't something I forget. Remember, I'm now the owner of said summer camp. By the way, I got a pretty tempting offer from a developer last week for that land."

Jackie was taken aback. She hated how nonchalant he could be about something so important. Her shoes slipped from her fingers and fell to the grass. "You're going to let someone destroy our summer camp?"

He had the grace to look uncomfortable at her reaction. "Jackie, it's not like that. I've worked with these developers before. They do great work and always try to preserve as much of the natural habitat as possible. Whatever they create, it's always nice. No one is using the land for anything these days. It just sits there."

"But won't they knock down the cabins?"

Jackie remembered walking through what was once her favorite cabin when they went out there for a picnic four years earlier. It had been the weekend of their class reunion.

"Mother Nature can take a real toll on vacant buildings over time," he said.

She didn't miss the evasiveness of his answer. "You can't let that happen, Owen. That camp is iconic. It doesn't matter that no one is using it right now."

Even she could hear the condescending tone in her voice.

The light in his eyes dimmed. He jammed his hands into the pockets of his dress slacks with a shrug. "We're still in the early stages of negotiations. I'm not in any hurry. I'll tell you what. If I decide to sell, I'll let you know. Maybe you and your friends could have one last picnic lunch on the beach out there or something. Things change, Jackie. People move on." He motioned toward Annie's house. "Losing Henry like this is a painful reminder of that, isn't it?"

At his mention of Henry, she felt a flush of shame. How could she fret about something as far removed from her current life as the old summer camp on a day like this?

"It is painful," she whispered.

"Say, how is your mom doing?" he asked.

She welcomed the subject change.

"I've thought about swinging by to say hello," he continued, "but whenever I drive by your old house, it never looks like she's home."

Jackie rubbed the back of her neck, trying but failing to loosen the muscles there. "You're right. She isn't home. After Dad's funeral, she got a few things in order, then headed back down to the small house she'd rented in Arizona for the winter. The owner let her extend her lease. Even though Dad was living in the memory care unit at the end, Mom says it's still too hard to be in the house, now that he's gone."

She felt the tears she'd worked so hard to suppress meander down her cheek.

"Aw, Jackie, I'm so sorry," Owen said. He stepped closer and wiped a tear away. "I know how much you loved your dad."

That did it. The tears flowed as if his thumb had flicked the floodgates open.

"Come here," he whispered. He pulled her back into his arms, and this time she didn't resist. She was too tired, and her head felt like it might explode.

Anyone who spotted her crying in Owen's arms would assume the tears were for Henry and his family. In a way, they'd be correct. But it was also the pain that refused to lessen over her father's death, along with her growing frustration over having to deal with his estate.

She didn't know how long they stood like that: her, crying and barefoot, in the arms of an old friend doing his best to offer comfort.

It felt so good to be held.

How long had it been since a man had wrapped his arms around her, for any reason?

Owen had attended her father's funeral. Had he hugged her then? All she could remember was the pain she'd felt at the sight of the woman on his arm that day.

Her friends always teased her about Owen. They thought the two of them could be more than friends, sure as they were that this man had always wanted more than just friendship from her.

And maybe that was how he *used* to feel. But he'd apparently moved on. What other reason could there be for him to bring another woman to her father's funeral?

She'd lost too much in recent years to take any more chances, no matter how natural it felt to rest her head against Owen's chest and listen to his beating heart.

First, her daughters had moved out, then she sold their childhood home and walked away from a stable, albeit stagnant, career.

Then her dad fell ill and faded away.

Mack's laughter proceeded thudding footsteps coming down the wooden stairs behind her. She pulled away from Owen again and brushed the tears from her face.

She didn't want her daughters to get the wrong idea.

"Jeez, Mom, are you all right?" Hailey asked. She dropped a hand on Jackie's shoulder. "Is your headache that bad?"

Mack picked her mom's heels up from the grass. "I'm sorry, Mom. As soon as Hailey said you had one of your headaches, I gave up on finding a scotcheroo bar."

"On finding Colton, you mean," Hailey teased, her hand still resting on Jackie's shoulder. "Hi, Owen. Hey, you have something on your shirt."

Jackie caught the look her daughters exchanged, then spied the black smear of mascara on Owen's shirt front.

She needed to squash any misunderstandings about this man before the girls got the wrong idea. They were constantly bothering her to either get back together with her old boyfriend, Ben, or get out and start dating again. She suspected it was because they worried about her, now that she lived alone with only a dog to keep her company.

"I was just saying a quick hello to Owen, but I've held him up long enough. I was klutzy and got my heel stuck between the boards on the step up there. He kindly got it out for me," she said. Then she turned back to her old friend. "It was good to see you again, Owen. Lynette will be happy to see Storm, too. It was nice of you both to come. Thank you, also, for coming to my dad's funeral. I missed speaking to you that day, and didn't give you a chance to introduce me to the woman who was with you."

Mack sighed. "Mom, give me the keys. I'll go get the car, then drive over to pick you and Hailey up so you don't have to get your feet back into these heels."

She could feel Owen's gaze on her as she again dug into her purse for the key fob. If she didn't take something for this headache soon, the nausea would surely set in.

"Wait," Mack said. "Hailey, do you have Mom's keys? You drove us here."

Jackie snapped her purse shut with frustration. "Really, Hailey? *You* have them?"

Hailey shrugged, thrusting her hand into the pocket of her black maxi skirt. "Oops. Guess so. Come on, Mack. We'll come pick you up, Mom."

Before she could stop them, her girls skipped away, leaving her alone with Owen again.

He still seemed to be studying her.

"What?" she said, uncomfortable under his gaze.

"Are you mad because I didn't come to your dad's funeral alone? That I had a woman with me?"

Jackie wished Mack hadn't hurried off with her shoes. She felt a burning desire to slink away, but despite her earlier protests, the soles of her feet weren't nearly as tough as they'd been when she was a kid.

"Don't be ridiculous. Why would I care who you were with?"

It was Owen's turn to sigh. "Never mind. I guess it was just wishful thinking on my part."

The back door creaked open again. She saw Storm in the doorway, wearing an impatient expression.

Ignoring the way her heart skipped a beat at Owen's confusing comment about wishful thinking, Jackie nodded in Storm's direction. "Looks like someone wants you."

Owen snorted. "Too bad it isn't the *right* someone. It was good to see you again, Jackie. Take care," he said, but the warmth had cooled from his words.

As he brushed by her on the way back to the stairs, she reached out and touched a finger to the smudge on his shirt. "I'm sorry about that."

He grabbed her hand and gripped it to his chest. "Don't worry about it. It's just a shirt."

Instead of pulling her hand away, she stepped closer. "I wasn't only referring to your shirt, but I am sorry if I ruined it. I meant . . . I'm sorry for trying to dictate to you what you should do with the old summer camp land. That's really none of my business. And I'm sorry for getting so emotional around you. I guess Henry's sudden death has left us all feeling unsettled. It really was good to see you, Owen. I miss the good old days, when we were the best of friends. But I know that was a long time ago."

Owen searched her eyes, then slowly brought her captured hand up to drop a light kiss onto her fingers before releasing her. "I'm still here for you, Jackie. All you ever need to do is ask."

A sharp blast of a horn cut through the charged air between them.

He turned to the stairs, but stopped and gave her one last look. "Your girls are getting impatient, and Storm will leave my ass if I don't get in there. But I do value your opinion about the land. Could I call you?"

Jackie nodded, but remembered he wouldn't have her cell number. "Call my old number at the house. Or swing by sometime this coming week. I have lots of work to do before I can head back to Minneapolis. My brother and mother seem to have deserted me, but there are still things that need to be settled for Dad's estate. I just want to get it done. Maybe I'll even convince Mom to put the house up for sale. I'd hate to do it, but like you said, change is part of life."

Another honk of the horn.

He nodded, then turned back to the stairs.

She thought she heard him say that not everything had to change, but she couldn't be sure.

Regardless, she was happy she had failed in her attempt to avoid Owen today. He was still her friend, even after all these years. And that was enough.

Wasn't it?

CHAPTER FOURTEEN

J ACKIE HEARD NIKKI BARKING inside the house as soon as she climbed out of her dad's old sedan. A decent night's sleep in the bed of her youth had helped to wipe away her headache, so today she'd tackle her dad's study. She'd worried there might be paperwork that needed attention in the small office.

Last night, after the girls headed back to Minneapolis in her car, her dinner had consisted of stale saltine crackers with peanut butter and an expired can of diet soda. She could do better, so she'd made it a priority to wake early this morning and go to the grocery store for fresh coffee to brew and bread to toast.

Her phone vibrated in her pocket, but whoever was calling would have to wait until she got her limited groceries put away and Nikki fed. The dog would wake her mother's neighbors if she didn't quiet down.

Ten minutes later, Jackie settled on the front porch with a steaming mug of coffee and jelly toast. She pulled her phone out and sighed, then tossed it onto the top of the steamer trunk that had served as a coffee table between the wicker couch and settee for as long as she could remember.

For the first time, she wondered if the trunk was empty.

She nibbled on her toast. The homemade chokecherry jam she'd found on a shelf in the basement also brought back memories of her childhood. Filling ice cream pails with the berries alongside her mother and brother, then spending hours in a steamy kitchen, turning the roadside fruit into her father's favorite spread, used to be a summer ritual. She sucked in her cheeks at the mere memory of how bitter the berries tasted straight from the bush. She could never resist her brother's dares to taste just one, even though she knew how awful they tasted in their natural state.

Maybe she should approach her tasks today a bit like the process of turning tart fruit into delectable jam. She felt bitterness toward her mom and brother for leaving all this for her to tackle alone, but perhaps going through her father's things, all by herself, would allow for some healthy reflection time.

Maybe this was how she'd finally heal.

She tossed the remaining piece of crust over the porch railing for the birds and picked up her phone. Had her mother decided what she wanted to do regarding the Ruby Shores house?

"Hi, honey. How is Annie doing?" Charlotte asked without preamble when Jackie called her back. "I felt awful for missing Henry's funeral yesterday, but I just couldn't bring myself to get on that plane."

"Hey, Mom. She seems to be holding it together, but we'll keep a close eye on her. How are things in Arizona?"

Her mother snorted. "Hot. Everyone warned me, but this heat is *brutal*. I'm enjoying an iced coffee by the backyard pool now because I know the temperatures will chase me inside by nine. Are you at the house?"

Jackie sipped her cooling coffee. "I am. The girls went back to Minneapolis yesterday, and I'm using Dad's car. I hope that's all right."

"You know it's fine. Drive it home. Sitting too long isn't good for vehicles. In fact, I've been trying to figure out how to get my car down here. The sedan that the owner of this house lets me borrow is a tank to drive. Do you think either of the girls would drive it down for me? Maybe bring a friend along for a little vacation? I'd pay to fly them both home again. They could stay as long as they wanted."

The question gave Jackie pause. How did she feel about either, or both, of her twenty-four-year-olds driving across the country like that? "Mom, does that mean you don't have any plans to come back to Ruby Shores for the foreseeable future?"

Her mother didn't respond immediately. Jackie could picture Charlotte sitting by a shimmering, aqua swimming pool and sipping a fancy iced coffee, wearing her favorite housecoat, far from the heartache of an empty house. Was it denial, or simply what her mom felt she had to do to move on herself?

"I may come up in the fall. My perennials will need to be cut back. I've always loved fall in Minnesota. Is the young man I hired to take care of my yard and plants doing a nice job?"

Jackie sat up straighter on the wicker sofa so she could better see the front yard over the porch railing. "The grass looks nice. He's keeping things trimmed, and your peonies are blooming. But the walkway isn't nearly as pretty without the annuals you always plant alongside it every year."

"And the basement is staying dry?"

She sank back into the cushions and took another sip of her tepid coffee. "It is. I checked yesterday, and my bonus prize was finding a jar of your chokecherry jam. I'm enjoying it on my toast right now."

Her mother chuckled. "Now that sounds delicious. We should can more again sometime."

A car drove by. An older woman strolled past them on the sidewalk with her dog. The world was waking up, and she needed to get to work.

"Mom," Jackie said, "what about Dad's things? How well did you go through his office after the funeral? I'm worried there might be things that need attention."

She heard what she thought was a sniffle. "I just can't do it, Jackie. I can't go through his things."

It was a discussion they'd had before.

"I know, Mom, and I'll handle it, if that's what you want. I thought I'd start in his office. What do you want me to do with everything?"

Another pause, then Charlotte cleared her throat. "Please know how much I appreciate your help, dear. Maybe when his clothes aren't hanging in the closet and his shoes aren't near the front door, I can stand to be there again. Would you be willing to pack up his clothes and personal effects? You could either donate them or have a rummage sale. Or is that asking too much? I know you miss him, too."

Jackie noticed that her mom never even mentioned Ron's name. Ron and their father's relationship had been contentious and complicated. In recent years, they'd had a reconcilement of sorts, but they were never as close as either Jackie or Charlotte would have liked.

So Jackie would handle things. It wasn't like she really had a choice. While donating everything sounded like the simplest approach, she imagined her father taking great offense at her giving his things away. He'd always worked hard to stretch his school administrator salary as far as possible, and he would want Jackie to do what she could to help Charlotte out financially. Not with Jackie's own money, but at least by selling his things.

"Actually, Mom, a rummage sale is a good idea. But what if I get rid of something of his that you would have wanted me to keep?"

"Don't worry about that, honey. I trust you. Use your discretion, and I promise not to question you later. I feel terrible putting all of this on you. Maybe if you let it sit, I'll feel up to it later. Probably not this fall, but maybe next summer."

Jackie hated the idea of leaving things in limbo for that long. Her father taught her to be a woman of action, and even though he was no longer here, she didn't want to disappoint him now.

"Let me do this for you, Mom. Maybe it will help us both move ahead. I'll tell you what. Anything I'm not sure about, I'll put it on one of the spare beds until I can check with you. And if I find anything in his office that I need help with, I'll call you about that, too."

"Oh, honey, you have no idea how much better I feel knowing you are handling this for me."

After hearing more about how her mother was filling her days in Arizona, Jackie promised to update her in a day or two and then hung up. She had work to do. Charlotte wasn't coming home to help, and apparently Ron's tenuous relationship with their father gave him a pass, too.

As she stood and gathered her empty plate and cup, she hoped she wouldn't uncover any proverbial skeletons in her father's closet.

Jackie looked up from the photo album in her lap when Nikki went into a barking frenzy. The dog was somewhere in the front part of the house. Then she heard the squeak of the screen door. Since Nikki calmed down, Jackie was sure that whoever was stopping by wasn't a stranger to the dog.

"I'm back here!"

The clickety-clack of Nikki's paws signaled the dog's approach, along with the slap of bare feet against the hardwood floor in the hallway.

"Knock-knock," Kit said, poking her head through the doorway. "Oh, wow, it's hot back here! Good thing I brought us refreshments."

Jackie sighed in relief when her friend held up two iced coffees. Condensation dripped off the tall plastic cups. Ever since she'd imagined her mother enjoying a similar beverage when she'd talked to her hours earlier, she'd been craving that exact thing.

"Bless you." Before accepting the cup, she closed the album and set it to the side so it wouldn't get wet. The flush on Kit's cheeks caught her eye. "Did you get sunburned?"

Kit dropped into a tattered recliner in the corner of the small office with a grunt. "No. Why? Are my cheeks red? That's probably because I'm so mad at that piece-of-work mother of mine that I could spit nails."

Jackie's breath hitched at Kit's words. Mia, Kit's mom, was a recovering addict, and they all knew she was only one poor decision away from another relapse. Mia had moved back to Ruby Shores to live with Hazel, Kit's grandmother, three years earlier. Initially Mia had done well with her recovery, but in Fiji, when they were all catching up, Kit had mentioned there was a new man in her mother's life.

He wouldn't be the first man to cause an upheaval in Mia's life.

"Is it bad? Did you finally meet the guy?" Jackie asked between sips of her iced vanilla latte. Most of the cubes had already melted, but it was still just what she'd needed.

"Oh, I met him," Kit said. She set her cup down and touched her cheeks. "Mom was pestering Hazel for money when I walked in on the two of them this morning. What is that woman thinking? Hazel is moving into her assisted-living apartment on the first of the month. She doesn't have extra money to throw Mia's way."

Nikki brushed up against Jackie's leg, then plopped her hind end down on her foot. She petted the dog's head but pulled her leg away. It was too hot for bodily contact. "I thought the plan was for both Mia and Marge to pay Hazel rent to live in her house, which would at least help with the cost of her new living arrangements."

Kit grabbed her cup and shook it, rattling the remaining ice. "That was the plan. But now Mia is thinking about moving to Denver with this guy she met at AA."

Jackie was sorry to hear that. "I think we know how that's worked out for your mom in the past."

"Which is why I look like I spent too many hours in the sun. I should have known Mia's grip on her sobriety would never last."

Jackie wasn't sure what to say. Kit had to feel caught in an endless loop where her mother was concerned.

Kit slurped the last of her coffee, then tossed the cup in the tall wastepaper basket Jackie had brought in from the kitchen. "Enough about that. I know you have lots you want to accomplish here. Put me to work. I need a distraction."

Jackie surveyed the messy room around them. She'd sorted paperwork into countless piles, but not much more than that. She wouldn't turn away help. "How long can you stay?"

Kit snapped her fingers. "Oh. Right. About that. I can stay as long as you need me—*if* I can catch a ride back to Minneapolis with you. Dean and Isaac wanted to go back for a big car show that's in town, and Dean has to work tomorrow. Besides, Chloe may be a very independent cat, but even she needs fresh food and water after a few days. Do you mind the company? Because I really don't feel like spending another night under the same roof as my mother."

"You know you're welcome . . . but the only problem might be that I'm staying through next weekend to have a rummage sale."

Kit stood and walked across the cluttered room to a closed closet door. "A rummage sale? Really? Those are a *lot* of work."

Jackie laughed. "You said you wanted a distraction! Can you spare another week? What about your job?"

Kit opened the door and flipped an overhead light on in the closet. "Since I needed almost two weeks for our original Fiji trip, and work has been really slow, I asked for a full month off. They were all too happy to give it to me. To be honest, I'm afraid things might wind down on our current project. There were rumors that the funding has dried up."

Jackie watched Kit with concern as her friend checked out the jackets hanging in the closet. "Do you think you might end up without a job? I know how important your research is to you."

Pulling a heavy parka off a hanger and slipping her arms into the sleeves, Kit nodded. "You're right. It has been important, but oversight and management of the project have shifted, and I don't have the same passion for it anymore. Maybe a change would be good for me. I'm not too worried. Since I'm a happily married woman now, my lovely hubby can support me for a few weeks—or months—if I have to make a shift. It'll be fine."

She zipped up the coat, spun in a circle, then swayed. "Shit. Today is *not* the day to play dress-up. This parka has to be made for forty below, not ninety above!"

Jackie tossed her empty cup, too, then held out a hand for the coat. Kit slipped it off and tossed it to her.

"That thing needs to go in the pile for the rummage sale," Kit said, turning back to the closet again. "If Charlotte spends next winter in Arizona, she's not going to need a heavy, man's parka like that one."

Jackie laid the coat on the recliner Kit had vacated, starting yet another designated pile. "You'll help me then?"

Kit tossed her arms into the air, her back still to Jackie. "Even prepping for a rummage sale sounds better than Hazel's house right now. But don't tell my grandmother I said that." She pulled another jacket down. "Hey, why don't we call Annie and Lynette? We could have a slumber party here tonight, just like we used to, but we wouldn't have to sneak the bottle of Boone's Farm in under sleeping bags. We could drink decent wine from actual glasses on your porch and sleep in proper beds."

Jackie hadn't thought about inviting people over. "That's a great idea! I bet Annie could use a change of scenery after everything she's been through, especially if that awful sister of hers hasn't gone home yet. But let's do takeout. I'm not cooking."

Jackie poured the last of the wine from the bottle Annie had brought over. She'd pulled it from the gift basket that Henry's work had sent to her house.

Annie picked up her wineglass and swirled the cool clear liquid around. "I need a favor."

"Anything," Jackie said as she set the empty bottle by the front door. "All you have to do is ask. We're here for you. Renee said to let her know, too, if she can help. Whispering Pines isn't too far away."

Annie raised her palm to Jackie. "Stop. You sound like every other person who stopped by the house after Henry's funeral. Everyone wants to help while in the moment. Most won't. But I know the four of you actually mean it. Right now, I don't want to talk about Henry, or how I'm doing, or anything like that. Please? I need a break from it all. I'm taking it a day at a time. So are the kids. I don't have to worry about work until mid-August. Other staff will take care of the things I normally handle over the summer. I'd rather hear what you three are up to. Distract me."

Jackie sat next to her again and picked up her own wineglass. "Fine. But you're the one who said you needed a favor. What is it?"

Annie took a sip of her wine, then closed her eyes and nodded. "Oh, right. I would appreciate it if one of you could come to Michael's wedding with me as my plus-one."

Kit froze with her wineglass halfway to her lips. "Michael's getting married again? Now? I didn't even know he was engaged!"

Jackie couldn't believe it either. While she'd never admit as much to Annie, she'd wondered if, after an appropriate time had passed following Henry's death, her old friend and Michael might try again.

One look from Lynette, who sat across the porch from her, told Jackie she wasn't the only one who had considered the possibility.

But if Annie was upset about Michael marrying again, she hid it well.

"When is it?" Lynette said. Jackie heard the plastic of Lynette's water bottle crackle.

"In August. Right before I have to head back to work. It won't be big. They are holding it in a local park. He's been seeing this woman named Tammy for about a year, and they'd talked marriage, but neither was ready to commit."

"Hmph, who does *that* sound like?" Lynette said, pointing her bottle at Kit.

"Hey, I married Dean! Eventually." Kit grinned. "But, ladies, come on. It's just the four of us. Aren't we going to talk about the elephant in the room? Annie, how do you *feel* about Michael marrying? Especially now, after . . . you know . . ." Her voice trailed off.

Holding her breath, Jackie hoped Kit's bluntness hadn't offended Annie. Henry's death was still so fresh.

"Do you mean now that Henry is gone, Kit?" Annie asked. Her expression was hard to read.

"I'm sorry, Annie. I shouldn't have said that. We all loved Henry, too. He was so good to you."

Annie reached for her hand. "Kit, it's all right. Really. This isn't a conversation I'd have with anyone else in the world, but you guys understand. I'm happy for Michael. Truly. Over the years, were there times when I questioned whether leaving Michael and eventually marrying Henry was a mistake? Of course. There is a chemistry between us that never completely burned out. Michael and I do still love each other, but we tried living as a couple once before, and aside from Ava and Colton, it was a disaster. *Could* we make it if we tried again? Maybe . . . down the road. But now—and please don't judge me—when I look at Michael, I see a forever-friend instead of a romantic partner. I hope I'm not one of those people who only wants what they can't have. For now, I just want the time and space to heal, because losing Henry almost killed me. I don't know if I'll ever feel whole again."

Kit, still holding Annie's hand, gave it a big squeeze before releasing it. "I get it. Our past is just that, and it's usually best to leave it back there."

Jackie fingered the photo album she'd brought out to the porch to show her friends. She thought about some of the pictures she'd thumbed through from her grade school and junior high years.

Was Owen someone she should leave in her past, too?

Annie noticed the album then and wriggled her fingers at Jackie. "I insisted we weren't going to talk about my sad situation any more tonight, and then I fell right back into it. What do you have there, Jackie? Did you find some fun pictures when you were cleaning house today?"

Jackie pulled the photo book off the side table and into her lap. "There are some fun ones. I thought you guys might get a kick out of seeing them, too." She'd stuck a torn slip of paper between the pages containing pictures from their senior prom, and now she flipped back to that section. "Check these out. We were just babies! I must say, Lynette, your Storm has probably changed the most."

Annie leaned over for a closer look, and both Kit and Lynette moved behind the others to see.

"It's getting too dark out here. I can't see very well," Kit complained. "I think I need new contacts. Glasses, too. Can we move inside to the living room? I want to look at the pictures. I also found two metal boxes in Glen's closet. One for each kid. Jackie and I peeked inside, but thought the four of us would have fun going through her box together."

Jackie swatted at a mosquito on her arm. "Yes. Let's go inside. But no one can go to bed yet!"

Ten minutes later, the four women settled around the coffee table in the living room, flipping through the photo album.

"Look at this darling picture of Renee and Owen," Lynette said, pointing to one photograph. "I wonder if Renee has any pictures from that night, since her parents weren't there to take any."

Jackie pulled the plastic covering back. The photograph was easy to remove from the page. "I could give her this one. It is cute."

"Here, I'm going out to Whispering Pines next week, I can take it to her. It looks like you have a bunch of group shots. Could I give her one of those, too?"

Jackie had no use for so many similar pictures. "Of course! She looks so happy in this one." She handed both pictures to Lynette. "You'll have to let us know what she thinks of them. You're going out there to talk business with her, right?"

"I am. I think if we put our heads together, we can come up with a plan. Then, when I get back, I've decided to make it official. I'm going to open an actual consulting office. I just need to find a location."

They met her announcement with screams of delight and hugs. Jackie headed for the kitchen to retrieve another bottle of wine. When she came back, she heard Annie mention how she'd love to go back to Whispering Pines, how she craved the quiet and solitude.

She set the open bottle down next to Kit, then turned to Annie. "Not to speak out of turn, but I bet Lynette would be happy to bring you along. And I *know* Renee would love to have you. Heck, I'd go if I could get away for any longer, but I've got important business waiting for me back in Minneapolis."

"Of course I'd love to have you come along!" Lynette jumped in. "I'd even let you drive, if you like."

This brought on a round of laughter. They all knew that Lynette didn't like to drive.

"I'll make sure Relic can take care of the dogs, and if so, I'm in," Annie said. "But just a minute. What big business do you have, Jackie?"

Jackie took a deep breath and poured herself a very full glass of wine. "Well . . . actually . . . I'm thinking about selling my pet adoption business."

"What?!" Kit looked stunned.

"But you've worked so hard," Annie protested.

Lynette was the only one who didn't look surprised. "Did someone approach you with an offer?"

Jackie had to lean over and suck some of the wine out of her glass before she could lift it without spilling. "How did you guess?"

Lynette shrugged. "People build and then sell businesses all the time. If they can get them off the ground in the first place, that is. Congratulations, even if you don't decide to sell. That is a hell of an accomplishment."

"But what will you do if you sell?" Kit asked.

Jackie shrugged. "I can stay on with them in a manager capacity if I want to, but I haven't decided. Hopefully I'll still do something with animals. Oh, that reminds me. Speaking of offers, when I ran into Owen over at Annie's house, he mentioned receiving an offer on the summer camp land."

Annie slouched in her chair. "Oh, *no*, not the camp, too! Why does it feel like everything is changing? Is it a developer wanting to turn it into just another cookie-cutter subdivision? At this rate, our little Ruby Shores is going to turn into a city."

Jackie carefully lifted her glass, still full of wine, and took another healthy sip. "That could happen. The subdivision part, I mean. Honestly, it was already such an emotionally charged day that when he told me about the possibility, I'm afraid I wasn't very nice to him about it. But he's so patient, he asked if we could talk about the land sometime. As if I might have better ideas about what he could do with it."

Lynette yawned.

Kit smirked. "Are we keeping you up?"

"No, I'm sorry. I just didn't sleep well in my little attic apartment last night," Lynette confessed. "It still feels strange, not having full access to my house anymore. But I hate the idea of our camp land getting bulldozed over, too. Maybe we could brainstorm ideas you could take to Owen, Jackie. Does he have to move quickly?"

Jackie pulled an afghan off the back of the couch and tossed it to Lynette. "It sounded like he has a little time yet."

A cell phone on the coffee table vibrated. Jackie glanced at the wall clock above Annie's head. It was after ten.

Kit snatched the phone up and turned it over. "Why would Dean be calling so late?"

As she watched her friend leave the room with her phone, Jackie hoped it wasn't more bad news.

"I hope nothing's wrong," Annie said, echoing Jackie's thoughts. "None of us need any more bad news."

Their conversation died away as they waited for Kit to return. Jackie noticed Lynette's eyes flutter closed, and poor Annie looked worn out. Maybe they should all go to bed. They weren't sixteen anymore, like they were back when these sleepovers were a regular occurrence.

Kit returned. Unlike her ruddy complexion earlier in the day following her fight with her mother, her face now looked drained of color.

Something *was* wrong.

"What happened?" Lynette asked, looking wide awake now. "Are Dean and Isaac all right? Chloe?"

Kit shook her head. "They are all fine. But there was a tornado."

Jackie set her wine back down on the coffee table. "In the Minneapolis area? I should call the girls. They're staying at my townhouse."

"No, in Iowa. Dean's mother called him. It touched down on his brother's farmstead. Everyone is all right, thankfully, but there's lots of damage. Dean plans to drive over first thing in the morning. He'll take Isaac, too, and see how they might help. The farmstead has actually been in Dean's sister-in-law's family for a long time. They are such a fun couple. I really like both of them. But this has his brother really shaken up."

Jackie suspected Kit might want to go with them to Iowa. "Why don't you take my dad's car? You could still get back home in time to go with them. Unless you're too tired to drive."

"Or had too much wine," Lynette said, motioning to the bottle in the center of the coffee table.

Kit shook her head. "I asked Dean if he wanted me to come. He said no. No one got hurt—at least in his family, he wasn't sure about neighbors. There will be lots of cleanup to do, but he knows I need to help Hazel get moved and give you a hand here, too, Jackie."

While Jackie appreciated Kit's loyalty, she knew she could handle this by herself. Or she could call her brother and insist he get his butt over here to help. "I'll be fine, Kit. And your aunt can help your grandmother."

Nikki whined. This was the time the dog normally went outside one last time before they both headed to bed.

Everyone was getting tired.

Kit rubbed a hand over weary eyes. "Honestly, there's always tension between me and Dean's mom anytime we're together. It's getting better, but Dean thought it would be best if I didn't go. At least until he has a better sense of how serious things are back there. He already talked to our neighbor at home about checking in on Chloe every other day until

I get back. So I'm afraid you're stuck with me, Jackie."

Jackie got to her feet and moved to Kit's side. She wrapped an arm around her waist and dropped her head to her shoulder. "There's no one else I'd rather be stuck with than you. Or you. Or you."

CHAPTER FIFTEEN

LYNETTE STOOD ON THE landing of the open staircase, looking up at her newly installed window. She couldn't believe how stunning the round, kaleidoscope-inspired stained glass looked. "Renee was right. You do amazing work, Seth. I can't thank you enough."

Renee's brother-in-law shrugged. "I lucked out with sisters-in-law, and I appreciate her making the connection between us. Most of this design is your doing. I'll admit, I had some doubts, but it all came together nicely. And thanks for your help, Taran. This project would have taken me twice as long without an extra set of hands."

"Happy to help," Storm said. "I'm just glad this one didn't knock me off the ladder this time."

Lynette couldn't believe he had pushed his thumb in her direction when he said that. "All right, for the record, I didn't push him off that ladder. He fell when he reached too far for my cat."

Seth looked from Lynette to Storm and back again. His eyes narrowed above a knowing smile. "I think that's an argument I'm going to choose to stay out of. Lynette, be sure to let me know if you have any trouble with the window. Any sign of a leak during your next hard rain, call me right away and we can get it shored up. But I think you'll be fine. This is a quality home, and there was plenty of room for me to secure everything up there. Whoever built this place didn't cut any corners. Do you know what happened to the original window?"

It was Lynette's turn to shrug. "Someone had already boarded it up when I bought the place. There was a terrible storm that rolled through Ruby Shores a few years back. The damage might have occurred then."

As Storm helped gather up the tools, he said, "Owen mentioned something about that." He handed a nail gun to Seth. "He said Kit's grandmother's old place suffered some pretty significant damage."

"It did," Lynette said. "Both her grandmother and Owen live near here, too. I heard Owen and his son were both a big help with the cleanup, though I was still living in New York City at the time."

Seth grunted as he used his free hand to pick up a large metal toolbox. "New York, huh? Never been. But I'd like to. What brought you back to Ruby Shores, if you don't mind me asking?"

"I sold my business," Lynette said.

"Here, let me help you with that," Storm said, taking the toolbox from him.

Lynette couldn't help but notice the way the muscles in Storm's arm flexed when he took the toolbox's weight.

Storm was stirring feelings in her that she used to worry might desert her once she crossed over the half-century mark. She needn't have worried.

Seth looked relieved. "Thanks. Don't tell Renee's sister, Jess, but you aren't the only one to tumble off a ladder. I slipped off one a couple weeks ago, and my wrist is still giving me trouble. But she doesn't need to know that."

Lynette laughed. "I'm actually heading out to Whispering Pines to meet with Renee. If I run into Jess, I'll keep that little tidbit to myself.

Promise."

The trio headed outside, where Storm and Lynette helped Seth finish loading his tools and extra-tall extension ladder.

"You have a beautiful home, Lynette," Seth said as he slammed the tailgate on his truck. "Call me if you need help with any other windows, or anything else. Maybe a vintage newel post for that staircase, or a mantel that's more appropriate for the year of the house. I have a shop full of items I've pulled from old buildings like this."

Even though he'd been addressing Lynette, Storm nodded and said, "Sounds like you've got some nice diversity in your business. Some of the renovations done here weren't true to the house's origins, so it's good to have someone we could reach out to for authentic pieces."

Something about the way he jumped into the conversation didn't sit well with Lynette. She didn't need a man to speak for her.

After promising to send him pictures of the light shining through the window the next time the sun peeked out from behind the day's heavy clouds, Lynette watched Seth drive away.

Storm stood next to her and said, "I'm going to run Shane and Dexter to the grocery store so we can get the fridge and shelves fully stocked before I leave. You probably don't have much in that little kitchen of yours, either, so I was wondering if you wanted to come along."

Her stomach growled at the mention of food. She'd enjoyed a donut and fresh coffee with her friends early that morning before rushing home to be there for the window install, but that was hours ago. He must have heard the rumble, because he laughed.

She returned his smile, deciding to let his overreach regarding her house go. After all, most of it was technically his, at least for the duration of the lease. He was leaving again in two days, and she didn't want to waste any of it arguing.

What she really wanted to do was get her hands on those arm muscles of his.

He reached for her, and her breath caught.

The slam of a door nearby had Storm pulling back.

"Taran, Taran, I have my grocery list ready to go," Shane said as he jogged down the back stairs and the path toward them. Dexter, Shane's live-in caretaker, followed at a more measured pace.

Lynette realized it was going to be difficult to find any alone time.

"Hold that thought," Storm whispered in her ear. "I have a plan."

Yep, he knows what I want.

The four piled into Storm's pickup and spent the next hour at the grocery store. Dexter spoke calmly to Shane to rein in the young man's excitement. He stayed by his side, but there was one time when she noticed his temper flare over something small Shane did.

Storm had gone back to grab ketchup in another aisle, so he didn't witness it.

It was probably nothing. Hopefully Dexter was competent at his job, and Storm was leaving his brother in capable hands. Lynette certainly didn't want to have to worry about Shane's safety or the caregiver's commitment, even though she'd be living in the same house.

After they returned home and fully stocked both the main kitchen and Lynette's small galley-style kitchenette upstairs, Storm grilled steaks on a backyard grill he'd pulled out of the garage. Lynette hadn't even noticed it there before.

By nine, Storm was encouraging his brother to turn in for the evening, reminding Dexter that Shane did best when they stuck to a strict sched-ule. Following orders, Dexter took Shane back to his room for his night-time routine.

That left Storm and Lynette alone in the kitchen.

He pulled the dishtowel he'd used to dry the dishes she'd washed off his shoulder and hung it on a drawer pull to dry.

How can I find such a simple act sexy?

She kept a close eye on him, wondering what would come next.

He reached for her right hand. "This looks good on you," he said, rubbing his thumb across the vintage ring he'd spontaneously slid onto her finger last summer at the ice cream parlor.

She used to wear a different ring on that finger, but she'd lost it in the lake at Whispering Pines. That had been a special family ring, too.

The only time she'd taken Storm's ring off during the months since was to have the prongs checked while visiting her favorite jeweler in New York. She would feel awful if she lost the stone out of his family heirloom. She'd expected one of her friends to ask about the ring, but none of them did. They probably thought it was just one of many she'd accumulated over the years.

"I still can't believe you let me wear it. If you ever want it back, all you have to do is ask."

He lifted her hand and dropped it onto his shoulder before pulling her up against his chest.

Her heart thundered. Could he feel it?

"I like these," he said, trailing one finger down her neck and the delicate skin her tank top didn't cover, stopping just above the black lace that peeked out above the jersey fabric. "Correct me if my memory is faulty, but there seems to have been some type of . . . *structural* . . . change here."

She shifted without thought, subconsciously hoping his finger would dip lower, but he continued to run it lightly across her bare skin. "You aren't wrong. To be honest, it was an impulsive action I've since regretted . . . but maybe it wasn't a mistake after all, if you like them."

His finger trailed up again until he gently lifted her chin, positioning her perfectly for a kiss. He bent down, stopping a breath short of her lips. "Nothing about you is a mistake. I'm only sorry it took me thirty-odd years to figure that out."

He jumped back with a gasp. "Shit!"

Lynette's eyes had drifted shut in anticipation of his kiss, but she snapped them open in surprise.

"Damn cat rubbed against my leg. Surprised me. How did that thing get down here?"

Laughing, Lynette scooped up the black cat. "This thing has a name. Ebony, did you sneak down here? Did I forget to close my door upstairs?"

Footsteps approached from the rear section of the house. "Everything all right in here?" Dexter asked. He had an empty glass in his hand. "Shane asked for ice water, and I heard a yelp."

He sneezed as he walked past Lynette.

"Are you allergic to cats?" she asked, concerned.

"Sure am," Dexter confirmed. "But if you keep her in your apartment, it'll be fine."

Lynette swung her gaze to Storm, who was eyeing the man closely.

"Dex," he said, capturing the man's attention. "This is ultimately Lynette's house. I know I rented the first and second floors from her for Shane's benefit, but she's free to come and go as she likes."

"That's not . . ." Lynette tried to interrupt, but he cut her off with a brief shake of his head.

"Is that going to be a problem?" Storm's attention was back on Dexter.

The man sighed. "Certainly not. I just need to know the ground rules. I'm sure we'll all get along just fine."

He filled Shane's glass with a pitcher of water from the refrigerator before bidding them both goodnight for the second time.

Once Dexter was gone, Lynette set Ebony down again.

"Storm, I'll stay upstairs when I'm home. I don't want to get in their way."

His features relaxed. "I know. I just wanted to be sure he is clear on where he stands in the pecking order around here."

She smiled. "Based on the way he hustled out of here, I think he got the message."

This time she put her arms around him first, laying her cheek against his broad chest. She loved how she could hear his heart beating under her ear. "I'm going to go up. It's getting late. Will I see you tomorrow?"

He wrapped her in a hug and rocked gently, side to side. "Woman, you drive me crazy. Yes, I plan to spend the whole day with you, and none of it here at the house. I'm paying Dexter good money to be here for Shane. Do I fit into your schedule?"

She squeezed him tight, then stepped back from his arms. If she stayed there any longer, she couldn't trust herself to head upstairs alone. "I'll have to rearrange a few things, but I think I can fit you in," she lied with a wink. She had no plans, and a whole day with him sounded like perfection.

"Glad to hear it. Go on upstairs then, and I'll lock up. Be ready to go at nine?"

She loved the earnest expression he wore. "I doubt I'll sleep a wink."

But she was wrong. Her head had barely hit the pillow before she drifted off.

It wasn't until sometime later, when a bright white moon shone through the open window above her bed, that something jolted her awake.

"What is that awful noise?" she moaned, pushing her hair out of her eyes as she struggled to sit up. A flash of black in the moonlight told her Ebony had leaped from her bed to the carpet below.

As the fog of sleep dissipated, the sound finally registered.

Somewhere below, a smoke alarm wailed.

Storm hadn't slept at the house. Lynette had assumed he would, but his absence was apparent when she ran downstairs in the middle of the night to see about the alarm.

Dex convinced her to keep the unfortunate incident to herself, insisting it would never happen again. He'd forgotten to turn a different alarm on that would have alerted him if Shane left his bedroom during the night. He insisted he was doing his best to learn Shane's routine, but had missed that one step.

Besides, the popcorn Shane had burned in the microwave wasn't really a serious risk, right?

But now, in the bright of day, Lynette was second-guessing her promise as she sat beside Storm in his truck. He drove slowly through the streets of Ruby Shores, pointing out landmarks here and there where they'd spent part of their youth together. She found his nostalgia both surprising and heartwarming. He reminded her of things she'd forgotten.

Telling him she wasn't getting good vibes off of Dexter would wipe the smile off Storm's face, and she hated to do that. They'd waited too long for this time together, with just the two of them.

If anything else happened, then she'd tell Storm.

With that decided, she turned her full attention back to the man by her side.

He pulled his truck into the weedy parking lot of the boarded-up building that, back in the '80s, had been the pizza parlor where they'd first met. He rolled down the windows and turned off the engine as he gazed at the eyesore.

"I remember your first day on the job," he said without turning to look at her. "You were too damn pretty for your own good. Smart, too. I knew I was in trouble."

He laid his hand on top of hers where it rested on the center console.

"That's a lie," she said. "You barely gave me the time of day, insisting that old battle-ax of a waitress train me in."

He laughed at that, squeezing her fingers. "That old battle-ax had a name. And Dorothy was a softy once you got past her prickly exterior."

Lynette thought back to those long-ago days. She didn't remember ever sensing anything even remotely soft in Dorothy. "You were the only one who got along with her."

"Not true. She liked Owen, too."

"Everyone liked Owen. He was nice. *You* were intimidating. At least at first. But after I got to know you better, you didn't scare me."

He sat quietly for a minute, then flicked his left hand at a mosquito hovering over his dash. "I probably *should* have scared you. Looking back, I'm afraid I took advantage of your innocence. God, Lynette, the way we couldn't keep our hands off each other . . . it's a wonder you didn't wind up pregnant."

Her breath hitched at his words. There was a time when she had thought she was pregnant with this man's child. But she'd never known for sure, and there was no getting at the truth now.

He shifted to face her. "I'm sorry I was such a terrible influence on you. I must have terrified your mother, with my long hair and tattoos."

She gave him a small smile, then turned her eyes back to the boarded-up business. "Honestly, how you looked was a big part of the fun. You were sexy as hell, as Annie likes to say, but you also scared my mom, and I liked that. It sounds so juvenile to admit that out loud, but it's true."

He shifted again, his eyes back on the building, too. "Did you know that Owen and I bought this building? We had big plans for it."

"This?!" she asked. "You did not."

He laughed. "Honest. We did. The old guy that ran it made a hell of a pizza, but he was a terrible business owner. His lease was coming due, and the building owners were more interested in selling it than locking things in with another lease, so we scraped together every penny we could and somehow bought it ourselves. We held on to it for ten years, and added other properties to our portfolio, too. Those were fun times. It wasn't until after we'd divested and went our separate ways that new owners turned this place into a laundromat. I'm sad to see it boarded up like this."

Lynette struggled to keep up. "You and Owen really did go into business together, then?"

He moved his hand away to rest his arm across the back of Lynette's seat. "We really did."

She sat with the information, trying to picture younger versions of both men working together. "Did you have a falling out?" she eventually asked.

Storm tugged at one of her silver curls that had escaped the updo she'd twisted onto the top of her head. "Nah. It wasn't like that. We were both married, and family obligations interfered with how we liked to work together. We both ran other successful business ventures, too. The marriages, though . . . neither of those turned out so well. But here we are, you and me, right back where we started."

He moved his hand to the back of her neck, gently massaging away the tension she hadn't even realized was there. She slid her hand from the console to his thigh.

He wasn't the only one brave enough to take calculated risks.

"What else do you have planned for us today?"

He gave her a cocky grin, then pulled his arm back and started the truck. Flipping on his radio to a local station playing '80s rock, he rolled up the windows before putting his sexy truck into gear and throwing gravel as he shot out of the parking lot.

He'd always been in a hurry when they were young, and adrenaline shot through her as her imagination skipped ahead to where he might take her.

Chapter Sixteen

Lynette's excitement shifted toward trepidation as Storm headed out of Ruby Shores on the road that would take them by the lake. In their younger years, there were plenty of places along the water that offered relative privacy where they could park, hop into the bed of his truck, lay on top of the thick sleeping bag he kept there, and learn every curve and plane of each other's bodies. The potential for discovery only added to the thrill.

Fifty-two-year-old Lynette had no desire to crawl into the back of this fancy truck to rediscover the nuances of her first lover's body. Beds worked better. Hopefully Storm felt the same.

Then another thought occurred to her. He'd mentioned he still owned the lake house where he lived as a kid. The same lake house she'd fled to when a stranger almost raped her. Storm knew she'd visited that house without him once: the night she took his pickup without permission and almost killed herself when she wrecked it.

But she'd never been honest with him about what drove her to do something so dangerous. He couldn't know how she associated that house with both his horrible mother and the horror of what she'd endured, as well as the trauma of what she'd had to do to escape.

Her breathing quickened, and she worried she might hyperventilate.

The music thrummed through the cab, and Storm remained oblivious to her rising panic.

She took a deep breath and closed her eyes. That awful night was far back in her past, and aside from discussing it with her four closest friends while at Whispering Pines last year, she'd never spoken of it with anyone other than the therapist she saw more recently in New York.

Her attacker was long dead.

Storm's mother, even if she really had been there that night and ignored a young girl's desperate cry for help, was no longer in the area. Storm had cut ties with her. The woman was irrelevant to their lives now.

There was nothing left for Lynette to fear.

Storm must love the house if he'd kept it these many years. He'd mentioned possibly selling it, but that didn't mean it wasn't still important to him.

When they passed the spot where she'd rolled his pickup, a shiver swept through her.

She glanced at Storm, then closed her eyes again. If he recognized the location, he gave no sign.

She was being ridiculous. What had Kit said two nights ago when they all spent the night at Jackie's mom's house? Something about the past being the past, and they should avoid drudging it up again.

She took another, extra deep breath. God, she was so sick of the same old track running through her brain of that awful night. It was time to let it go.

Telling Storm the truth might be the only way she could put it behind her.

But that scared her, too.

She unbuckled her seatbelt as he pulled into the driveway, trying to ignore the little voice in the back of her mind telling her that if she was going to build something real with Storm, she needed to tell him everything. She opened her eyes and the house of her nightmares loomed large.

"Do you remember this house? I know it's been a long time, and it looks different since I added new siding and put on a metal roof. Excellent alternative to shingles—snow buildup was a problem in the winter, and I'm just not here often enough. I . . ." His voice trailed off. "Lynette, what's wrong? You look like you've seen a ghost."

She forced a smile. "I'm fine. It's just that my memories of this place are . . . shall we say . . . complicated."

His expression shifted as he realized what she meant. When she reached for the door, he put his hand on her knee to stop her from getting out of the truck. "I'm an ass. I should have remembered about that night."

Her panic ratcheted back up at his words. Had someone told him what really happened?

"I forgot how you snuck in here to 'borrow' my truck that night." He made air quotes with his fingers when he said the word *borrow*, then gave her knee a playful squeeze. "Look, Lynette, I'm sorry things got so sideways after that night. It took me a while to understand just how lucky we all were that you weren't seriously hurt. It could have been so much worse. You ruined my truck, sure, but in the scheme of things, that wasn't what was important. It was an accident. I never understood why you took it, but I know you well enough to understand that you wouldn't have if you'd have had any other choice."

She hiccupped, unable to control her emotions.

"Oh, hey, hey . . . I had no idea bringing you out here would upset you like this. Wait here."

He jumped out of the truck and ran around to her side. He opened her door and scooped her out of her seat like a child. When he let her legs down but held tight to the rest of her, their bodies were flush from head to toe. His arms, one around her shoulders and the other around her waist, were like steel. He held tight as she wept, and her frustration over the explosion of feelings coursing through her escaped through the burning tears.

They stood that way until there were no tears left in her.

His arms loosened as she quieted.

When she looked up into his eyes, sure she must look an absolute fright, he stepped away and pulled his cotton T-shirt off, using the hem to wipe underneath her eyes and nose. She tried to duck away, hating for him to soil his shirt, but his arm went around her waist again, and then she couldn't have gotten away, even if she really wanted to.

A giggle bubbled up, jumping over the lump that remained in her throat. "What, no fancy hankie today?"

A grin replaced his frown. "Sorry. I'm only a proper gentleman when attending funerals or weddings."

His mention of *weddings* made her stomach do a funny little flip.

Once he seemed satisfied with the state of her face, he tucked his shirt into a back pocket of his jeans. "This wasn't how I imagined our date ending, but I can take you home if you'd like."

She didn't like that idea at all. The warmth of his bare chest under the palms of her hands finally registered. He'd brought her here because it offered them a privacy they wouldn't find at her house. She wasn't naïve. He'd brought her here for sex—something she wanted, too.

But before they could go inside, there was something she needed to do first.

Hating to lose contact with his gorgeous, chiseled chest, she stepped away, promising herself they'd get back to that soon. Now, she took his hand and shook her head. "I don't want to go home. I want to see your lake house and all the renovations you've done to it since the one time I was inside when we were kids. But first, there's something I need to talk to you about. Can we walk?"

"We can do anything you want to do, Lynette," he said. "But can I have one proper kiss first? That's the only way I can stop staring at your lips and anticipating where I think both of us want to take this date."

He wiggled his eyebrows at her in what he probably thought was a flirtatious way, but really just made him look ridiculous. She held tight to his hand, then stepped forward so she could kiss him again like she'd wanted to ever since he'd caught her on the stairs up to her apartment a few days earlier.

When his free hand cupped her bottom and he tried to pull his other hand from hers, she stepped back and turned toward the path down to the lake.

"Come on."

She tugged him by the hand and he stumbled after her, a pained look on his face.

"You are still a bit of a tease, aren't you?" he said, but when she spun around to protest, his smile told her he was kidding. He kissed the knuckles of her hand, still clasped tight in his, then nodded toward the path. "Let's talk. Everything else can wait."

———❧———

Storm's lake house appeared well-kept from the driveway, but weeds had invaded the beach.

"Sorry, I never come down here anymore," he said, pulling fists of tall weeds out of the sandy soil and tossing them away from the water's edge.

She watched him for a couple of minutes, then spied an old wooden bench poking above the growth. Walking over to it, she noted the vegetation was much sparser, and the wood looked like it might hold them if they sat down. She tested it out while he went on pulling weeds. It seemed sturdy enough.

"Storm. Here. Sit with me. And you better put your shirt on in case the mosquitoes get bad."

He halted and looked her way. "Huh. Never noticed that bench before." He pulled his T-shirt back on as he came closer, then gave the open spot next to her a dubious look. "Is it rotten?"

She bounced a little, and when it didn't splinter, she patted the open spot.

He sat gingerly, as if expecting to break through upon contact. It held.

"Fishermen might have pulled it down here," he said, still looking curiously at it. Eventually, he settled, even stretching his legs out in front and crossing his booted feet.

Lynette was comfortable in the heat with her sandals on, but he had to be roasting in jeans and those heavy boots. She felt a twinge of guilt.

"Thank you for your patience with me. I never considered you a patient guy when we were younger."

He shrugged, then dropped his arm across the back of the bench behind her. "Life has a way of knocking some of the zap out of all of us. I've learned not to rush something good."

When his other hand slowly reached for her breast, she playfully slapped it away.

"This is going to take longer if you keep messing around."

He laughed and pulled his hand back. "Fine, I promise I'll try to behave. You're just so distracting in your pretty white blouse. You know I can see the lace of your bra underneath it, right?"

She snorted. "You are incorrigible."

"Guilty as charged. You were saying . . . ?"

She let out an enormous sigh. "I wanted to talk to you about what really happened that night. The night I took your truck without permission. But you need to promise you won't interrupt . . . and that you won't fly off the handle."

He stiffened next to her. "I promise . . . but you're scaring me, Lynette."

"I know. To be honest, I vowed to never tell another soul about what happened. And I didn't, for a very long time. But it ate at me. I can see now how much damage that did to my psyche. I drank to drown the memories. Until last year, when I almost drowned myself."

He uncrossed his ankles and dug a heel into the sand. "Does this have something to do with that stunt you pulled at Whispering Pines last summer?"

"You promised not to interrupt."

He squirmed. "Sorry. Continue. I won't say another word."

And he didn't.

She told him how bored she had been at the after-graduation party on that long-ago night—a party he couldn't attend, as he was older.

Told him how she climbed into a stranger's pickup truck simply because her anxiety levels were sky high and she had recognized him from the pizza parlor. How she knew almost immediately that she'd made a huge mistake and was in real danger.

Storm sprang to his feet and paced along the lake's edge, oblivious to the water he kicked up with his boots. "I'll kill him," he muttered.

She could either stop and assure him that wouldn't be necessary or pretend he'd done as she'd asked and stayed quiet. She chose the second option and continued speaking.

"When he parked at the lookout above the beach, I knew I was out of time, and almost out of options. I'd kicked some kind of tool on his floorboard earlier. If he got me out of the truck, it was game over. I worried he'd do more than just rape me . . . he might kill me."

Her words had fallen to a whisper. Storm came back to her and sat down again, clasping both her hands. But he stayed quiet this time, so she drew the strength from him she needed to continue talking. Telling Storm was so much harder than it had been to tell her girlfriends last year. After a steadying breath, she met and held his gaze.

"Storm, I let him think I was into him. It was so awful. The only other person I'd ever been with was you, and he was *nothing* like you."

His breath hissed. "Did he actually . . . ?"

"No!" she said. "But I let him think he'd get his way. I insisted we stay in the truck instead of going out to the picnic table, though. Said it would be too buggy."

Storm almost laughed at that, but he choked it off. None of this was funny.

"I kept thinking about that wrench, or whatever I'd kicked. When I told him I needed to get my pants off over my shoes, he let me bend down, and that's when I grabbed it. It was a good thing he was smoking weed when he picked me up. He might have been so much harder to fool if he wasn't stoned."

"Jesus, Lynette," Storm groaned.

She nodded. "I know. Dumb. Horrible. But the one thing I did right was to realize I needed to fight to get away from him. I let things progress a little more, all while gripping that heavy tool in one hand like my life depended on it. Because it probably did. Then, for a split second, a beam of moonlight illuminated his disgusting face, and his eyes were closed."

"I'm not even going to ask what you were doing to him to make him close his eyes."

"I did what I had to do to survive. Never forget that."

He fell silent again, but she could read what she thought was respect, and not revulsion, in his eyes.

It was time to push through the worst of this part of the story.

"I swung that damn wrench as hard as I could, and I'll never forget the way it cracked against his forehead. He slumped, and I didn't wait around to see if I'd killed him. I jumped from his truck, being careful to take anything I'd brought into the pickup with me, and adjusted my clothes. Then I remembered my prints were on that wrench, and if I'd killed the bastard, I didn't want there to be any ties to me, so I made myself go back and wipe it clean. The door handles, too. Then I left."

She stopped for a moment, watching him struggle to process it all.

Finally, he gave her a brief nod. "You ran to my house from the look-out, didn't you? It wasn't too far, and he probably wouldn't think to follow you there. Because I'm going to guess you didn't kill the piece of shit, right?"

"Right."

She shivered, and he ran warm hands over her arms.

"And when no one was home, you remembered where I kept my keys—and you took my truck."

"Wrong."

This gave him pause. "Wrong? What do you mean?"

"I mean that I'm pretty sure your mom was home, but she didn't open the door for me. Her car was in the garage, and I thought I saw lights flick off inside when I first knocked and yelled for help."

He stopped trying to warm her arms and scooted back on the bench. "Look, Mom isn't a good person. I know that. But even she wouldn't ignore a cry for help."

She didn't argue with him. She knew the truth. Maybe he'd believe her in time.

"I was panicking, sure that he'd recovered enough to chase me down. When I saw a car on the road by your house, I was convinced it was him. Whoever it was drove on by, but it spurred me to action. Yes, I knew where you kept your keys. All I could think to do was take your truck and get as far from that madman as possible. I tore out of the driveway and headed for Ruby Shores with my fingers crossed. But there was one more hiccup."

She waited, curious if he'd guess. When he shrugged, she sighed.

"The truck was almost out of gas!"

He grunted. "That happened often, leading up to payday."

"Yeah. Luckily, Donna taught me to always keep an emergency twenty in my wallet. I figured if I could just get to that old gas station on the edge of town, I might get home in one piece."

Storm rubbed his face with both hands. "But you nearly didn't get home in one piece. How did you end up in the ditch that night, Lynette?

The rollover could have killed you. The condition of my truck afterward still haunts me, and not because I cared about the damn pickup. I cared about *you*."

She wished he'd have told her that after the accident. But like so many other things that happened during that time, he'd stayed away and she'd misinterpreted why.

"My mind was still playing tricks on me," she said. "I saw headlights coming up fast behind me and I was sure he'd found me. I didn't slow down for the corner, and suddenly I was flying. And that's all I remember until I woke up in the hospital. I'd survived my foolishness, but I knew you'd never forgive me for wrecking your truck. When Mom insisted we leave town and start over somewhere, I hated it, but what option did I have? It wasn't until recently that I found out why she was so adamant that we leave like we did. She finally told me the truth."

A seagull screeched overhead, drawing her eyes upward.

Storm said, "Why do I have the feeling I'm not going to like what she told you?"

"You're right. You won't. Remember last summer when we went for ice cream, and I asked you if you knew about the money?"

He gave a slow nod. "I had no idea what you were talking about."

"According to Donna, your mother paid her to take me away. And since we always lived paycheck to paycheck, my mom was in a world of hurt financially after I wrecked your truck, and with the medical bills and everything. Your mother didn't press the issue around the damages, and she gave Donna ten thousand dollars to leave—on the condition that I never speak to you again. That was a lot of money for us back then, but I honestly never knew about the money or its conditions until my mom told me last summer."

The bench underneath them gave an ominous crack, as if it was about to collapse under their weight.

Which seemed ironic to Lynette, because she felt so much lighter now that she'd told Storm everything.

Well, everything except the worry that had her so anxious that night in the first place—the concern that she was pregnant with Storm's baby. She'd never know if that was true, because after the accident, she bled heavily for days. If there had been a baby before the accident, there wasn't one after. Her speculation would undoubtedly hurt him, so she kept that part to herself.

Not every secret deserves to see the light of day, no matter how much time has passed.

She stood, then turned back to face him. When she extended a hand, he took it, and as she yanked him to his feet, one of the end boards on the bench finally collapsed.

They laughed, but he grew somber again.

"It seems my mother has some things to answer to from that night."

Lynette had no desire to confront the woman. If Storm wanted to, that was up to him.

He drew her close, and they stood together, lost in the terrible revelations she'd spilled.

Eventually, he straightened and stepped back. "Now I'm going to hunt that monster down and kill him."

She didn't need to see his expression to know he was serious. But the Universe had protected him from having to take another's life.

"While the tiniest part of me appreciates you being willing to kill for me, that won't be necessary. He's long dead."

"*You* killed him?" Storm gasped. Apparently the idea of him committing murder in the name of her honor was more believable than her doing it herself.

She only shrugged, unable to resist keeping him wondering about her a little longer.

But she underestimated his ability to see into her soul. She could tell the moment he was on to her.

"No way," he finally said, giving one of her silver ringlets a light tug. "You did what you had to in the heat of the moment, but you aren't a cold-blooded killer." This time he captured her hand. His touch was light. "In fact, you're not cold at all. You're a survivor, and my biggest screw-up in life was letting you get away the first time."

He brushed a light kiss across her cheek, but seemed willing to let her take the lead. He hadn't made her feel shameful for her foolish actions on that long-ago night. He'd listened, and she could tell he believed her. What more could she ask for?

She pulled him gently toward the path back up to the house.

When they reached the yard, he paused, but never released her hand. He fished a set of keys from his pocket and put them in her free hand, wrapping her fingers around them. "Keep those."

"Your keys?"

He nodded. "Yep. Keys to this house, and the one on Nantucket. There are keys to your house on there, too, but I'm sure you already have your own set."

"But I don't understand. Why are you giving me your keys?"

He let go of her. "Because I never want you to be locked out of my home again. Now, I know telling me what happened that night was hard. Do you want me to take you home?"

She shook her head and held up the keys. "Now that I've told you, I want to finally put it all behind me. Which key opens this front door?"

He crossed his arms over his chest while raising his eyebrows. "Are you sure? We don't have to go in. When I planned today, I had no idea what you'd endured out here that night. You aren't going to find milk and cookies waiting inside for you."

"Which key, Storm?" she repeated, jangling the keys in his face.

He chuckled, then took the keys back and crossed to the front door, unlocking it.

When he stepped to the side so she could enter, she couldn't believe what waited for her.

"Did you do this?" she asked, kicking off her sandals and walking barefoot across the red rose petals scattered on the hardwood floor. "Because it's so much better than milk and cookies."

"I did. Keep following the rose petals. I'll be right behind you."

Flattered that he'd even think to go to this much trouble, she ventured down the hallway while he disappeared into another part of the house. The heady scent of roses surrounded her while a wash of classical music suddenly filled the air. The roses led her to a closed door. She stopped, not knowing whether she should go any farther, but then curiosity got the better of her and she opened it.

More petals crossed the room, but instead of ending at the massive king-sized bed, they veered off toward yet another doorway. Inside was a bathroom. But not just any bathroom. White marble covered the floor, while a deep-navy tile, shot with silver, stretched from floor to ceiling. The stunning tile reminded her of the dark, silver-entwined fabric of the dress she'd worn to prom on the arm of a much younger Storm, and of their restless desire as young lovers.

She suspected the decades between those early days and now would only enhance the pleasure she'd find in his arms.

Her eyes scanned the rest of the room. A glass-enclosed shower, easily large enough for two, gobbled up one corner. He'd placed a free-standing soaker tub strategically under a window, allowing for a stunning view of the lake beyond. All the hardware was shiny chrome, and a narrower door likely hid the commode.

A shimmery negligee and matching robe hung on a velvet hanger from a hook beside the shower. Propped up on the white vanity top was a note with her name on the front.

She giggled as she picked it up, not caring that she probably sounded like the teenage Lynette who Storm first seduced—though his earlier approach basically relied on beer and not this kind of romantic assault on her senses.

While most things about Storm had changed and matured, his penmanship had not. His handwriting looked like the same chicken scratch he'd used to write out their schedules at the pizza parlor all those years ago.

His note invited her to take as much time relaxing in the bathroom as she'd like, and he'd be waiting for her when she came out.

The tub beckoned her. She turned on the faucets. Petals covered the bottom of the bath. A crystal bottle of what looked like bubble bath sat on a shelf above the tub, and as steaming-hot water flowed in, an explosion of floral scent surrounded her. Even with the door shut, the music played in here, too, piped in through some invisible speakers.

Storm was full of surprises. Well, she could play at his game, too. He expected her to pamper herself for a bit, then wrap her body in that gorgeous lingerie and join him on the bed. He probably even had candles and champagne waiting for her, too, since he was going all in.

The tub also looked big enough for two.

She slipped out of her clothes, down to her pretty matching-bra-and-panties set. He wasn't the only one who loved decadent undergarments. A drawer in the vanity revealed a variety of toiletries she could use, like a razor and hair ties, but she'd come prepared. All she needed to borrow was the new toothbrush and toothpaste.

Once the tub was full, she positioned herself on the edge with her left foot carefully positioned so the first thing he'd see when he looked at her body would be the little blue tattoo that still danced on her inner thigh.

The butterfly that matched his.

She figured it was about time the two butterflies got reacquainted.

Taking a moment to settle her nerves, she removed the pins from her hair and let her head fall back, shaking out her curls. It was probably a snarled mess, but she didn't care. They could wash it together.

"Storm, are you out there?" she yelled, doing her best to sound more confident than she felt.

"I am" was his only reply.

"Say, can you come in here for a minute? I need a little help with something."

The door swung open on silent hinges, and their gazes met and held through the steam rising from the tub.

"Are you sure you're still up for this?" he asked. She noticed he was still fully clothed.

She appreciated his concern. "I am. Say, I love this tile you picked out in here."

His eyes flicked to the walls, and he grinned. "Ever since you talked me into taking you to your prom, I've especially loved this dark navy color. Throw in some silver and I'm a goner."

He was describing the fabric of her prom dress. He hadn't forgotten either.

She lifted her leg slightly and ran a light hand down her thigh. "I even shaved for you," she said with a wink.

He groaned when he spied her tattoo.

"You kept it," he said, his voice husky with need.

"Of course I kept it," she said with a laugh, and when he reached out to touch the tiny butterfly, she captured his hand and slid into the tub, careful not to smack her head or push a wall of water out onto the bathroom floor.

As he towered above her beside the bath, she spied a bamboo back brush on the ledge between the wall and tub. Bubbles almost reached her neck, so she removed her wet bra and let it dangle over the ledge, still feeling self-conscious. She held the brush up to him.

"Care to join me? I could use a little help washing my back."

Storm growled and ripped his shirt over his head, tossing it into a corner. Then he tried to shimmy out of his pants.

She laughed at his obvious eagerness when he half-tripped getting out of his jeans. "Weren't you just saying how you've learned not to rush something good?"

Free of his clothing, he stepped into the tub and sank down into the water with her. His large body made it a tight fit. "I promise not to rush round two."

Chapter Seventeen

Whispering Pines Resort

R ENEE STOOD BY THE office window, looking out. Lynette could tell by the way she was twisting her hands that her friend was nervous.

Is she afraid to take a deep dive into the financials for this place with me?

"How's she doing?" Renee asked, motioning beyond the multi-pane glass.

Oh. She's worried about Annie.

"This will be good for her. Thank you for not minding that I brought her along," Lynette said. The old desk chair underneath her groaned in protest when she pushed back far enough to cross her legs. "I can't imagine what she's going through."

Renee nodded. "Unfortunately, I can. It feels a little like when you are in a small boat, out on the water. When everything is calm around you, you can convince yourself that you can almost handle the nonsensical tragedy of losing someone you love. But then a speedboat powers by, and even though they might be halfway across the lake, its wake throws you off balance, and it takes time for things to settle again. She'll have good days and bad days. And it's impossible to guess when she'll feel like herself again."

Lynette got out of the noisy chair to stand beside Renee. "I'm so sorry. I should have been there for you when you lost your first husband. *We* should have been there for you. I know how much Annie appreciates the distraction of spending time with us."

Renee touched the glass, drawing Lynette's eye to the mullions that divided the pane. The wood peeking through the peeling white paint looked dry, or possibly even rotten. The cost of upkeep alone on a resort like this had to be daunting.

"Don't apologize," Renee said. "Our lives all looked so different back then. Sometimes it's hard to believe that Jim's been gone for almost seventeen years. You know, legend has it that Whispering Pines is a wonderful place for people to come to heal from the blows life often hits us with . . . and I believe it."

Rows of what looked like black ledgers on shelves under the window caught Lynette's eye. She stooped down for a closer look. "A cynic would think that was nothing more than a catchy advertising slogan, but I believe there is something special about this place, too. It's good for Annie to sit in the sunshine out there, in the peace and quiet. There's no rush, but I'm sure she has some decisions to make. Hey, what are these? Old financial ledgers?"

Renee glanced down at her and laughed. "Spoken like a true business-woman. No, they're actually guest books. Believe it or not, they date back as far as 1926. I haven't spent much time going through them, but what I have looked at is pretty neat. Lots of entries are men-only for the first ten years. Someone took the time to put them in chronological order."

Lynette groaned as she straightened. The stiff muscles she'd suffered after her time at the lake house with Storm had lessened, but weren't yet back to normal. She smiled at the memory.

"What's that mischievous little smirk for?" Renee asked, narrowing her eyes.

Lynette twisted from side to side, then shrugged. "I may be a tinge bit stiff . . . but a girl shouldn't kiss and tell."

This pulled a shriek out of Renee. "Good thing the only kind of girls we are these days are Kaleidoscope Girls. And Kaleidoscope Girls are *required* to tell each other when they have hot sex with an old boyfriend!"

Julie wandered in right then, eyes wide. "Annie had sex with Michael?! Wow. That sure happened a lot faster than I would have guessed."

Lynette wasn't sure she'd heard Renee's daughter correctly. *Annie and Michael?*

"Julie! Why would you say something like that?" Renee looked horrified.

But Julie just looked at her. "Mom. Come on. We're all adults here. Do I want to hear about any sex *you* are having? Of course not." She shivered, as if to emphasize the point. "But I enjoy a little gossip just as much as the next person."

Renee grabbed Julie by the upper arm and pulled her to the window, pointing at Annie where she relaxed in one of the red Adirondacks on the beach. From this distance, they could just tell that she was dabbing at her eyes with a tissue. "Does that look like someone who ran into an old boyfriend's bed, only a week after her husband's funeral? And, by the way, Michael is Annie's ex-husband, not just ex-boyfriend."

Julie had the grace to blush. "Sorry. I guess I shouldn't eavesdrop."

"No, you should not," Renee said. "And it's nice of you to join us. We've been waiting for you for fifteen minutes."

"Relax, Mom. I was checking the new guests in to the Gray Cabin. Two sisters. And get this. They said someone way back in their family actually *started* this place. That's why I took more time with them. Isn't that fascinating?"

"*This* place?"

"Yeah, Whispering Pines. They didn't really know much more than that, so I don't know if they are the family Celia bought the resort from or not."

Renee's expression had quickly gone from irritated with Julie to intrigued. Lynette found the possibility interesting, too, but if they didn't focus, they wouldn't get any work done. She was here to help with the future of the resort, not to dig into its history. She walked back to the chair behind the desk, sat down, then motioned to the other two chairs across from her.

"How about if we leave the history of this place to someone in your family who likes to act as a historian? Meanwhile, I'm here to help you figure out how the two of you can work to keep this amazing place *in* your family."

Renee finally left the window and took the chair nearest the wall. "While I've dreaded this session because I'm worried there won't be any suitable answers, it's still better than talking about my friends having sex in front of my daughter."

Lynette laughed, and it was Renee's turn to blush.

"What I meant was *talking* about the sex in front of my daughter . . . not the sex itself."

Julie took the only open chair, then grabbed Renee's knee. "Just stop, Mom."

Lynette tapped her Montblanc against her notepad. She never did important business without her signature pen, and helping Renee and Julie figure out how to lower the stress of keeping Whispering Pines in their family was very important business indeed.

"One last thing, then we'll start," Lynette said, eyeing mother and daughter across the desk. "It was me. I had the hot sex with an old boyfriend."

"God, Lynette!" Renee cried, dropping her forehead onto the desktop.

"But," Lynette quickly added, winking at Julie, "I'll save your mother the embarrassment of telling you any more, at least in front of her. Catch me after dinner, and we'll talk."

Renee laughed, assuming—incorrectly—that Lynette was kidding. "Where do you want to start?"

Lynette pulled the cap off her pen with a nod. "Let's start with the revenue you can earn when you rent every cabin out, and then what your vacancy rate has been running in the summer months."

Both Renee and Julie pulled their chairs closer to the desk. Everyone was anxious about making this work.

Lynette and Julie now sat together beside the smoldering fire in the pit in front of the three small cabins. Annie was staying in the same cabin she'd used the summer before, and she'd turned in early. Renee had excused herself when Matt returned from a twelve-hour shift.

Before leaving her daughter alone with one of her oldest friends, she'd shaken a finger at Lynette with the stern warning to behave.

Both Lynette and Julie were still chuckling about it.

Lynette never enjoyed being told what to do. "So, Julie, should we talk business or sex first?"

Julie burst into hiccupping laughter. "I understand why Mom likes you so much. She needs someone like you in her life."

"We *all* need each other in our lives," Lynette clarified. "I don't know where I'd be without Renee and Annie. Jackie and Kit, too. To be honest, my very best friend is my mom, but she's traveling the world with her new beau, so I'd be awfully lonely these days if not for the four of them."

"Donna has a *beau*?" Julie asked, wriggling her eyebrows. "That must be new, because your mom never mentioned anyone when she was here last summer."

Lynette pulled a marshmallow out of the torn bag at her feet. She'd already eaten so many that she'd probably wake up with a bellyache in the morning. But it was better than a hangover. Sitting around a campfire always made her crave a cocktail. True to her word, she hadn't had alcohol since the previous summer when she vowed to never drink again, but that didn't mean the desire for it was gone. She jammed the marshmallow onto a roasting stick and held it close to the dying embers as she contemplated Julie's question.

"I think Donna had a thing going with him for much longer than she let on. He used to live next door to her in New York City. They'd planned to travel together, but then the pandemic hit, and I yanked her out of the city and dumped her into our big old house in Ruby Shores. I'm glad she finally admitted that living out the rest of her days with her daughter meant she had to give up on dreams she'd already put off for far too long. I do miss her, but I'm happy for her at the same time. Does that make sense?"

Julie reached for the marshmallow bag and roasted one of her own before replying. Once the little treat was a toasty brown, she slid it from her roasting stick and nodded her head. "Is that your subtle way of telling me that living and working beside my mother might not be what's best for either of us, now that I'm an adult?"

The young lady is perceptive, Lynette thought, smiling.

"Honestly, Julie, that isn't why I mentioned Donna. But you make a good point. I built a successful business alongside my mother in New York City. It was always the two of us against the world. We made a good pair. We lived in separate apartments, but in the same building. We grew to be very codependent, and I don't think it was great for either of us. I loved getting to spend so much time with her, and we do good work together, but in some ways it stifled both of us."

Julie licked her sticky fingers, considering this, then frowned. "You don't think me and Mom could work together to make this place even better?"

Lynette sipped her water and then relaxed against the slanted backrest of her chair, contemplating the stars above. She didn't want to overreach, nor did she think her own experiences should sway Julie and Renee too much. Instead of answering Julie directly, she pointed toward the heavens.

"Look at the countless number of stars up there. Every single one is unique. And even though each one looks so tiny from here, in reality they could represent whole worlds."

Julie propped her roasting stick against the side of the firepit. "Smart *and* philosophical."

Lynette sighed and brought her gaze back down to meet Julie's. "I don't want to push too hard. This consulting stuff isn't as easy when you know the people you are trying to advise."

"Pretend you don't know us. Pretend we just met this morning, and after having a look at the books and hearing more about how things work around here, just give it to me straight," Julie said. "I can take it."

Lynette studied her friend's daughter for a minute before responding. "Fine. Here's what I think. Renee and her sister Jess were smart to establish the retreats they run out here during the off-season. If she can devise a third income stream, beyond the summer rentals and the retreats, it would be even better. That should more than cover the cost of maintaining things—barring some huge unexpected expense—but she'll never get rich off of it. Except maybe if she sold it."

Julie nodded. "She's not looking to get rich. This resort technically belongs to Mom, but it really is part of our extended family. I think that's why Jess and Val help with the retreats and take almost nothing for the time they put in."

"I think that's how it should be. If your whole family, beyond just the four of you, benefit from Whispering Pines, they should somehow help keep it going, too."

Julie picked her stick back up, but instead of reaching for another treat, she tapped it against the bricks of the fire ring. "But . . ."

It was then that Lynette realized Julie already knew the answer to the biggest question hanging over their earlier discussion in Renee's office. "But Whispering Pines, as amazing and special as it is, simply isn't big enough to support both of you, if you want to do adult things like renting or buying a place of your own, saving for your own retirement, and all those other adulting things we all faced at your age."

"Ouch," Julie said, grasping at her chest in mock surprise.

"This doesn't surprise you, does it?"

She shook her head. "Of course not. I'm young, but I'm not stupid.

I've helped Mom with almost every aspect of getting this place up and running again, and I've always known it couldn't be the place I'd spend my career."

Lynette smiled. "You didn't really need me to tell you all this, did you?"

The thickest log in the pit split into two halves along the haphazard line that glowed through its middle. She watched the way Julie followed the sparks as they floated up and into the sky.

The symbolism was easy to spot.

"No. I already knew I needed to split off and make my way on my own, but this gives me the push I needed to get started. We all love Whispering Pines, and I want to help Mom keep it, but I'm also getting a little antsy to try something different. I just have no idea what that might be. I love getting to be outside so much here, and I don't even mind some of the grunt work, like turning the cabins over between customers. But I also want to find something lucrative that can support the 'adulting' I need to do."

Lynette thought back to when she was Julie's age. That was when she'd also started working toward her dream of a boutique—which she'd then started, grown, and eventually sold. But not knowing how she could make it happen had scared her silly. She'd had to learn to push through that fear. Julie would, too.

"I don't have any simple answers for you, Julie, but I know you'll figure it out. You impressed me today. You have a knack for both business and the hospitality industry. Let me think about it, and if any brilliant ideas come to me, I will let you know. Donna was integral to my success. Maybe Renee will be for you, too."

Julie sat with that for a bit, using her stick to prod the dying embers in the pit. "I *will* figure it out. But hey, I saw that yawn you tried to hide. You can't go to bed without getting to the *sex* part of the discussion you promised me."

"I'm not sure I promised you that," Lynette said with a grin. She was thoroughly enjoying this one-on-one time with Julie. Renee was lucky to have a daughter like her. "Besides, a lady should never kiss and tell. Well, not tell too much, that is. So I'll give you the very abbreviated version. I dated a guy when I was a senior in high school. He was a couple years older, my boss at work, and looked like the typical bad boy that most mothers would hate to have their daughter drag home."

A small flame rekindled thanks to Julie's ministrations. "Donna didn't like him?"

Lynette considered this. "Not exactly. I think he scared her. Or, together, we scared her. We couldn't seem to keep our hands off each other. Have you ever dated anyone like that?"

Julie blew out a sigh. "I wish."

Lynette laughed. "Be patient. You will, as long as you don't settle. But it wasn't like Donna could judge my boyfriend too harshly. She had a terrible track record with men. We were awfully young, though. It was almost like our passion was too big for us to handle back then. I also did something really stupid one night, and it ended with me totaling his pickup. This is from that night." She pointed to the faint scar on her cheek. "We moved away after that, and I doubted I'd ever see him again."

"Wait," Julie said, wriggling her bottom in the deep-seated chair. "Was he the one out here at Whispering Pines last summer? The one named Storm? He carried you from the boat after . . . you know . . ."

"One and the same. He was also at Annie's house after the funeral, but you might not have recognized him in his suit and tie. I never would have thought someone could change that much from how he looked in his early-twenties to his early-fifties."

"I didn't see him at Annie's, but I thought he looked, I don't know, striking, maybe, when I met him last summer. Huge guy. What was he like as a kid?"

Lynette took a deep breath and closed her eyes, drawing forth an image of the Storm who'd taken her to prom and stolen her virginity that very night. "Long, silky black hair. My hair was always curly and frizzy like this," she said, yanking on one of her silver curls. "I was jealous of his silky hair. He wore all black, already had tattoos, and he was lanky."

"Are we talking about the same guy here?" Julie asked.

"Surprisingly, yes. Everything about him changed. Except, to be honest, that chemistry between us. That seems to have only gotten better."

Julie clapped her hands together. "Tell me more."

Lynette was about done with her sharing. But there was one important thing she wanted to get across to this younger woman. "The one constant I'm seeing in Storm is how protective he is of the people he loves. Our relationship burned too bright when we were kids. There was lots of sex and beer, not necessarily in that order, and we're both lucky some mistakes we made back then didn't screw up the rest of our lives. He protected me then from a man my mom was dating. When someone else hurt me, I didn't dare tell him because I knew he'd probably kill the guy. His impulse control was far from developed back then. We went our separate ways, and we both grew up. But he has a younger brother who really needs him, and Storm is his protector. I also know that he'd do the same for me, if it ever came to that again."

Lynette paused at the sound of a car pulling into the lodge's parking lot.

Julie glanced that way, too, but she didn't look concerned, despite the late hour. "It seems like Storm, along with Matt, came to your rescue last summer."

The woman's insight made her smile. "You are right. He did, didn't he? He's still protecting me. We've both done a lot of living in the decades since we were together as kids. Somewhere along the line he learned how to romance a woman, too. At least, I find his methods romantic. So that's the truth of it. It wasn't poor Annie reuniting with a lost love, it was me. In fact, I just found out that Annie's ex is getting remarried soon. So even if those two wanted to reconnect down the road, now it won't happen."

Julie nodded, considering all this. "Time moves on. Maybe now it's her son who finds himself in a love triangle."

Surprised, Lynette tried to remember which of Annie's sons was which. "Relic?"

"No," Julie said. "Colton. The older one. I think he might have a little crush on one of Jackie's daughters. But I think the *other* twin might like Colton."

Lynette slapped the arms of her chair with both hands. "Get out! Does Jackie know? Or Annie?"

Julie laughed. "I have no idea. This is just me speculating based on what I saw at Annie's house the other day." Then she waved at something beyond the meager light cast by the fire. "Hey, Nathan. How was your date?"

A young man stepped up to the fire. "Hey, cuz. It was fun. The food was good, too. You'll have to check it out sometime."

Lynette wasn't sure who this guy was—besides, apparently, Julie's cousin—but they must have discussed his plans for the evening in advance.

"Nathan, this is Lynette, Mom's friend from back in the day. They called themselves the Kaleidoscope Girls."

Lynette pushed up out of her chair and extended a hand. "Hi, Nathan. I'm Lynette Howe. Yes, I'm an old friend of Renee's. We go all the way back to our days at summer camp as twelve-year-olds."

Nathan seemed surprised at Lynette's extended hand, but he took a step forward to shake it. "I'm Nathan Rand, Julie's cousin. Have you met my mom? Jess?"

Lynette could see the resemblance now. "Sure. I met her out here last summer. You look like her."

He shrugged. "Better to look like *her* than my dad."

"Seth?" Lynette asked. The young man's off-the-cuff remark had caught her off guard.

Julie groaned. "Seth is his *stepdad*."

Sensing a touchy subject, Lynette sat back down. "Sorry about the handshake. A little too formal around a campfire, but old habits die hard. Are you renting a cabin out here?"

"Not exactly. Renee is letting me rent half the duplex for cheap so I can afford to work on a book I'm trying to write. I hope I can finish it in a year."

This was news to Lynette, but as the fire popped at their feet, the spark of an idea came to her. She met Julie's eye with a wink.

I think I just figured out who can give Renee a hand around here, once in a while, if Julie moves on to start her own career.

Chapter Eighteen

JACKIE WEAVED THROUGH HER mother's crowded garage as best she could. Little rectangular pricing stickers covered the fingers of her left hand. "Mom suggested either donating Dad's stuff or selling it in a rummage sale. 'Whatever is easiest,' she said. And what do I do? I pick the harder option, because in my mind that's what Dad would have done. He'd have hated for me to just give all his stuff away. Remind me to never *ever* again volunteer to set up and then run a rummage sale. Did you see the weather forecast? Rain. If we can't move these tables out to the driveway, people will trip over things inside the garage because it'll be so crowded."

Kit added a handful of dress shirts to an already overburdened hanging rack. She turned and only took two steps before the creak of twisting metal stopped her. Before she could reach the rack, it snapped in two and all the neatly hung clothes tumbled to the floor. She opened her mouth, and Jackie knew that a blue streak of curse words quivered on the tip of Kit's tongue.

"Stop," Jackie said. "If you complain, too, we may have to call it a night and go find that last bottle of wine we didn't get to when Annie and Lynette stayed over."

Kit snorted as she stooped to pick up the heap of clothing. "You can bitch, but I can't?"

"Right," Jackie said. She kicked the worthless clothes rack she'd uncovered in her mother's laundry room. "How will we hang these shirts now? We can't fold these."

"I think Grandma Hazel has a heavy-duty rack in her basement. It's too late to run over there now, but I'll grab it early tomorrow morning. We're opening at eight?"

"And if I have my way, we'll close by ten. I'd much rather be at Whispering Pines with Renee and Lynette and Annie this weekend."

Kit picked up the last couple of items that had fallen to the garage floor. "Me, too, but this needs to get done. I have an idea: we stay at full-price until noon, then everything goes to half-off or 'make an offer.' Because, remember, anything left when you close the doors will still need to get hauled to a donation location. Let's finish this the right way, so our hard work is worth it. And why, by the way, are you so crabby tonight?"

Jackie stepped over to the shoe rack that held at least a dozen pairs of her father's shoes. She picked up a brown suede loafer. It was the type of shoe he'd always worn around the school. "I'm *crabby* because I'm about to pawn all my dad's personal items off to complete strangers. I hate this. He should still be here with us. Getting rid of his things just makes it even more real. He's gone forever. After working hard for his whole life, this is all there is to show for it?" Jackie slowly spun in a circle, taking in the contents of the crowded garage.

She hated the look of pity Kit gave her.

Her fingers went to the necklace at her throat. It was always a relief to feel the chain there, and the weight of the pendant, which housed a small part of her dad's ashes.

"I'm sorry, Kit. You're giving up time with your own family to help me, and I'm being miserable company. I promise I'll be better once this is over."

Kit looked around them. "I think we've done enough for tonight. You've put in some long days, sorting Glen's things into the different 'keep,' 'sell,' or 'donate' piles. We priced almost everything out here. We can do a few last things in the morning. I'll run and grab the hanging rack, and then we'll open the doors. I suspect many of your customers will come because they knew Glen personally. Maybe it'll be a good day, with lots of reminiscing with folks who appreciated your dad."

Jackie unstuck the rest of the stickers from her fingers and flicked them into the small trash can she'd set under the table. "I do like to think that's what will happen, versus a bunch of vultures who never knew Dad, just sweeping in here and looking for a good deal on his things."

"I vote we go inside and treat ourselves to gigantic bowls of ice cream," Kit suggested. "Hey, we never had time to look through those metal boxes I found in your dad's closet. You know, the two with you and your brother's names on them. Do you think going through that now would make you feel better? Remember, you aren't selling anything in that box. You get to keep all those things, if you like."

Jackie did like that idea. "Ice cream first, then Dad's box. If the things in there are too hard to look at when I'm already a wreck, we'll close it back up and I can take it back to Minneapolis with me to open again when I'm feeling stronger."

After Kit made sure the outer doors into the garage were closed and locked, Jackie flicked the lights off.

Nikki was happy to see them. The border collie led the way to the kitchen, no doubt hoping for some late-night kibble. Instead of dog food, she received a scoop of vanilla ice cream. Not that she complained.

They sat at Jackie's parents' table with their massive bowls of ice cream and toppings, and Jackie had to admit she felt much better.

"Good idea, Kit."

Kit raised a heaping spoon, as if making a toast. "Many hands make light work, and everything is better with ice cream. Say, I heard from Dean. He called when you made that run to the store for more pricing stickers. The tornado damage is more severe than his mother led him to believe. Her house actually has some damage, too. He said it reminded him of the damage Hazel's house sustained when that storm tore through Ruby Shores, right before we were supposed to go to Hawaii."

"That stinks," Jackie said. "Still no injuries, though?"

"Right."

The way she said it made Jackie suspect there was more. "But . . . ?"

"His mom doesn't have any injuries from the storm, but she is having some cognitive difficulties that Dean wasn't aware of until seeing her again in person. According to his brother, she's been getting more forgetful over the past year. Dean may need to stay a little longer than he initially thought. He wants to make sure she's still all right on her own."

Jackie felt for Dean. She knew how hard it was to see a parent's mental acuity slip away.

"His employer is being accommodating, then?" she asked, sprinkling more peanuts on the top of her ice cream.

"Not particularly, but Dean said he doesn't care. This is too important, and if they can't understand this at work, he says 'Screw 'em!' "

Jackie knew exactly how Dean was feeling. It was an emotion she'd entertained often during the year leading up to quitting her corporate job. Luckily, now that she was her own boss, she had more freedom.

But, a voice in the back of her head whispered, what if she *sold* her business?

Then what?

Nikki pawed at her dinner bowl. Jackie realized she'd forgotten to feed the poor thing, and ice cream was an inadequate substitute. She'd been too involved in getting ready for the sale.

Kit scraped the bottom of her bowl with her spoon. "This was such a good idea."

"It was," Jackie agreed, finishing her ice cream, too. "But I'm too tired to go through that box tonight. Do you mind if I just throw it in my car and look at it later?"

Kit stood and picked up both of their bowls, taking them to the sink while Jackie got up and filled Nikki's bowl with kibble instead of ice cream. "Of course I don't mind. Tomorrow will be a busy day, and you just never know who might show up. So we should both get some beauty sleep."

Something in the way she said it alarmed Jackie. "Kit . . . what did you do?"

After she'd stowed the dishes in the dishwasher, Kit threw in a pod and started the machine, a small smile tugging at the corner of her mouth. "I have no idea what you're talking about."

Kit never was much of a liar.

By eight the next morning, Jackie figured out exactly what Kit had done. A sizable crowd waited for access to her father's treasures when she rolled open the garage door. The sky looked threatening enough that she wasn't sure she should put the tables out. But the garage was already so crowded, she figured it was worth the risk.

She glanced at the table they'd established for people's purchases. Kit was already busy taking money from happy shoppers. When Jackie pulled at one end of a table to move it outside, taller items swayed, nearly falling over and creating a big mess.

"Here, we'll get that," came a voice from behind her that she knew well.

She turned to see Owen. "I wouldn't have pictured you as a man who spends his Saturday mornings hunting for treasures at garage sales."

He laughed, and she realized she might have stared at him for longer than necessary. He looked good in a snug green T-shirt that brought out the blue in his eyes and soft-looking jeans that hugged him in all the right places.

"To be honest, the best Saturday mornings are on the lake with a fishing pole in my hand. But a little birdie let me know you had some nice tackle for sale this morning, so here we are," he said, motioning to the young man who had stepped up beside him.

Jackie grinned, genuinely happy to see Owen's doctor son. "Well, hi, Adam! It's nice to see you. How have you been?"

Owen frowned. "And here I thought you'd be happy to see *me*."

"Stop. I'm happy to see you both," Jackie admitted. Someone jostled into her from behind. The rain was holding off, and the garage was too congested. "Could I bother you to move these three long tables out onto the driveway?"

Owen moved to the first one, but Adam eyed the sky. "It still looks like rain. You sure you want to do that?"

Just then, a stray raindrop landed on Jackie's cheek. "I'm *not* sure, but it's just too crowded inside. I think I'll have to take my chances."

Both men nodded, and soon all three tables were outside. The flow inside the garage opened up. Jackie moved a few things too susceptible to water damage back inside.

Owen had mentioned fishing, so she sent him into the back corner where they'd set out her father's three large soft-sided tackle boxes. Each box held numerous neatly organized sleeves filled with jigs. Adam seemed more interested in the table piled with tools.

With both father and son occupied, Jackie hurried over to Kit and bent to whisper in her ear, not caring that she was still busy with customers. "You told him to come?!"

"I called him. He likes to fish, and your dad had some amazing fishing equipment," Kit said, not bothering to keep her voice down.

Someone tugged at Jackie's arm. "Say, you're Glen's daughter, right? Can you do any better on this putter? I'm looking for one for my grandson, but I would never pay ten dollars for a gold club."

Jackie knew the high-end putter originally cost ten times that, because she'd given it to her father for Christmas a few years earlier, but before she could respond, she thought she heard Owen yell for Adam to come over. Then what initially sounded like a squabble near the tackle quickly escalated into an argument.

"What in the world?" Jackie left the haggling customer and the quality putter to hurry back toward the raised voices. "What's happening?"

An elderly man with watery, red-rimmed eyes said, "This jackass thinks he can buy up all three tackle boxes, but I had my eye on the biggest one. Just couldn't walk as fast as him."

Jackie looked between the old man and Owen, who now held a tackle box under each arm, his foot perched possessively over the largest box on the garage floor. He was motioning for Adam to pick it up before someone nabbed it.

"Owen, you don't have to buy all three! That's too much tackle for one man."

He grinned, as if enjoying himself. "It wasn't too much tackle for your dad. Sorry, buddy, you know how this works. I beat you to these, fair and square."

The old man banged his cane on the floor three times, then spun nimbly away as he mumbled under his breath. Jackie suspected the cane might be more for show or to garner sympathy. The guy was probably a pro at reselling quality items he picked up at rummage sales for cheap. Jackie had heard of people making a living that way.

Other shoppers were also eyeing the tackle boxes Owen and Adam held, looking disappointed over missing out.

"Seriously, Owen, what are you going to do with all that?"

He shook his head. "We'll talk about it later. For now, can I stash these inside?"

Confused, she shrugged. "Sure, I guess."

"Hey, Dad, did you see that John Deere mower over there? I'll need a rider, right?" Adam said, over the large tackle box in his arms.

Owen nodded. "Mine's on its last leg after all the heavy mowing we've done at the old camp. It wouldn't be a bad idea to buy a replacement." He strained to see the price listed on the large sign Kit had hung from the steering wheel. "That seems like a fair price if it works."

"Of course it works," Jackie insisted. "Dad didn't have anything that wasn't in good working condition."

"I suspect that's true. I remember him being very *persnickety* about his lawn equipment."

"Persnickety," Kit said. Jackie hadn't heard her come over. "That's a great word."

Adam put the big tackle box back on the floor under Owen's foot again and hurried over to the lawn mower before the slow-moving guy with the cane tried to nab that deal, too. "Mind if I pull it farther away from the garage and try to start it?" he called back to Jackie.

She waved for him to go ahead.

"Kit, can you handle this for a minute? I need to run inside with Owen quick."

Someone had knocked a stack of jeans off the corner of a table. Kit picked them up and refolded them as she said, "Yep. No one looks ready to pay at the moment."

Jackie looked toward the cash table and froze. "Kit," she hissed, "where's the money box?"

"Relax, Jackie. I pulled the bills out of it and put them in my fanny pack, then put the box under the table. If someone wants to steal a handful of coins, we'll let karma strike them down. I used to help Hazel with rummage sales when I was a kid. I know all the tricks of the trade."

Both Jackie and Owen laughed. Jackie was impressed with Kit's obvious expertise.

"Let me get that one," Jackie said, pushing Owen's foot off Adam's discarded tackle box.

She and Owen went inside and stowed all three tackle boxes in Glen's old office.

Jackie brushed her hands together. "Seriously, why do you want all that?"

"Actually, I don't."

This ticked her off. "You made me miss a sale? Lots of people out there wanted these. Why would you do that?"

He grabbed both of her hands in his. "Jackie. Slow down. You priced that tackle way too low. Your father is probably turning over in his grave right now! I couldn't let you sell it for that. The vultures were circling, so I had to act fast."

His explanation struck her as funny, and she relaxed, enjoying the feel of her hands in his. "He's not."

This shut him up for a second. "He's not what?"

"Turning in his grave." She fought to keep a straight face.

"Okay . . ." he said, clearly not following. "Why does your face look pinched?"

"Dad can't turn in his grave because we had him cremated."

He looked stunned. "Jackie, it's just a saying. I didn't mean to upset you."

Finally, unable to maintain the somber look, she let out a bark of laughter. "I'm just messing with you! But now what am I going to do with all that fishing tackle? Mom wants all of this stuff gone. And she didn't care how I got rid of it. Despite what she said, Dad would have hated for us to donate it all."

Some of her enjoyment over their exchange ebbed away when he dropped her hands. It had felt so natural, she'd practically forgotten he was holding them. Then Owen squatted down and pulled a plastic sleeve out of one of the tackle boxes. He flipped the shallow sleeve open, revealing row upon row of small squares. Each square housed a fancy jig of some sort. There were at least ten more plastic sleeves in this container alone.

"Jackie, each one of these jigs can cost around ten bucks, sometimes more, sometimes less. Take that, times however many are in each of the three large tackle boxes and you are talking serious money here."

She felt stupid. "I had no idea."

"Happy to help," he said, standing back up so he could grin down at her. "If you'd like, I can figure out a way to get you more money for these. I'm not sure how yet, and it probably won't be full retail, but it'll be a heck of a lot better than your asking price."

He pulled the stickers off the three boxes and stuffed them in his pocket.

Adam came rushing in. "Jackie, Kit needs you outside. Someone has an issue with a microwave or something?"

Jackie dropped her head. She'd thought thirty dollars for a brand-new microwave, still in the box, was fair. Was someone going to try to talk her down on that, too?

"I better go," she said.

Owen was petting Nikki, who'd found them in the office. "Right behind you. I'll make sure she doesn't sneak out behind us."

The three hurried back into the garage. Crabby Man, as Jackie had secretly named him, was standing next to the cash table with Kit, leaning heavily on his cane. Someone had taken the microwave out of the box, and it was open on the table.

"Tag says 'new.' So how do you explain this?" the old man said, pointing inside the microwave with his cane. It was impossible to miss his accusatory tone.

Jackie nodded. "It was still in the box."

"Then why does it look like a bowl of spaghetti blew up inside of it?!"

She should have double-checked inside the unsealed box.

Owen, still behind her, picked the empty microwave box up off the floor. "Look, buddy, she's just trying to sell her old man's stuff. Why don't you cut her some slack?"

The irate customer turned to Owen. "Who are you calling old, you jackass?"

Before Owen could even respond, Adam stepped forward and placed a hand on the man's shoulder. "You probably don't want the microwave, Mr. Carson. But I thought I saw a nice minnow bucket out here on one of the tables on the driveway. Can I show you that one?"

The man seemed to deflate like a balloon with a tiny hole in it. "Oh, hey, Doc, didn't notice you. A minnow bucket, you say?"

Jackie watched in amazement as Owen's son steered Crabby Man away from the decidedly not-new microwave and down the driveway to a bright-yellow minnow bucket that surely *was* new—she could see the original tags on it.

Kit must have slipped into the house and back again, because she held a roll of paper towels in one hand and a bottle of cleaner in the other. She grinned. "Oops. We probably should have opened this before the sale started."

Jackie nodded, then glanced again at Adam and Crabby Man before turning her attention back to Owen. "That was amazing. How was he able to calm him down like that?"

Owen gave a one-shouldered shrug. "What can I say? The kid makes a good doctor. I'm assuming that crotchety old man's one of his patients."

Kit pulled a wad of paper towels off the roll. "Remember how good he was with Hazel?"

Jackie thought back to the night they'd found Kit's grandmother sitting in a chair in her backyard after that terrible storm, blood dripping down her face. Adam had handled that situation beautifully as well.

"You should be proud," she said.

Owen nodded, understanding her perfectly. "I am. Of both my boys."

Adam must have sealed the deal, because Mr. Carson, formerly known as Crabby Man, walked away from the sale carrying the yellow minnow bucket in one hand while he twirled the cane in his other. Jackie blinked twice to make sure she was seeing what she thought she was seeing. When Adam handed her a five-dollar bill, she passed it on to Kit for safekeeping.

"Patient of yours?"

"You know I can't divulge that kind of thing," Adam replied with a grin.

"Well, regardless, thank you. He was certainly ornery."

Kit slammed the microwave closed. "You mean crabby? Like you last night?"

Jackie narrowed her eyes at Kit. "I wasn't *that* bad."

Kit turned to Adam. "She was. Trust me. So, what will you give me for the lawn mower?"

CHAPTER NINETEEN

J ACKIE LET NIKKI BACK in, chuckling when the border collie slid the final three feet to her breakfast, served up in a doggy dish bearing the name *Hoover*.

"I wish I was as happy as you are every morning, Nikki," she said, patting her dog's haunches as she snarfed up her breakfast, tail wagging the whole time. "But coffee helps."

Once she'd filled both travel mugs and rinsed out Charlotte's coffee pot, she made a special point of unplugging it so she wouldn't have to circle back to double-check when they were already five miles from the house.

They had their bags packed, and as soon as she could wash out Hoover's food dish and round Kit up, they'd be on their way.

"I wonder if little Hoover is enjoying Arizona with Mom," she said, sipping her coffee as she waited for Nikki to finish eating.

Once the dog started pushing the empty bowl across the floor, Jackie picked it up and washed it out. She'd probably come back to Ruby Shores at least a couple more times this summer, to spend time with Annie and keep an eye on this house, but she couldn't leave a dirty dog dish on the floor, old coffee in the pot, or milk in the fridge.

After checking to make sure Kit had unloaded the dishwasher as promised, she picked up both travel mugs and went in search of her friend.

She found an animated Kit on the wicker sofa on the front porch. She had one foot propped up on the steamer trunk and her free hand waved madly, seeming to punctuate her words. When she spied Jackie in the doorway, she mouthed *Sorry!* to her, held up five fingers, and kept right on talking.

Jackie went to load Nikki into the car while she waited. The dog balked when she tried to coax her into the travel crate in the backseat, but a doggie treat was enough to convince her.

She did her best to ignore the half dozen boxes containing her dad's things that hadn't sold in the rummage sale. They'd lined them up along the outer walls of the garage. She still felt sad about purging the house of all but the most special items from his life. The next time she came back, she'd drop these boxes at the thrift store.

Owen had taken the tackle home to figure out a better way to sell it. She looked forward to the excuse of talking to him about it in the future.

Kit appeared on the upper landing of the stairs between the garage and the kitchen as Jackie opened the big garage door. "Sorry I held us up. I did lock the front door. Are we ready to go?"

Jackie noticed her friend sniff at the air, the way Nikki did when she caught a whiff of food in the kitchen or a rabbit in the backyard. She laughed. "Yes, I have a mug of coffee for you, too. It's already in the car. Get in, and let's go. I've had enough of this place for a little while."

"Yes!" Kit did a fist-pump as she bounced down the stairs and around to the passenger side of Glen's sedan. "Thank you for the coffee. I see you got Nikki in her crate."

Once Kit fastened her seatbelt, Jackie backed out of the garage. She made absolutely sure she'd closed the garage door, then headed down the street that would take them to the highway and back to the Minneapolis–St. Paul metro area. They rode in companionable silence until they'd left the town's outer limits.

"You must have had an interesting phone conversation back there. You looked pretty intense. Is it your mom again?" Jackie asked. She flipped the lid of her travel mug open and took a sip of steaming coffee.

Kit sighed. "No, that was Dean. And I'm not sure I'm ready to talk about what he told me."

Intrigued, Jackie tapped the clock on the car's dashboard. "No worries. You have two hours to get ready, but you've got me curious, so you aren't getting out of this car until you spill it. Your conversation, that is. Not your coffee."

She knew something was up when Kit met her weak attempt at humor with nothing more than a brief nod.

"Will the girls be at your townhouse?" Kit asked.

She's stalling, Jackie thought. It was her turn to nod. "Yes. They'll be around, but maybe not home when I get there. Mack is searching for a job, and Hailey is on a rotation of three twelve-hour shifts this week. She works today."

Kit had to wrestle her mug out of the cup holder. It was a tight fit. After she took a sip, she checked Nikki in the backseat. "I can't believe the girls are twenty-four and college graduates already. Is Hailey enjoying nursing? I know she thought about switching out of that field earlier in her college days. And I'm sorry Mack is having trouble finding a job."

They continued to discuss the girls. Jackie shared her concerns over how serious Hailey was about her boyfriend. She worried her daughter was too young.

"Weren't you about her age when you married Todd?"

She flipped on the blinker to pass a moving truck. "Exactly my point."

They debated the moves her girls were making in this post-graduation season of their lives for the next half hour. When they passed a sign declaring the next rest stop was in fifteen miles, Kit asked her to stop when they reached it.

Jackie frowned. "I have to pee lots more often than I used to, too—thank you, menopause—but it seems like you have to go all the time. Do you have a bladder infection?"

"Don't think so," Kit said, tapping her coffee mug. "I probably just drink too much. I'm always thirsty."

Nikki barked in the backseat. Jackie used the rear-view mirror to check on her, but nothing looked to be wrong. Kit spun in her seat to check her, too. "Maybe you can let her out at the rest stop. Aw, I'd hate to ride in that tight little box, too, girl."

Jackie supposed she could try. She had one more treat in her pocket if she had to bribe Nikki to get in again after a brief stretch.

"Okay, I'm ready to talk about it now," Kit said, surprising Jackie.

"Talk about what, exactly?"

Kit shot her an exasperated look. "My phone call. I'm freaked out, and I think I could use some advice."

Jackie checked her speed, set the cruise control, and relaxed in her seat. Traffic was lighter on this stretch of road, and she should be able to give Kit most of her attention. "Advice is what I do best."

Kit snorted. "I hope so, because Dean dropped a bomb on me this morning."

"What kind of bomb?"

Her friend sighed. "The bomb where he tells me he thinks we should sell everything, quit our jobs, and move to Iowa."

"He did *not*. Why would he do that?"

Kit pulled her mug out again, and Jackie could hear the liquid sloshing around inside. "Oh, the laundry list of rationales was long. His brother and sister-in-law are going to need lots of help to rebuild. His mother wants to move into an apartment building where two of her girlfriends already live. That would leave the house he grew up in vacant, and she's trying to convince Dean to buy it instead of selling it to a stranger. There's a big shop on her property, and it would be the perfect place for him and Isaac to rebuild old cars."

Kit was right. This *was* a bomb. If Kit left Minneapolis, there would be no one in the area Jackie considered a friend. Something told her Mack and Hailey didn't plan to stick around for long.

She must have gotten lost in her thoughts for longer than she thought, because Kit snapped her fingers at her.

"Hey, Jackie, where'd you go? I thought you were going to give me advice. What am I supposed to do now? I don't want to live in *Iowa*, near his *family*!"

Jackie did her best to shift from thinking about how Kit's leaving might affect her, to what it would mean for her friend's way of life. "Well . . . what does Isaac think?"

"I asked Dean that, too. According to my husband, all Isaac sees is a kickass shop for them to work in. He's done with high school and hasn't decided about college yet. He has no ties to this area other than me and Dean."

No hurdle there, then, Jackie thought.

"Is Dean thinking he'd work for his brother in Iowa?"

Kit blew a raspberry. "No. He'd have to find a new job. But that doesn't seem to worry him. Apparently, if it took us a while to find work, his mother would just hold off on expecting any payment from us for her house."

Jackie considered this. A few days ago, Kit had mentioned some dissatisfaction with her own job. Jackie reminded her of this.

Nikki whined behind them.

"I know, girl," Kit said, smiling back at the dog. "I have to go potty, too."

Jackie doubted that was why Nikki was complaining, but she kept them on topic. "What if a move to Iowa opened up some fun, new opportunities for you? You've been at the same job, and in the same townhouse, for a long time. Dean moved in with you when you got married. You were quick to convince me to move to Minneapolis when I wanted to start a new business. When I faced the possibility of some big life changes, you encouraged me to go for it. But when you are the one facing these kinds of decisions, it's scary, isn't it?"

"Terrifying."

There was another sign for the rest stop—just one mile ahead now.

"Don't miss it," Kit reminded her.

Another thought suddenly occurred to Jackie. "Kit, when was the last time you had a checkup?"

Kit looked at her like she was nuts. "Jackie, I'm having an existential crisis at the moment, and you're worried about whether I'm overdue for a pap or a mammogram?"

Jackie turned on her blinker and tapped the brakes to turn off the cruise. "That's not what I said. Do you remember Todd's mom?"

"Maybe you're the one who needs a checkup. Get tested for ADHD. You can't focus on *anything* this morning."

Jackie slowed as they approached the parking area. She pulled into a spot and parked.

Kit unbuckled her seatbelt and reached for her door handle, but Jackie stopped her.

"You have to go to the bathroom all the time, you just said how thirsty you always are, and a few nights ago you complained about your eyesight. I think you've lost weight, too, but you haven't mentioned being on a diet."

Kit froze, then dropped her head back with a moan of frustration. "God. How could I be so stupid? You're right. The signs are all there. Todd's mom had diabetes, didn't she?"

Jackie prayed she was wrong, but something told her she wasn't.

"She did. But she was Type 2, and when she focused on her eating, and getting enough exercise, she controlled it without too much trouble. I don't know how she's doing these days with it, because we lost touch after the divorce, but she missed the signs at first, too."

Kit covered her face with both hands. "I'm a scientist. How did I not notice?"

Nikki let out a piercing yelp, surprising them both.

Dropping her hands and opening the car door, Kit moaned as she stepped out of the vehicle. "Life just keeps handing us lemons, doesn't it?"

Jackie climbed out from behind the wheel and met Kit's gaze over the top of her dad's old car. "I guess so, but that's why we need to stick together. Life with friends means helping each other make lemonade out of these lemons."

Kit scratched at her neck as she considered Jackie's words. "That sounds great and all, but I'm afraid that if your diagnosis to explain my frequent bladder issues is correct, my lemonade days may be behind me."

By the time Jackie dropped Kit off at home, her friend had already made an appointment to see her primary care doctor. She also promised to give Dean's request serious consideration, and to keep Jackie posted on everything.

Once Jackie reached the townhouse complex she was calling home these days, she pulled into one of the visitor parking spots. Her daughters had taken over the second stall of her garage after Lynette got her boxes out of there, so that left no space for her dad's trusty old sedan.

She hated having to snap a leash on Nikki to take her inside, but rules were rules. She missed living in a single-family home like the one she'd given up in Chicago, but she'd been hesitant to purchase in this area.

Four years here, and the city still didn't feel like home.

It took her three trips to get the car unloaded. Neither of her daughters were home at the moment, but empty cereal bowls in the sink and two coffee cups on the island meant they were probably coming and going, living their own lives, today. This place was a hub for her tiny family, but it wasn't exactly what she'd always envisioned to be their home.

She checked the time. Mack was hopefully out job hunting, and Hailey's shift normally lasted until eight on the day shift. Deciding to pass on preparing a family dinner, she set her dad's metal box on the kitchen island and pulled up a stool.

The original plan to open it with her friends had sounded fun, but now she was glad to have time alone with the things her dad had felt important enough to stash in a box with her name on the outside.

The mechanism to open and close the top was difficult to pull loose. When it finally popped open, she got to her feet so she could have a better look inside. Everything looked jumbled together.

"What did you deem worthy of saving, Dad?" she asked, her voice echoing around her. Nikki was probably snoring away in her bed in the other room by now, tired after the ordeal of a two-hour drive in her hated crate.

An envelope protruded above everything else, so she pulled it out first. It was a letter made out to Charlotte and Glen Turner, in her own handwriting. The postal stamp was dated 2005. This was the letter she'd sent her parents informing them she was divorcing Todd. She hadn't been able to tell them to their faces, or even call them with the news. She'd known how disappointed they would be.

Why had her dad kept it?

She set it aside without rereading it, unwilling to revisit that painful chapter in her past.

She reached in, and her fingers snagged on a ribbon. She pulled a cheap plastic medallion out of the box. Expecting it to be one of her many track medals, she laughed when she spied the pine trees engraved on one side of the gold-colored circle, and *First Place* on the other. This would have come from her days at summer camp, though she couldn't remember what contest she might have taken first place in. When she held the prize in her hands and closed her eyes, images of her and dozens of other young girls screaming as they competed in things like sack races and swimming relays flooded her mind.

Those were the good old days.

The door opened and both her daughters came barreling into the kitchen, talking a mile a minute. When they spied her at the island, they froze. She'd have sworn they both looked guilty.

Mack was the first to speak. "Oh. Hey, Mom, we didn't think you were back yet."

"Hi. I wondered where you were, Mack. And Hailey, I thought you had to work until eight tonight. It's why I didn't put anything in for dinner."

Hailey pulled out the stool next to Jackie and plunked down on it. She yanked her work badge off and tossed it onto the island. "I switched shifts with someone. What are you doing?" She reached for the divorce letter.

Jackie snatched it away. She didn't remember exactly what she'd written in it, but she was sure it wasn't something her daughter needed to read.

"Jeez, sorry," Hailey said, looking wounded.

"No, I'm sorry. But I don't want you to read that," Jackie explained. "But look at this. I won this when I wasn't even a teenager yet, at summer camp."

Hailey accepted the medal, turning it over in her hands. "This was in there? Where did you get the box?"

Jackie shrugged. "It was my dad's. We found it in the closet in his study. There was one with Ron's name on it, too. I didn't have time to look inside until now. I just started going through it. I've been dying to know what things Dad kept about me. Mom has never been much of a saver. After I moved out of the house the first time, she cleaned out my room and only kept one box of my things. I found that box in the attic last week, but there was nothing too special inside. Mom's idea of what was important didn't always match up with mine."

Mack came to stand on Jackie's other side and pulled the box closer.

She reached inside and pulled out what looked like an old ring box. The once-blue velvet had faded to a worn purple.

"Oh, jewelry!"

But when she opened it, tiny teeth spilled onto the island.

She recoiled, but Jackie laughed.

"My baby teeth," she said, picking one up and holding it up to the light.

"That is *disgusting*," Mack said, grimacing. "I was hoping for a diamond ring that me and Hailey could fight over."

Jackie gathered the teeth and put them back into the ring box. "Pull something else out."

Next came Jackie's graduation programs from both high school and college. Those didn't hold the girls' interest, but they took more time with the wedding invitation.

"I've never seen this," Hailey said. A mix of emotions played across her face. "What were your wedding colors?"

Jackie had to stop and think. "Peach and burgundy."

"Huh" was all Hailey said as she put the invitation back in its envelope, but Jackie could tell her daughter wouldn't have approved of that color combination.

"Have either of you talked to your dad recently?"

Both girls shook their heads.

"We'll hear from him on our birthday," Mack said.

Neither of them seemed to want to discuss Todd, and Jackie didn't press.

Mack pulled out a folded piece of paper. She unfolded it and laid it on the island, attempting to smooth the creases out with her hands. "Aw, this is cute. Mom, you never told us you won first place in a talent show in 1981. What was your talent? And what grade would you have been in?"

Jackie picked up the yellowed certificate. She didn't have to do the math to answer Mack. "I can't believe Dad kept this! It was the end of fifth grade, and we sang a duet."

"Wait, wait, wait," Mack cried. "*You* sang? You can't sing!"

Jackie laughed and waved the award certificate in Mack's face. "This is proof that I can. Or I could."

Hailey looked just as skeptical as her sister. "What did you sing? Did you sing with Annie or Lynette?"

Shaking her head, Jackie tried to remember the details of that long-ago talent show. "Have you two heard of Sonny & Cher? We sang 'I've Got You Babe.' It was something, let me tell you!"

Mack frowned. "You sang that with Annie or Lynette?"

"No, it needed to be sung by a man and a woman. Or, in our case, a girl and a boy. Owen was my partner. Do you guys remember him? I ran into him at Annie's, after Henry's funeral. He's also the one who held that surprise party for me when I turned fifty. You might have met him there."

Both girls nodded, and then Mack smiled a smile that Jackie didn't particularly care for.

"Mom, do you mean to tell us you've had a little something going with Owen ever since the two of you were kids?"

Jackie refolded the certificate and placed it on top of the divorce letter. "Don't be ridiculous. He's a friend. He has always been nothing more than a friend."

Mack scoffed. "Mother. I'm not a child. I saw how that man looked at you the other day. Even if you don't want to be more than friends with him, he looked like he wanted to whisk you away somewhere and—"

"Stop right there, Mackenzie Marie," Jackie said, cutting her daughter off. "We are not having this discussion right now. What else is in the box?"

"Fine," Mack said, reaching in and pulling out a packet of what Jackie could see were the annual Christmas card photos she always sent, held tight with a rubber band. "But we *will* talk about it. Here."

Jackie took the bundle, snapped off the rubber band, and held the top one, setting the rest down. It was a collage of photos, and included a sunny snapshot of Jackie with her girlfriends in Arizona.

"Ah, this was when we went to Annie's parents' to celebrate turning fifty. Say, that reminds me. I'm not really excited by this idea, but your grandmother asked me to tell the two of you she'd love it if one or both of you could drive her car down to her in Arizona. You could stay for a visit, then she'd pay to fly you back."

Mack looked intrigued, but Hailey did not.

Mack reached for the card and studied the Arizona snapshot. "I'd do that. I'm kind of striking out around here on my job hunt, and I need a break. Would you want to come, too, Hailey, or won't that work in your timeline?"

"Timeline? What kind of 'timeline' do you have, Hailey?" Jackie asked. She felt like she was missing something, but she had no idea what that something might be.

Hailey shot a look at Mack, then turned to her mother with a smile. "Mom, I've been wanting to talk to you about something, but I was waiting for the right time."

Never a good way to start a conversation, Jackie thought, bracing for what might be coming.

"I'm moving to Reno. With Evan. I gave my notice at work yesterday. Evan got a great job out there, and he's already found us an apartment."

Jackie could see the uncertainty in her daughter's eyes as the words tumbled out of her mouth.

"Reno?" she repeated.

Her brain struggled to process as quickly as Hailey was speaking.

"With Evan? The same Evan who took a job here in Minneapolis, so you followed him here? Hailey, that was just two months ago. Neither of you have been at your jobs long enough to move already. And I know you two are serious, but moving in together . . . are you sure you're ready for that?"

Hailey practically bristled at the question. She'd never liked to have her actions questioned. "Of course I'm ready for it, Mother. We've been dating for four years already."

Jackie remembered at least two temporary breakups between Hailey and Evan within that four-year time period, but she knew it wouldn't help to rub those in her daughter's face.

"And don't try to talk me out of it, because my mind's made up."

Before Jackie could fashion a response to that snippy comment, a phone rang. Hailey pulled hers out of the pocket of her scrubs. "There he is now. If you two will excuse me, I need to talk to him. He's signing the papers for the apartment today."

Jackie watched her leave the room, then swung her gaze back to Mack.

"Did you know about this?" she demanded.

Mack looked sheepish as she shrugged. "Mom. You know better than to ask me that. I can't break the twin code."

Nikki wandered in and pushed her head against Mack's leg.

"I should take her out," Mack said, probably happy for the excuse to escape, too. "Then I think I'll call Grandma and see if I can't get that ball rolling."

A minute later, Jackie found herself alone once more, but the quiet no longer felt comfortable. It felt lonely.

Hailey had decided to move across the country without even consulting with her. Kit might move to Iowa, and Mack was eager to escape Minnesota, too, even if it was only temporary.

Or could a trip to Arizona turn into something more for her other twin, too?

She sat for a moment, then gathered up the memorabilia her father had saved from some of the highest, and lowest, points in her life. He was no longer here to save anything she might do in the future, or to offer her his advice.

She was on her own.

Her cell phone vibrated with an incoming email. With a sigh, she opened the app, surprised to see quite a few messages that she'd missed.

The first one was from the party wanting to buy her pet adoption business. Had she given their offer any further consideration? Because they'd love to proceed.

Another was from Owen. He'd listed an initial batch of her father's tackle in an online auction, complete with quality photos, and was happy to report that bids had already far exceeded the price she'd slapped on them for the rummage sale, and there were still three days of bidding to go. She laughed, happy to see he'd found a good solution to her dilemma.

The third email she checked was from the daughter of one of her favorite customers. It was a courtesy note, letting her know that her customer had passed away and the daughter would keep the basset hound Jackie had helped her mom adopt. Since the hound was already thirteen years old, it probably wouldn't be for long.

A wave of sadness hit. The situation reminded her of little Hoover, the dog her father had adopted late in life. Hoover had outlived her new owner, and now she was living with Charlotte in Arizona.

Jackie missed her dad. She missed her mom, too, but she had no desire to move to Arizona.

But what if she moved back to her hometown?

Both Annie and Lynette lived there now.

Kit was probably going to go to Iowa with Dean and Isaac.

Her girls were moving on with their own lives.

Maybe it was time she, too, made a big change in her life.

She'd done it before, and she could do it again.

But this time she'd be going home. There were people in Ruby Shores who meant the world to her.

Could she find happiness there again, like she had when she was young?

She thought she could.

But first she needed to speak to her lawyer. She had a business to sell.

Chapter Twenty

LYNETTE ARRIVED AT THE Crystal Café five minutes early. Annie had parked her car out front already.

She'd been excited when Annie was free to grab lunch. They'd only talked on the phone a handful of times in the weeks since getting back from Whispering Pines, and she wanted to make sure her friend seemed to be doing all right as she acclimated to what her new life looked like.

The first thing Lynette noticed when she entered the new restaurant was how different it smelled. Kit's aunt had sold her home-style café to two younger women who'd relocated to Ruby Shores from California during the pandemic.

Lynette recognized the parallels with her own life.

The smell of fresh baked goods at the Crystal Café had been an integral part of her childhood and teen years. The new owners hadn't changed the establishment's name, but it was looking to Lynette like they'd changed almost everything else.

The glass display cabinet that used to contain a mouthwatering as-sortment of pies, rolls, and breads was gone. So was the cash register, along with the familiar *ping* you'd hear anytime a satisfied customer paid. A complete gut job was the only way they could have transformed the restaurant's interior so dramatically. Lynette guessed there were half as many tables now, and they weren't full of customers the way they used to be, despite the noon hour.

When Marge was running the place, there was always a wait to get in.

A woman dressed in all white with a long black ponytail greeted her, losing points when she addressed Lynette as "ma'am." Lynette knew that wasn't fair, given the woman looked thirty years younger than her and Annie, but it still irritated her.

The hostess knew Annie by name and led Lynette right to her.

Annie got to her feet and gave Lynette a warm hug. Once they were both seated again, Lynette started to say something about all the changes to Marge's restaurant, but Annie cut her off.

"I *know*," she said with a wink. "More change. And things don't run as smoothly as they did under Marge, but the food is good. Different, but good. It may remind you of New York."

Lynette flipped the menu open, then dug a pair of cheaters out of her purse. She had to admit—the selection on the new menu was a pleasant surprise.

Once they'd placed their orders and were alone again, Lynette clasped her hands on the tabletop and looked Annie in the eye. "I promise we won't talk about you during our *entire* lunch, but how are you doing? How are the kids?"

Annie sighed. "Asking for time off until mid-August might have been a mistake. I need to keep busy. I insist on taking Nora to the swimming pool on every sunny day. She's bored—we go so often—and getting permanently pruned little fingers and toes."

Lynette understood. Annie had always worked hard. Leisure time would be difficult for her right now. "I never want the summer to go by too fast, but you only have a few weeks until mid-August. That reminds me. Is Michael still getting married?"

"He is," Annie said. "Can you go to the ceremony with me?"

Was that a flicker of apprehension in Annie's eyes?

"I'm planning on it," Lynette confirmed. "I haven't been to a wedding since Kit and Dean's. It's hard to believe that was almost four years ago already. Are you still feeling all right about Michael marrying again?"

A server dropped off their beverages, and Lynette ripped the paper off her straw. Her first sip of iced tea was divine, boasting the perfect balance of mint and lemon. Maybe there was hope for this place after all.

"I'm fine with it. He seems excited, and Colton thinks the woman he's marrying will be good for him. Ava is more reserved when I ask her about them as a couple. My guess is Ava has harbored a not-so-secret hope that someday her parents would get back together. Not that she'd ever wish Henry to be out of the picture, but that's what happened. Relic doesn't say much. Because Henry was his father, Relic and Michael's relationship has always been more precarious."

Lynette nodded. The blending in Annie's family meant complications. Then she remembered Julie's comments while the two of them had visited around the firepit at Whispering Pines, about Colton and Jackie's twins. If she said anything about that, would she be betraying Julie's confidence? She decided to keep Julie's speculations to herself. They might not even be true.

"Well, hopefully the wedding ceremony goes off without a hitch and the couple lives happily ever after," Lynette said. She took another sip, realizing that if she didn't slow down on her iced tea, she'd need a refill before their meals arrived. "Aside from your ex, how are other things? Are your two pups all right? When do you get your cast off?"

Annie dumped a packet of sugar into her iced tea, and Lynette had to fight the urge to scold her for ruining perfection. "I see my primary care doc next week, so hopefully I'll be cast-free for my ex's wedding. Daisy and Lemon are good. I'm guessing Relic won't take Lemon with him when he goes back to school in the fall. It's so hard to take care of a dog, given how busy he is with classes and work. I don't mind. The two dogs enjoy each other's company, and I hate the idea of roaming around that big house all by myself once Relic is gone again. The experts all say not to make any big financial decisions like moving for at least a year after losing a spouse, but I'm pretty sure I will want a smaller place someday. Maybe next summer. Somewhere that feels like a fresh start. Does that make sense?"

Their food arrived, and Lynette turned her plate for easier access to her endive salad.

"I think it makes perfect sense. My apartment in New York City, before we moved back to Ruby Shores, was luxurious, but small. So when we moved into our big old house in town here, I never did fully acclimate to the feeling of so much space. It's one reason I agreed to rent most of it to Storm for his brother."

They continued to visit while they enjoyed their meals of fresh vegetables and lean chicken.

"Say, have you done anything about finding a location for your new consulting business yet?" Annie asked as she tried but failed to stab a mushroom on her plate.

"It's funny you should ask. Have you ever noticed the storefront across the street? I don't know what used to be in there, but it's sat vacant since the days of the pandemic."

Annie strained to look over Lynette's shoulder and out the window behind her. "The one with the red front?"

Lynette turned around to make sure they were talking about the same one. "Yes. It could use a fresh coat of paint around those front windows, but yes, that one. You don't know who owns it, do you?"

Annie laughed. "As a matter of fact, I do. The place has been home to a few different businesses through the years. If I remember right, there is one large office, a smaller space out front for a receptionist, and a small waiting area. The pretty woodwork sticks out in my memories. If no one made the mistake of painting over it, you'd love it."

It sounded surprisingly perfect to Lynette, but she needed to be careful not to get her hopes up. "Is there any chance you have the owner's number? I'd love to see it sometime."

"Why don't I just call her? She works a block over. I bet if she has time she'd show it to you now."

"Now?"

Annie nodded and pulled out her phone. "One second."

The conversation lasted more like two minutes, but Lynette could tell she was going to get to see the inside of the building today.

Annie's grin when she hung up confirmed it. "She'll meet us there in ten minutes."

"Perfect," Lynette said, reaching for the check.

But Annie beat her to it. "Oh no. After everything you've done for me this summer, this is my treat."

When she resisted, Annie reminded her to just say "thank you." They both laughed at the reference to one of Lynette's favorite sayings.

While they waited for the server to return to take Annie's card, she asked Lynette when Donna had gotten back to town.

"Back to town? No. She's still floating around the canals of Venice, last I heard. But she is planning to come back in September. What made you think she was back?"

"Huh," Annie said. "I swear I've seen her cute aqua convertible around town more than once. It's not like there are any other Mini Coopers like hers in Ruby Shores."

Annie was right. Donna's car was certainly a standout. "Someone else must have got one just like hers?"

Annie shrugged. "Must have, because I know I saw it. Once at the post office and another time outside the liquor store. I thought that was pretty strange, since I know you don't want any alcohol in your house anymore."

Lynette didn't like the little river of apprehension that traveled down her spine. When she got home, she'd check Donna's car in the garage and make sure it hadn't moved an inch.

Someone cleared their dishes, and she reached for the wallet in her purse to fish some bills out for the tip. But there was no cash. At all.

Impossible.

She'd picked up a few hundred in cash before their trip to Whispering Pines, and had barely spent any of it.

She sighed. "I'm so sorry, Annie, but I seem to be out of cash. Do you want to cover the tip, too, and I promise to buy next time?"

"No problem at all," Annie said, handing the ticket and her card to the server as she passed by.

Without the cash register up front, the transaction was quick and silent. But Lynette missed the charm of it all.

Ten minutes later, a fresh sight charmed and delighted her. Annie had been right. This office space could work. The woodwork, along with plaster medallions in the ceiling around the light fixtures, was stunning. Thank goodness no one had ruined what appeared to be hand-carved wooden trim with paint.

The unease she'd felt at the end of their lunch dissipated, and was replaced with a new enthusiasm over finally taking a real step toward getting her consulting business off the ground.

Lynette's excitement only lasted as long as it took her to drive the short distance back home. When she opened the garage door, she was relieved to see her mother's cute little convertible in the far stall. But upon closer inspection, she noticed little splashes of mud on the fenders behind the front wheels.

Donna would never put her Mini Cooper away dirty before leaving town for an extended period.

Who the hell had driven her mother's car? *She* certainly hadn't.

She needed to sort this out.

After closing all the garage doors, she headed for the back entry to the house, but pulled up short when she noticed the open door to her she-shed. No one else was supposed to have a key to her shed, and she always kept it locked. No sense tempting curious neighbor kids, or even Storm's brother, by leaving it open.

She heard the music first, before she could see whether anyone was inside. Through the window, she could see the small television she'd mounted in one top corner was on.

"What the . . . ?" she said as she pushed the door open all the way.

"Oh, hi, Lynette," Shane greeted her. "This is a good show. Did you come out here to watch it with me?"

His bright smile made her glad he'd cut her off before she got the cuss word out. Next to him sat a bottle of the sparkling water she stored in her little refrigerator, along with a bag of chips he must have brought from the main kitchen.

"Here, want some?"

She took the chip bag from him and looked inside. It was practically empty. How long had he been out here? And, more importantly, how did he get the door open?

"Shane, I'm glad you're enjoying the show, but do you remember how Storm said you weren't going to come in here? That this was my special place?"

Shane's face fell, and she feared he might cry.

Where was his caregiver? He wasn't supposed to be left alone like this.

He pushed off the sofa, knocking the bottle over and splashing her plush area rug with the mineral water.

"Oh no!"

She hated the way Shane cringed, as if she would slap him for accidentally spilling the water.

"It's fine, Shane. You can help me clean it up, and then we can go find Dex. How does that sound?"

His smile returned, and thanks to the spare roll of paper towels she kept in the shed, she'd cleaned up the mess in short order.

When they got in the house, Dex was still nowhere to be found. She checked her watch. It was two o'clock.

"Shane, you usually take a quick nap in the afternoon, right?"

"I do," he said, yawning. "I think I'll go lay down now."

Lynette watched him walk up the stairs and turn down the hallway toward his room, but before he disappeared out of sight, he stopped and pointed to her stained-glass window, high above them. "That's really pretty, Lynette. It reminds me of those tubes you look through and the glass sparkles like magic."

She laughed. "Those are called kaleidoscopes, and that's exactly what it's supposed to look like. I'm glad you like it."

"It's perfect for a castle house."

He headed back for his room, leaving Lynette both charmed and concerned.

She pulled out her phone and tried Dex's number. Storm had given it to her in case of emergencies. It went straight to voice mail. Frustrated, she knew she'd just have to wait until Dex returned from wherever he'd disappeared to and confront him. Or was she out of line to think it was her place to question Shane's caregiver?

Deciding she would interrogate the man when he bothered to show his face again, whether or not it was her business, she stomped out to the front mailbox and gathered the handful of envelopes from inside. She'd have loved to take the mail out to her she-shed and relax with a cup of tea while going through it, but she couldn't do that until she got to the bottom of this mess.

Instead, she detoured to her office, not caring that this wasn't technically the part of the house she was supposed to be in these days. Her bank statement was the top envelope, so she tore it open, chastising herself again for not switching it to paperless. Letting the statement sit in her mailbox wasn't the most secure practice in this day and age.

She unfolded the statement, scanned the entries, then gasped at the low balance. That couldn't be right. Then she checked the transactions more closely. The rent check for the house was missing, but her mortgage payment had come out like clockwork.

She hadn't overdrawn her account, but it was close.

It wasn't like she was living month by month, but she'd invested most of her funds and didn't have extra cash flow each month.

Dex still wasn't back, so she decided it was time to call Storm. Things weren't working out quite as he'd hoped, and now his brother's caregiver was in the wind.

Chapter Twenty-One

Lynette woke to the melody of birdsong and bright sunshine streaming through the curtain-free window of her bedroom. Today promised excitement. She had an eight-o'clock appointment to sign the papers on her new office space, and then Annie would meet her there to help her clean things up.

She began preparing a mental list of all the things she wanted to do with the space, but as the last remnants of sleep cleared away, she froze.

This wasn't her bed anymore.

Her bed was upstairs in the attic.

"Morning," came a growly voice beside her, accompanied by a heavy arm falling across her midsection.

This was Storm's bed now, as he'd claimed her old room as his own for those few times he expected to stay at the house he'd rented for his brother.

Storm pulled her closer and rolled on top of her. "I could get used to this."

Lynette could, too, but based on the slant of the sun, she suspected she didn't have much time before she'd have to leave the house for her meeting. She checked her phone.

"Oops, sorry, but I'm going to be late if I don't get a move on it."

She tried to push him off, but he was too heavy.

"What time is it?" he asked; he'd buried his face in her hair, muffling his words.

She pushed at his shoulder again. "A quarter after seven."

He let out a disappointed sigh and rolled off her to sit up, swinging his legs over the side of the bed. "I'll start the coffee."

Lynette watched as he shuffled naked toward the attached bathroom.

"And I could get used to *that*," she teased.

A grunt was his only reply. Apparently Storm wasn't a morning person.

They still had so much to learn about each other.

When she'd called Storm three days earlier about her growing concerns over the quality of care that Dex was providing to Shane, as well as the missing rent payment, she hadn't expected him to jump on the first flight out of Nantucket the next morning. He'd transferred the rent money before he even boarded the 6:00 a.m. flight.

He kept a garage near the Minneapolis airport where he stored his truck when he wasn't in Minnesota, so it didn't take him long to get back to Ruby Shores.

Within minutes of his return, he'd sat down with Dex and Lynette to discuss her concerns. The younger man was no match for the intensity of Storm's interrogation, and it didn't take long for him to admit to both a gambling problem and leaving Shane unattended. He still denied driving Donna's car, but when Storm insisted he follow him out to the garage, the man couldn't deny the mud on the Mini Cooper.

Storm had established a checking account Dex was to use for both groceries and paying the monthly rent. When he'd foolishly borrowed money from the account for an evening of blackjack at a local bar, he'd lost it all. He was out trying to win it back when Lynette had come home to find Shane alone.

Storm fired Dex on the spot, along with a threat that if he didn't return the money he'd taken within two weeks, they'd notify the authorities.

As the man sped away in his battered Nissan, Storm had turned to Lynette with a frown. "Yeah, I'm never going to see either him or my money again. I'll take it as an expensive lesson."

When Lynette had asked him where he'd found Dex in the first place, he admitted the man was someone his mother had recommended. Shane's care was the only thing he'd reached out to her about in years.

Today, he had an appointment scheduled for around the same time as Lynette would sign on her new lease. He was meeting with someone at an agency who could hopefully find him a more reliable caregiver for Shane.

Lynette held her breath while turning a key in the locked door to her new office space. She couldn't believe this was finally happening. She'd dreamed of this moment for two years, ever since moving back to Ruby Shores. The seed of the idea had germinated even earlier, when she was becoming more and more unhappy with the day-to-day running of her online boutique while still in New York.

Donna planned to come home for a visit soon, and she couldn't wait to show this space to her.

She stepped into the front waiting area and gazed around the space with a fresh eye. When she'd first toured this space, the arrangement of the rooms and the majesty of the high ceilings and gorgeous wood trim enchanted her. Now she could see there were plenty of issues she'd overlooked in her initial excitement.

Old, broken furniture littered the front room. Three massive, dented metal filing cabinets claimed the wall behind a receptionist's desk. Snagged beige fabric upholstered the half-wall that sectioned the front area in two.

This would all need to be gutted.

Wandering back to the larger office, she discovered more junk. Cheap bookcases, their shelves bending under the weight of heavy plastic binders, suggested the space's last tenant sold insurance.

"Hello! Are you in here, Lynette?"

Relieved to hear Annie's voice, she dropped the cracked blue binder she'd pulled down onto the massive wooden desk that dominated the back office, raising a cloud of dust on impact. Sneezing, she hurried out front.

"Annie, I'm so glad you're here! This might be more work than I'd expected."

She pulled up short when she saw Annie wasn't alone.

"Surprise!" Renee yelled, rushing forward to catch Lynette up in a hug.

Still standing next to Annie was Renee's daughter, Julie, along with Annie's daughter and son-in-law. Stunned speechless for a moment, Lynette studied their smiling faces.

Annie dropped a large plastic bucket with rags and cleaning supplies poking out of the top onto the rickety front desk. "Our tour of this place was so fast, I doubted you noticed how much work it would take to clean it up."

Lynette laughed. "You're right about *that*."

Annie inclined her head. "I know you, Lynette. You are a dreamer and a doer. But you are used to having minions execute the minutiae for you."

"So you brought the minions for me!" Lynette rushed forward to give each of them a quick hug so they knew she was kidding. "I can't believe you're all here! This would take me weeks to clean up by myself."

Renee walked around the perimeter of the front room. "This isn't so bad. You should have seen the inside of the lodge at Whispering Pines when I first visited the resort after Celia passed it on to me. I know it could have scared me away, but I was lucky to have help from Julie and the rest of our family. We didn't want you to tackle this alone either. It won't take long with all of us here to help."

Lynette, still standing next to Julie, dropped a thankful hand on the younger woman's shoulder. "I can't believe you drove over here to help. Who's watching the resort? Matt?"

Julie shook her head. "Nathan. We liked your idea of asking him to help, and he was more than happy to give it a shot. Today is a test run. We have a few folks checking out. And since you so generously came to Whispering Pines and helped us brainstorm on things, we wanted to return the favor in some small way."

Ava stepped forward and pulled a roll of trash bags out of her mother's bucket. "And Grandpa Michael asked for some time with Nora, so we took him up on it today. We didn't think having Nora underfoot in here would be real productive."

Lynette couldn't argue with that. "It's so nice of you to give up your Saturday to help. And speaking of alone time with Nora, I'd like some of that, too, please. Remember, you promised I could be an honorary grandma to her, but I've been slacking in that regard."

Ava grinned as she snapped open a trash bag. "Anytime. The other thing we talked about was you helping me figure out that side gig I've been dreaming of, so I *might* have an ulterior motive for being here. I hope to get my name on the top of your new customer list."

Lynette hadn't forgotten, and she was glad to hear that Ava was keeping her dream alive.

Renee whistled for everyone's attention. "There are quite a few of us, Lynette. So do what you do best and put us all to work. Then you can buy us dinner tonight."

"I'd be more than happy to do that," Lynette said. "Let's get started!"

Annie had also thought to borrow Michael's truck while he watched Nora. Within an hour, they'd loaded most of the broken furniture Lynette wanted to get rid of into the truck's bed.

The massive desk in the main office was the only thing that wouldn't fit. She hated the clunky thing, but maybe she'd settle for using it for the time being. The top was wood, which was fine, but the body was an industrial green metal that looked like it came out of an old warehouse. It didn't fit the vibe she envisioned.

Ava had emptied the filing cabinets into garbage bags, running them out and tossing them into the trunk of their car. She promised to haul them to the recycling place in town on Monday. As she tied the last bag of random paperwork that the previous tenant hadn't bothered to dispose of, she caught Lynette's eye. No one else was nearby at the moment.

"I really appreciate your help," Lynette said.

Ava nodded. "It's fun to do this kind of thing once in a while. Oh, and hey, I wanted to mention that if you need any help to set up your social media, I work with that kind of thing at the bank. We aren't a big regional or national bank, and someone has to do it. I've learned through trial and error, and I'd be happy to apply some of that here to help you."

Her kind offer surprised Lynette. "To be honest, I hadn't thought about that part yet—which is silly, because I built my primary business online over the past twenty years. I'm going for something simpler here, but you're right, I still need an online presence. Give me a week or two, and we can talk again, all right?"

Ava hoisted the stuffed plastic bag over her shoulder. "Of course. But I have one request. Don't tell Mom, okay? She's so concerned with me trying to fit more into my life, on top of my full-time job, Nora, and my marriage, that she thinks I'll spread myself too thin. And the last thing I want to do right now is give her anything else to worry about."

Daniel returned after stowing one last busted chair into the truck and offered to take the bag outside for his wife.

"I understand," Lynette told her when they were alone again. "How do you think Annie is doing? I can't really get a read on her. She keeps telling me she is taking it all day by day, and she hates how empty the house is, but I need to know if there's more I can do to help her through this awful time."

Ava turned to find her mom. She was across the room, using a broom to sweep the walls. Because Annie was so short, she had to jump to reach the corners. The tall ceilings made it difficult for someone her size. They both smiled at her efforts.

"I think she's doing as well as we can expect," Ava said, keeping her voice low. "I know spending time with Nora helps. Two-year-olds are so fearless, you can't wallow in your own thoughts when you're trying to keep them safe. I think that's why my dad wanted time with her today. He's hurting, too. My dad and Henry used to be best friends before all the crap with my mom. They were working on rebuilding their relationship recently, and I think they were getting to a good place. Dad feels lost without Henry, too."

Lynette hadn't stopped to consider how Henry's death would also affect Michael.

Fifty years of living inevitably resulted in lots of complex layers.

Lynette gazed around the dusty space that would soon be her new office, and knew how lucky they all were to have each other.

A full day of work in her new office space, followed by a quick dinner at a trendy restaurant on the edge of town that served pizza and pasta, had left Lynette exhausted. After paying the tab and thanking everyone yet again for their help, she stopped in the ladies' room to rinse a smear of tomato paste from the front of her shirt before heading home. The shirt was already dirty from the dusty work in her new office, but she didn't want it ruined. It was a favorite from their girls' trip to Maui a few years earlier.

As she rubbed at the spot with a wet paper towel, she heard muffled crying coming from one of the stalls.

Is that Annie?

Caught between feeling like she was intruding and concern for her friend, she tossed the ineffective towel in the garbage and padded softly toward the stalls. She had to bend low to see if she recognized the shoes of the occupant behind the only closed stall door.

The door swung inward and Annie stepped out, freezing when she spied Lynette.

"I thought you left," she whispered, swiping at her tear-streaked face.

"I thought *you* left. Oh, honey," Lynette said, stepping forward to wrap Annie in a hug, but the shorter woman managed to avoid her.

Hurrying to the sink, Annie splashed water on her face, then ripped a paper towel from the dispenser to dab at her eyes and cheeks. "Don't worry about me, I'm fine. Really. Today was fun. I enjoy being around people. It's going home to an empty house that gets me sometimes."

Lynette took the towel from her and gently removed a streak of mascara at the woman's temple. Up close, she noticed the exhaustion in Annie's eyes.

"Come home with me," Lynette offered. "We could hide out in my she-shed, drink wine, and watch a movie. It isn't late."

Annie smiled. "As delightful as that sounds, I still need to return Michael's truck, run Nora home, and then hurry home before Daisy or Lemon have an accident in the house. If they haven't already. Michael already offered to make a trip out to the landfill tomorrow with any junk we stashed in his pickup. And you need to spray that, or it'll stain," she said, poking at the stubborn spot that remained behind the wet splotch on Lynette's shirt.

Lynette tossed the paper towel. "Are you sure?"

"I'm sure," Annie sighed. "This is my life now. But thank you for letting me be part of your fun today. I'm excited for you."

Together, they walked back out to the parking lot. It was difficult for Lynette to watch Annie drive away. Her brave face and assurances didn't negate the fact she'd been quietly sobbing in a bathroom stall five minutes earlier.

When Lynette got home, she found a note from Storm tacked on the door to her upstairs apartment, letting her know he'd taken Shane out to the lake house and they'd be back by ten. She appreciated his thoughtfulness. If it wasn't for the two of them, she'd be facing an empty house, too, and she was starting to realize how much she enjoyed their company.

After feeding an irate Ebony a late dinner and spraying spot treatment on her shirt, she treated herself to a long, hot shower. When she noticed it was still only eight, she decided to give both Kit and Jackie a call. They hadn't spoken since the sleepover, and she had lots of news to share with them.

Her conversation with Ava about how Michael was hurting over Henry's death had also reminded Lynette that she couldn't ever afford to take her closest friendships for granted.

After pulling on a soft yellow shorts set of cool cotton, she wandered out to her she-shed with her phone and charger. She flipped the small air-conditioner on and settled into her comfortable couch, thinking again how she never seemed to spend enough time in this quaint little space.

Jackie's name was ahead of Kit's on her phone, so she tried her first, but there was no answer.

Kit picked up after three rings, sounding breathless. "Hey, Lynette, it's good to hear from you. I've been meaning to call you. I have lots of news."

Laughing, Lynette settled her heels on the velvet ottoman, relishing in the feminine energy of her surroundings. "Well, I'm glad I called, then. I have news, too. But you start."

Kit shared Dean's crazy idea about relocating their little family to the farm fields of Iowa that had been home for him as a boy. But Lynette didn't think Dean was the only one excited about the idea. She heard a new sense of enthusiasm in her friend's voice that was missing when they'd discussed life while on their Fiji trip.

"You're moving to Iowa, aren't you, Kit?" she said, beating her friend to the punch line.

"Do you think it's stupid to pick up and move?"

Lynette knew Kit would appreciate an honest answer. She took a few seconds to consider the question.

"No, it's not stupid," she eventually said. "A little impulsive, maybe, but you've talked about how your townhouse is too small for the three of you. And I think it's great that Dean and Isaac have found a shared passion around vintage cars. That kid *needed* a male role model in his life. It speaks volumes that Isaac will move with you. He's eighteen now, right?"

"He is. But neither Dean nor I have new jobs yet," Kit countered.

Lynette could tell her friend was afraid of such a massive change.

Who wouldn't be?

"You mentioned your job might wind down, right? Kit, you've dedicated yourself to your monarch research for years now. You've done plenty to help the butterflies. Maybe it's time to help yourself grow in a new direction. Change is scary . . . but sometimes necessary. Give yourself time to figure out your next steps. That's what I've been doing. Oh, by the way, that was one thing I called to tell you about. Remember how I said I wanted to start a real consulting business?"

"Sure," Kit said. "And you'd be great at it. I've been talking your ear off, so now it's your turn. Tell me more."

Lynette shared how Annie helped her secure the new office space, and how everyone, including Renee and Julie, came to help her clean it up.

"Is Annie doing all right then?" Kit asked.

Lynette sighed. They were all worried about their friend.

"She probably wouldn't appreciate me telling you this, but I caught her crying in the bathroom at the restaurant after we finished up today. It's tough for her, but she seemed like she was doing okay for most of the day. I think we just need to keep making sure she knows we're here for her. That's all anyone can do."

She could hear Kit talking to someone else, probably holding a hand over her phone. "Sorry about that, Lynette. Isaac came in to take one of the kitchen boxes I just finished packing."

"Wait, you're literally packing to move right *now*?"

"Well, I'm just starting with the easy stuff. We are driving over there tomorrow. I haven't actually been back with Dean since this came up, and I need to see his mom's house again so I can decide what to take from my place here to a farmhouse in the middle of nowhere. I'm not sure my white living room furniture will be a good fit."

Lynette hoped Kit's good-natured chuckle meant she was content, despite her reservations, with the decision to move.

"But I do want to get back up to Ruby Shores again this summer. Or in the fall. I told Dean I'd move, but only on the condition that I could come visit all of you whenever I wanted."

Lynette got up and went to her mini-fridge, relieved there was still one bottle of her mineral water inside. Shane hadn't drunk or spilled all of it, it seemed. "Jackie is going to miss you in Minneapolis."

The line went quiet, and she thought she might have lost Kit.

"Well . . . about that," Kit finally said. "Have you talked to Jackie recently?"

"No, I hadn't talked to either of you since we spent the night at her mom's, so I'm calling you both tonight." Lynette did her best to cradle her phone between her ear and shoulder as she unscrewed the top of her water. "I actually called her first, but she didn't answer."

"I won't spoil her surprise then, but she might miss me, even if I stayed here."

Lynette wasn't sure what she meant by that, but she'd just have to try Jackie again when she finished talking to Kit. "Girl, I am excited for you guys. I hope you consider Iowa to be a chance for a new adventure. When you got married, Dean moved into your place. This time you can move into a place that feels new for both of you."

Kit snorted. "Except we'll be moving into the house Dean lived in as a kid."

Lynette just laughed. There was only so much encouragement she could come up with on the spot.

"I probably should go help the boys load the truck," Kit said. "But there is one more thing I wanted to update you on. I had a health scare."

Lynette sat up and put her bottle of water off to the side. Her mind flashed to the heartbreaking scene in Fiji when Annie learned of Henry's heart attack.

"Is it serious?" she whispered, afraid to hear what Kit might say.

"It's frustrating, is what it is," Kit said. "Turns out I have diabetes. Diabetes! Type 2. Can you believe that? And it took Jackie to point out what should have been a litany of telltale signs for me to see it. I'm a *scientist*, for God's sake."

"But you aren't a *doctor*. Cut yourself some slack. So what does that mean? Are you on shots, now? Pricking your finger constantly? Uncontrolled diabetes is dangerous."

She heard Dean's voice in the background, and then Kit said, "Take a breath, Lynette. I'll be fine. Yes, diabetes is dangerous if you don't manage it, but I promise I'm learning lots and have things back under control. These things happen. It sucks, but we aren't kids anymore. We'll all probably face some health issues at one point or another. That's life."

"I suppose it is, but we don't have to like it," Lynette said, hating the news that Kit had a chronic condition that could affect her for the rest of her life.

"I'm sorry, Lynette, but I have to go. I promise to update you after our visit to Iowa. But give Jackie a call. She's got lots going on, too."

After they'd said their goodbyes, she tried Jackie again, but again, no luck.

She'd try her tomorrow.

A vehicle pulled into the drive, and she knew Storm and Shane had returned. She flipped off the air, unplugged her phone, and went out to meet them, careful to lock the door behind her. She didn't need any more surprise guests.

Shane's clothes were dirty, and he looked tired, but he also wore a smile. "We had fun, Lynette. I helped my brother clean up the bushes around our house by the lake. I'm going to go take a shower now, then go to bed. See you tomorrow."

"I'll be up in a minute, Shane," Storm said.

Lynette thought Storm looked even dirtier, and maybe more tired, than Shane. Maybe she shouldn't have kept him up so late last night.

He took a step back when she went in for a hug. "I stink," he said.

But she didn't care. He'd clean up, and they could share a bed again tonight, though their tired muscles probably wouldn't allow for anything other than sleep.

The ongoing reminders of Henry's death, and now the news of Kit's diagnosis, made her even more thankful that Storm was back in her life.

They'd wasted enough time apart.

Chapter Twenty-Two

Jackie pulled into Lynette's driveway, hoping she'd catch her friend at home. She had missed Lynette's call the night before, and instead of calling her back, she'd thought it sounded like more fun to surprise her this morning.

She needed to drive over to Ruby Shores anyhow. Her brother had finally agreed to help her with some maintenance items at their parents' house. Ron wouldn't get in until the next day, but Jackie had felt the need to get out of Minneapolis.

She'd tentatively accepted his apology for making her handle so many things on her own related to their father's estate, but she wasn't completely convinced he'd show. Her brother's memories of Ruby Shores, particularly during his high school years, were more jaded than Jackie's.

During her drive back to Ruby Shores, her mind had bounced between the list of things she and Ron should address and the worry over her daughter's announcement that she would follow her boyfriend across the country. Jackie was terrified that Hailey was making a big mistake, but there was no changing that girl's mind. Her daughter needed to experience life on her own for a while.

"Either it'll work out or she'll come running home to me with her tail between her legs," Jackie said, turning off her car. When she realized she was talking to herself again, she knew coming here had been the right decision. She needed a friend. Maybe Lynette could help her make some decisions she was considering, too.

Jackie didn't feel nearly as decisive as Hailey.

She recognized Storm's truck parked on the street and wondered why he might be in town.

No one was outside, so she made her way to the back door. Before she could knock on the outer screen, the door swung inward and the unmistakable scent of chili wafted out to meet her.

A man she didn't recognize stood behind the mesh screen, smiling at her. "Hello."

"Hi," she said, unsure whether this was Storm's younger brother or the caretaker Lynette mentioned was living here, too. "I was wondering if Lynette was around."

Heavy footsteps approached from what Jackie knew to be the kitchen. Storm appeared, holding a long wooden spoon stained with what looked like tomato sauce, a kitchen towel draped over his shoulder. "Hey there, Jackie. Good to see you. Shane, let her in."

Shane's eyes narrowed. "Is she a stranger?"

Instead of showing irritation at his brother's question, Storm looked impressed. "She is not a stranger, but it's a good question to ask. Jackie is a friend of Lynette's. And of Owen's."

Jackie smiled. "I thought *we* were friends, too, Storm." She let his mention of Owen go without comment.

"And she's a friend of mine," he clarified with a wink.

"If you say so," Shane said.

He held open the screen door so Jackie could come in.

"My show is almost done, so I'm going to go finish watching it before the chili is ready." The younger man gave Jackie a curt nod, then headed down a hallway in the opposite direction from where Storm had come.

"I don't think he likes me much," Jackie said, watching him go. "He was friendly at first, but he seemed disappointed when you introduced me."

Storm pulled the towel off his shoulder and bent down to wipe up a splash of sauce that had dripped onto the light hardwood floor below. A small black cat wove through his booted feet to lick the spot he was trying to clean.

"Scram," he growled, but to no avail. The directive seemed to have zero impact on the cat. After a few more licks, she sauntered off a bit, then sat on her haunches and stared at the two of them.

"Let me guess. Ebony?" Jackie asked, entertained.

"The one and only. And don't let my brother hurt your feelings. He was hoping you were delivering a new book he ordered yesterday. He's not patient. What can I do for you? Lynette didn't mention you were in town."

Jackie took three tentative steps in Ebony's direction and reached down to allow the cat to sniff her fingers. "Lynette doesn't know I'm back in Ruby Shores. I wanted to surprise her. Is she not home?"

Storm raised his eyebrows. "Technically she lives upstairs, and I don't keep track of her comings and goings."

"Oh. I'm sorry. Is there an outside set of stairs or something I can use to get to her door, then?"

It was Storm's turn to smile. "No, the only stairs are inside, but it doesn't matter. I'm just giving you a hard time. She told me she was going to take a well-deserved nap in her little she-shed out there. I don't think she's used to all the testosterone in her house."

"Too much testosterone would exhaust me, too," Jackie said, deciding there was some family resemblance between the two brothers after all: both of their smiles revealed slight dimples in their chins. "But a nap? I've never known Lynette to be a napper. She must not be sleeping well in the attic."

Storm shrugged, then pointed toward the backyard with his spoon. "You'll have to ask *her* about that."

If she'd been talking to anyone other than Storm, she would have sworn he blushed. But she doubted anything embarrassed him. The kitchen must be hot, given the eighty-degree day and the cooking she'd interrupted.

"I'll go wake her up."

"Come back for chili later if you're hungry" was all he said as he turned and clomped back toward the kitchen.

Did the man ever wear anything other than boots?

Jackie let herself out, and when Ebony skirted through her ankles and down the stairs, she let out a yelp.

If Ebony ran off, Lynette wouldn't be happy.

Jackie ran after the feline, but Ebony was too crafty. She disappeared into the rose bushes that ringed a water fountain. Jackie went in after her and cursed when a thorn ripped a narrow scratch all the way down her arm. Something darted off to her left, and she hurried after it, only to see a white and gray bunny bolt around the corner of the garage.

"Ebony!" Jackie hissed. She stayed bent over at the waist, even though she was now outside of the cover of the rose bushes.

"Jackie? What are you doing here? And why are you whisper-yelling at my cat?"

Straightening, Jackie spied Lynette, standing in the doorway of her shed.

Ebony sat at Lynette's feet, staring out at Jackie as if taunting her.

Lynette's mussed curls made it look as if she'd been doing exactly what Storm said.

"Since when do you nap?"

"Since when do you sneak around people's backyards and yell at their cats?" Lynette countered, a teasing note in her voice. "Now, come here and give me a hug. This is a nice surprise! First Renee and Julie yesterday, along with Annie's daughter and family, and now you. And here I thought life in Ruby Shores would be quiet and, frankly, boring."

Given who was making chili in her friend's house right now, Jackie suspected Lynette's life was anything but boring these days.

Lucky girl.

When she reached the lavender-painted door, Lynette caught her up in a quick hug, then waved for her to come inside. "The air is on."

Jackie whistled as she took it all in. Her friend's she-shed was smaller than she'd expected, but also much more opulent. "This is incredible! Wherever did you find that mini pink fridge? And this rug? The windows look like something out of a fairy tale, with their little criss-crossy things, too."

Lynette laughed. She collapsed onto a gorgeous sofa, tossing what looked like a cashmere throw over the arm. More evidence of her nap. The vivid fuchsia of the throw would have rivaled the richest peonies back at Jackie's mother's house.

"That pretty throw might have to come home with me."

"I'll get you one for Christmas," Lynette offered as an alternative to theft. "Help yourself to something cold."

Jackie was more than happy for an excuse to look inside the vintage-inspired refrigerator. "Fancy waters, even!" She removed two, handing one to Lynette before twisting the cap off hers.

Lynette accepted the bottle, then shook her head. "Imagine coming out here to find Shane, Storm's brother, sitting out here by himself, watching the television and drinking one of these."

Jackie sat down on the other end of the couch. "What was he doing in here? This is a *she*-shed! You may need to hang a sign on the door, warning the boys to keep out."

After taking a drink of the water, Lynette sighed. "The poor guy was probably bored in the main house. I try to keep this locked, but I'd forgotten about the board full of keys hanging inside the kitchen. Actually, that's where Shane's previous caregiver also found the keys to Donna's Mini Cooper."

Jackie's jaw dropped. "Something tells me that taking Ms. Donna's pretty little convertible out for a joy ride might have contributed to the 'previous' in *previous caregiver*?"

"And to Shane sneaking in here," Lynette confirmed. "But that mess is for Storm to clean up. I'm so glad to see you! Surprised, but glad. What are you doing back in Ruby Shores again so soon?"

Jackie settled deeper into the sofa, slipped her feet out of her flip-flops, and brought them up to rest on Lynette's fancy tufted ottoman. "Do you mind?"

"Of course not," Lynette said, swinging her own feet up to rest next to her friend's.

"I'm not even sure where to start," Jackie admitted. "The easiest part of your question to answer is that Ron is coming over tomorrow. We have a bunch of things that need fixing over at Mom's, and I finally shamed him into coming home to help. I also really wanted to get out of Minneapolis for a while."

The air-conditioning unit kicked on, adding a low hum to the background of their conversation.

"I remember feeling like that sometimes in New York. Too many people, too much traffic, too much noise . . . just too much of everything."

Jackie considered this. "I understand what you're saying, but in my case, it's almost the opposite. Kit left this morning for Iowa. Did you know they're moving?"

Lynette nodded, but didn't interrupt.

"Hailey is moving to Nevada. I think it's a big mistake. Mack is driving down to Arizona in my mom's car, and something tells me she won't hurry back. And in other big news, I agreed to the sale of my company and decided not to stay on with them as a manager. I'm done working for people, even though I can't afford to be done *working*."

Lynette patted Jackie's hand where it rested on top of the sofa between them. "Minneapolis isn't home for you, is it? Are you thinking about moving back to Chicago? I know you built a nice life for yourself there."

Jackie hadn't considered returning to Chicago. She admitted as much to Lynette. "I'm not sure where home is anymore."

Lynette swirled the water in her green bottle. "Move back to Ruby Shores. This was home for you, once upon a time."

Ruby Shores held more appeal for Jackie than Chicago. She'd been considering it, too. But what would it mean if she were to move back to her hometown at this age? Her parents didn't even live here anymore. Her father was dead and her mother had run away. She had no family in Ruby Shores.

"We could be your family," Lynette said, as if she had read Jackie's mind. "We *are* your family. I'd love it if you lived closer. And I think

Annie could really benefit from having more of us in town. She puts on a good front, but I know she's hurting."

At the mention of Annie, Jackie could have kicked herself. How dare she feel sorry for herself because her daughters were leaving again and Kit was moving away? They all had good reasons to make those changes, even if she didn't agree with all of them. Annie, on the other hand, had lost her husband, and he was never coming back.

"The other night was so fun, having a slumber party at Mom and Dad's," Jackie said. She let her head drop back. Even the ceiling in Lynette's little shed sported fancy details, including a plaster medallion around a light fixture dripping crystals. "You should call this place your mini-château instead of a she-shed."

Lynette laughed. "That sounds fancy."

"This *is* fancy! Just think, if you added a bathroom and a little kitchen, you could practically live out here. Have you ever slept out here overnight?"

"No. But I might try that. I could open the window and fall asleep to the sound of the water fountain."

Jackie noticed the way the crystals above cast tiny prisms of light against the upper walls of the old shed. "I want a mini-château of my own. Maybe Annie would, too. She hates living in that big house by herself now. I know Relic is around this summer, but he'll leave soon."

Lynette tossed her arm across the back of the sofa. The ring on her finger caught Jackie's eye, just as it had done when they'd been hiking in Fiji.

"That's pretty. Where did you get it?"

"From Storm, actually. Believe it or not, I found it in a locked box out here."

"Here?" Jackie struggled to imagine Storm spending time in this fancy little place.

"Well, yes, but before I transformed it from a garden shed. Remember the tarot cards I brought to Whispering Pines? I found them in the same dusty old box."

She explained to Jackie how the box used to belong to Storm's great-grandmother.

Jackie held Lynette's hand and tilted her finger so she could get a better look at the setting. It was simple yet elegant. "Storm gave you a family heirloom. What does *that* mean?"

"Mean?"

She could tell Lynette knew exactly what her question meant, but she was being evasive. "Are you two engaged?"

Lynette snorted. "Me and Storm? That's ridiculous!"

But Jackie didn't think it was a far-fetched question. "Are you sleeping with him?"

"There isn't all that much sleeping, per se."

She slapped the couch. "So *that's* why you needed a nap!"

Lynette shrugged. "What can I say? We aren't as young as we used to be, but that man still makes me feel like no one else ever could."

"But you wouldn't marry him."

Lynette crossed her ankles, and Jackie noticed three silver rings on her friend's toes. "All I'm saying is it's definitely not an engagement ring. In fact, some people might think it's cursed. Storm's grandmother was wearing it when she drowned."

Jackie recoiled. "That's a little morbid."

"It honestly doesn't bother me. At least not much. Before his grandmother wore it as her wedding ring, it belonged to Sybil. Sybil originally owned this place. I knew her when I was a girl, and I really liked her, but you know how it is. She intimidated me a little. If she was still alive, I'd love to sit down and visit with her. According to Donna, she was a fascinating woman. I'm honored that Storm thought to ask me to wear her ring."

Given this backstory, Jackie suspected the ring meant the two were more serious about each other than they might want to admit.

A shrill whistle caught their attention.

"Let me guess," Jackie said. "Storm? He seems like a guy who could whistle loud enough to be heard through closed windows and over the noise of an air-conditioner."

Lynette swung her legs off the ottoman and pushed out of the comfortable sofa. She went to the door and stepped outside. "I'll be right back."

Jackie noticed the little smile on Lynette's face. Her friend was in deep with that man. Again.

While she waited for her to return, Jackie studied the many personal touches and items of comfort around her. There was even a small section of one wall that boasted a shelf full of books. She remembered Lynette saying she wanted something like Renee had in the comfortable little library room at Whispering Pines. That had to have been her inspiration.

She crawled, somewhat clumsily, up from the couch and went over to check Lynette's selection of books. Maybe she could borrow one for a few days. She couldn't remember the last time she'd relaxed with a good book. A scrapbook rested on the top shelf, and she'd just reached for it when her friend returned.

"Don't touch that!" Lynette yelled.

Jackie pulled her hand back. "You scared me!"

"Sorry," Lynette said with a giggle. "I didn't want you to see that until I get our pictures of Fiji in there."

That made the scrapbook irresistible, and Jackie pulled it off the shelf despite Lynette's warning. "Now I *have* to look."

"Fine," Lynette caved. "But grab your shoes, too, and bring it inside. Storm wants to feed us. You can look at it after we're done."

Remembering the delicious smell of chili had Jackie's stomach rumbling with hunger. All she'd eaten was a stale donut with her gas station coffee that morning. She checked her watch. "I didn't realize how long we visited."

Lynette adjusted the thermostat on the wall. The air-conditioner fell silent. "Just think. If you lived here, we could hang out in my mini-château and talk like this all the time."

Jackie had to admit the idea had plenty of appeal.

Jackie and Lynette entered the kitchen.

"Take a seat," Storm said from the stove.

Shane was already at the table, along with another man whose back was to them. The man glanced toward the door, then pushed away from the table and got to his feet.

Owen looked as surprised to see Jackie as she was to see him.

"I didn't know you were back," he said with a broad smile.

"Neither did we, until I caught her crawling through the bushes after my cat," Lynette joked.

Owen's head swung toward Storm. "What is it with these women, always chasing cats around our neighborhood?"

"Damn cats," Storm said, carrying a large steaming kettle to the table.

It occurred to Jackie that Lynette had put Storm up to this when she'd run inside to talk to him. But that was only a few minutes ago, so maybe Jackie was the latecomer to this little get-together and not Owen.

She stepped back to set Lynette's scrapbook on a nearby sideboard. "I'm intruding. I should go. You didn't plan on me for dinner."

"Baloney," Lynette said, grabbing her by the hand and pulling her over to the table. "Look, there are five place settings. Sit here, next to Owen. I always sit at this end of the table."

Shane put his water glass down. "Last night you sat there," he said, and everyone laughed when he pointed to the chair Lynette had pushed Jackie into.

Jackie wasn't dumb. This was all a little too convenient. Not that she minded. It was fun to see Owen again.

Once everyone was at the table, Jackie tasted her chili.

"Storm, this is delicious. It reminds me of my dad's chili." She touched the pendent at her neck, expecting the all-too-familiar ache to bloom in her heart again. Instead, fun memories came to mind, of family game nights and Super Bowl parties, where the celebrations wouldn't have felt complete without a big pot of Glen Turner's chili.

Easy conversation flowed around the table. Owen shared about the success he'd had in selling most of Glen's old tackle. "Swing by sometime, Jackie. I have an envelope of cash for you. Speaking of, Taran, I kept the best pieces for us to buy. Thought you might want to pick some up for yourself."

"I love fishing," Shane said, earning a chuckle out of his big brother.

"We'll come look tomorrow," Storm said. "Thanks for thinking of me."

Lynette cleared her throat. "Speaking of tomorrow, did you guys know the fair is in town? I convinced Storm he should take me up there for greasy fair food and some dancing in the beer gardens. He tried to get me past the bouncers when we were kids, but he wasn't able to get us in."

Storm scooped up a heaping spoonful of chili with a shake of his head. "I can't believe I let you talk me into going to the fair, Lynette."

"Can I come, too?" Shane asked. "I think I like the fair."

"Not this time, bud. I'm taking Lynette out on a proper date. I've arranged for someone to take you to that new movie you've been wanting to see, and then out for ice cream. How does that sound?"

Jackie watched the two men interact, impressed with how Storm clearly cared about his brother. Some men would have shipped him off to a group home years ago. But not Storm.

Lynette turned to Jackie and Owen. "You two should come with us. We could make it a double date."

Jackie's pulse quickened at the suggestion. "But I'm helping Ron at the house tomorrow."

Lynette waved away her excuse. "You've done all the work on that place for months. Your brother is just now stepping in to help? Screw him. The two of you can get some things done during the day, but come evening, get your short shorts and halter top on, tease up your hair, and watch for us to pick you up at seven. We'll pretend it's 1988 again, but this time the bouncers will *have* to let us in."

Jackie never could resist Lynette when she was in a fun mood like this. "Why not? I'm in if you're in, Owen."

He was taking a sip of his beer. He tilted his bottle at her. "I've been in all along. *I* wasn't the one that needed convincing."

Chapter Twenty-Three

J ACKIE FLINCHED. HER TOWEL caught on the scab forming over the scrape she'd earned the day before while chasing Ebony into the rose bushes. Trimming a hedge of lilacs alongside the garage at her folks' house had meant additional slashes to both her forearms. The new scratches were all superficial, but at first glance, she looked like she might have tangled with Lynette's cat—and lost.

She checked the time. At this rate, she'd be late for her first official date with Owen Jameson.

It had been years since she'd spent a full morning and afternoon with her brother, but he still knew her well enough to comment on how jittery she seemed.

Luckily, Ron had dinner plans with his old buddy Bruce. Jackie declined his offer for her to tag along, but she insisted he text her a picture of the man. She knew Kit would get a kick out of seeing the guy she once had a huge crush on, back when they were in high school.

When Jackie mentioned she'd be out late, her brother didn't ask questions. He probably assumed she was doing something with Lynette or Annie. What would her big brother say if she told him about her actual plans for the evening? To Ron, Owen would probably always be his little sister's nerdy sidekick.

But Jackie knew better.

She blasted her wet hair with the blow dryer, then slapped on mascara and a tiny spritz of perfume. It wasn't like she was going out with a stranger. Far from it. Owen had grown up beside her, long before she was even old enough to wear makeup.

God, why am I so nervous?

She'd considered dating him once or twice during high school. If she was honest with herself, she even remembered feeling a little jealous seeing Renee on his arm when the two went to prom together. It was a blind date, and nothing came of it, but still.

Transitioning from platonic friend to boyfriend had always felt too risky for Jackie. In high school, they'd drifted apart, and Owen had never been more than a special friend from her grade school days.

Until now.

She smiled, remembering their winning duet when they'd mimicked the iconic Sonny & Cher. Would she even have remembered that special day if her dad hadn't kept their certificate? Did Owen ever think back to their victory on that fun afternoon of their last day in fifth grade?

Jackie dug through her suitcase, trying to decide what to wear. They were going to the often dusty, always bright and loud county fair. An evening at the fair used to mean a new pair of jeans—Jackie never would have risked shorts on rides where countless people had puked, regardless of what Lynette had said about fair attire—and a cute top. Back then, Jackie wore a size two, and she could rock a new pair of Guess jeans like few others.

She laughed when she pulled out the only pair of jeans she'd packed. The size had an extra one in front of the two, and the built-in comfort stretch usually meant they'd look a little too baggy after an hour of wear.

The mom jeans weren't going to cut it. After tossing them aside, she decided the pretty coral sundress she'd purchased for Fiji but never wore would be the better choice.

It wasn't like they'd be riding the Zipper or the Tilt-A-Whirl.

The short, fluttery sleeves did nothing to camouflage her scraped arms, but it was too hot to wear long sleeves.

The doorbell rang as she struggled to shove a pearl stud through her ear.

When had she gotten so lax on wearing makeup and jewelry? She couldn't remember the last time she'd worn earrings. Her special pendant was the only jewelry she wore anymore.

She found her sandals in the bottom of her suitcase, then hurried to the door.

Owen stood there, his back to her. He wore dark jeans and a simple black shirt.

Was he remembering their early days of friendship, too, as he waited for her on the front porch?

She joined him on the porch, and when he turned to her, she appreciated how his understated clothing complemented his tanned skin, salt-and-pepper hair, and bright blue eyes.

But she worried when he didn't return her smile.

Instead, he studied her face for so long that she held her breath. Was he disappointed in how she looked? His eyes swept down the length of her, but when their eyes met again, her worry evaporated.

"You look stunning," he whispered, extending his hand.

"Oh, stop," she said. "Or don't."

He laughed, and with a slight tug, he brought her closer. Then he stepped closer still, until their bodies nearly touched.

"Jackie, I've waited an incredibly long time to take you out on a date. I admit, the county fair wouldn't have been my first choice. But then I thought back to all the fun we used to have when our moms would drop us off out there in the early afternoon. We always had just enough money to buy a ride pass, have some cotton candy, and play a game or two. They'd pick us up hours later, and no one worried that anything bad could happen to us. Granted, maybe they should have worried a little, but that was a different time. And, if I remember right, I think I'm still one up on you in the water gun race."

Jackie rested both hands on his chest. "You know that's not true! I always beat you twice as often as you beat me! How can you not remember that?"

He captured her hands and held tight. "Maybe you're right."

His eyes wandered down to her lips, and the importance of their long-running competition faded away.

"I remember everything about those days, Jackie," he said, meeting her gaze again. "You made my childhood special. I always felt like the luckiest kid in our class, because you told everyone we were best friends. When did that change? And why?"

Jackie tried to pull back. Her excitement over the upcoming evening plummeted.

He must have read the disappointment in her eyes. "Shit. I'm sorry. I didn't mean to bring that up now. Actually, I never intended to bring it up. You still drive me a little crazy, I guess. Can I kiss you?"

"Kiss me? Why?"

Jackie would have slapped her own forehead at such a stupid response if her hands weren't still stuck in his.

He laughed. "Because if I don't kiss you before we go pick up Storm and Lynette, I won't be able to follow a single string of conversation. I'll be too worried about when, or even if, I'll finally be able to kiss you after waiting for forty years."

She snorted, hating how unladylike it made her sound. "Owen, there is no way you've been waiting forty years to kiss me. Do you mean to tell me you've wanted to kiss me since we were twelve years old?"

He grinned as he nodded, his mouth moving ever closer to hers.

This Owen reminded her of the much younger version of her old friend, the one who loved to tease her.

Had that been twelve-year-old Owen's way of flirting with her, even back then? If so, she'd missed it.

What else had she missed out on?

His grip on her hands loosened, and she pulled one free, wrapping it around to touch the back of his neck and easing her fingers up into his thick hair. He accepted her invitation, finally touching his lips to hers, softly at first, but with a growing pressure that spoke of a man whose almost limitless patience was reaching its end.

They were going to be late for their double date.

"Tell me again why you're driving? I thought Lynette said they'd pick us up," Jackie said. She tried to check her reflection in his side mirror, but with no luck.

"You still look perfect," he said, grinning over at her with a smile that made her cheeks heat.

Her hand went to the hair framing her face. "If Lynette even *suspects* we're fifteen minutes late because we were necking on my mother's porch like a couple of horny teenagers, she'll never let us forget it."

He shrugged. "I don't need Lynette to help me remember that. I used to dream of sitting with you on that porch—*alone*—and doing what we just did . . . and more."

"You better not have been thinking about *more* when we were twelve."

Owen burst out laughing. "I can tell you are a mother to girls. Trust me, twelve-year-old boys think about way more than you can even imagine."

He pulled into Lynette's driveway. Jackie spotted her friend and Storm holding hands by the water fountain.

"They're so cute!"

"Do not let Taran hear you call him *cute*," Owen warned, turning his truck off. "And to answer your earlier question, I don't know why Storm asked me to drive. Not that I mind. Do you want to wait here?"

"Sure," Jackie said. That would give her a second to fix herself up again. Her face had to be red from his stubble.

He was back before she could shove her powder compact back into her purse.

"Guess they're driving separate. You don't mind, do you? Storm decided he needs to have his truck, too. Says he's worried that the woman he hired to keep Shane entertained tonight might be in over her head."

"Why would I mind?" Jackie said.

But it bothered her a little. This was feeling more and more like an actual date all the time.

Why does that make me so nervous?

She'd known Owen for most of her life.

But this was a different Owen, and now they were both experienced, unattached adults.

"Oh, and Lynette is claiming eating too many mini-donuts on an empty stomach will make us too sick to drink beer in the beer gardens, so she wants to grab a decent dinner at some restaurant downtown that used to belong to Kit's aunt. Are you all right with dinner first?"

Jackie sighed. Their friends were up to something. "Lynette wouldn't be drinking beer, no matter how many little donuts she eats. But that's fine. Dinner sounds great."

A civilized dinner for four sounded like the buffer she needed to catch her breath.

Fifteen minutes later, Jackie sipped her white wine while she listened to Owen and Storm debate whether he could have gotten her even more money for her father's old tackle. Owen had sold the last of it to Storm earlier that afternoon.

Jackie shook her head. "No way. Storm, I was so clueless, I was practically *giving* that tackle away at the rummage sale. But Owen and his son stepped in and saved me from being the fool."

"Yeah, if Owen wants to ride to Jackie's rescue, let him," Lynette said, winking at her old flame.

"Jesus, woman, you are exhausting," Storm said, but his smile suggested otherwise.

Jackie searched for a new topic. "Hey, Owen, what's the latest on our summer camp land?"

She immediately realized her slip.

"I meant *your* land, not ours."

"No, it's ours," Lynette corrected her. "And I was hoping we'd talk about this, because something Jackie said yesterday sparked an idea for me."

Jackie tried to think back through everything they'd discussed, but she had no idea where Lynette was going with this.

"But first, tell me you didn't already sell it, Owen," Lynette said.

"The man buys and sells land for a living," Storm said. "If he stands to make enough profit, and he's comfortable with what the buyers intend to use the land for, why shouldn't he sell it?"

Lynette laid her hand on his forearm. "Oh, hush. This is a good idea. Wait and see."

Storm sighed and picked up his whiskey on the rocks. "Sorry, man. I tried."

Owen had opted for a diet soda—the same as Lynette—when they'd ordered their drinks. He took a sip, then shook his head. "I haven't sold the land. I told Jackie I'd talk to her first about it before accepting any offers, and we haven't had that conversation yet. The potential buyers aren't in a hurry. What did you two come up with?"

He was looking at Jackie when he asked.

"Lynette, what did we talk about that gave you an idea?" Jackie said.

Lynette tapped the sides of her soda glass with her fingernails. "Remember when you said you'd love to have a mini-château like mine?"

"What the hell is a mini-château?" Storm asked.

Laughing, Jackie shook her head. "That's just a fancy word I made up for her she-shed. Lynette fixed it up so nice. I'd love to live in something like that—only a little bigger, of course."

Owen helped himself to a piece of bread out of the basket in the middle of the table. "Is your idea to turn the land into some kind of fancy, glamping vacation getaway? I kind of doubt that would work."

This seemed to give Lynette pause. "No, that wasn't what I was thinking . . . but that might be an idea to explore, too."

Storm shook his head, clearly not as intrigued by the idea as Lynette.

"Here's the deal," she said, grabbing a slice of bread, too. "As much as I enjoy having you and Shane in my house, I'm not loving living in my attic. And, as previously noted, my shed isn't big enough to call home. Annie is unhappy in that big house of hers where she raised her family with Henry. Jackie here isn't feeling at home in Minneapolis, either, so I'm trying to convince her to move back here to Ruby Shores."

Owen dropped the butter knife onto the tabletop with a clatter. "Back here?" he asked, looking crestfallen.

His reaction wasn't what Jackie would have hoped for.

"Wait," Lynette ordered. "Please don't interrupt. I've been dying to talk to all of you about my idea. What if you held on to the land, Owen, and developed it yourself? Or maybe you and Storm could work together on it. I'd raise my hand, but I just committed to getting my consulting business off the ground and I don't want to spread myself too thin."

"Develop the land . . . how?" Owen asked, his buttered bread forgotten on his salad plate.

"You'd have to keep the cabins," Jackie interjected.

Lynette squinted her eyes, as if considering this. "I hadn't gotten that far. No. Listen. Here's my idea. What if we built a bunch of cute little cottages near each other, and each of us could live in one? Jackie, remember how we talked about how fun your sleepover was the other night? I agree. It was a blast to sit around and talk for hours, like back in the good old days. But then, when we got too tired, we each had a bed of our own to sleep in. This could be kind of like that. Or like our trip to Whispering Pines, except you wouldn't have to bunk with Kit. Close, so we can be together as much or as little as we like, without being too close. And I'm thinking no kids. Fifty and over, or some such requirement. Jackie, I was even thinking of those darling little cottages at the resort we visited in Fiji. You know, the one where Renee stayed before but they didn't have room this time, so we hung out on the beach? Where the owner's son hit on me?"

That last bit had Storm sitting up straighter in his chair.

"Nothing happened. Don't worry. He was a dweeb," Jackie assured him.

"Well then," he said, as if that made him feel any better.

Jackie smiled. Jealous Storm was kind of cute, but she remembered Owen's warning not to call his big, burly buddy that to his face.

"Remember how we thought the pretty colors of the cottages looked like a kaleidoscope when you put them all together?" Lynette added. "Your land would be the perfect place to build a Midwest version of them. Maybe some of the cottages could be seasonal or temporary rentals. And you could sell some of them. I'd prefer to buy." She sipped her soda before continuing. "Then my imagination really started churning. What do people our age want out of a home? What do we want to do with our time when we aren't working? Travel, maybe? But sometimes we can't because we have animals. Jackie here could offer some kind of pet-sitting business or something."

Storm finished his drink, then shook the ice cubes in his glass. A nearby server approached, thinking he might want a second, but he declined. "Lynette, next you're going to suggest a shuffleboard area and bingo."

She laughed. "No, I'm not envisioning some kind of retirement community, exactly, but it could be a place for people like us to live our best lives before we hit retirement age. There could be HOAs for the cottage owners, to cover things like snow removal and mowing. Things we don't want to worry about anymore."

"That's great, Lynette, and I admit you have me a little curious, but that sounds like lots of ongoing work," Owen said. "I'm not at the point in life where I want to be tied down to something like that."

Lynette chewed and swallowed a bite of bread. "I'm a few steps ahead of you, Owen."

"Welcome to my world, buddy," Storm interjected.

"You'd hire a manager," Lynette continued, ignoring Storm. "Someone to oversee the entire operation. Give her some leeway to figure out what she might do with the cabins that are out there. Handle rentals. Oversee maintenance for the grounds."

Jackie was doing her best to keep up with Lynette. It felt like her friend had an entire pot of cooked noodles in front of her and she was tossing them randomly against the wall to see what might stick. "You said 'her' as if you might already have someone in mind. It better not be me. I know I need to figure out my next career move, but I'm with Owen. That sounds like more than I'd want to take on right now."

Storm took a drink out of Lynette's glass. "Jackie, I thought you had a relatively new business you were running in Minneapolis."

"I did, but I just signed the papers last week to sell it to a larger player in a related, but slightly different, space. I hadn't planned to get out of it, but it was getting hard on my heart. When you're dealing with both dogs and people who are elderly, you can guess what caused most of the churn in my customer base."

"Oh" was all Storm had to stay to that. He clearly hadn't considered that angle before.

"Can we focus here, folks? I'm trying to make a very important pitch to Owen, and you keep straying off course," Lynette said, pulling her glass away from Storm. "My idea for someone who might be interested in something like this is our friend Renee's daughter. Julie! She's helping

Renee run Whispering Pines right now, but that arrangement has some serious drawbacks."

Jackie nodded. "I like Julie. She seems whip smart. Do you think she'd ever move to a place like Ruby Shores?"

"That sounded like a dig on our little town, Jackie."

That wasn't how she'd meant it at all. "Sorry, Lynette, I didn't mean it as a dig. And I guess if Julie lives full-time out at Whispering Pines, Ruby Shores wouldn't seem like too sleepy of a place for her."

"Did you mention any of this to Julie yet? Or to her mother?" Owen asked. Jackie thought he looked skeptical.

"Of course not. I wanted to talk to you first, Owen. And I appreciate any thoughts Jackie and Storm might have, too. This is barely past the brainstorming phase."

Their food arrived, and Lynette sat back to give the server room.

"You said you wanted to brainstorm ideas, Owen," Jackie reminded him.

Owen smiled up at the server after he placed a steak in front of him, then turned back to her. "I guess I did. I just wasn't prepared for the whirlwind that is Lynette."

That raised a laugh around the table, and the four old friends dug in to both their meals and the interesting concepts Lynette had raised.

"I can't believe they ditched us like that," Owen said as he handed Jackie a fluffy cone of cotton candy.

They'd already walked up and back down the midway once. Her feet were getting sore.

A stray piece of the spun sugar floated loose and caught in Owen's hair. Jackie picked it off and popped it into her mouth. "*I* can believe it. In fact, I think that was the plan all along. They've manipulated us, my friend. First the song and dance about coming up here to the fairgrounds and partying like we were back in the eighties. Lynette knew that would pique my interest. Then Storm asking you to drive, too, 'just in case'? They set us up."

Owen shoved his wallet into his back pocket, then helped himself to a strand of cotton candy. "For what?"

Jackie wondered how men could be so obtuse sometimes.

"Storm doesn't do shit like this. He doesn't manipulate. He just tells it to you straight. You don't get any games with him."

She laughed. "That's probably true, but Storm is now part of a couple. And the other half of his couple is used to getting what she wants."

Owen licked his fingers, and she lost her train of thought for a minute.

"What does Lynette want?"

"She wants me to let this happen," Jackie said, thinking out loud but not caring whether Owen heard her.

They were passing by a now deserted booth, and Owen pulled her gently into its shadow. According to the sign hanging across the front of the white pop-up cover, you could get "3 pairs of sunglasses for $9.99" there, but it was late, the display was empty, and no one was paying any attention to Jackie and Owen.

"Why would Lynette care if we finally agreed to . . . I don't know . . . date?"

Jackie loved his hesitation. "You're cute when you're nervous," she said, bopping him on the nose with the cotton candy.

He groaned. "Don't tell me *I'm* cute, either. That doesn't just apply to Storm."

"I disagree." She moved the cone of sticky candy away from his face and behind her back. "You've always been cute. Storm is more the dark, mysterious type."

He reached around her, trying to score another chunk of pink fluff. She held it farther back, and it became a bit of a flirty tickling match.

"Great, you pretty much called me a fluffy little puppy and Storm a bad-ass guard dog."

Jackie gave up and allowed him to tear off another large piece.

She feigned disgust. "And here I was, just about to remind you how much I love dogs. And there is nothing in this world cuter than a puppy. Except maybe you."

She shoved the last of the cotton candy into her mouth, noting the way some strands stuck to her lips. This was getting messy.

He noticed, too, and dropped the wad he'd pulled off onto the grass. One minute she was laughing up at him, and the next he'd pulled her tight against him, and he was doing an admirable job of making sure her lips were free and clear of the sticky strands of candy.

Jackie had no idea how long they stood there in the shadows, kissing each other as if they were the only two people at the fairgrounds. But then a group of kids started calling out that "the old dude should get Grandma a room!" When their jeers penetrated the fog of lust surrounding them, they pulled apart, laughing.

"Did those snot-nosed kids just call me an old dude?" Owen asked, wiping at his mouth with the back of his hand.

Jackie shook her head and laughed even harder. "No. I'm sure they said 'silver fox,' not 'old dude.' But I think they called *me* a grandma, so you should go punch the little shits in the face."

"Nice try on the 'silver fox' line," Owen said, reaching for her hand. "But they got one thing right. We should go. I hate to think of myself as some desperate old dude, groping you in the shadows like a starved teenager."

She entwined her fingers in his. "I think the term we used earlier was 'horny.'"

He laughed. "Don't remind me. Woman, you drive me crazy. I promise that I never usually act like this."

"I'm not complaining," she assured him.

Then the undeniable scent of mini-donuts wafted by them, and she knew she had to have the one thing she'd never been able to deny herself at the fair, even when they'd come here as kids. She tugged Owen along behind her, and he didn't resist.

"Are you taking me to the pot of gold at the end of the rainbow?"

Jackie stopped and glanced back at him. "What are you even talking about?"

He pulled his hand from hers so he could wrap an arm around her shoulders and pull her against his side. Then he pointed to a long line of people up ahead, and the popular food truck they were all visiting on their way out of the gates. The flashing sign above the donut truck boasted a big black cauldron with golden donuts spilling out of the top. A neon rainbow shot out of the middle of the cauldron and up into the night sky.

She laughed, and he dropped a kiss onto her parted lips.

Then he sighed. "Are you really going to make us wait in that line before we can leave?"

She put her arm around his waist, and out of nowhere, a memory of her mother and father at that long-ago Maine beach with their arms around each other flashed into her brain. They'd looked so content in that moment.

It was exactly how she felt with Owen's arm holding her close now.

"We never *ever* left these fairgrounds without donuts. I think it would be bad luck to start now," she said, pointing to the flashing sign above the food truck.

He sighed. "Who am I to push our luck?"

Together they joined the line. It moved faster than she remembered. The people schlepping the donuts were old pros. Maybe they were even the same ones that had served them up bags of greasy, sugary delicious-ness when they were kids.

Once Jackie held a toasty-warm bag in her hand, she allowed Owen to escort her out to the parking lot. But unlike the fair visits of their childhood, he was the one driving her home, and she couldn't wait to see what other surprises the night would hold.

CHAPTER TWENTY-FOUR

J ULIE PULLED INTO A parking lot overlooking a public beach. Crowds dotted the stretch of sand between the vehicles and the shoreline. She crawled out from behind the wheel and scanned the area for a bathroom. Laughter competed with the squawk of seagulls above, and the sun burned hot in the clear blue August sky.

She was still ten minutes from Owen's property where she'd be meeting Lynette and the others, but her bladder needed immediate attention.

The slam of a heavy metal door rang out, and she headed for the concrete brick building at the far end of a wide pathway. Given all the people coming and going from that area, she'd likely find the bathrooms there, and maybe something cold to drink. She'd forgotten her travel mug filled with ice water on her mother's kitchen counter when she'd left Whispering Pines two hours earlier.

The phone call that had proceeded this trip was the only thing she'd been able to think about for the last few days. Lynette's excitement about a tentative project had been palpable, even over the phone. Julie was trying to reserve judgment until talking with Owen in person, and seeing the land in question, but it was hard not to catch Lynette's excitement herself.

Lynette knew of the dilemma Julie found herself in, and she was trying to help her find a way out of it.

Julie loved the energy of this beach, and the lake reminded her of the one that Whispering Pines was on. But she should get back on the road, since she'd hoped to arrive ahead of Lynette so she could look around by herself first.

She'd pinned the location of the camp to Maps in her phone, but Matt had also sketched out a rough guide for her to follow. He'd visited the area once before with Renee, when Kit and Dean got married. Using both resources, she had no trouble finding the way to her mother's old summer camp. There was even a sign, its lettering faded, that marked the turnoff on the main road, but weeds nearly obscured it. She could have easily missed it.

The sign reminded her of the first time she'd traveled the gravel path to Whispering Pines, except this was a paved road. Potholes made for a bumpy last half mile.

Hoping she was in the right place, she parked beside a pickup that might have been around since her mom went to camp here. Julie doubted the truck belonged to Lynette, Owen, or Jackie.

This time when she exited her vehicle, the buzz of a lawn mower greeted her. Fresh-cut grass lay in shallow piles on the ground. It seemed as if too much time had passed between cuttings. She doubted that whoever was mowing would object to her having a look around.

A split-rail fence delineated a circular area that might have once been a tended flower garden, but any remaining perennials and wildflowers had to fight for space against choking weeds.

A nasty, grinding sound caught her attention, and the buzz of the mower cut off.

"Someone ran over something they weren't supposed to," Julie said, feeling a pang of sympathy for the person mowing. She'd run over her share of things that mower blades weren't built to handle, setting her back hours while doing lawn care at Whispering Pines.

From her position by the fence, she could spy a variety of old buildings. A few log cabins dotted the perimeter, while a yellow clapboard structure looked like it might have served as an office at one time.

"Can I help you?"

Julie jumped. The male voice rang out from somewhere near the closest cabin. She spun around to see a guy walking toward her. He'd hacked the sleeves of his T-shirt away, and sweat stained the fabric nearest his underarms. Large headphones hung around his neck. He was pulling off a pair of gloves. Dark glasses hid his eyes, but she could tell he'd been speaking to her.

He'd obviously been on the mower, so he mustn't be a random stranger wandering the property.

She was the wandering stranger.

Julie raised a hand in greeting. "Hello. I'm here to meet Owen Jameson, the owner of this place. I think Lynette and Jackie, friends of mine, are supposed to be with him. But I'm a little early."

He tucked his gloves into the front pockets of his threadbare jeans, then pushed his glasses up, exposing a ring of dirt above and below his eyes.

Despite the dirt, there was something arresting about the man. She could see now that he might be older than she was, but not by much.

He nodded, but she couldn't tell if he'd been expecting her today, too. "I'm Adam. We should have mowed out here last week, but we didn't, and now I'm paying the price. It's always harder when this place gets away from me. You probably heard me hit something with the mower just now. You'd think I'd learn."

"What did you hit?" she asked. "I mow as part of my job, too, and the worst thing I ever ran over was a metal dog leash. It wrapped tight around the axle and gouged one blade beyond repair."

He winced. "Ouch. I hit the frigging base of what I think was once a flag pole. And I'm not the first one to do it. My brother warned me it was there, but I got so engrossed in my book, I got distracted."

It surprised her when he pointed to the headphones. She'd imagined him listening to hard rock or something. He pulled a phone from his back pocket, then glanced her way. "What time did you say you were meeting them?"

She hadn't said, but the guy seemed relatively harmless. "At two."

"Huh. It's only one thirty. Why'd you get here so early?"

His question irritated her. Like it was any of his business.

"Being prompt is important. I wanted a cushion in case I had trouble finding it."

He nodded, as if finding her answer satisfactory.

"Do you know Owen?"

He put his sunglasses back down again. "Sure. Why would I be mowing his place if I didn't know him? He mentioned having a prospective buyer for this place. You look too young to be the interested party."

So much for being friendly. She decided he was definitely being rude now. Did he have a problem with the possibility of Owen selling? If she was ever in charge of this community-type place Lynette had explained to her and this guy worked for her, she wasn't sure she'd be able to keep someone like him on. Sure, he looked like he might be handsome underneath the dirt and sweat, but his attitude grated on her nerves.

Deciding his assumption as to her approximate age didn't deserve a response, she spun away with nothing more than a quick wave and a suggestion he go fix his mower. As tempted as she was to turn around to see if he'd followed her instructions, she kept her eyes on the yellow building. If it was locked, she could at least look through the windows while she waited for the others.

But the shuffle of footsteps coming up beside her meant he didn't want to let her roam around on her own.

"Why don't I show you what's here while you wait? That'll save you all some time," the man who'd said his name was Adam suggested, walking alongside her now.

"That isn't necessary. I can get a first look at things on my own."

She sensed his shrug as he pulled up. "Fine," he said. "Have a look around. But keep an eye out for the momma bear and cub that I noticed when I drove in an hour ago."

He spun away from her this time, and she couldn't quite decide if he was serious or not as she watched him retreat.

"Really?" she yelled after him, hating herself for seeking clarification. But the headphones were already back in place, and she was on her own again, like it or not.

The front door to the yellow building was locked, so she wandered around it, peeking in through the windows. It looked mostly empty, except for a desk and one lone chair in the middle of the room that she could see through the glass.

A crunch of tires signaled another arrival, and she hoped it was Lynette and Jackie. She also hoped Owen was friendlier than the guy he'd hired to mow. Their brief encounters at Whispering Pines the previous summer hadn't given her much of a chance to get to know him.

She circled around to the front of the yellow building, then waved when she recognized Lynette.

"You're early!" Lynette hollered in her direction.

Julie jogged back to where she'd parked, careful to watch her step so she didn't fall and make a fool of herself. "So are you guys," she said. She slowed as she got close. Running up to possible future employers wasn't the professional image she'd hoped to portray.

When Lynette grabbed her into an exuberant hug, she understood this wasn't likely to be a formal interview.

"Lynette, can't you see you're embarrassing the poor girl?" Owen said, stepping forward after shutting his car door. "You'll have to excuse her. She's convinced she's come up with the perfect game plan for this place, and assures me you'd be the perfect person to run it if we can make the various pieces fit."

Julie attempted to smooth down her hair after stepping away from Lynette, but a strand of it had caught in the bangles around Lynette's wrist.

Owen looked hesitant to help, so Jackie stepped forward with a laugh. "For God's sake, Lynette. Chill."

Once free, Julie pointed at her car. "I brought a résumé along. Would you like to see it?"

Owen opened his mouth to respond, but Lynette waved away her suggestion. "Give him one before you leave, if you like. But it isn't necessary. I'll vouch for you."

With that, Lynette held out an arm, and Julie could see she would have to allow this vivacious woman to show her around. She wasn't as easy to resist as Adam.

A phone rang, and Jackie stepped away. "You guys start without me. I need to take this."

Lynette hardly acknowledged her friend, instead hauling Julie by the arm toward the first cabin—the cabin where she feared Adam was probably still trying to get his lawn mower started again.

Sure enough, as they rounded the corner, there he was, down on his haunches, working on the mower.

"What did you hit this time, son?"

Adam glanced their way, then tossed the tool in his hand to the ground in what looked like frustration. "I told you to cut that old pole down flush to the ground, but obviously that didn't happen."

Julie pulled her arm out of Lynette's, watching the men with worry. Had Owen meant "son" in a literal sense, or as more of a broad term older men sometimes used to address younger, less experienced men?

Lynette rested her hands on her hips. "Adam, you are a doctor, for crying out loud. Why aren't you wearing gloves while you work around sharp blades? And why, by the way, are you even out here mowing? Are those school loans too much to cover on your doctor's salary?"

"Resident salary," Owen corrected her. "And my son here has decided he needs the tax break from home ownership, so he's doing what he can to save up and buy me out."

Adam *was* his son. Why hadn't he bothered to mention that fact when Julie asked him if he knew Owen?

As if he could read her mind, Adam shot her an apologetic smile. Her stomach did a funny little roll, and she worried the leftover pizza she'd inhaled for breakfast might have been past its prime.

Lynette was staring at Owen. "What do you mean, buy you out? Really, Owen, if you already had other plans for this place, why didn't you just say so? I'd hate it if we wasted Julie's time asking her to drive all the way over here on her day off."

Owen rolled his eyes, and Julie noticed for the first time how much Adam looked like this man. How had she missed it?

"He couldn't afford to buy me out of *this*," Owen said, gesturing around them. "He wants my house. The house where I grew up, and where we stay when we're in town these days."

Lynette's shoulders visibly relaxed. "Owen, I'm familiar with your house. We're practically neighbors, after all. Well, that's a relief. I was worried for a minute there. But, wait . . . if Adam buys your house, where will you live? And does Jackie know?"

Julie wasn't sure why Jackie would care, but the question seemed to put Owen on edge. He glanced over his shoulder, but Jackie must have still been on the phone, back by the cars.

"She *doesn't* know, does she?" Lynette went on. "I swear to God, Owen, if you break her heart after all the effort I put in to getting the two of you together, I'll never forgive you."

Adam sat down on the quiet lawn mower, looking surprised. "I *knew* there had to be some other reason you were so adamant about going to that rummage sale at Jackie's parents'. It's not like you make a habit of helping women sell off their fathers' estates, but you made sure no one took advantage of her on the tackle. Now it's all making sense. Speaking of, it's too bad Kit drove such a hard bargain on that lawn mower. We should have paid her what she wanted for it, since this thing might be toast."

Owen raised one hand, and both Lynette and Adam fell silent. Even Julie could sense the change in him. "That's enough out of both of you. Yes, Adam, Jackie and I are dating now. No, Lynette, I haven't mentioned to Jackie the possibility of selling my house. Not yet. Please let me do that. I don't want you interfering any more."

Lynette seemed to wipe all emotion from her expression, though Julie suspected a giggle was fighting to get out. "Yes, sir. My lips are sealed."

Jackie rounded the corner, apologizing for needing to take the call. "What did I miss?" she asked Owen as she reached his side.

"Nothing important," he said, glancing quickly at Lynette.

She coughed, and Julie was sure Lynette was close to losing control of her emotions.

"Julie, are you ready for the grand tour?" Owen said. "Adam, you're welcome to join us and hear all about Lynette's wild ideas, if you like. I hadn't found time to update you before today, so I'm sorry if this is all coming as a surprise."

Julie looked over at Adam, expecting him to be looking at his father, but their gazes snagged. She widened her eyes at him, wondering whether he caught her silent question. He couldn't have just told her who he was?

And he's a *doctor*?

For the first part of Owen's tour, as Lynette shared her vision, Julie felt torn between listening to them and sneaking glances at Adam, who'd left the mowing for another day and fallen in behind them. But eventually, her intrigue around the various things Lynette mentioned as possibilities captured her complete attention.

After showing her each log cabin, the nearby lake and waterfall, the lodge where her mother and friends had spent so much time during their summer camp days, and the building she'd correctly guessed was the office, Owen led them over to the undeveloped portion of his land.

As they stood before a section of land where Lynette and Jackie discussed matching cottages, Julie inhaled deeply, trying to take it all in. The familiar scent of pine made her think of home, but, surprisingly, none of this caused her to worry about moving on from Whispering Pines.

Instead, she was seeing how she could use the skills she'd learned while helping her mother reopen their family resort as a jumping-off point for what Owen and the others might create here.

Thanks to Lynette, who'd already helped her mother so much, Julie might get the chance to be part of this, too.

As if Jackie could somehow follow Julie's train of thought, she put a comforting arm around her shoulders, leaning in close. "You can see it, too, can't you?"

Julie studied the stretch of land before them, then nodded. "I think I can, and I want to be part of it."

Their brainstorming continued until Julie felt nearly faint with hunger. It was getting late in the day.

Jackie captured Owen's hand while Lynette talked on about how they should reach out to their old friend Wendy to see if she'd ever be interested in offering art classes out of a cabin here. "I'm sorry to interrupt, Lynette, and I agree we should keep Wendy in mind, but I think we could all use some food. By the time we're done eating, Julie probably won't want to drive home in the dark. If you'd like, Julie, you could crash at my mom's place. I'm staying there while I'm in town. You can drive home in the morning."

Julie felt torn. Did Jackie really want a spur-of-the-moment overnight guest, or was she just being nice?

"That's probably a good idea. The deer make the roads around here dangerous at dusk," Adam said.

Jackie nodded, as if that decided it.

Julie smiled. "You know, Jackie, you remind me of my mother. I can take care of myself, and I don't want to impose."

Adam shook his head. "It's better to be safe."

"Would you like to get cleaned up and join us for dinner somewhere, Adam?" Lynette asked.

He checked the time on his phone, much as he'd done earlier when Julie first arrived. "I'd love to, but I have a shift that starts at ten tonight. I should probably get home and take a nap after I shower. Dad, what should I do with the mower? I'd need a hand to get it onto that old trailer if you want me to haul it in to the repair shop."

Owen shook his head. "If you can limp it into the equipment shed, I'll deal with it tomorrow."

Adam said his goodbyes, and Julie had to admit she felt a touch of disappointment when he didn't give her any extra attention.

Lynette offered to ride back to town with Julie, and they arranged a restaurant where they'd meet. Throughout the drive and the lengthy dinner, they continued to talk possibilities and opportunities.

Julie wasn't sure what to think of Owen. He was obviously entertaining many of the ideas Lynette and Jackie discussed, but he seemed slightly reserved, as if he was still trying to decide whether to go this route. Adam had mentioned something about a potential buyer, and she knew selling would be a simpler route for Owen to take.

But every once in a while she'd catch the way he looked at Jackie, and her womanly heart suspected that he would ultimately do whatever would make Jackie the happiest.

It was the same way Matt often looked at her mother.

Julie hoped she'd find that kind of love someday, too. But for now she had a career to focus on.

By the time the sun had set and Jackie was showing her the spare room she could sleep in, Julie was still surprisingly awake. Jackie didn't look tired, either.

"Are you all talked out yet?" Julie asked, unsure whether her host might be ready to turn in for the night.

"Hardly. That darn Lynette has my head spinning. You, too?"

Julie laughed. "Like a top. What if we grabbed something to drink and sat out on the porch? We could visit about something other than business, too."

"I'd like that."

Jackie's dog wandered up and nuzzled Julie's hand. Their own dog was basically living at her grandparents' house these days, and she missed having Molly around.

"And can Nikki join us?"

Jackie laughed. "Just try to stop her. I'm going to change into something more comfortable. Would you like some wine? I think there's a bottle of red in the kitchen."

Red wine sounded awful to Julie. "It's getting late. I could get us ice waters instead, if you like?"

"I like," Jackie said, leaving her to change.

Minutes later, the two sat on the front porch in semi-darkness. What shone through the living room window provided enough light, and Nikki sat on the floor next to Julie. The dog's tongue hung out of the side of her mouth in ecstasy whenever Julie rubbed the top of her head.

Jackie grinned. "Careful, or she'll sneak into your backseat when you leave in the morning."

"How are Annie and Kit doing?" Julie asked. She felt like she'd gotten to know all of her mom's old friends a little during their visit out to

Whispering Pines. "I can't imagine how Annie is coping."

Jackie took a long drink of her water, then relaxed back against the wicker sofa. "Annie is doing all right. It's obviously hard for her, and it'll be worse when Relic leaves again for college. As we mentioned, we haven't talked to her yet about whether she might be interested in a cottage, but if we get past the talking stage and decide to actually move ahead, she'll be the first one we talk to."

Julie agreed a fresh start in a new home might be healthy for Annie. "And Kit?"

"Believe it or not, Kit is moving to Iowa."

Julie listened with interest, then felt a twinge of sadness when Jackie mentioned Kit's diabetes diagnosis.

Eventually, when they'd exhausted their discussions about Annie and Kit, Jackie cleared her throat. "I just realized we haven't talked about whether your mom might ever be interested in a cottage. She is, after all, one of the Kaleidoscope Girls. I hate when she sometimes feels left out."

The thought had already occurred to Julie, but she doubted a move like that would ever work for Renee. "Probably not, given her ties to Whispering Pines, and Matt's job. But . . . and I don't mean to overstep . . . if I managed the project and lived on-site, she could stay with me anytime. That way, she could still feel like a part of it all."

"Oh, I like that idea," Jackie agreed. Nikki whined, and she let her dog out to go to the bathroom. "And who knows? Maybe Kit would want to rent a cottage for a few weeks each summer. Given their big move to Iowa, she probably couldn't buy here, too, but we'd talk to her about it."

"If you buy one, would there be room for your daughters?" Julie asked, thinking back to the twins she'd spent time with at Annie's house after Henry's funeral.

Jackie sighed. "I'd be sure to always have a room for them. I'd maybe even build a three-bedroom cottage. But they both have other plans these days. Mack drove my mother's car down to her in Arizona, and for now, she's job searching down there. I'm not sure if she'll stay, but she might. And Hailey followed her darn boyfriend across the country."

Nikki came back in and laid down near Julie again, then rolled over so she could scratch her belly. The dog had a filthy yellow tennis ball in her mouth. She must have found it in the grass. Jackie just shook her head.

"You don't like Hailey's boyfriend?" Julie asked.

Jackie considered the question for a moment, then shook her head. "It's not that I don't like him. I just don't think either of them is ready for the level of commitment it takes to live together."

Julie thought she understood that. "Maybe it'll help if they aren't around other people they know. If they only have each other to rely on, their relationship could grow."

Jackie slapped her thigh, and Nikki got to her feet. "Time will tell."

"And if it doesn't work out and she comes home, something tells me Colton would be happy to nurse her broken heart."

But the moment Julie saw the blank look on Jackie's face, she knew she'd said too much.

"Wait. What do you mean? Did Colton ask Hailey out? If he did, she never told me," Jackie said, sounding hurt. "After Henry's funeral, when we were all at Annie's, Hailey said something about *Mack* having a thing for Colton."

Julie shook her head. "That was just me speculating. I thought he acted interested in Hailey, but he probably knows she's dating someone. I need to quit talking so much. To be honest, I wasn't very nice to Owen's son today, before you got out there. I keep getting myself in trouble."

Jackie had stood as if to go to bed, but she dropped back onto the couch. "I'm surprised you didn't find Adam intriguing. I mean, he looks so much like Owen, and he's a doctor."

Julie laughed. "I thought he was a hired hand, taking care of the grounds out there, and doing a poor job at that. He didn't mention being Owen's son when I asked him if he knew the owner. I thought he was rude. But maybe I misjudged him."

"It can take a little while to warm up to the Jameson boys. My friends tried to get me to date Owen when we were kids, but he was firmly in the friend zone back then. The first time I ever saw him in a different light, actually, was when he took your mom to prom. I might have even been the tiniest bit jealous. But then came graduation, and we all headed off in different directions. We didn't have our first date until a couple weeks ago, and even though it's still really new, no one has ever made me feel like he does." She scoffed. "It only took us forty years to get to this stage."

Jackie stood again, not bothering to hide her next yawn. "I'm going to call it a night, but I just remembered something. When I was going through my dad's things, I found some pictures from our senior prom. I pulled a couple out for your mom, and Lynette was supposed to bring them to Whispering Pines to give to her, but she forgot them here. Will you take them to her?"

"I'd love to!" Julie said. She picked up both of their water glasses to take inside. "I remember Mom mentioning a prom night way back when, but I've never seen any pictures. I'd love to see the dresses you all wore."

Jackie held the door as Julie juggled the glasses, her cell phone, and Nikki's slobbery ball. "Well, it probably won't surprise you to hear that we tried to all wear bright colors, because we very much wanted to look like the inside of a kaleidoscope when we danced together on the dance floor."

The ball slipped from Julie's fingers, and Nikki bounded after it. "Of course you did," she said with a laugh. "Now I'm going to go try to sleep, but I'm sure I'll lay there and stare at the ceiling, trying to figure out the best way to get all of you Kaleidoscope Girls your own pretty little cottages, all in a row."

Chapter Twenty-Five

LYNETTE TOSSED A THIRD and a fourth dress onto her mussed comforter, worried she'd have nothing appropriate to wear to Michael's wedding the next day. Back when she was running her business and she needed to dress up for an event, all she had to do was walk down to the sample room. She would always find something stunning. But since those days were in her past, and she'd procrastinated on picking up something new for the occasion, one of these would have to do.

Why was it so hot? She scooped her silver mass of hair up onto the top of her head, secured it with an old-fashioned rubber band because it was the only thing handy, then pulled an ice-blue silk scarf from the top drawer of a lingerie chest she'd found in her attic.

She wrapped the silk around the topknot to keep her hair out of the way and slipped out of the pink terry-cloth robe Donna had left behind. The goal was to never have anyone see her wearing the robe, but it was too comfortable to stow away.

The breeze from the ceiling fan brought relief to her flushed, heated skin as she rummaged through other drawers in the chest for a proper bra and panties to wear under a dress. The shapewear in the bottom drawer would have made the dresses fit better, but Lynette couldn't imagine stuffing herself into any of it.

Tomorrow's weather forecast called for sun and eighty degrees. Shapewear was out of the question.

Instead, she pulled on an ivory bra-and-panties set that would provide her with enough support while still helping her feel pretty. If Storm was the one taking her to Michael's wedding, she'd have opted for the sexy black set he'd gifted her as part of her birthday present. But she'd be going with Annie, and her sole job would be to see that her friend enjoyed the day.

Annie swore she was happy for Michael, but Lynette couldn't help but wonder if there was still unfinished business between the two of them. How could there not be? He was her ex-husband and the father to two of her three kids.

But Annie's Henry had only been gone for two months. It was much too soon for her friend to move on already.

At the very least, she hoped Annie had a knock-out dress to wear for the event—and thankfully she wouldn't still have that orange cast on her wrist.

Which brought Lynette back to her own selection of dresses, fanned out across her bed. The little black dress was one of her go-to outfits, but it reminded her a little too much of all the black attire they'd recently worn to Henry's funeral.

The black one went back into the closet.

Lynette fingered the glittery red fabric of the dress she'd worn to her old company's New Year's Eve party when she'd been back in New York for her consulting gig. She knew the rich color provided an eye-catching contrast to her silvery hair, but it seemed a bit much for a summer wedding. Someone had also told her once that wearing red to a wedding was insensitive, as the bold color might draw attention away from the bride.

That left the much more subdued pink wrap dress, or the ruffle-tiered halter neck number in fern green. Both were lightweight chiffon.

She picked up the pink one and slipped it over her shoulders, wrapping the belt around her waist. The style resulted in a plunging neckline, and as she checked her reflection in the full-length mirror in the corner, she worried it might be too revealing.

Someone tapped on her door, surprising her.

"Lynette, are you home?" Storm's voice came through the closed door.

She glanced around her messy attic space. She hadn't been expecting any company. Not that Storm would even notice.

"Hi!" she greeted him as she pulled the door open. "I didn't think you'd be around today."

When his mouth tilted up on one side in that half smile that always kicked her pulse up a notch or two, she almost wished he'd interrupted her while she tried on the sexier, red dress. He didn't seem to mind, though. His gaze traveled down her front, and he let out a little whistle of appreciation.

"Where are you off to in *this*?" he asked, stepping into her apartment. He reached around to place his hand on the small of her back and pull her closer. "Because wherever you are going, I want to come, too, so no one else gets the chance to try this."

Her breath hitched when he ran the fingers of his free hand from her collarbone down to the place where the two halves of the bodice came together between her breasts.

She captured his fingers in hers. "What makes you think I'd let anyone else touch me like that?"

His eyes darkened, then narrowed, and he dipped his head toward her. "That's a relief," he said, brushing a light kiss against her lips. The hand on her back, however, pulled her ever tighter against him.

He straightened slightly and noticed the second dress on her bed. "If you aren't wearing this out with me, I might like that one better. It isn't as revealing."

"Why, Taran Gage, I never would have considered you the jealous type," Lynette teased, enjoying the warm strength of his arm around her and the way their bodies so easily molded against each other.

"Then you don't know me very well," he said, dropping another light kiss on her—this one in the valley between her breasts.

Lynette was afraid he was right. She pulled away, and he didn't resist. "You're probably right. We don't know each other very well. But I'm having fun getting to know you again."

He grinned, then stepped over to her bed and the other dress. "Seriously, what are you getting dressed up for? I was hoping to take you for a drive this afternoon."

Lynette went back to the mirror to check her reflection again. "I need to figure out what to wear tomorrow. I'm going to a wedding with Annie. Her ex is getting married."

He walked back over to stand behind her. He stood close enough that she could feel the heat from his body, but he didn't actually touch her again. "In that case, since you're going out with Annie, wear this one. It hugs you in all the right places. It looks pretty on you. But I only have one request."

As if he couldn't quite resist touching her, his fingers found the knot holding the blue silk around her hair. He loosened it, then slowly wrapped the length of icy-blue fabric around his wrist as it slid from her hair.

Lynette couldn't understand how such a simple act could bring a flush of color to the skin across her chest. She imagined how the satin-smooth fabric of the scarf would feel against her naked skin.

"Are you going to grant me my wish, Lynette?" he whispered.

She gave her head a little shake, trying to pay attention to what he was saying instead of how what he was doing with his hands was making her feel. "What's your request?"

"That you leave your door unlocked when you return from the wedding and wait for me in your bed wearing nothing but this blue silk scarf."

When he tickled the swell of her breasts with the tail of the scarf, she shivered.

A door slammed on the floor below them, and Storm dropped his hand, allowing the silk to slide off his wrist and pool onto the floor. "Damn, woman, you make me forget myself. I came up here to see if you wanted to go get ice cream and go for a drive, and the next thing I know, I'm tempted to scoop you up and toss you onto that bed."

She loved that she enticed him like that. No other man had ever made her feel as desirable as Storm always did. Twirling from side to side so her dress swished around her thighs, she grinned at him. "I'm always a sucker for ice cream. But only if it's coconut flavor."

He grimaced. "If that's what it takes. Now, come on. We'll sneak out of here before Shane catches us and insists we bring him with, and once we get you that disgusting ice cream, we can swing by that land of Owen's that you can't seem to stop talking about. I'd like to see for myself what has you so excited."

"Why don't you bring Shane along, too?" Lynette suggested as she loosened the belt on her dress. "That man loves his ice cream."

"He does," Storm said. "But I've narrowed down the list of potential new caregivers for my brother to two. One is here now, and I'd like to give them some space to see how they get along."

Lynette slipped the pink dress off, and pretended not to hear him suck in a breath as she went to her closet to hang it back up, wearing nothing but the delicate ivory lingerie. Then she picked up the halter-style dress, purposefully brushing against him ever so slightly on her way back to the closet. Once both dresses were hanging back up, she dipped down gracefully to pick up the scarf from the floor.

"You are *killing* me here, you know," he hissed, his gaze never leaving her.

"Good," she said, dropping the scarf onto her pillow as a silent promise to grant his wish the following evening. "Now, if we're going out to the old summer camp, I'm afraid I'm going to have to slip into something a little more practical than this."

She tried to pass by him again to retrieve a pair of capris and a short-sleeved shirt from the laundry basket of clean clothes on a nearby chair, but this time he didn't let her by. Instead, he wrapped both arms around her waist and walked her back slowly until the wall beside the door got in the way. His kiss wasn't gentle, though he still kept it brief.

When he pulled away, Lynette delighted in the short gulps of air he took, as if fighting for control.

"Get dressed," he ordered, one hand on the doorknob. "I'll meet you at my truck in five minutes."

When he was gone, Lynette skipped back over to her bed, turned around, and fell onto it, laughing as she gazed upon the dingy, dropped ceiling. Time with Storm always made her feel young and desirable again.

What more could a woman want?

———❦———

Lynette climbed out of Storm's truck and slammed the door, careful not to knock off the extra scoop of coconut ice cream from the top of her sugar cone. The cloud of dust his tires stirred up as they'd arrived at her old summer camp hung just above their heads in the still air. She held her cone away from the haze.

"Feels like rain," Storm said, coming around the front of the truck to stand beside her. "We could sure use some. It's dry."

She nodded. A drip of melting ice cream trailed down her knuckles, and she did her best to lick up the mess. "And hot. But I spent countless hot days and nights out here as a kid. Want some?"

The look he gave her when he pushed his sunglasses to the top of his head made her laugh. "*Ice cream*, Storm. Ice cream. Try this. I love the coconut flavor because it reminds me of some of my travels."

He looked skeptical, but he bent down and licked her cone. After a beat, he sighed. "Fine. I'll admit it isn't as bad as I'd imagined."

Lynette stretched up to steal a quick kiss from him. When she playfully licked at his lips, the lingering taste of coconut made her imagine traveling somewhere tropical with this man.

He let her have her fun, then dropped an arm over her shoulders. "You better show me around this place before I forget why we came out here."

She nodded and took a couple steps, then pulled up. "Did you grab Owen's keys? I think I left them in the cupholder."

He dug in a pocket, then pulled out a ring of keys and shook them. "Got 'em. Hey, it looked like you were giving Owen a piece of your mind back there at his house when we swung by for these. What was all that about?"

Lynette snagged the keys from his finger and resumed walking toward a nearby cabin. "He still hasn't told Jackie that he's considering selling his house to his son, Adam. This is just a second home for him, and he has another place out East. I worry that he'll take off about the time Jackie finally moves back here to Ruby Shores, and history will just keep repeating itself."

"What history?" he asked, keeping in step with her.

"Storm, don't pretend that those two haven't been dancing around each other like shy little teenagers for as long as you've known them. We're all convinced that Owen has had a thing for Jackie since we were kids, but she's always ignored us whenever we brought it up."

Storm removed his arm from her shoulders when they reached the first cabin. "Want me to unlock it so you don't get melted ice cream all over everything?"

"Sure," she said, handing him back the keys.

"What is it with women? Always meddling in everyone else's business. It's so much easier to not get involved." He had to finagle the lock, but it finally snapped open. He swung the door wide and motioned for Lynette to enter ahead of him. "Sure, I'll admit Owen used to have a thing for Jackie."

"Used to?" Lynette said, frowning back at him.

Once they were both inside, he pulled the door shut. "You aren't going to stay out of it, are you?"

She popped the last of her cone into her mouth and shook her head, but she couldn't speak again until she'd chewed and swallowed. "What kind of friend would I be if I let those two keep missing out on at least *trying* to find out if there is something special between them?"

He wiped something from the side of her mouth. "The kind that doesn't meddle."

She made a scoffing sound. "That's not how female friendships work."

He took off his sunglasses and walked the perimeter of the empty cabin. "Well, that's how we men stay friends: by staying out of each other's business. Tell me about this place. Is this the cabin you slept in as a kid at summer camp?"

She shook her head. "Not this one. We were in Cabin 7. I think this was Cabin 8. My friend Wendy's sister was the counselor over this one. Her name is Stella."

Storm unlocked one of the four windows and slid it open. A chunk of plaster broke off and fell to the floor. "Does your grand plan call for knocking these older cabins down, or do you have some ideas about how to use them again? Because they don't seem to be in too tough of shape structurally, aside from some chinking that's long overdue."

"Chinking?" Lynette laughed. "What's that mean?"

Storm picked up the piece of plaster from the floor. "It just means fixing and replacing this material between the logs where there is obvious wear and tear."

"That's good to hear. Because I hope to save these old cabins. These little buildings were an integral part of so many kids' childhoods. We'd like to see if maybe we could use them for seasonal things, like art classes for kids in the summer, or countless other little businesses. It would take some work, but I think we could turn this into something real again."

Storm's phone rang, and he pulled it out of the pocket of his jeans. He held up one finger, then stepped back outside. Through the screen, Lynette could hear his end of the conversation, and she guessed it was

Shane's caregiver calling to check in. She closed and locked the window, then followed Storm back outside, locking the door behind her. She wandered slowly toward the next area she wanted to show him while he finished up on the phone.

When he caught up to her again, he captured her hand in his.

"Everything all right at home?" she asked.

He nodded. "Sounds that way. Show me more. Because I'm intrigued. I like this place. The energy. It's good."

Lynette squeezed his fingers. "Do you really believe a place can have an energy to it? Because I do. I think that's why Jackie was so quick to loop us all in when Owen mentioned selling it. We'd hate for this land to be turned into just any other typical subdivision. It's special, and we hope to help keep it that way."

"Yeah, sure, most places have an energy to them. Sometimes it's promising. Other times, it practically repels you. In fact, those kinds of feelings helped guide both me and Owen back when we were investing in properties together. It almost always paid off to note that first gut feeling we got when we visited a place."

She nodded as she continued to walk him around the property, pointing out different areas where she and the other women envisioned various things.

After she'd pulled him all around and talked his ear off for nearly an hour, she noticed the sweat stains down the back of his shirt and the flush to his face. In her excitement, she'd forgotten all about the heat, but he looked on the verge of heatstroke. It didn't help that he wore long, dark jeans and a black T-shirt.

Then she had an idea.

"I have one more thing I want to show you," she said, tugging him toward the lake.

He resisted, shaking his head. "Can it wait? I need a cold shower. My head is throbbing. I know how excited you are, and I appreciate you showing me all of this, but it must be pushing ninety out here. Aren't you hot?"

She pulled harder at his hand. "I'm hot, but I know how to fix it. I promise. Do you trust me?"

It didn't matter how hard she pulled. If he didn't want to follow her, there was nothing she could do about it. He was too big and too strong.

But she also knew it wouldn't be hard to convince him. She glanced around, already sure they were completely alone but confirming it one last time. Then she dropped his hand and pulled her blouse over her head.

"What the hell are you doing, Lynette? Someone might see you."

She took three steps backward, moving away from him and toward the relief she knew to be just down the walking path behind them. She flicked open the button to her shin-length cotton pants, knowing it was the easiest way to seal the deal. Then she spun around and headed for the water, never bothering to look behind her to make sure he followed.

"Who knew you'd turn into an old prude, Taran Gage?"

Before long, she could hear the telltale splashing of water. The lake was just beyond the trees ahead, and the waterfall wasn't far beyond that. Storm said nothing, but she could hear his footsteps behind her.

When she broke out of the shade of the trees and onto the shale and sand beach, she paused so he could come up to stand beside her. His shirt was already in his hand, and he tossed it to the ground. She dropped hers on top of it. Soon, both wore only underwear.

Lynette groaned. "Shoot, I forgot to change out of these! I need to wear them under my dress tomorrow. I can't wear them into the lake."

Stepping behind her, Storm made quick work of her bra clasp, and added it to their growing pile of clothing. She automatically covered her chest with her arms, then hurried for the shoreline, still wearing her underpants.

She heard Storm chuckle as she waded into the calm water.

"I thought you didn't want to get those wet," he said.

"Too late. I'll have to find something else that goes with blue silk," she said, relishing the coolness of the water against her hot skin. "Are you going to join me?"

Her answer came in the loud splashing beside her. Storm ran past her, and when the gentle swells reached his waist, he dove under, kicking water into her face. She laughed, drenched, knowing he wasn't intentionally trying to drown her. When he resurfaced, his sunglasses still shielded his eyes.

"You are going to lose those!"

When she pointed, he looked surprised. "You had me so flustered, I forgot I still had them on." He floated onto his back. "This is exactly what I needed. I'm sorry I doubted you."

"Apology accepted. Hey, want to race?"

He looked her way, though she wasn't sure he could actually see her, given the water streaming down the front of his sunglasses. "Race? Where to?"

"To the falls. They're just down that way. You can hear them, right? We could walk there, but because I'm now completely topless, even *I'm* not quite that brave. We aren't far from town, and the grass is long. Owen said his son Adam was coming out to mow again tonight."

He swam back to her side. "Show me. But let's not race. I couldn't let you beat me, but I'd also hate to lose my sunglasses."

She laughed. "Follow me, then. The falls were always my favorite spot out here when I was a kid."

"Why?" he asked.

"You'll see. Come on."

She swam away from him then, moving perpendicular to the shore, loving the silky feel of the water against her nearly naked body.

Storm looped back to shore to place his sunglasses on their pile of clothes, then waded back into the water. Twelve-year-old Lynette never could have imagined herself practically skinny-dipping in this lake with a beautiful man she'd loved for over thirty years.

Her arms were tiring when the falls came into view. She ignored the burn in her muscles, powering on, until she reached the pool at the foot of the falls.

When she attempted to stand up, the water was deeper than she'd expected, and she sank below the surface. The sensation brought back memories of that awful, drunken night at Whispering Pines when the lake engulfed her, but she didn't panic. She wasn't alone this time. Storm caught her outstretched hand and pulled her easily toward the more shallow waters. When they could both stand, he caught her up against him and took a moment so they could both catch their breath. He rested his chin on the top of her head, and she liked the way his hairy chest felt beneath her cheek.

Once his breathing eased back to a normal level, he nodded toward the falls. "What are they called?"

"Diamond Falls. Legend has it there are diamonds buried here. I admit, we've dug around looking for some before, but wouldn't you know, we've never found any."

He laughed, then kissed the tip of her nose. "I can tell that life with you would be easy."

It seemed a strange thing to say.

"I *like* easy," he said.

"Umm . . . okay," she said, feeling unsure. She tilted her head back to look at his face.

His eyes grew round. "Wait. Hold on a second." He took a big gulp of air, then pulled out of her arms to dip below the surface. He must have had to sit on the lake bottom for his head to disappear like that.

Had he stepped on something and hurt his foot?

He came back up, water sluicing off of his muscular chest and arms, wiping at his eyes.

She noticed his little butterfly tattoo and laughed. "What the heck are you doing? Did something poke your foot?"

He shrugged. "I think I found that diamond you've been searching for. At least I hope I did."

Maybe he had sunstroke after all.

But then his other hand came up out of the water, and between his forefinger and thumb, he held a large diamond ring in a simple platinum setting.

She froze, looking between his hand and his eyes.

"Lynette, I've loved you since the first time I laid eyes on you. You came waltzing into the pizza shop without an ounce of experience and dared me to hire you. I was two years out of high school, but I still let you talk me into prom. You were irresistible, and the way you blew in and out of my life when we were kids left me wondering what had just happened. But I never forgot you. And frankly, I never want to live without you. Ever again."

Storm was proposing to her.

Here.

At Diamond Falls.

"But you have a son, Storm. I've never even met him. My mom barely knows you. Heck, I sometimes feel like *I* barely know you. We've been back in each other's lives for such a short time. This is all happening so fast . . ."

He didn't look put off as she tried to process the shock of seeing him standing in front of her with a diamond ring. "That's not true, Lynette. It's been a year since we rescued you when you foolishly tried to drown yourself in that little dinghy."

She huffed. "I was *not* trying to drown myself."

"I think Donna would approve of this. She's coming home in a couple weeks for a visit, right? I'll talk to her about it then. And yes, I know you haven't met Phoenix yet, but that's easy to solve, too. I'll get him here to Ruby Shores, so the two of you can get to know each other. Promise."

Storm had obviously been thinking this through, anticipating her fears.

Why was she feeling so blindsided?

He grasped one of her hands with his free one and pulled her closer to him. "Look. Lynette. I can see that I've surprised you. But our situation isn't all that different from Jackie and Owen's, except we've at least had the nerve to find out if we're compatible, right? And we are. We always have been. We were just way too young when we were in each other's lives before."

A trickle of water tickled her lips, but before she could lick at it, he bent down and kissed the moisture away.

"Are you going to make me get down on one knee? Because I'm happy to try, but I might drown."

The reality of what was happening finally sank in. Here she was, a fifty-two-year-old woman, standing bare-chested in front of the man she'd loved longer than anyone else on Earth aside from her mother and best friends, and he'd just proposed to her.

She couldn't quell the shiver of happiness that coursed through her.

"But you have to ask me properly."

He smiled, as if confident in her answer now. He took three steps closer to shore, pulling her by the hand with him. Then he sank down in the shallows on one knee, the falls at his back, and he held the ring up to her again.

"Lynette Marie Howe, would you do me the honor of becoming my wife?"

A spark of light—just to the left of the falls—pulled her eyes away from Storm and the ring. She couldn't find the source, but it hadn't been her imagination. Maybe it was the ghost of the Indian priestess that Wendy used to tell them about as kids, signaling to her to accept this diamond being offered to her by the most special man.

She looked back into Storm's eyes. "How can you be sure it'll work?"

He sighed, then struggled to get back onto his feet. She laughed as she helped him up, then stared into his eyes again.

"Lynette, the only thing I'm one hundred percent sure of is that I've spent enough of my life without you. Changing that is easy. All you have to do is say yes."

"But where will we live, and what about Shane . . . ?"

He gently laid a finger to her lips, silencing her. "We'll figure it out," he said. "Just trust me."

Trust wasn't something that came easily to Lynette. But with the water sparkling behind him, she decided Storm was worth taking a chance on.

"Yes," she finally said, holding her left hand out to him.

"Really?" he said, looking as surprised as she felt.

When she nodded, he moved to slide the ring onto her finger.

And he dropped it.

"Shit," he muttered, dipping below the water's surface yet again.

The water swirled above where he'd disappeared, and he was down for so long that she worried.

But then his hand popped out first, holding the dripping ring aloft, followed by the rest of him. "I told you to trust me," he laughed. "Now let me get this damn ring on your finger before I lose it again."

CHAPTER TWENTY-SIX

LYNETTE HELPED HERSELF TO a piece of wedding cake and a flute of sparkling water, then searched the tables for a familiar face. She spied Ava and her husband, Daniel, at a table on the edge of the setup. Little Nora was probably riding through the crowd on her grandfather's hip.

"Is this seat taken?" she asked, her hand on the back of an empty plastic folding chair.

Ava glanced up at her with a smile that was nearly a grimace. "Let me guess. Mom ran off to talk to Dad."

Lynette sighed. "Can you blame her? The poor guy just got jilted at the altar. He's bound to be upset."

Daniel shook his head. "I suspect he might feel a little relieved about Tammy after the sting fades. They were rushing things. Ever since Henry died so suddenly, Michael's been acting . . . I don't know . . . off. When he let Tammy crank up their wedding date, I told Ava something was up."

Ava put her hand on top of his. "No one needs to hear you say *I told you so*, honey."

Daniel shrugged, then took a sip from his champagne flute. He grimaced.

Lynette grinned. "Not good?"

"Don't tell me you *like* the champagne. It tastes like something out of a box we would have drunk in high school," he said.

She ran her finger around the rim of her flute. "I picked the sparkling water option. I don't drink anymore."

"Well, I'm not going to drink anymore today," he said, getting to his feet. "If you ladies would excuse me, I'm going to go find Nora and get some food into her. No one wants to experience a hungry, tired two-and-a-half-year-old. I think we've all experienced enough drama for one day."

Ava watched him go, then turned to face Lynette. Ava grabbed Lynette's left wrist. "I quit yesterday, but you can't tell Mom."

"Quit what?" Lynette said. For a moment there, she thought Ava had noticed the new rock on her left ring finger—the one she kept trying to keep hidden until she had a chance to tell Annie that she was engaged.

"My job. I quit my job at the bank. Daniel is a little freaked out by it, but I couldn't take it anymore."

Lynette, still feeling out of sorts following her own surprise engagement and then Michael's nearly runaway-bride situation today, struggled to focus. "You quit your job, but you don't want your mom to know . . ." She spoke the words slowly.

"Right. You know how badly I've been wanting to open an online boutique, but it never seemed like it was the right time. I had to work to cover our mortgage, but I hate all the travel they require me to do, and daycare is so expensive. Daniel and I have talked a lot about it, especially after what happened to Henry. Life is too short. He wants me to be happy. So my last day is in two weeks. Then we'll be able to pull Nora out of daycare, and we'll put our house on the market. Daniel can't cover the mortgage on his salary alone, and I know it'll take some time before

I can turn a profit. How long did it take you to earn a paycheck in your business?"

A server came by with a bottle of champagne and offered to refill the two women's glasses. Both covered their flutes with their hands, and the man moved on.

"Back up," Lynette said. "Where will you live?"

Ava chewed on her lower lip. It was a nervous habit Lynette recognized; a tic she'd inherited from her mother.

"You don't have any place to go yet, do you?"

Ava shook her head. "But we'll find something less expensive. Don't worry. We will make sacrifices so we can build a life we are happier with over the long haul."

"I'm not saying what you did was a bad thing, Ava. Impulsive, maybe, but you're right. The time will never be perfect. But I don't understand why you want to keep this from Annie."

A set of hands dropped onto Lynette's shoulders. "Keep *what* from Annie?"

"Oh, hi, Mom," Ava said, patting the chair Daniel just vacated. "Sit. Did you talk to Dad? How is he doing?"

Annie squeezed Lynette's shoulders, then sat as her daughter directed. "Michael is coping with it. I can't quite tell if he's broken up about Tammy's last-minute decision to call off the wedding, or just embarrassed that she waited so long to do it. All I know for sure is that he is bound and determined to get his money's worth out of all this."

Annie made a big circle in the air above her head, and Lynette cringed at the scenery. Guests continued to mingle, filling their plates with delicate finger sandwiches, mints, and cake. The gift table sat empty now. Michael and Tammy had instructed everyone to please take back any gifts they'd brought, along with their sincerest apologies for having them go to the trouble of buying the supposedly happy couple a gift in the first place.

Did Storm expect something like this? Not to be left at the altar, of course, but the white-linen-covered tables, fancy food, and a live band tuning up beside a small dance floor?

"Lynette? Where did you go, girl?" Annie said, snapping her fingers in her direction.

"Sorry," she said. "This day has just been full of so many surprises. It's really got me thinking."

"Mom, promise me you aren't going to worry about Dad," Ava said, wrapping her arm around her mother in the chair next to her. "You have enough on your plate. None of us want you to worry about us right now."

Annie sat up taller in her chair, eyeing her daughter with what looked like suspicion to Lynette. "Ava, honey . . . do you have something you want to tell me?"

Ava seemed to search for an answer, so Lynette jumped to her rescue. "Storm and I are engaged," she blurted out, waving her finger and the new diamond ring in Annie's direction. She hadn't planned to tell her like that, but poor Ava was looking desperate.

Annie stared at the ring, then up at Lynette. Then she burst out laughing.

Lynette wasn't sure how to take her friend's laughter. "Are you *laughing* at me, Annie?"

"Of course I'm not laughing at you, Lynette. I'm *thrilled* for you! This deserves a toast!" She jumped to her feet. "I need a glass. Be right back."

Ava grabbed Lynette's hand to better see the engagement ring. "Impressive. Who's the lucky guy?"

Some of Lynette's anxiety ebbed away when Ava's question made her think of Storm. "An old friend I dated in high school. We ran into each other last year, and we've been getting to know each other again ever since. But it's all very new, and more than a little nerve-racking."

Ava released her hand and nodded knowingly. "And now this debacle has you wondering if you even want to *have* a wedding, am I right? Oh, Lynette, don't let my dad's impulsiveness scare you off."

"So you're admitting impulsiveness runs in your family?" Lynette teased, placing her left hand back in her lap. She still wasn't used to wearing a ring on that particular finger, and it felt odd.

"Maybe a little. But remember, you promised not to tell Mom."

Neither Lynette nor Ava had noticed Annie return with a new flute of champagne.

The excitement in Annie's expression faded away, as did the color in her cheeks. She set her flute down on the table and, not watching what she was doing, only got half the base onto the surface. When she let go, it tumbled silently onto the grass, and Lynette wasn't even sure Annie noticed.

"You did it, didn't you?" Annie said to her daughter. Her disappointment was obvious. "You quit your job. And then you told my friend behind my back, instead of coming to me about it."

Her chest heaved, and Lynette could see the tears building in Annie's eyes. Lynette moved to get up out of her chair and go to her friend's side, but Annie stopped her.

"Don't get up. I don't want to talk to either of you about this right now. Ava, I warned you about quitting your job, but I suppose Lynette's fairy tale has clouded your vision. You'll never be able to afford that house of yours now."

She turned to Lynette. "You're welcome to leave now. I know you only came today because all of you feel sorry for me. I'll find a ride home. Now, if you'll both excuse me, I'm going to go find my granddaughter. I need a big hug from a little girl who isn't going around behind my back, keeping secrets."

Lynette watched her dear friend stomp off.

Ava looked over Lynette's head at someone and stood. "Dad, she's not doing okay today. I need to go check on her."

Michael moved to Ava's side. His tie hung loose around his neck, and he'd ditched his suit jacket. He carried a crystal lowball filled with what looked like a neat whiskey, but Lynette thought his eyes looked clear when his gaze met hers.

"Thanks for bringing Annie today. I appreciate it. I know this is all a lot, on top of what she's already going through. If she just said anything that hurt you, please ignore it. Henry's death has hit us all hard, but her especially. Ava, honey, I'll go talk to your mom. You should find your husband, and the two of you can take Nora home. I'm going to send the band packing. This little charade has gone on long enough. I thought we could just make a party out of it, marriage be damned, but I'm tired. Enough is enough. Lynette, I heard Annie send you away, but will you please stick around until I can talk to her?"

Lynette could see the man was hurting, and though she didn't know him well, she knew this was not the way he'd expected his day to turn out.

"Of course I'll stay. Annie may still pack an emotional punch, but I can take it."

With a thankful grin, Michael went in search of his ex-wife.

Ava gathered both her purse and the tiny beaded one Lynette knew Annie had gifted to her granddaughter for what was supposed to be a special day in all of their lives. "I know Mom doesn't approve of my choice to pursue my dream career, but that won't stop me. Can I call you tomorrow? I thought maybe I could be of some help to you in your office, in exchange for some guidance."

Lynette watched the area behind Ava for Annie's return. She hated if she'd done anything to upset her friend's already fragile psyche. "That would be fine, Ava. But on one condition. You can never ask me to keep a secret from my friend ever again. I won't do it."

Ava bent and brushed a quick kiss on Lynette's cheek. "I won't. Besides, you never agreed to keep this secret. This is all on me, running my mouth. Mom is lucky to have such a special friend like you."

But Ava was wrong.

Lynette was the lucky one.

She only hoped Michael could calm Annie down enough that she'd get the chance to tell her that.

CHAPTER TWENTY-SEVEN

Michael's wedding fiasco left everyone shaken. He calmed Annie down enough that she agreed to a ride home with Lynette, but Lynette didn't want her friend left alone. Annie had refused to come home with her. She could have stayed with Annie for moral support, but her friend didn't invite her in. It was a relief to find Relic's car in the driveway. He'd also attended the almost-wedding, but he'd left earlier.

"Are you sure you're all right, Annie? It's been a day," Lynette said when Annie snapped off her seatbelt.

"I'm just tired. And disappointed for Michael. And upset with Ava. But she's a grown woman, and I need to let her make her own mistakes. That's how *we* learned, right?"

Lynette watched her go, then backed out of the driveway with a shake of her head. She wished Annie had more faith in Ava. Ava's chances of success would improve if she had her mother's support.

The one thing Lynette looked forward to after such a strange day was the silk scarf still waiting for her on her pillow, and a late-night visit from Storm.

But even that fell apart when she found a note and a white rose on her pillow in the spot where she'd left her scarf. Storm apologized for having

341

to take a rain check, but something urgent had come up, and he'd be back later the following day. He'd borrowed the silk scarf so he could be sure they'd use it later.

Lynette collapsed into bed with an exhausted smile, enjoying the night sounds floating through her open window. Moonlight washed across her coverlet. She'd have welcomed the warmth of Storm's arms—but, at that thought, she couldn't help wondering how Michael felt tonight.

Had the jilted man drowned out his disappointment with enough wedding champagne and gifted whiskey to fall into a dreamless sleep?

Alcohol as an avoidance tactic was one Lynette had used for so long that, eventually, it nearly killed her.

Or, since Michael's partner wasn't willing to fully commit, maybe he welcomed an empty bed, relieved to have dodged what could have been a disastrous marriage.

Her mind shifted to Annie. Her dear friend had shared her bed with Henry throughout a long marriage, but now she slept alone, too.

Is the door open again for Annie and Michael to find their way back to each other?

Lynette couldn't help but wonder if it was that possibility that had her old friend so upset, instead of Ava's hasty departure from a well-paying job to chase her dreams.

These thoughts stayed with Lynette as sleep finally claimed her, and she spent a restless night imagining many happy endings for Annie in the years to come.

Her eyes fluttered open to the unexpected scent of bacon wafting through her open window. The kitchen sat two floors below her attic bedroom, and someone was cooking breakfast. She sat up and spied the single white blossom Storm had left her. She'd placed it in the short glass from her bathroom before falling asleep. Plucking it out of the water now, she held the rose under her nose and inhaled deeply.

Waking to the smell of bacon and roses was a winning way to start any day in her book.

But Shane's caregiver had to be the one preparing breakfast downstairs, and with Storm gone, she'd settle for breakfast in her attic kitchenette.

Sadly, without bacon.

She crawled out of bed, donned her mother's pink robe, and shuffled to her bathroom. She'd taken the time the night before to wash off her makeup and brush out her hair, so her face was naked and natural. In keeping with the morning ritual she fought to maintain, she smiled at her reflection in the mirror while brushing her teeth. No matter how pronounced her wrinkles and blooming age spots might appear in the soft morning light, age had taught her that every day she got out of bed was a blessing.

She started a pot of coffee, then opened her refrigerator. The scaled-down size worked for her. It was mostly empty. Still practically drooling over the scent of bacon, she reached for the carton of milk and checked the expiration date. Cereal would have to do.

Just as she was about to douse the flakes with milk, a knock sounded on her door.

"Lynette, are you up, honey?"

She glanced back at her unmade bed: the comforter was falling off the mattress, half of it trailing onto the floor. Was she still asleep? Because that was the only way it could be her mother on the other side of that door.

"Lynette," came the voice again. "Wake up. I know you got in a little late last night. Breakfast is ready downstairs."

"Mom? Is that you?" Lynette said, hurrying to the door that separated her attic apartment from the rest of the house.

She flung the door open, and up came Donna's arms.

Lynette fell into them. "I can't believe you're home already! You said you'd be back in early September."

Donna held Lynette tight, rocking her back and forth in her arms. "When my only daughter gets engaged for the first time in her life at fifty-two, a herd of elephants couldn't keep me away."

Lynette pulled back. "But . . ."

Donna nodded, dropping her arms. "Storm called me last week. We talked for a long time. He said he hoped to propose to you soon and asked if I'd give you both my blessing."

The coffee pot sputtered behind her, and Lynette feared she needed a cup even more than she'd first thought. Her mother wasn't making any sense. "I don't understand. He didn't tell me he'd already discussed this with you."

Donna motioned toward the coffee pot. "Pour me a cup, too. I couldn't find any coffee downstairs. I know you always function better once you have some caffeine, and I'm guessing this engagement has you a little off your game."

Lynette couldn't believe Storm had already reached out to Donna, before even asking her to marry him. Why hadn't he told her?

"I said yes, you know. When he asked me. The day before yesterday. Or did you already know that, too?"

Donna chuckled. "I suspected you would, but no, I haven't talked to Storm again. Except a quick text to tell him I was getting in last night. He let his brother and the woman taking care of Shane know I'd be arriving around six. I enjoyed sleeping in my old bed again. Traveling the world is as wonderful as I'd hoped, but not all mattresses are created equal."

Lynette filled two mismatched mugs, then handed her mother the one that wasn't chipped. "I still can't believe you're here! But it is so good to see you. We have lots to catch up on, aside from my engagement. What about Chester? Did he come with you?"

After a sip of her black coffee, Donna shook her head. "Not yet. He wanted to fly home to see his son. But he'll come for your wedding."

Lynette choked on the hot liquid in her mouth. "Don't rush things, Donna. We just got engaged, and you're already talking about the wedding!"

Donna set her cup down. "I don't think I'm the one rushing things, dear. Storm suggested he didn't want a long engagement when he first called, so I just assumed we'd need to make quick plans."

"I haven't even met Storm's son yet," Lynette said. She wrapped her hands around her steaming mug to warm them. Her hands always felt icy when she was nervous. "How can I marry the man before I'm even sure his son likes me?"

Donna unplugged the coffee pot, picked her mug back up, and motioned toward the apartment door. "I'm sure the boy will love you, Lynette. Besides, Storm mentioned his ex has Phoenix most of the time, though I could tell that bothers Storm a bit. Now, why don't we go down and eat before things get cold? I put the bacon and scrambled eggs in the oven to keep them warm, but they won't keep forever. Nice robe, by the way. I thought I'd donated that thing before I left."

Lynette stepped over the heels she'd kicked off the evening before, but Donna picked them up and set them neatly beside the door on their way out.

Mom really is back, Lynette thought with a smile.

"Say, how did the wedding go yesterday?" Donna asked. "Annie's ex was getting married again, right? I remember him from that Thanksgiving we spent at her house a couple years ago. Michael, was it? Nice man. Handsome, too."

Lynette paused with her hand on the newel post at the top of the stairs, glancing back at her mother. "He *is* a nice man, but believe it or not, the bride got cold feet and left him at the altar."

"She did not," Donna whispered, pulling the attic door closed.

"She did. We knew something was up when the music started and the bride walked toward her groom wearing jeans. Michael was waiting for her in a handsome suit, and his face went as white as the gown we all expected to see the bride in. She apologized to the crowd, kissed Michael on the cheek, and said goodbye. I felt awful for him, left standing alone in front of family and friends like that. But once the shock wore off, he invited everyone to stay and enjoy the food, since the caterers had everything set up already. It was the strangest couple of hours ever."

She could hear Donna on the stairs behind her as they made their way down. When they reached the landing between floors, a rainbow of bright colors splashed across the pale wooden floors.

"I wanted to tell you how much I *love* your new stained-glass window, honey," Donna said, admiring the work of art high above their heads. "The picture you sent me didn't do it justice. It truly looks like a pattern in a kaleidoscope."

Lynette studied it, again. "I love it, too. Renee's brother-in-law exceeded my expectations with his work. That reminds me. I've only told Annie about our engagement. I still need to call Jackie, Kit, and Renee. This will be a shock to them. It sure was for *me*."

The doorbell rang just as the two women reached the base of the stairs. Lynette glanced down at the old bathrobe she wore, then around the front hall, expecting to see either Shane or his caregiver appear to answer the door.

She really should have taken a moment to get dressed.

Donna pushed past her, headed for the door. "No need to call Jackie, dear. I suspect this is her joining us for breakfast."

The surprises just kept coming.

Sure enough, when Donna swung the door open, Jackie was standing on the front step holding a plate of rolls. She raised them higher and smiled at them. "I couldn't arrive empty-handed."

Lynette shook her head. "I didn't even know you were still in town, Jackie. And since when do you have fresh rolls baked up in the morning?" She adjusted the hem of her robe, self-conscious next to Jackie's casual yet sophisticated outfit and combed hair.

"Since never," she said with a laugh. "But Donna called me when she got to town yesterday, so I had time to prepare. How was the wedding? Shoot, I should have thought to call Annie and bring her with me this morning. She'd be excited to see you, too, Donna."

Donna accepted the plate from Jackie and motioned her inside. "Head back to the kitchen. Lynette has lots to update you on, but we need to eat before my breakfast is cold."

Jackie held an arm out when she reached her side, and Lynette automatically slipped hers through. "You look stunning this morning, Lynette," Jackie said, nodding at her pink bathrobe. "I'm going to have to get myself one of those.”

“Shut up,” Lynette said, bumping her friend with her hip. “I wasn’t expecting company this morning. Those rolls look delicious, but why did you bring so many? Mom, is Shane joining us for breakfast?”

Donna shook her head. “No. He’s at an appointment with his caregiver.”

“Are the others here yet?” Jackie asked, her eyes scanning the rooms on the main level as they made their way back to the kitchen.

“The others?” Lynette said, pulling Jackie to a stop. “Who else is coming? I really need to run upstairs and put some clothes on.”

But the sound of the back door told her she was too late.

“Hello!” Storm’s voice boomed from the back portion of the house. “Lynette? Donna?”

“We’re right here!” Donna yelled back, hurrying around Jackie and Lynette for the kitchen.

Lynette was sure she’d heard Storm talking to someone. “I can’t go in there like this,” she said, spinning away from Jackie when her friend tried to grab her hand.

“*There* you are, Lynette,” Storm said.

She stopped, her back to both Jackie and Storm. “I’ll be right back. I need to run up and get dressed. Mom didn’t tell me anyone else would be here.”

“Hey, Storm,” Jackie said. “I’ll go see if Donna needs help in the kitchen.”

Lynette took two steps toward the stairs, but Storm was quicker, wrapping his arms around her waist before she reached the landing. He nuzzled the side of her neck, and she couldn’t help but laugh. She spun around to face him. “*Storm.* Seriously. I need to get out of this robe and into something decent. We have guests!" Then she slapped his arm. "And you couldn't have thought to tell me that Mom was coming two weeks early? *And* that you'd already talked to her about us?"

Storm held her loosely but was apparently not going to let her go completely. She thought he looked tired but happy. "I'm liking you in pink," he said, his fingers toying with the top of the robe's zipper.

"Storm!" she hissed again. "Knock it off! Let me *go*."

He sighed, then released her. "Fine. But if you aren't back down here in two minutes, I'm coming up after you. And then we'll *both* get in trouble, because once I'm up there with you, they'll have to wait for us to come back down and breakfast will surely get cold."

She gave him a light shove, then sprinted up the stairs. Knowing he probably wasn't kidding, she changed in record speed and was still twisting her hair up into a knot when she slid through the kitchen door mere minutes later.

At the table waiting for her was one more surprise.

Storm stood behind a boy of roughly ten years old, a possessive hand on his shoulder. "Lynette, I'd like you to meet Phoenix. My son."

Lynette gave up on her hair, ignoring it when it tumbled back down around her shoulders, and muttered, stunned, "Your son . . ."

Donna, who must have already met the child while Lynette was upstairs, slid a heaping plate in front of the boy.

Phoenix thanked her, then swung his eyes back to Lynette. He raised a friendly hand in her direction. "Hi, Lynette. It's nice to meet you. Dad already told me all about you during our drive over from Minneapolis this morning. He picked me up at the airport last night."

Lynette glanced between father and son. How much had Storm told the boy? If he'd told him they were planning to marry, Phoenix didn't look upset about the news.

Jackie, standing near the microwave heating the rolls she'd brought, froze, her eyes locked onto the large diamond on Lynette's left hand.

"Lynette. Storm. Do you two have something to tell us?"

Phoenix scooped up a forkful of eggs, looking at the two women. "They're getting married."

"I can see that," Jackie replied.

"I was going to call you . . ." Lynette started.

Donna stepped between them and pointed at Jackie with a wooden spoon. "Didn't I tell you we had news?"

The microwave beeped, but Jackie ignored it, rushing to Lynette's side instead. She grabbed up both of her hands, studying them. "First he gives you a family heirloom, and then he puts a honking diamond ring on you, and I have to find out you're getting married over family breakfast?"

Lynette didn't even know how to respond to that. Everything was happening too fast.

But Jackie laughed and caught her up in a big hug. "I'm *thrilled* for you!" Then she spun on Storm and hugged him, too. "And I'm a little worried about you. But I suspect you can handle her."

Storm assured Jackie that he would do his best.

After that, everyone settled around the table and the small talk commenced as they all tried to get to know each other a little better. Lynette replied when spoken to, but it wasn't until Jackie asked her about Michael's wedding that the table went quiet. When she reported that the wedding didn't actually take place, Storm got to his feet and went over to the stovetop for the rest of the scrambled eggs. He brought the kettle back to the table and offered everyone seconds. When he reached Lynette, he caught her eye.

"And Michael's runaway bride has you feeling a little freaked out. Am I right?"

The man was more perceptive than she gave him credit for. "Maybe a little."

She passed on more eggs, so Storm returned the kettle to the stove, then crouched beside her chair and spun her to face him. "Lynette, that's *their* story. Not ours. I promise not to pressure you. If you want to wait to actually get married, that's not a problem. I'm not going anywhere."

She could read the sincerity in his words and see it in his eyes. Suddenly, she knew she was tired of waiting for a life with this man, and she shook her head. "If Phoenix doesn't mind having me for a stepmother, I say . . . why wait? I wonder how long it takes to get a marriage license and an appointment at the courthouse."

There was a clatter of silverware next to her, drawing Lynette's eyes to her mother. "What's wrong? You seemed fine with me marrying Storm when we were upstairs."

"I *am* fine with that, but I hate to see you marry in some sterile courthouse setting. You deserve more than that," Donna said, looking distressed.

Storm, still crouched in front of Lynette, nodded. "I agree. I don't want to wait, either, but you deserve something more personal than the courthouse."

Jackie cleared her throat. "What if you got married here?"

"Here?" Lynette repeated, looking at her friend.

"Yes, in the garden out back. The rose bushes are so full and beautiful this time of year. A friend of my parents is a retired judge. I'd be happy to call him and ask if he still performs marriage ceremonies. Unless you want a church wedding, or a proper minister."

Lynette turned back to Storm. "We haven't even talked about what we want."

He gave her a reassuring smile, then struggled back to his feet. "I want what you want, Lynette. To be honest, marrying you in the backyard of this house—a house that means so much to me and my brother—would be nice. But only if *you* like the idea, too. I don't need a big fancy party, and as long as whoever performs the ceremony can make it legal, I'm good with it. I did the whole big church wedding once before, and this guy here was the only real thing to come out of that."

Jackie clapped her hands together. "I get to plan another Kaleidoscope Girl wedding! First Kit's, and now yours."

"Maybe wedding planning could be your new gig," Lynette joked. Her excitement was growing.

Her friend shrugged. "Doubtful. But for you, I'm willing to do whatever it takes to pull a beautiful wedding together quickly. When we're done here, we need to go see Annie. We can call the others from her house. How soon do we want this to happen?"

Lynette looked back at Storm questioningly.

He shrugged. "Phoenix is here. Your mom is here. I'd vote for as soon as the rest of your friends can get to town—if that works for you, of course. I'll make sure Owen is in town, too, so he can stand up for me."

For a split second, Lynette wondered how she could pick which of her friends to ask to be her maid or matron of honor. But then her eyes fell on Donna, and she realized there was no decision to be made.

"Mom . . . will you stand up for me?"

Donna reached across the table for her hand. "It would be an honor, dear."

Storm snapped his fingers. "It's decided then. Let the wedding planning begin. But, Lynette, I need to warn you about something."

Her gaze swung back up to meet his. "Warn me?"

He gave her one hard nod. "If you try to pull that 'runaway-bride' crap on me, I won't let you go nearly as easily as it sounds like Michael did. You said yes, and I'm holding you to it."

And though a smile softened his words, Lynette knew he meant it.

But she couldn't imagine ever wanting to leave his side again.

CHAPTER TWENTY-EIGHT

J ACKIE SLAMMED HER CAR door and glanced at her watch. After a busy morning ensuring everything was proceeding as planned for Lynette and Storm's big day, she worried she was late joining the rest of the Kaleidoscope Girls in helping the bride into her wedding gown.

As she stepped onto the immaculately manicured lawn of Lynette's backyard, someone called her name.

She turned to see Owen jogging in her direction, and her heart did a slow rollover in her chest at the sight of him. He looked even more handsome in a light charcoal suit than he had in black at Henry's funeral.

"You already look properly dressed to play the role of best man," she said with a smile.

He stopped a few feet from her. "And you look more beautiful than ever. Has anyone ever told you that green is your color?"

She gave him a little curtsy at the compliment, then got down to business. "Tell me we don't have any hiccups here."

This seemed to confuse him for a moment. "Hiccups?"

"Problems regarding the wedding, I mean. The way you came running over here has me worried. Did the chairs and cake get delivered?"

Owen visibly relaxed. "I think so. I guess I didn't pay much attention, but Donna is running a tight ship around here at the moment, and I didn't hear any rumblings of trouble."

"Thank goodness," Jackie said, relieved.

"No, I just wanted to catch you before you head upstairs to help Lynette get ready. Your other friends are already up there, by the way."

Jackie wasn't surprised she was the last to arrive. "I better hurry."

He put out a hand to stop her before she rushed off. "I just wanted to be the first to tell you I've decided what I'm going to do with the land out by the lake."

"The summer camp land?"

When he nodded, she held her breath.

"I've talked things over with my lawyers and accountants, and even though there are certain risks, I'll move ahead with Lynette's ideas. We might even talk to Julie again about the manager role today. She arrived with Renee and Matt about twenty minutes ago."

Jackie exhaled, relieved. "Owen, that is fantastic news! Lynette will be so pleased. Should we go tell her together?"

Owen laughed. "Not right now. I already told Storm, but I asked him to keep quiet about it until I could talk to Lynette after the wedding ceremony. I don't want to do anything to distract from their big day."

Unable to help herself, Jackie flung her arms around Owen and hugged him tight. When she loosened her grip and tilted her head back, his face was oh so close to hers, and she kissed him, not caring if she'd have to touch up her lipstick once she got upstairs.

He kissed her back, but then pulled away, pointing to the house behind them. "I've kept you long enough, and I know what a stickler you are for staying on schedule. You better get up there."

She shrugged. "Dad taught me to never be late. Good luck up there, and remember to keep your knees bent. You don't want to pass out during the ceremony and face-plant into one of Donna's rose bushes."

"I'll keep that in mind. Now, go."

It was hard to leave him when he looked so dapper. But if she didn't hurry, she'd miss helping Lynette into her dress.

She let herself in through the back door and hurried up the stairs to Lynette's attic apartment. The ceremony was supposed to start at two, and it was almost one o'clock; maybe the bride was already in her gown. The couple had opted to forgo any photographs beforehand so that they'd first see each other when Lynette walked down the aisle.

But she needn't have worried. Lynette was just stepping into her wedding gown when Jackie burst through the door.

"Nice of you to join us, Jackie," the bride said, but even from the doorway Jackie could see the twinkle in her eye.

"Hi, everyone," Jackie said. "Sorry I'm a little late. What did I miss?"

Renee laughed and shook her head. "Only Lynette's second attempt to get into this thing."

"I decided I better pee quick before getting into it," Lynette said. "This way, I can make it through the ceremony without a potty break. Maybe."

The women in the room, all at least Lynette's age or older, chuckled knowingly.

"I still can't believe you bought this at a thrift store," Renee said, pulling the dress up while Lynette held Donna's hand to balance.

Annie, standing nearby with a long white veil in her hands, nodded. "And it wasn't just any thrift store. It's a thrift store that's in the same building where that dress shop used to be back when we were kids. We all went there before our senior prom to buy our dresses, remember?"

Renee moved behind Lynette and started working on the zipper and buttons that ran up the back. "And those were all such pretty gowns! I'm still so thankful you thought to invite me over to your prom when my own plans fell apart. There, how does that feel?"

Lynette shifted around inside her dress, making sure nothing felt uncomfortable. "About as good as a dress covered in old, heavy lace can feel, I suppose. Thanks for the help, Renee. You, too, Mom."

The door to the attic apartment opened again, and Jackie's mother hurried in, carrying a small bouquet.

"Oh, Mom, that is so *pretty*," Jackie said, stepping forward to take the bridal arrangement. "Lynette, look at this. Mom used some of her dried peonies she keeps in the basement to make this for you. Isn't it perfect?"

"Oh, Charlotte, it *is* perfect!" Lynette cried. "Thank you for doing that for me."

Charlotte smiled at the bride. "It was an honor, honey. I didn't have fresh peonies in my yard since it's too late in the summer, but the dried versions are pretty, too. Speaking of pretty—you look absolutely *beautiful*."

Jackie handed the bouquet to Lynette so she could have a closer look, and a strand of diamonds around the bride's wrist caught her eye. "That's gorgeous," she said, pointing to the bracelet.

Lynette grinned. "An early wedding gift from Storm. He gave it to me last night beside the fountain, under the moonlight."

Annie moaned. "Storm is sexy *and* romantic, then?"

Everyone laughed. Annie had been vocal about how sexy she'd always found Storm for most of their lives.

"I know how to pick them," Lynette said, winking as she handed the flowers back to Jackie so she could finish getting ready.

Donna hugged Charlotte. "My daughter looks beautiful, doesn't she? She's almost ready, but we can't go downstairs yet. I have something old for you, Lynette."

Lynette laughed and held out her arms. "Isn't a vintage dress enough 'old' for this bride?"

"Nope. Now if I can just find what I did with it . . ." Donna said, her voice trailing off as she searched a variety of bags on Lynette's bed.

"Donna, do you mind if I give Lynette a little something 'borrowed' while you look?" Kit asked. As she stepped forward, Jackie noticed a thin silver chain dangling from her fingers.

"Of course not, dear. You go ahead."

Lynette eyed Kit's hand, and Jackie saw a tear escape the corner of the bride's eye. She lunged for her purse and the miniature stack of tissues she'd stashed inside of it as Kit moved to stand behind Lynette.

"You gave each of us one of these when we were kids, Lynette, and somehow I kept mine for all these years. I wore it with the silver gown you gifted me for Dean's daughter's wedding, and I thought it only right that you wear it today, on your own wedding day."

Jackie plucked out lots of tissues, because Kit's thoughtful gesture had them all on the verge of tears.

"I found it!" Donna yelled, holding what looked like a string of pearls in the air. "Kit, I hope you don't mind, but I brought a necklace for Lynette, too. With the open neckline of the dress, I think she can pull off wearing two."

"By all means," Kit said, using the tissue Jackie had handed her to dab at Lynette's eyes.

"Pearls? Mom, did you buy me *pearls*?" Lynette asked, watching her mother approach after Kit moved aside.

Donna smiled. "I did not. Before you get too excited, I should tell you they aren't even real. They're plastic. But my sister, Irene, loved to wear these anytime we played dress-up as kids, and they are about the only thing I have left that belonged to her."

Lynette's eyes widened in shock. "Except for the teddy bear. But Ebony destroyed her."

A loud meow came from the bed, and Jackie couldn't help but laugh. She hadn't noticed the cat until now.

"These belonged to your sister?" Lynette asked as her mother placed the strand around her neck. The iridescent string hung slightly lower than the butterfly necklace.

From where Jackie stood, the pearls looked genuine.

"They did," Donna said, and Jackie worried that one tissue wasn't going to be enough to handle the tears welling up in the mother-of-the-bride's eyes.

Jackie shot a look at her own mother, and Charlotte, reading her daughter's expression, nodded back. Donna needed a distraction.

"Say, Donna, Jackie mentioned that your old friend Raven Black came for the wedding, surprising Storm and Shane. I'd love to say hello to her before the ceremony starts," Charlotte said. "Lynette is almost ready to go, so why don't we give these girls a few minutes alone?"

Donna took a deep breath, then turned to Charlotte. "That's a splendid idea. And I'll introduce you to Chester, too. We're having so much fun, traveling the world together. You'll love him."

Jackie watched the two older women head down the stairs, their voices trailing off. She checked her watch again. They were due downstairs in ten minutes and needed to hurry.

"Annie, did you bring the other present?"

Annie gave a start, then set the veil down while Renee put the finishing touches on Lynette's hair. "Yes! Right here!" she said, pulling a small wrapped box out of the purse on a chair next to her.

Lynette eyed it with a sideways glance. "You guys are spoiling me."

Renee stepped out of the way so Annie could hold the gift out to Lynette, but she pulled it back at the last minute.

"What do you say?" Annie asked, earning a round of laughter out of the five old friends.

Lynette inclined her head at Annie. "Thank you."

"Exactly," Annie said, finally giving her the box. "Kit gave you something borrowed, and Storm gave you something new. The pearls from Donna are your something old . . ."

"That just leaves something blue," Lynette said, dropping the silver wrapping paper to the floor. She popped the top of the blue velvet box open. "Oh my. These are stunning."

Jackie stepped forward and took the box from Lynette. "Just like you, my friend. Annie, get that veil on her, and I'll get these earrings in her ears."

Lynette laughed. "I knew putting you in charge of keeping us on schedule today was the right choice, Jackie. Thank you, all, for these beautiful sapphire earrings. They even have little stars on them! The perfect finishing touch for my bridal ensemble."

The accent she placed on the words "bridal ensemble" had them all giggling again.

Once the veil and earrings were in place, Jackie suggested Kit and Annie accompany her out to the backyard to make sure everyone else was ready to get started. Renee would walk Lynette downstairs and hand her over to Donna for their walk down the aisle together.

When they reached the back lawn, Jackie was relieved to spy the judge she'd arranged to marry the happy couple, standing near the fountain—where the wedding would occur—and chatting with Storm. The man was an old friend of her father, and the sight of him helped Jackie relax.

The guest list was small, numbering only twenty, and Lynette had insisted that her four oldest friends, along with Wendy, fill one of the two front rows of chairs. Storm's son and brother, along with Shane's caregiver, sat in three chairs across the aisle from them, with Raven and Donna's Chester filling the last two chairs. The remaining eight guests were scattered among the other rows.

They were ready to start.

As Jackie waited for the woman they'd hired to handle things like photographs and music to key up the processional song, she bent over to whisper in Annie's ear. "Lynette told me what happened at Michael's wedding. How is he doing?"

Annie sighed. "He'll be fine. Maybe Tammy leaving him at the altar will be a good thing. He was shocked, of course, and I haven't talked to him since the day it happened, but Ava tells me he seems to be recovering quickly."

Kit caught Jackie's eye, as if scolding them to hush. But since the music hadn't started yet, Jackie ignored her.

"I can't imagine ever doing this again, can you?" she whispered into Annie's ear, but then she worried the question might make her feel bad. "Oh, I'm sorry, Annie, that wasn't very sensitive of me to say."

Annie tapped Jackie's knee, then pointed toward the three men standing in front of the small gathering of friends and family. "It's fine, Jackie. I'm doing all right. But Owen is certainly looking handsome today in his wedding finery, don't you think? I saw the two of you kissing just before you came up to Lynette's apartment. Maybe another wedding isn't so out of the question for you at some point."

Jackie snorted, and Kit shot her another look. She'd been about to scold Annie for spying on her when the strains of *Canon in D* filled the air. It was the same music Jackie had used for her wedding to her first husband.

She'd leave the whole marrying-later-in-life thing up to Kit, Renee, and Lynette.

Once was probably enough for her.

Jackie was glad she'd kept a tissue for herself; she teared up listening to Lynette and Storm recite their vows to each other. She'd made it through Lynette's walk down the aisle, the judge's welcome, and Donna's reading without a single tear. But when the two once-young lovers pledged the rest of their lives to each other, the tears came.

She felt someone's gaze on her as she dabbed away the pesky moisture. It was Owen, and when their eyes met, he winked.

The lighthearted gesture helped her regain her composure.

The judge motioned to Storm's son to bring up the rings, and Jackie held her breath, praying the boy wouldn't drop them into the thick grass. She knew Storm had already dropped Lynette's ring into the lake while proposing to her.

But she needn't have worried. Phoenix safely handed them off to the officiant, then took his seat again.

The judge held up a simple band of gold for the guests to see. "Taran asked that I thank his aunt, Raven Black, publicly on his behalf for offering him his great-grandfather's wedding band to use in his marriage to Lynette today."

Jackie grinned as the judge continued to use Storm's legal name. It sounded strange to her ears, but she knew it was the proper thing to do.

Then she wondered, for the first time, whether Storm and Shane's mother knew about today's wedding. The couple hadn't invited her.

Once the bride and groom exchanged rings, Storm turned and motioned for someone to come up front. Shane got to his feet and went up to stand beside Owen. He looked incredibly nervous, but Owen placed a comforting hand on his shoulder, and Shane visibly relaxed.

Then, incredibly, Storm's younger brother began singing a jaw-dropping, a cappella rendition of "Amazing Grace."

Jackie gave up on her one flimsy tissue and let her tears flow. Aside from his own, there wasn't a dry eye in the backyard by the time Shane finished, not even Storm's.

The time-tested hymn is fitting for both weddings and funerals, Jackie thought.

Shane gave a shy little bow, then returned to his seat.

Annie's granddaughter, Nora, picked that exact time to let out a yelp in the chairs behind them. Annie spun around and tried to quiet the girl, but they couldn't really expect the two-year-old to stay still for so long. Jackie peeked over her shoulder to see Ava stand up with the irate toddler, as if to take her away, but Lynette laughed through her happy tears.

"She's fine, Ava," Lynette said. "We aren't being fancy today. Bring her over here and let her splash her hand in the fountain. That might keep her happy until we finish."

Ava looked torn, but when she glanced down at her mother, Annie nodded and pointed to the fountain. "It's Lynette's day. Do as she asks."

The short reprieve turned out to be the perfect note to get people smiling again.

The judge pronounced Taran and Lynette married, and invited the groom to kiss his bride.

Storm made a show of taking Lynette into his arms and dipping her low for the kiss, but when he tried to straighten, he fumbled, and Donna had to rush forward to help Lynette stand back up. With a hand on his lower back, Storm turned to Owen. Even from her seat, Jackie could hear him hiss "Damn back!" to his best man.

CHAPTER TWENTY-NINE

Lynette and Storm made their way back down the makeshift aisle without incident, but Jackie suspected Storm was masking his back pain. Owen escorted Donna out, and when he passed by Jackie, he grimaced and put a hand to his lower back, a surprisingly accurate imitation of Storm after kissing his new bride.

Jackie laughed out loud.

"What's so funny?" Annie asked.

"Us," Jackie said, shaking her head. "None of us are as nimble as we used to be, and we can either laugh in the face of fate, or curse it. As far as I know, cursing fate never got anyone anywhere."

"Did you drink some of the wedding wine before this shindig started?" Kit asked, looking confused.

"Come on, let's go congratulate the bride and groom," Jackie said. Her friends clearly weren't understanding her today, but she enjoyed having an inside joke with Owen.

"Be there in a minute," Kit said, then headed over toward Dean and Isaac.

Annie picked her purse up off the grass, then waved at little Nora by the fountain. "I'll be there in a second, too, Jackie."

Jackie sighed. Coming to things like this alone always felt a little strange, but at least she was among friends. She wanted to catch Shane while he visited with his brother and Lynette over by the cake table.

She caught Lynette's eye as she approached the happy couple. "Did you have any idea Shane could sing like that, Lynette?" she said, before turning to address Shane directly. "That was incredible. I had no idea you were so talented."

Shane's cheeks flushed, and he took a step closer to Storm's side. She felt bad; she hadn't meant to embarrass the man.

"I didn't know he could sing like that either," Storm admitted. "I mean, I knew you liked to sing in the shower and around the house, but when you asked me if you could sing today, I wasn't sure what to expect. And it certainly wasn't that!"

"You liked it?" Shane asked. His brother's approval was clearly important to him.

"I did, Shane. I loved it. And I love you," Storm replied. He gave Shane a side hug before swinging his gaze to Shane's caregiver. "I assume you had something to do with this?"

The younger woman nodded. "I heard Shane singing around the house, too, so I encouraged him to keep at it. I know I haven't been here long, but I majored in music therapy, and I know how beneficial playing instruments, singing, and even just listening to music can be. In fact, he's so talented, you might get him into one of the facilities in Minneapolis that helps their residents develop their musical skills."

Jackie noticed the way Storm bristled at the woman's suggestion.

"Shane doesn't belong in a facility. He belongs in a normal home, with a little help," he said.

The caregiver frowned. "I'm sorry. The word 'facility' was a poor choice. They're more like group homes. Some people can thrive in that environment."

"I love music, Storm," Shane said. "I want to sing at more weddings."

Storm seemed to ponder this, then turned to Lynette. "Would you mind if I visited with her a little more about the types of homes she's talking about?"

"Of course I don't mind," Lynette said. "I'll visit with some of our guests while you're gone."

Once Storm was out of earshot, she rolled her eyes. "Being asked permission by *him* to do something is going to take some getting used to."

Annie joined Lynette and Jackie. "Thank you for being so understanding when Nora misbehaved, Lynette. Ava feels terrible."

Lynette shook her head. "Don't you give it a second thought. She's darling, and no one minded a bit."

Jackie looked around the backyard, wondering what had become of Owen. She was excited for Lynette to hear his news. She spied him near the back door. He was alone, a drink in his hand. She waved him over.

He made his way back to Jackie and her friends, snagging a glass of white wine from the refreshment table as he passed, which he handed to her.

"You didn't have to get me wine, Owen," Jackie said, but, seeing Lynette frown at her, she quickly added, "Sorry. Thank you, Owen. That was nice of you."

"Better," Lynette said with a wink. "Are you having fun, Owen?"

"Watching your husband get a kink in his back when he tried to dip you was certainly a highlight," he replied with a wink.

"You caught that?" Lynette laughed. "He was hoping no one noticed."

Everyone noticed, Jackie thought, but she kept her mouth shut.

"Say, actually, I wanted to visit with you about something," Owen said.

Jackie reached for his hand. "You are going to be so excited, Lynette."

"If these two have decided to get married, too, I'll need that necklace back right away, Lynette," Kit said.

Jackie hadn't even noticed Kit's return to the group, but it was hard for her to pay attention to much else when Owen was nearby.

Why had it taken her so long to realize the effect he had on her?

"Ha-ha, Kit. Don't be ridiculous," Jackie said.

Owen grinned, seeming not to mind Kit's joke. "Does someone want to find Renee so I can update all five of you old summer camp friends all at once?"

"Wait!" Lynette cried. "Is it the land? Are you going to keep it and develop it like we discussed?"

He drained the glass in his hand. "Way to steal a guy's thunder. Storm is going to have to be on his toes to stay ahead of you."

She pretended to elbow him in the stomach. "Tell us!"

"All right. Yes, you guessed it. I'm keeping the land. In fact, I was wondering if you guys thought it would be all right to offer Julie the manager role today, in person. Wouldn't it be more fun than calling her up on the phone?"

Seeing the confusion on both Annie's and Kit's faces, Jackie gave them a quick summary of how Owen planned to develop the land, thanks to Lynette's ideas and encouragement.

"Cottages? We could all live right next to each other?" Annie said. Her smile looked more genuine to Jackie than any she'd seen from her friend since before that dreaded phone call in Fiji. "Count me in!"

"But what would you do with your big house?" Kit asked.

Annie shrugged. "Rent it out to Ava and her family."

"I thought they already had a house."

Jackie felt sorry for Kit. The woman had so much going on in her own life, between her health issues and moving to Iowa. "I promise to catch you up on everything, Kit, but just go with it for now, all right?"

Before Kit could answer, Renee came by with Matt and Julie. "You guys are all looking pretty excited over here. Did I miss something?"

Owen squeezed Jackie's hand and smiled at her, then turned to the bride. "What do you think, Lynette?"

Lynette fanned herself with her hands. "I think you should take Julie over to my she-shed and have a little chat with her. I left it open today in case anyone wanted to get out of the heat for a few minutes."

"Julie?" Renee said.

Jackie could see the moment when the dots connected for Renee.

Julie smiled, as if she might know what Owen wanted to talk to her about, and she walked purposefully toward Lynette's shed, with Owen close behind.

"Is he about to poach my daughter from me?" Renee asked.

"He certainly is," Jackie confirmed.

Renee didn't look overjoyed, but Lynette reached for her, and Renee joined hands with the bride.

"Renee, this is best for both of you. We've talked about it. You agreed you could make it work out at Whispering Pines without her, especially now that your nephew will be there for the next year to help as needed."

Kit rubbed her forehead. "I hate living all the way over in Iowa. I'm so lost."

Jackie and Lynette did their best to bring not only Kit but also Annie, Renee, and Matt up to speed on Owen's decision.

Owen and Julie weren't gone long and, based on their matching smiles, Jackie suspected Owen had his first employee officially on board to help him with his project.

Julie had what looked like a card envelope in her hand.

"Is that for the newlyweds?" Jackie asked.

"No, it only has Lynette's name on the front. Owen said it's Storm's handwriting. We found it tacked to the door of her shed. Which, by the way, is nothing at all like any shed I've ever been in."

Owen glanced at the envelope in Julie's hand. "Lynette, don't open it until we get Storm back over here. I'll go get him."

Lynette took the envelope from Julie and turned it over in her hands. "Maybe I should open this later . . . in private."

Owen wasn't gone long. Storm smiled when he saw what Lynette was holding.

"Open it," he urged.

Lynette looked unsure. "Storm . . . you already gave me a present last night."

"This is different," he assured her.

With a shrug, Lynette slipped a finger under the seal and opened the envelope, careful not to tear anything that might be inside. She pulled out a sheet of paper and unfolded it, holding it farther away from her face.

"Here," Annie said, reaching into the purse on her wrist and pulling out a pair of reading glasses. "Use these."

Jackie glanced at Owen. "A bad back and failing eyesight," she whispered to him. "I guess that's what you get at a geriatric wedding."

Lynette stuck her tongue out at her, then settled Annie's glasses in place. "I heard that."

Everyone quieted to give Lynette a chance to read Storm's note. She handed the glasses back to Annie, but said nothing at first.

"What does it say?" Kit asked, making Jackie wonder again why the woman was always so impatient.

"You're really willing to move my she-shed for me?" Lynette asked Storm.

The groom shrugged. "If you decide you want us to move out of this place and buy one of the cottages Owen will build, then yes. I know how much you love having that little space all to yourself, and it's unique. You did a marvelous job with it, and something that size wouldn't be that hard to move."

Lynette obviously loved her new husband's thoughtful offer. She threw herself into his arms, and Jackie almost laughed at the man's pained cringe, but stopped herself.

"Where are you two going to live, anyhow?" Annie asked. "Storm, I thought you had a place in Nantucket. And this is Lynette's house, even though she's renting most of it to you right now."

Lynette put an arm around Storm's back. "We're still working on that," she said. "I haven't been to his house in Nantucket, but that's where we'll spend our honeymoon. We don't have to decide right away. The only thing I know for sure is that I'm taking some of the money I earned from the sale of my business and buying one of Owen's cottages."

"And what about your husband?" Owen asked with a grin.

"Oh, he can live with me out there when we are in Ruby Shores," the bride replied.

Everyone laughed.

"What kind of floor plan do you think you'll want?" Jackie asked.

With that, Storm groaned. "We've already started debating that, and

Lynette was quick to inform me that it'll technically be her cottage, so she'll design it. Since I don't want to argue on our wedding day, I'm going to invite the gentlemen to accompany me over to the hors d'oeuvre table for some sustenance, then to the other side of the yard to discuss fishing."

As he turned to leave with Matt and Owen, Lynette stopped him. "Where did Phoenix go?"

He motioned toward the garage. "He asked Isaac to show him Kit's Mustang. My kid loves old muscle cars, too."

Jackie snorted. "Imagine that. Kit, you guys drove the Mustang? From *Iowa*?"

Kit nodded. "We did. Which is why we won't be able to stay too late today. It's a long drive back, and if the old girl breaks down on the interstate, we don't want to be caught out there after dark."

After the men moved off, Wendy joined the bride and her friends. She held a large wrapped gift that had to be a wall hanging of some sort, given its shape and size. "This is for you and your new husband," she said, handing the present to Lynette. "I don't think Storm would mind if you opened it without him."

Annie rubbed her palms together. "Oh, I bet I know what this is."

"Shh," Wendy said. "Let her see for herself."

Lynette unwrapped it, and Jackie took the paper from her to avoid making a mess. A bright smile told them all that Lynette loved what she saw. "Did you paint this?" she asked, spinning the frame around so everyone could see it.

"I knew it! A kaleidoscope! She gave one to Henry and me when we got married, too," Annie said.

"I'll find the perfect spot for it in my new cottage," Lynette said.

Donna came by and offered to take the painting into the house.

"New cottage?" Wendy asked.

The question launched Lynette into yet another telling of Owen's plans for the old summer camp land.

"An art class?" Wendy said, when Lynette mentioned her idea of a class Wendy might want to offer out of one of the old cabins. "Well, maybe . . . but I'm also intrigued about the cottages. Are you seriously considering buying one, Annie? Because I sure miss seeing you at work all the time."

"Maybe. I'm not loving life in my big old house these days."

Wendy nodded. Jackie remembered Wendy was also a widow, so she likely understood how Annie was feeling.

Storm returned, and when Lynette looked at him expectantly, he nodded. "As wonderful as this day has been, we should probably get going. I just checked again with Donna, and it still works for her and Chester to get Phoenix to the airport tomorrow. Their flights are within an hour of each other, so she'll be sure he gets on the correct plane, too."

Lynette laughed. "Grandma Donna. I never thought I'd see her that way, but those two have certainly hit it off already."

Jackie wondered if Lynette and Phoenix would also manage to build something of a relationship, now that she was married to the boy's father. She hoped that would be the case.

The couple thanked them all for their help in pulling their special day together so quickly, then said their goodbyes.

Kit and family left shortly after the newlyweds, and as Jackie wished them luck on their drive home to Iowa, she said, "Text me so I know you made it back."

"Yes, Mother Jackie," Kit joked, hugging everyone.

Eventually, only Jackie and Donna—along with Owen and Renee's family—remained. Charlotte had gone home shortly after the ceremony with a headache, but Jackie suspected she was simply wanting to have some time in the house by herself. Her mother had spent so little time there since her husband had died in January.

The caterers would be back soon, so everyone pitched in to tear things down as required by the rental contract. Once they'd returned Lynette's backyard to normal, Julie approached Jackie and Owen. She thanked them both again for the opportunity to manage Owen's new project.

Renee and Matt had followed Julie over, and Matt joked that his step-daughter better plan to keep a room open for Renee at all times because he knew she didn't want to miss out on any more Kaleidoscope Girls fun. He'd help Renee's nephew, Nathan, keep the lights on at Whispering Pines. When both Julie and Renee ran inside to use the bathroom before their drive home, Matt shook Owen's hand and gave Jackie a hug.

"This will be good for both of them," Matt said. "I appreciate you taking a chance on Julie. I know she's young, and relatively inexperienced in some things you'll need her to work on, but I know she'll do right by you. And this will take lots of pressure off Renee, too. Thank you."

Jackie was so happy that Renee had found someone like Matt, after losing her first husband so young. "That's what friends are for," she told him.

"Exactly. Owen, we need to get another fishing trip on our calendars, too. Something tells me Lynette won't interrupt the next one with a cry for help."

Jackie laughed. He was right. Lynette was in a much better place now, and her future looked bright.

"Tell the girls I went to get the car, would you?" he said, waving a goodbye.

Once she and Owen were alone again, Jackie decided she should check to see if anyone had bothered to lock Lynette's she-shed back up.

"Doubt it," Owen said. "There is a ring of keys on a hook in the kitchen. I bet we need that to lock the door. I'll be right back."

Jackie nodded her appreciation, then made her way over to the shed. Sure enough, the door was closed but not locked. She stepped inside and closed the door behind her. It was blessedly cool inside.

Owen wasn't gone long. He rapped softly on the door, and Jackie opened it to him, welcoming him inside. He collapsed onto Lynette's sofa and yanked off his tie.

"I can't believe you kept that thing on until now," Jackie said, taking it from him and hanging it carefully over a nearby chair so it wouldn't wrinkle.

He patted the sofa next to him, and she sank down onto the comfortable cushion with a sigh. She kicked her shoes off and snuggled into his side.

"Lynette really did a nice job on this. Storm made the right call by offering to move it for her."

Jackie smiled. "He sure did. He scored lots of points with that one. When I first saw this place, I told Lynette it was more like a mini-château than a she-shed. It was the same day that she tried to convince me to move back to Ruby Shores, actually."

She thought she might have felt Owen tense up.

"And have you decided about that?" he asked.

If he'd asked her before today, she'd have admitted that no, she wasn't yet sure. But now that he planned to move ahead with developing the summer camp land, the idea of buying one of the cottages and making it her own—kind of like this little gem Lynette had made—had convinced her that the move was the right thing to do.

"I have. I'm going to buy one of your cottages. Annie will, and hopefully Lynette, too, and maybe even Wendy. She was certainly curious about it. I know Kit probably can't buy one, given all the changes they're navigating right now, but she'll visit. And Julie's ties mean Renee can visit anytime she wants, too. So, yes, I think moving back to Ruby Shores is the right thing for the next season in my life. I suspect Mom will sell her house to live in Arizona permanently, so I won't be any closer to her. But my girlfriends are as much family to me as my mother and brother are, and living near as many of them as possible sounds amazing. Besides . . . that would put me closer to you, too."

Owen was definitely tense now.

She sat up and put some space between them. "Is something wrong? Do you not want me to move back here?"

Not that long ago, Owen's thoughts on where she lived wouldn't have mattered to her. But things were different between them now.

At least, she'd *thought* they were different.

He undid the top button of his dress shirt, probably to give himself time to gather his thoughts. "Something has been weighing on my mind about us, Jackie. Lynette's been on my case to talk to you about it."

She worried she knew what was coming and got to her feet. If he was about to end things between them, she'd need a quick escape. She couldn't decide whether escape felt so necessary because she'd hate for him to see her fall apart when he broke her heart, or because she would kill him for making her feel so vulnerable. He reached out and wrapped his fingers around her upper leg. The tiny building wasn't big enough for her to move much farther away from him.

"Jackie, it isn't you. It's a promise I made to Adam months ago. He'd like to settle in Ruby Shores permanently after he finishes up all his residency requirements. But that's only if he can buy my old house from me and make it his own. I never really expected to spend so much time in Ruby Shores. As you know, I still have a house out in South Carolina. Our plan was that I'd sell the house to him and move back out East, and he'd keep a room for me anytime I wanted to visit. But it wouldn't be more than once or twice a year."

"You're *leaving*?" Jackie asked, confused. "But you just agreed to develop the land."

He nodded. "I did. And I hired Julie to be the boots on the ground. Technically, I could handle project oversight remotely most of the time. But now I'm pretty sure that's not what I want anymore."

She wasn't sure what he was telling her.

He sighed. "All I know for sure is that I've waited almost forty years to tell you I love you. And I do. I love you, Jackie. We'll figure the rest of it out, if you still want to. We're kind of like Lynette and Storm, but we are different, too. They were a couple before, and even though it was a long time ago, it was serious even then, despite how young they were. They aren't starting from scratch. Not like us."

He gave her leg a light tug, and she sank down next to him again.

"I love you, too," Jackie said. Saying the words out loud didn't scare her as much as she'd thought it would. "And don't you see, Owen? We aren't starting from scratch. I used to consider you my very best friend in the entire world."

He kissed her on the forehead. "Those are the words a ten-year-old would say."

She laughed. "Friendship can often be the best foundation for something more. If something *more* is what you want."

Owen pulled her close, then carefully shifted their bodies, so he was half on top of her.

" 'Something more' is what I've always wanted where you were concerned, Jackie."

When he kissed her this time, it was so much more thrilling than the chaste kiss he'd dropped on her forehead a moment ago.

Too soon, she heard Lynette's mother outside, talking to someone, and the rattle of what sounded like an old-fashioned lid to a metal garbage can. She turned her mouth away from his and gently pushed against his chest. "We should go. I'd hate for Donna to come looking for us and find us in here, making out on her daughter's couch."

Owen chuckled. "We could lock the door and pull the curtains."

"Didn't you say Adam is working a twelve-hour shift today? I'm sure Donna is ready to call it a day. She'll catch a flight out tomorrow, and take Phoenix to the airport, too. We should go."

Owen stood, then pulled Jackie up next to him. "Since Charlotte is home, are you worried what she'll think if you don't come home tonight?"

His question gave her pause. But then she laughed. "I'll text her to let her know I'll be back in the morning. She'll probably assume I'm staying at Annie's or something to give her time in her house alone."

"Will you correct her?" he asked. She could see her answer was important to him.

"Do you *want* me to?"

A nod would mean Owen was taking this budding relationship seriously. He'd always liked Charlotte. But a shake of his head would mean he wasn't yet ready for that level of commitment.

He nodded.

"I'll just skip all that, then, and tell her I'm staying at your place tonight."

He opened the door, glanced around them to make sure everything was in order, then waited for her to leave in front of him, chuckling the whole time. "Well, that might get the tongues wagging around here."

Chapter Thirty

J ULIE RUSHED AROUND HER new apartment, picking dirty clothes off her bedroom floor and shoving them into her closet. She checked the time on her phone and nearly panicked when she realized she still had to clean her bathroom.

Owen had put her on his payroll shortly after Lynette and Storm's wedding, but she'd worked remotely for the first month until he could retrofit this building from its earlier life as the old summer camp offices into a two-bedroom apartment.

As the official manager of the new Diamond Falls development, Julie now called this apartment her home.

The job was even more demanding than she'd expected, but she felt like she'd met each challenge head-on, and Owen seemed pleased with their progress to date. Beyond these apartment doors, she was holding her own.

Why was it, then, that inside the privacy of her new home, she was living like an irresponsible slob?

She was going to have to pull herself together in all aspects of her life if she wanted to truly succeed around here.

The rumble of the lawn mower beyond her windows meant Adam was heading to the equipment shed after mulching thick layers of fallen leaves yet again. At least one of them was staying on schedule. His respect for schedules was how Adam, when he wasn't playing "lawn boy" out here, managed a career as an actual *doctor*.

Even though her toothpaste-stained sink demanded attention, Julie couldn't help but peek out the mini-blinds as Adam passed by on the mower.

Sunglasses hid his eyes, and she thought his hair could use a trim, though the length did nothing to distract from his good looks. His hand tapped against his thigh, and she guessed he was listening to music today, instead of a book or podcast, through his noise-canceling headphones.

His head swiveled in her direction and she jumped back from the window, hoping desperately that he hadn't noticed her lurking there. Ever since she'd discovered he was the owner's son, she'd done her best to keep things professional between them.

The alarm on her phone went off. She groaned, dashing into her bathroom to give it a quick scrub. She'd only given herself a fifteen-minute cushion to ensure she was up front to meet their guests when they arrived.

Ten minutes later, she sat at the desk in her brand-new office, as if she'd been sitting working that way for hours instead of rushing around like a crazy woman. Owen wasn't in his larger office across the hall, and she wasn't sure where he'd disappeared to, but she knew he'd be there for their planned presentation to Jackie and Lynette. He was a professional, after all, and the two women were his first official *paying* customers.

Maybe he was in the equipment shed, talking to Adam.

She heard the slam of car doors and took a deep breath.

Show time!

The first voice she heard was Owen's.

She hurried outside—and bumped right into Adam.

He had to grab her by her upper arms to keep her from falling back onto her bottom.

Mortified, she shrugged off his hands. "I'm so sorry! I should have been watching where I was going, but I was trying to get out front to meet Jackie and Lynette."

He grinned, but his laughing eyes made her nervous, so she looked down. Small bits of dried leaves clung to his white T-shirt. "No harm done," he assured her. "Good luck with your presentation. And remember, this is just practice. Jackie and Lynette are already a lock. This will help you perfect your pitch to help sell the cottages in the buildout of the second cul-de-sac."

When he talked like that, he reminded her of his father.

"Right, right," she said. She wasn't sure what had her more nervous—almost falling over Adam, or impressing two of her mother's oldest friends, one of whom was also her boss's girlfriend.

Adam kept walking, and Julie realized she was now officially late for her first presentation.

But if Owen noticed, he gave no sign, greeting her instead with a friendly nod. "Are you ready to show our esteemed guests what we've accomplished so far?"

"I am," Julie said. "Hello, ladies!"

Jackie laughed and hurried up to pull her into a quick hug. "Oh, *stop*. You're acting like we're real customers. And, Owen, I hope you don't really consider us 'esteemed guests.' " The drawl she placed on the last two words forced a nervous smile out of Julie.

"Yeah, Owen, if it wasn't for the two of us, none of us would even be standing here right now," Lynette chimed in. "Besides, we're practically family, not guests."

Owen laughed. "Fine. If you want to play it that way, then let Julie show you the updates we've made to the old camp office while I go return a phone call with one of our contractors. Then I'll meet you in the community room to go over the blueprints."

Jackie grabbed his hand and planted a kiss on his cheek, leaving a small smear of pink lipstick behind. "And that's for keeping me away from this place for two months while you got down to business. The wait has been killing me!"

Julie grinned at Jackie's antics while also wishing she could feel a little more comfortable around Owen. She loved working for the man. He was patient with her countless questions and always kind to her. But he was also whip smart, and she'd heard him demand better out of a contractor who'd missed a deadline. She'd vowed to never be on the receiving end of a conversation like that with Owen. He could be intimidating.

Lynette pulled Jackie back from Owen, then turned to Julie. "Lead the way, girl. And, Owen, if your mug will be on a camera of any kind, stop in the bathroom and clean that lipstick off your face. It isn't your shade."

His face flushed, and Jackie laughed.

Ten minutes later, Julie had finished showing the two women her new apartment, reasonably certain neither had noticed the streaks of dust she'd failed to eliminate during her abbreviated cleaning session.

"If you think my apartment is nice, wait until you see what Owen did with the old lodge over here!"

"Lodge?" Lynette said. "There was never a lodge out here."

"She means the mess hall," Jackie said, walking toward the building that housed the new offices. "Julie, when we were kids, that was where we ate every meal."

Julie and Lynette followed.

"And made our infamous kaleidoscopes. Jackie, remember how Wendy sent me and Kit to the office for supplies that day, and it ended up being the same day that money disappeared? At first, everyone assumed we stole it. That mess was the only dark spot on what was otherwise an amazing summer at camp. It was the year we first met Kit."

Fascinated, Julie tried to imagine this place back in the '70s and '80s. She suspected not much had really changed until now.

She pulled the door open and motioned for Julie and Lynette to enter. One of them whistled.

"Pretty impressive makeover, isn't it?" she said in an inside voice. She could hear Owen talking in his office and didn't want to interrupt him. He probably wasn't expecting them to be here already. She'd moved the two women through her apartment awfully fast. "Let's go into the community room. I've got things ready for you, and I'm sure Owen will join us in a minute."

She led the way, and when she motioned for them to take a seat at the long wooden table they'd saved when cleaning out this building, both Jackie and Lynette grinned as they settled on a matching bench. Aside from a good cleaning and screw-tightening, they'd left the table as it was, complete with initials carved into the wood by long-ago campers.

Jackie felt under the table. "I hate to admit this, but I'm kind of sad you scraped away all the old wads of gum."

Both Julie and Lynette laughed.

"Sorry to keep you waiting," Owen said, strolling through the door with rolls of blueprints under one arm.

Jackie shook her head. "You didn't. We just sat down. I *love* that you kept this old table. I probably ate plenty of pancakes and hot dogs at this very one, or another of the similar ones that used to fill this part of the mess hall."

"Mess hall?"

"That's what they used to call this place," Julie offered.

Lynette tapped her palms on the time-worn tabletop. "Enough small talk already. I'm dying to see what you've planned so far."

Jackie rolled her eyes. "Sometimes you're as impatient as Kit."

Owen held up a hand to stop the bickering. "Julie, let's start with the very tentative plans we have for some of the cabins. Then we'll discuss the cottages."

She nodded and pulled out a simple map, drawn from a bird's-eye view of the old summer camp buildings. "Most of our attention has been on this building and my new apartment, and then the cottages, so there's still work to be done on figuring out the most effective uses of the various log-sided cabins that date back to your days at summer camp. Your friend Wendy has committed to running a variety of art courses out of this cabin near the main road from May through September. From what I can gather, there's a genuine need for something like that around the Ruby Shores area."

Both Jackie and Lynette nodded.

"I'm not sure if Annie mentioned this to either of you, but she called and asked about the possibility of bringing someone in to teach stained-glass classes."

"Annie is teaching stained-glass classes?" Lynette asked, surprised.

Julie laughed. "No. Annie wants to *learn*, not teach. I suggested my Uncle Seth might be interested in something like that."

Lynette snapped her fingers. "Yes! He did a phenomenal job with my kaleidoscope window. He'd be the *perfect* choice if he can teach, too. I'd consider taking a class with him. I've always thought about making jewelry with colored glass, but never knew where to start."

"That still leaves lots of open cabins," Owen chimed in. "Jackie, I haven't mentioned our idea to Julie for another of the cabins. Why don't you share with these two what you were thinking?"

Jackie pointed to a cabin on the edge of the camp. "What if I established some type of doggie daycare out of this one? It's a popular concept in the bigger cities, and no one is offering anything like that around here. I think there might be a market for it."

Lynette sighed knowingly. "And you already miss working with your pups, don't you? No room for cats at your daycare?"

"No cats," Jackie said with a laugh. "In my limited experience, cats prefer to hang out at home, alone, all day, whereas some dogs benefit from more social interactions. I might want to try it."

Julie tapped her pen against the map. "I like that idea, but have you ever considered opening some kind of service where people could board their pets while they travel? Maybe even when they travel south in the winter, to escape the brutal weather we get up here?"

Jackie nodded. "That was actually what I wondered about initially, but these cabins wouldn't be big enough for something like that. I'd need a much larger building."

"What about the old place that used to be the pizza restaurant where I first worked with Storm?" Lynette suggested. "Owen, you worked there, too. It's vacant."

He nodded. "I know that building well. It could work. But now we're getting sidetracked. Let's bring it back to this place. Julie, anything else with the cabins?"

"Not yet." She turned to the two women. "If you'd like, we can show you the blueprints for the cottages now."

Both Jackie and Lynette leaned forward on the table, clearly eager to see the schematics.

Owen unrolled another of the tubes he'd brought in, anchoring both ends of the paper with small weights placed on the table for just such a purpose. "Talk them through it, Julie."

After spending long hours poring over these designs, this was the area Julie was most comfortable discussing. She stood to make it easier to walk them through the neighborhood-level drawing first, before they got to the individual cottage blueprints.

"There will be five cottages in this first cul-de-sac. I'm going to point out which one each of you are buying, but if you disagree with anything, now is the time to speak up."

Both women nodded again.

"This first cottage would be Annie's. She's requested a fenced-in backyard for her two pups, Daisy and Lemon, and this yard would be the easiest to fence. There will be three bedrooms, whereas some of you requested only two, but her rooms will be on the smaller side, so the overall footprint doesn't get much bigger. Annie doesn't want a large master, and the other bedrooms could be for her kids and grandkids when they come out for a visit. Her only other request is a special nook inside her living room to display her kaleidoscopes. Apparently she'll be bringing her entire collection from her larger house."

"Of *course* she is," Lynette laughed. "That looks perfect for Annie, but I'm sure you'll walk through this with her, too, right?"

"Certainly," Julie agreed. "Then this second cottage will be Kit's."

Jackie raised her arms in the air, much like a track star might do after being the first to cross the finish line. "I still can't believe Kit talked Dean into buying a cottage! We all expected her to just come for a visit once in a while."

Lynette pointed to what would be Kit's cottage. "Well, remember, that condo they lived in was Kit's when they got married. So when they sold it, what they did with the proceeds should have been up to her. She earned this."

"I don't think Dean put up a fuss at all," Jackie added.

"Did Kit have any special requests for her unit?"

Julie shook her head. "Not really. She only wants two bedrooms. This will be a second home for them, so she's not sure how often they'll be here. Her only ask was that we incorporate a butterfly garden somewhere nearby. She said that butterflies are near and dear to her heart."

"Her work involved butterflies, didn't it?" Owen asked.

"Yes, before she moved to Iowa," Jackie confirmed. "When we were kids, that area next to where we park—the one you cleared out and planted over with grass—used to be a butterfly garden. But it got too overgrown, choking out the best plants."

Julie was understanding why Owen had warned her it might be difficult to keep this meeting on task. She tapped the map to get their attention, then pointed to a round circle in the middle of their cul-de-sac.

"*This* is where we are proposing the butterfly garden will go."

Lynette frowned. "I have a question. Maybe it's nothing, but does the color-coding you used mean anything? The cottage you said will be Annie's is red, Kit's is orange . . . by the way, did you know Kit's favorite color is orange?"

"Based on her hair color," Owen said. "I'd have guessed that."

"As a matter of fact, the colors do mean something," Julie said. "I was going to save my proposal for the outside colors to be used on the cottages until later, but we can get into that now if you like."

"Sure," Jackie said. "Does this mean Annie's cottage will be red and Kit's orange? That would be a *lot* of orange."

Julie laughed. "Don't worry. I didn't take it that far. I was thinking these could be accent colors, with all the cottages being a bright white. We could use these colors on things like front doors, maybe even shutters or window boxes, depending on what you all prefer."

Jackie and Lynette both gave the proposal some thought.

"We thought white would give it all a level of cohesiveness, while the pops of color could provide some differentiation."

Julie appreciated Owen's clarifying comment. It helped to know he had her back if she missed something important.

Then Jackie leaned closer and pointed to the purple cottage on the other end. "Is this one mine?"

"It is," Julie said, wondering whether Jackie had just made a lucky guess, or if she'd caught on to where Julie's inspiration for the colors had originated.

"But your favorite color is green, not purple," Lynette said.

Jackie nodded. "I know, but the blue undertones in my skin wash me out if I don't get the right shade of green. That's why I wore purple to our senior prom. The dress shop didn't have any green gowns that worked for me."

"No way," Lynette whispered. "This navy one is mine, then, right? Renee and Owen wore yellow, but since she isn't buying a cottage, will this one be Wendy's?"

Julie still found it strange that Owen took her mom to prom. "Yep, that's Wendy's."

Jackie laughed. "I can't *believe* you thought to take the color of dresses we wore to prom as the basis of your color scheme! You used the photograph I sent home with you for your mom, didn't you?"

Julie grinned. "I did. I thought about calling each of you to talk about your favorite colors, but then I figured you must have liked the colors of your dresses or you wouldn't have picked them. We can always change these, but I thought it was a fun place to start."

"Well, color me impressed," Jackie joked. "I think we follow. Now, show us the individual cottage blueprints."

Owen pulled the weights off, rolled up the first map, then presented Jackie and Lynette with their blueprints. Each cottage would be a little different, and he took the lead in walking them through the more detailed drawings. Julie was still learning her way around blueprints.

An hour later, she could tell Jackie and Lynette were approaching the point of information overload. A rainstorm had moved through while they were looking over the blueprints.

"I think that's probably enough for today. We'll wait until we have a sunnier day to go back and look at the actual lot sizes. They've marked them off. But do either of you have any other overarching questions we might answer right now?"

Owen stood and stretched.

"I have one," Jackie said. "When can we expect to move in?"

"We're still shooting for early next spring," he said, dropping his arms. "But you both know things like weather and material availability could change that."

Lynette nodded. "I think we all have some flexibility in that regard. Spring sounds like the perfect time for a fresh start, side by side with our besties."

Julie loved the sound of that. "The one thing we are more comfortable about planning is a day next summer for the grand opening celebration. We're thinking July eighth. It's a Saturday. Do either of you know of any conflicts with that date?"

Neither could think of anything.

"That's right around the time we always came here for summer camp. The first half of the summer was for girls at camp, then the boys would come during the second half," Jackie explained.

"Seems like the boys will invade our space this time, too. Some things never change, do they?" Lynette smiled. "How do you want to celebrate?"

"We'd include everyone's families, and hope that most people could make it," Julie said. "We'd cater in some great food, and we thought some games of some sort might be fun, but that's as far as we've gotten. Do you have any ideas?"

"There used to be an old softball field, just past the last of the cabins," Lynette said. "Is that still there?"

"It is," Owen said. "It's overgrown and would need to be cleaned up, but we don't have any immediate plans to develop that portion of the property."

"We should totally play a big game of softball!" Lynette said. "Like we did out here when we were kids. Remember how we first met Kit on the softball diamond?"

"Well, that's where *you* met her," Jackie said. "Before that, I caught her snooping through our cabin."

The way the two women laughed, Julie suspected it must be an inside joke.

"Softball it is then," Owen said. A phone rang back in his office.

"And that's my next appointment. Ladies, thanks for letting us walk you through all this, and I'll swing by your mom's place this evening, Jackie."

He hurried out of the room to catch the phone, and Julie began gathering up the rest of the blueprints.

"Hey, Jackie, wasn't that the same game where you got your first period? Kit and Wendy came to your rescue that day." Lynette slapped her leg as if she'd just said the funniest thing imaginable.

Jackie threw a pencil at her. "Shut up, Lynette. Some things are best forgotten."

Lynette easily deflected the pencil. "At least I didn't mention that tidbit in front of Owen. You can thank me now."

Julie slid the blueprints into protective tubes while the two women continued to reminisce about their long-ago days at camp. It was easy for Julie to imagine the countless shenanigans the Kaleidoscope Girls would conjure up in the future, when they all lived side by side. She suddenly worried that her mother would have so much fun when she came here to visit her old friends that she'd never leave.

Chapter Thirty-One

J ACKIE MOANED OVER THE delicious forkful of her mother's famous mashed potatoes.

Charlotte laughed. "I'm happy to hear I haven't lost my touch! It's so hot in Arizona right now that we eat more salads than comfort food."

Jackie swallowed. "I wish Mack had made the trip back with you. I miss her. How do you think she's doing?"

Her mother helped herself to another sliver of roast beef and an extra scoop of peas. "Mackenzie is fine, honey. Still trying to find a more professional job, but her two part-time gigs provide her with enough income to keep up with her student loans and car insurance."

"Mom, you can't let her live with you, rent free, indefinitely."

"Why not? *You* are." Charlotte raised an eyebrow to emphasize her point.

Jackie pushed back from the table before she could give in to the temptation to eat a second helping of potatoes. It was amazing how much easier it was to stick to healthier eating habits, now that a man she loved often saw her naked. She took her plate to the sink, then spun back to face her mother.

"That isn't exactly true, Mom. I may not be paying you in cash, but ever since Dad died, and you headed South, I've been pouring plenty of sweat equity into this place. It's a big house, and the wear and tear is showing. Besides, I offered to pay you once my lease was up in Minneapolis."

Charlotte pushed the peas around her plate. "I know, I know. I'm just teasing you. Besides, you're already paying rent for that storage unit for your things. Seems we're both still in a transition phase, doesn't it? But back to Mackenzie. I suspect that once she feels more financially stable, she'll get a place of her own. She's made a couple friends, and they're already talking about renting an apartment together down the road."

Jackie missed both her daughters terribly, but she didn't want to be the type of mother who tried to hold them back from living their own lives. Her parents had never done that, and she wanted to give the girls that same sense of freedom, now that they were young adults. Even when she feared the moves they were making were too risky.

She rinsed the dishes, put what she could in the dishwasher, and filled the sink with soap and water to clean the rest by hand. Her mother brought her plate over, too, and together they made quick work of the messy kitchen.

"Feels like old times, doesn't it?" Jackie said. She spied the two dog bowls, empty now, and piled those in the dishwasher as well. Nikki and Hoover were off somewhere in the house, now that their favorite activity—eating—was over until tomorrow.

Charlotte sighed. "Yes . . . and no. In a way it's good to be back, but it also reinforces some decisions I've been making lately."

Jackie had been expecting this conversation ever since her mother had returned from Arizona that first time, for Lynette and Storm's wedding. "Why don't we go out to the front porch to talk? It's a lovely evening."

"I'll grab a bottle of wine," Charlotte said. "You bring the glasses."

The mention of wine made Jackie wonder just what decisions her mother had been contemplating. She suspected it was something more important than repainting the yellow in the kitchen that she'd always despised.

Once they were settled on the porch with wine in hand and dogs at their feet, Jackie jumped right into the deep end.

"Have you finally decided to sell the house, Mom?"

"I have. And I appreciate the work you've already done to clear out some of the *stuff* we've accumulated over the years. Especially your father's things. I couldn't face that task, and I'm sorry to have burdened you with it."

Jackie sipped her wine, realizing how her feelings around that particular task had evolved. "It's all right, Mom. Really. At first I hated the idea of going through Dad's things, and I was mad at you for putting it on me. But once I got going, I realized it was a helpful way for me to process my grief. I still miss him, every day, but it hurts a little less than it did. Besides, I had help. First Kit helped me pull that rummage sale together, then Owen saved me from practically giving away so many of Dad's hobby-related things."

Hoover sat up, barked, then laid her head back down on Charlotte's right foot. "Hoover might be slowing down, but she still has ears like a bat."

"She's not much *bigger* than a bat," Jackie pointed out.

Charlotte laughed. "Thanks for reminding me about the tackle. I need to thank Owen for the check he sent. It came in handy."

Jackie set her wineglass down. "Mom, are you having some money troubles?"

"Who isn't these days?" Charlotte raised her glass to emphasize the point. "Seriously, hon, I'm fine. But I hit a bit of a snag today regarding this place."

"What do you mean?"

"The foundation. It needs to be reinforced—replaced, even—in the northwest corner of the house. Your dad knew it needed work, but we didn't get around to it before he got sick. Lots of houses in this area are having foundation issues."

Why hadn't her parents mentioned this to her when it first came to their attention?

Probably because she was off in Chicago, and then Minneapolis, living her own life.

"I know Lynette had to pour a ton of money into fixing the foundation over at her place," she said. "I wish you would have told me."

Charlotte shrugged. "What, and have you deal with it like everything else? It's been weighing on me, knowing that each year it was getting a little worse, so I had someone come over and look at it for me today. He confirmed what I already knew. He's willing to do the job, but he's booked out for another month and isn't sure the weather will allow him to get it all done yet this winter."

Jackie thrummed her fingers on the wicker armrest. "Is it absolutely necessary to fix it before you sell?"

"I believe so. I discussed the situation with a friend of mine who sells real estate—she's one of the best in town—and she thought I'd come out ahead financially that way, despite the cost of the repairs."

"Can you afford it?" She wasn't privy to her mother's financial records, and she wasn't in the best place to potentially help her mother out, either, but she'd do what she could. She'd ask Ron to help, too.

But Charlotte nodded. "I can make it work. You need to trust me on this."

"But the topic seems to have you upset. What am I missing?"

Charlotte snorted. "You'll think I'm being foolish."

"Try me."

Her mother pushed to her feet, disrupting Hoover's nap. She walked to the screen and motioned toward the front lawn. "The contractor told me today that all the vegetation around the foundation would need to be removed. Jackie, I've spent *years* tending to my bulbs and bushes. They'll ruin it all, and it breaks my heart."

Jackie knew how important her mother's flowers and garden were to her, even though she'd done little to care for them since her husband had died. She sipped her wine and considered the problem.

Then an idea sprung to mind.

"You know, today I went with Lynette out to our old summer camp land. Owen and Julie walked us through their plans for the development of it, including the cottages."

Charlotte turned to face her daughter. "I love the idea of you living near your girlfriends. That sounds so lovely! If only I was lucky enough to have friends like that. Have they started building yet?"

Jackie finished the wine in her glass and set it down. Then she stood and headed for the screen door at the top of the stairs. "Mom, let's look at your plants."

"Why? I already feel terrible about the state they're in because of my neglect, and now I'm sad because they'll be destroyed."

"Maybe not." Jackie pushed open the door. "Come on. I have an idea. Put the dogs in the house, please, then meet me over by your peonies."

A minute later, Charlotte joined her on the grass. Autumn had arrived, and the peony bushes looked spent.

"When is the best time to transplant these, Mom?"

"The peonies?"

Jackie shook her head. "All of it. Well, maybe not the regular, run-of-the-mill bushes, but any of the flowering plants you love so much."

Charlotte got down on her knees. "Fall is the best time to transplant peonies. After they go dormant—like this—but before the ground freezes. You cut them back, dig them up with care, then get them straight into the ground at their new location."

Jackie made her way to one of the two front corners of her mother's house. "What about these tall flowers? They are gladioluses, right?"

Charlotte grunted as she struggled back to her feet. "Right. Those grow from bulbs in the summer. Some bulbs sprout and flower earlier in the spring. Jackie, are you thinking about transplanting some of these? But where would you replant them? You said your new place won't be ready until next spring."

The sound of a car pulling into the driveway captured Jackie's attention.

She loved the way her heart still skipped a beat whenever Owen arrived.

Charlotte glanced his way, but her attention went right back to her flowers. "It was a good idea, though. I wish it would have worked."

Owen climbed out of his car and jogged over to the two women. "What are you two up to?"

Jackie motioned toward her mother's plants and the house's foundation. "Mom got bad news on her foundation today. It needs to be repaired."

He cringed. "That seems to be a common theme. I've been keeping a close eye on mine, too, and I'm worried it might need some work. I hope neither of us has as much trouble as Lynette did with *her* foundation."

Charlotte nodded. "And they'll trample my plants, ruining them when they start work. Jackie was just quizzing me about the possibility of relocating some of these, but I don't think it'll work."

Owen squatted down. "Why not? They're perennials, right? My mom used to say fall was the best time to dig up bulbs if you wanted to divide them. Wouldn't this be similar?"

"Digging them up would be the easy part," Charlotte said. "We could take them out, but where would we put them?"

"I'd love to use these to give me a head start on my landscaping at the cottage," Jackie said.

"And we could probably store the summer flowering bulbs in a cool, dry place until next spring," Charlotte said. "But the spring-flowering bulbs and these peony bushes would have to be replanted yet this fall. The bulbs need to be in the ground over the winter in order to bloom in the spring."

"And there's no way you could plant anything in the ground surrounding your new cottage, Jackie. Not yet, at least. The foundation hasn't even been dug."

But she didn't want to give up on her idea. "A simple solution for one of the peony bushes would be to transplant it next to Dad's headstone, where we buried his urn. I think that would look nice."

She thought her mother paled at the suggestion, but she didn't verbally object.

Owen nodded. "But that would only be one or two . . ."

"What if we replanted the rest of the peonies and the spring bulbs somewhere else on your land, Owen? Mom, could we plant them somewhere on a temporary basis, and then move them again when my cottage is done?"

Charlotte considered this. "I doubt they'd all survive, but some might, which would be better than nothing."

Jackie turned to Owen. "What if I dug these up now and put them in the ground around one of the old cabins, or your new offices, before the ground freezes?"

He smiled. "Why not try? As Charlotte says, it would be better than nothing."

The relief on her mother's face brought a smile to Jackie's.

"That would be so wonderful, honey. Thank you."

She hugged her mother. "Mom, sometimes it's the little things that make all the difference. And this way, when you travel back here to see me in the summer, you can say hello to your favorite plants, too."

Charlotte, complaining about mosquitoes, headed back inside.

Owen took a few steps back and checked out the front of Charlotte's house. "I can't imagine someone else living here."

"It's taken me time to get used to the idea, too," Jackie said. "But I suspected Mom would decide to sell, even before she confirmed as much to me tonight."

The two stood there for a minute, contemplating the changes to come. The air was warm and still, but the humidity remained high after the earlier rain shower.

"I could use a walk, and I know Nikki could, too. Interested?" she asked.

He nodded. "Very. I spent too much time behind my desk today. Why don't you go grab the dog? I'll switch my shoes."

She hurried inside and found Nikki's leash on the hook by the front door. Both dogs came running, and she quickly realized Hoover wouldn't want to be left out. "Mom, where's Hoover's leash? We're taking them for a walk."

Owen laughed when she rejoined him with both dogs in tow.

They walked in silence for a block, enjoying the beautiful summer evening. A few people were outside, puttering in their yards or stretching their legs. The scent of burning leaves perfumed the air, and geese honked high above, already heading for a warmer climate ahead of the upcoming winter.

"I saw Adam's car out at the camp today, but I didn't see him. How is he doing?" she asked.

He nodded, part of his attention on preventing Hoover from getting herself tangled either in her leash or between Nikki's much longer legs. "He attempted to clean up some of the leaves out there today."

Jackie had been wanting to ask Owen about where things stood with his house, but he didn't seem to pick up on the openings she provided. She'd need to be more direct. "Have the two of you talked any more about whether he still wants to buy you out?"

Conceding to the lack of leash-walking skill the smaller dog possessed, Owen scooped Hoover up and tucked her under his arm. When Jackie shot him a look of disapproval, he shrugged. "What? She's going to hurt herself."

"She's getting fat," Jackie countered. "She needs exercise."

Owen patted his flat stomach. "Don't we all."

She sighed. "I feel like you're avoiding the subject of your house."

He kicked a stick that lay across the sidewalk, then picked it up in his free hand. "I probably am."

Nikki stopped and squatted. Jackie was glad she'd grabbed a roll of pet waste bags.

"Why?" she asked, after she'd cleaned up after her dog.

"Because. Adam still wants to buy my old house. Once he does, I'll feel like an interloper, staying there. I know he envisions some updates, and then getting started on a family of his own to live in it."

Jackie laughed, despite the pebble of doubt lodged near her heart at the thought of Owen possibly living out East on a more regular basis. "Is he even dating anyone?"

Owen grinned. "No, but can I tell you a secret? Promise to keep it to yourself."

Jackie had to yank back on Nikki's leash when the border collie tried to go make friends with another dog tied up in someone's yard. "Why, Owen, do you have gossip to share?" she said after she got the dog back under control.

"I do . . ."

Hoover spied the other dog then, and let loose with a round of barking, but none of the other dogs paid her any attention, as she was still tucked safely under Owen's arm.

"Spill. I'm a *vault* with secrets."

He laughed. "Okay, well . . . Adam has a crush on Julie, but she doesn't seem to feel the same."

"*Our* Julie?"

"Well, technically Renee's Julie, but yes. You hadn't guessed as much?"

Jackie shook her head. "No! The only thing Julie ever said to me about

Adam was how rude she was to him when she first met him. I think she felt bad. But I rarely see them around each other. He must be a little older than she is, right?"

"Yes, but not by that much. I feel bad for the guy. Like father, like son, I guess."

Jackie pulled up short, much to Nikki's dismay. "What's that supposed to mean?"

Owen stopped, too. "You know what it means, Jackie. I've had a thing for you since we were kids, but after we got to junior high, you barely gave me the time of day."

"Well, I know, but . . . that was before," she spluttered. Her own foolishness through the years didn't sit well with her now.

He gave her a warm smile. "I know things are different now. But I doubt Adam wants to wait decades for Julie. He isn't as patient as I am."

She sidled closer to him and stole a kiss, not caring if the guy buzzing by them on a bicycle noticed. "I appreciate your patience. Maybe I could do some matchmaking. Julie isn't dumb. Adam would be quite the catch. He's a doctor, for crying out loud, and almost as handsome as his father."

Owen put Hoover down and wrapped an arm around Jackie as they walked. "Flattery will get you everywhere," he said, giving her a squeeze.

The time suddenly felt perfect to ask him the question she'd been losing sleep over lately. "Owen, when my cottage is ready . . . would you ever consider moving in with me?"

There was the slightest hesitation in his step, but he continued on, his arm still solidly around her waist. "Are you sure that's what you want? Because it was just a few hours ago that you and Lynette joked about men invading your space out at your old summer camp. I know she was joking about Storm, but I'm a guy, too, last time I checked."

"No kidding," she laughed. "But yes, I'm very sure. I was just waiting for the right time to mention it. Am I going too fast? Is that a level of commitment you aren't ready for yet?"

He shook his head. "Hell, Jackie, I'd marry you tomorrow if I thought that was what you wanted, but I suspect you like things as they are between us right now. We're still getting to know each other."

He was right. Lynette might jump quickly into marriage with her old flame, but life had made Jackie more cautious. "The only thing I don't like about us right now are the nights when we're apart."

"All right, then. I appreciate the offer, and my answer is yes. I'd love to move in with you when your cottage is ready. But I'm not a freeloader. Should we buy it together?"

She shook her head. "I haven't even thought that far ahead. Of course, I know you aren't a freeloader—that goes without saying. All I want to know right now is that we're both ready to move ahead in this relation- ship. And it sounds like we agree."

He dropped a kiss on Jackie's lips, then released her so he could pick up Hoover again. The dog's stubby legs had to move three times as fast as Nikki's to keep up, and she was at risk of tripping over her tongue with all the panting.

Jackie's phone rang in her back pocket, and she recognized the ring tone. "Oh good, that's Hailey! It's been almost a week since I last talked to her. Mind if I take this?"

"Of course not," Owen said. "Go ahead."

But the moment she said hello, she knew something was wrong. She could barely understand her daughter through the sound of gulping tears. She tried to calm the girl for nearly five minutes before Hailey hurriedly said goodbye, promising to call again later that night.

"That didn't sound good from this end," Owen said, glancing at her with concern.

Jackie didn't answer him immediately. The things Hailey had said between the waves of tears had her mind reeling. She had to fight the urge to run home, pack a bag, and catch the next flight to Reno. Owen could surely get her to the airport in Minneapolis as quickly as possible.

But that was exactly what Hailey had begged her not to do.

Finally, she realized he was still waiting for an answer. She laughed, but this time there was no humor in the sound. "My little cottage is getting crowded all of a sudden. That was Hailey. She asked if she could move home."

Epilogue

A WAVE OF DÉJÀ vu hit Jackie when she spied Annie and Kit making their way over to the refurbished softball diamond, reminding her of Kit's first game with them as kids.

Now Kit carried a large cardboard box, while Annie flung her arms around as if sharing an exciting story. They weren't yet close enough for Jackie to hear their conversation.

Jackie had the balls and bats ready to go for both teams, thanks to Annie's access to the used sports equipment at the high school. There was a pile of old softball mitts for anyone who might not have their own. She'd even thought to pull a first-aid kit together at the last minute, using her flamingo-covered bag from Fiji, in case someone needed a bandage or wrap.

She plopped down on a wooden bench to wait for her friends. It was the same bench where she'd cheered on her teammates during those special days of camp. A protective overhang used to shield the bench and ball players from the summer sun, but now only the benches remained to delineate each dugout. The bleachers behind home plate were gone, too, but Julie had set up collapsible camp chairs for today's spectators.

"I can't believe he's here!" she heard Annie say to a red-faced Kit, still carrying the large box.

Jackie ran over to help. "You can't believe *who's* here? Let me help you with that, Kit. What's in the box?"

Kit didn't argue, and sighed in relief once Jackie had hold of the box. "No idea. Wendy caught me when she pulled up in her big Suburban and asked me to bring it over here for her."

The box was taped shut; otherwise, Jackie would have peeked inside.

"Was her sister, Stella, with her?" Jackie asked.

Annie grinned. "Yes! They're excited to coach the teams today, just like they did when we were kids. They even took the roster and split everyone between two teams and assigned positions."

It was Jackie's turn to feel relief. She'd worried that would still need to be done once the rest of their family and friends arrived. Wendy's prep work meant they could start playing right away.

"And you'll never guess who else was with Wendy and Stella," Annie said as Jackie dropped the box on the nearest dugout bench.

Jackie shrugged. "Is it . . . Scott? You know, the cute guy camp counselor we met out here when we were kids and Wendy reconnected with a few years ago? She hasn't said much about him lately, and I didn't want to ask."

This gave Annie pause. "You're right . . . I wonder if they're still an item. But no! You're close, though—this is someone else that was out here when we went to camp."

Jackie was out of ideas and fiddled with the edge of the tape, still curious what might be inside.

Treats?

"Just tell her!" Kit said. "She's obviously not into guessing games today."

"Fine," Annie said, tossing her hands up. "It's Pratt!"

Jackie forgot about the tape and mystery box. "Pratt? Oh, wow . . . how can he still be alive? Wasn't he old when he was in charge of the camp counselors?"

Kit laughed. "He just told me he's seventy-six years old and still umping games for a local slow-pitch men's league in Ruby Shores. That would have put him in his mid-thirties when we were kids. Which I suppose seemed old back then."

Jackie couldn't believe Pratt was here. "I didn't think Wendy kept in touch with him. She never seemed to like him when he was her boss, even though she tried to hide it."

"Stella kept in touch. When she heard about today's game, she knew he'd love to take part. Just like old times," Annie said. "And speaking of old times—or maybe *old-timers*—here come some of the guys now. It looks like Renee and Lynette are with them, too."

It wasn't long before everyone, including Wendy, Stella, and Pratt, arrived at the field to play what would hopefully be the first annual Diamond Camp softball game. The camp used to be called Camp Barefoot, but bare feet didn't hold the same universal appeal as diamonds.

It surprised Jackie when George and Lavonne, Renee's parents, showed up to watch.

"We had to see what Julie was up to over here in Ruby Shores," George said, waving at his granddaughter when Jackie greeted them both.

Kit's grandmother, Hazel, along with Annie's son-in-law and granddaughter, Daniel and Nora, filled more of the spectator chairs.

A shrill whistle cut through the air, and Wendy waved her arms to get everyone's attention. It wasn't easy, but eventually people quieted enough for her to speak.

"Hi, everybody! Thanks for coming out to play a little friendly game of softball on this beautiful summer afternoon!"

Kit snorted. "Friendly? Who are you kidding? Jackie will be sure to keep things competitive!"

Offended, Jackie plunked both hands on her hips. "I am not that competitive," she insisted.

Owen, standing next to her now, reached over and tickled her under her arms. "Since when?"

The shriek of another whistle shut them up, and Jackie noticed Pratt was holding a red whistle in his mouth. She'd have sworn it looked exactly like the one he'd used to corral them as kids.

"I can already see that keeping this hodgepodge mix of players focused on the game is going to be nearly impossible," their old ump complained. "Reminds me of when you ladies were all snot-nosed little kids."

This man used to intimidate most of the camp kids, but Jackie had always looked beyond his gruff exterior. She knew he was having as much fun as everyone else.

The whistle also reminded her of another fun day, last year in Fiji, when the captain called them back onto the catamaran for more island exploring and that delicious buffet lunch. Later that same day, Annie's life had shattered.

So much had happened in the year since that trip.

Wendy laughed, pulling Jackie's attention back to the game. "We better get to it then. Stella, do you have team rosters?"

"I do," said the other woman standing beside her sister, holding up a clipboard. Jackie hadn't run into Stella for years, but she didn't seem to have changed much.

"Great," Wendy continued, taking the list from Stella. "Let's make this quick. Here's the deal. We've assigned teams, positions, and batting order. We put a lot of thought into this, and no one can switch or make changes without our approval. Questions?"

Stella smirked. "She might be stretching the truth a little. We printed out the list of names Julie emailed her and made all the assignments during our ten-minute drive over this morning."

Pratt rolled his eyes and tapped at his wristwatch.

"And without further ado, here we go," Wendy said. "Hey, Stella, open the box, will you?"

Stella pulled out a pocketknife and split the tape in two. "We've got shirts for everybody!"

Annie jumped up and down with excitement. "Finally! We never got team shirts when we were kids. I never thought that was fair!"

Jackie met Lynette's eye, and they burst into laughter.

"Annie, you were always the eternal optimist, trying to make life fair for everyone," Lynette said. Turning to Jackie, she lowered her voice. "Isn't it great to see Annie so happy? What a difference a year can make."

Wendy cleared her throat. "Julie gave us size estimates for everybody, so when I call your name, Stella will fish your shirt out for you. And remember, no switching teams or positions. Let's start with the Kaleidoscope team! Stella will coach you. Now, pay attention so we can whip through this quickly. I'll call out your names based on your batting number in the lineup. Colton, shortstop; Hailey, third; Matt, right field; Lynette, you'll be in center; Dean, we put you out in left; Adam, you'll be on the mound; Isaac, catch for him; Robbie, we hear first is where you rock; Phoenix, play in between first and second base as the rover; and last but not least, Jackie, you are on second."

Ten people crowded around Stella as she tossed out orange T-shirts. Jackie caught hers midair and grinned at the bright image of a kaleidoscope on the front. When she flipped it around, she loved seeing HOWE across the top with a bold number seven below it.

"This is great!" she yelled. "Is this from our cabin number, Wendy?"

Wendy shot her a big grin. Stella, it turned out, had been wrong about the time that had gone into preparing for this game.

"All right, does everyone on the Kaleidoscope team have a shirt and remember their position on the field? Don't worry about remembering the batting order. We'll keep you straight on that."

Kit held her mitt high in the air. "What's the name of *our* team, Wendy?"

Jackie laughed. Kit was as impatient as ever.

"How about the Monarchs?" Wendy yelled back, and Stella pulled out a black shirt with a big, orange monarch butterfly on the front.

"That's perfect!" Kit shouted back.

"We thought you'd approve. Here are the positions for my Monarch team!" Wendy referenced her clipboard again. "And we'll kick things off with you Kit, on third."

Jackie nodded. "Kit was always great on third. I can't believe you remembered that, Wendy."

Wendy grinned at her again. "Renee, you're out in left field; Julie, second base; Storm, right; Relic, you'll catch for your sister, Ava, who I know from watching her play ponytail league can pitch a wicked fastball."

Jackie watched as Annie's oldest and youngest high-fived each other.

"Owen, your height will serve us well on first," Wendy went on. "Annie, I remembered you like shortstop; Shane, we thought you'd have fun playing center field, next to your big brother."

Shane grinned and pointed at Storm, who returned the gesture.

"Any questions?" Wendy asked. "Stella, did everyone get a shirt?"

"Everyone but you and me, sis," Stella said, tossing a black T-shirt to her.

Shane raised a tentative hand.

Wendy noticed him. "Yes, Shane. What's up?"

"I have a special request . . ."

Wendy glanced at Storm, as if worried Shane might ask to switch things up after she'd specifically said they couldn't.

"Can I sing the national anthem for everybody?"

Wendy's surprise was obvious, but she'd heard Shane sing at Lynette and Storm's wedding. "Can you sing it without the instrumental?"

He nodded.

Jackie glanced over at Storm and Lynette. Their grins warmed her heart.

"Everyone, take off your hats, please," Storm said, before nodding at his brother.

Shane cleared his throat, spread his feet a little wider, and clasped his hands behind his back. When he sang, everyone went still.

Jackie listened in amazement. Lynette had mentioned how Shane was thriving at his new group home. Storm had worried about his brother for months after enrolling him in the music-focused program, but it seemed to Jackie that it had been the perfect choice.

When the last notes faded away, everyone cheered and donned their caps again, and Pratt gave a quick puff into his whistle. "Let's play ball! We'll play five innings. It's too damn hot to play any more than that."

Stella's Kaleidoscopes had first ups, but Ava got things moving quickly with that wicked fastball Wendy had mentioned by striking out the first three batters—Colton, Hailey, and Matt—one, two, three.

Feeling slightly humiliated for her humbled teammates, Jackie grabbed her mitt and ran out to second, doing her best to get everyone fired up to face the Monarchs. "Come on, guys, we got this! We got this! Don't let Ava show you up, Adam!"

Adam tossed a softball to Jackie. "She set the bar pretty high. I'm not sure I can keep up with that!"

Jackie grinned. She'd forgotten how good Annie's daughter was on the softball field. Despite Kit's and Owen's earlier teasing about her competitive nature, all she really wanted to get out of today's game was a fun time for everyone.

"Balls in!" Pratt yelled, motioning for Kit to enter the batter's box.

Kit swung the bat in a circle a time or two before settling it on her shoulder. Grandma Hazel yelled her encouragement from the sidelines. Jackie loved how that woman was always there for Kit—when Kit was a young girl, deserted by her parents, and even now that she's a grown woman.

Kit swung and missed Adam's first pitch. "Just getting the rust out!" she yelled, holding a hand out toward the pitching mound while she adjusted her feet.

She let the next two balls thump into Isaac's catcher's mitt, waiting for the perfect pitch.

"Two and one," Pratt announced.

Kit still had a little wiggle room with one strike and two balls.

But, impatient as she was, she swung up and hard at the next pitch, even though it was coming in low. She connected, but the ball popped high into the air, heading straight for her husband in left field.

When he made an easy catch of it, Kit stuck her bottom lip out and pointed toward the outfield. "You're on the couch tonight, buddy!"

Laughter rippled across the field. Jackie loved to see the comradeship building.

Adam's pitching was accurate, but not as fast as Ava's, and Renee got ahold of one, slamming it right past her son on first base for the first double of the game.

Jackie stood just behind her friend on base. "That's okay, Robbie, that's okay. Don't feel bad about your old mom sneaking one by you like that!"

Robbie shook his head at her. "Jackie, cut the smack talk. We're on the same team!"

Renee laughed. "Us old ladies have to stick together!"

Adam looked over his shoulder. "Renee, can your daughter hit a softball?"

Both Jackie and Renee grinned. Ava wasn't the only daughter of a Kaleidoscope Girl who knew her way around a softball diamond.

Renee shrugged. "I guess you'll just have to find out. Pitch the ball already."

Adam might have underestimated Julie, because the ball came in flat. Julie swung hard, and the line drive screamed toward him, smacking him square in the nose. By some miracle, he bobbled the ball but then caught it, holding it up in his mitt.

Jackie spied the horror on Julie's face before she noticed blood dripping onto the sand at Adam's feet.

Renee was quick to respond, rushing forward to the young man's aid.

"Somebody grab my flamingo bag!" Jackie yelled.

Julie spun back toward the fence and scooped up the bag. Jackie had mentioned the kit to her earlier, but she doubted Julie ever imagined she'd be the one to hurt another player.

As Julie rushed forward to help, Jackie couldn't help but wonder if this would quell Adam's interest in the young woman. He was crouched down and pinching the bridge of his nose while Renee hovered above him. Julie fell to her knees in front of Adam.

"Mom! Get back! I've got this!"

Renee raised her palms, and Jackie could about imagine what she was thinking, being pushed aside like that. Julie's mom, still concerned, walked slowly backward toward second base.

When she was back on the bag, Jackie bumped her with her shoulder. "Jeez, Mom, get out of here," Jackie whined, mimicking a bossy daughter voice she herself knew all too well. "I've already been blowing off this handsome doctor's advances for months, and now I probably broke his nose. I should be the one to clean him up."

But Renee didn't seem to pay Jackie any attention, watching as Julie helped Adam to his feet and held a wad of gauze against his still-gushing nose.

"Are you going to be all right, son?" Owen yelled from the Monarchs' bench.

Adam waved a bloody hand at his dad. "I'll be fine. I don't think it's broken."

Jackie noticed Grandma Hazel push clumsily out of her chair to stand and walk toward the fence behind home plate, concern etched into her features. "Do you have that trusty doctor bag of yours close by, Adam? I can go fetch it for you!"

This brought a round of laughter from many, and it helped dissipate the tension that always surfaced with a hurt player on the field. Hazel's comment reminded Jackie of the night Adam had rushed forward with said "doctor bag" to help the elderly woman after a tornado nearly leveled her home.

Julie was walking Adam off the field, keeping one arm around his waist. "You guys keep playing. I'm going to take him to my apartment for some ice."

Stella checked on her player as he came off the field, then hustled out to the mound. "Anyone else on my team able to get a softball across the plate? We're going to need a new pitcher."

When no one responded, Kit got off the bench and walked out to the plate, pointing to Dean in the outfield. "My hubby is shy. He actually pitches in his old man beer league back home."

Stella pointed both hands toward left field. "Come on, man, we need you! Phoenix, I'm going to send you out to take Dean's place. We can function without a rover."

Jackie caught Renee watching her daughter as she led Adam back for that ice.

"I wonder if she'll finally get up the nerve to tell him how she really feels," Renee said.

Pratt blew his handy-dandy whistle again as he wiped sweat from his brow.

"Wait. What did you say, Renee?" Jackie whispered, not caring that Storm was heading for the batter's box.

Renee sighed. "Don't tell Julie I told you . . . but she has a huge crush on Adam."

"She does?!"

"Well, don't look so surprised. He seems like a great guy. He's handsome—at least when his face isn't all bloody—and he's mature. What's not to like?"

Jackie smiled. "And points for being a doctor."

"Right. But he's also Owen's son, and he works out here some. She doesn't want to screw things up professionally."

Storm didn't move a muscle with Dean's first pitch.

Renee looked closer at Jackie. "Why does your face look so funny?"

Jackie held her glove under her chin. "Same face my momma gave me. What's funny about it?"

Renee narrowed her eyes at Jackie. "Do you know something you aren't telling me?"

Dean threw a second pitch, and Storm swung and missed. The catcalls were ramping up.

Jackie gave a quick nod. "I do. But you can't tell anyone. Owen said Adam really likes Julie, but he thought the feelings weren't reciprocated. He even said, and I quote, 'like father, like son.' I don't have to tell you how bad *that* made me feel."

Renee threw her head back and laughed. "Well, if the two of them don't figure each other out over a bag of ice, you and I may need to do a little matchmaking."

Jackie grinned. "Count me in."

The crack of the bat pulled their attention back to home plate, and they both watched Storm's pop fly sail toward Matt in right field for an easy catch.

"What the hell!" Storm yelled. "Why is it you can't catch a damn fish, Blatso, but you can catch a softball like that?"

Jackie loved the proud look in Renee's eyes when she sent Matt a thumbs-up, even though he'd ended the inning and left her stranded on second. "That's my man!"

Pratt blew his whistle again. "That puts us at the top of the second. Score zero, zero. Lord help us all."

The bats got hotter during the second inning. Two Kaleidoscope runners got on base, Ava struck one out, and then Robbie stepped up to bat.

Jackie knew Robbie had played a lot of baseball as a kid, and the Monarchs didn't have anyone covering second because Julie was still with Adam. Annie tried to cover both short and second. She grinned when she saw Renee shift out in left field to provide Annie with more backup. She hoped it wouldn't be enough. The Kaleidoscopes needed to get some scores up.

Crack!

Robbie connected with Ava's well-thrown pitch, and they all watched as the ball sailed clear out into the backside of center field, well behind Shane. All three runners made it around the bases, and the Kaleidoscopes were on top, at least for the time being.

The Monarchs couldn't match them run for run, but Ava also slammed out a home run, bringing in Relic, and the inning wrapped up at a score of three to two.

Julie and Adam returned at the top of the third inning. Adam grabbed an empty lawn chair next to Hazel while holding a bag of ice against his face. He wouldn't be returning to the game, but Julie ran out to cover her position on second again.

Since Jackie had popped out for their third out in the second inning, they started off the third at the beginning of the lineup again. Colton was first up, and when Ava's first pitch came in unusually slow and high, he only caught a piece of it. The softball dribbled past his sister, but Ava made no effort to stop it. Owen rushed forward from first base to grab the ball. Ava, finally in motion, headed for the sidelines. She barely made it beyond the baseline before bending over and throwing up everything she'd eaten at the barbecue before the game.

Everyone froze—aside from Colton, who jogged to first, careful to avoid the mess but unsure how else to respond.

Ava straightened, and though Jackie thought she looked a little green, she was smiling. "Sorry, guys! I guess the term '*morning* sickness' shouldn't be taken too literally. Wendy, I'm out. Put Relic in for me. He's got a great arm."

Jackie ran from the bench over to Annie at short and swung her friend up and around, whooping with joy. "You're going to be a grandma again?!"

Annie laughed and struggled against Jackie's arms. "Sure am. But I wanted to let Ava and Daniel tell everyone. I doubt this was the way they'd hoped to share their good news, but there you have it!"

Pratt gave three long blows into his whistle, fighting to maintain control. "Wendy! Make your lineup shifts and let's keep moving!"

Wendy ran out onto the field. "Congrats on the baby news, Ava! Relic, you heard your sister. Get on the mound. Annie, can you catch for your boy? We'll just have to operate with the shortstop position open."

Jackie released Annie so she could run back to home plate.

"I can cover if my knees don't complain too much," Annie said, crouching down in front of Pratt when Hailey stepped into the batter's box.

Getting no chance to warm up his pitching arm, Relic wasn't as tough from the mound as his sister, and the hits started flying.

By the end of the third inning, the teams were all tied up. The Kaleidoscopes squeaked out one run and held the Monarchs in the fourth.

Relic's pitching had improved with each batter, and in the fifth and final inning he'd only allowed one run to come in by the time his big brother got up to bat. He'd already struck out Isaac and Phoenix, but there were three runners on base. If Colton got a good hit, it would be that much tougher for the Monarchs to catch them with their last at-bats.

"Come on, little brother, lob one in here, nice and easy," Colton taunted Relic. "Make my job simple."

"In your dreams, bro," Relic said. He wound up and hummed one right past Colton.

Colton swung so hard at the second pitch, Jackie was afraid he might fall over from the effort.

"Two strikes!" Pratt announced.

Annie pounded the catcher's mitt, giving her youngest a target to aim for. Jackie wondered how many times Annie had played like this with both Relic and Colton through the years. Ava, too.

When the pitch came, Colton was ready. He got a solid hit, and it sailed toward Shane in center field. Jackie held her breath, torn between hoping at least some runners could score for her team while also wanting to see Shane make a big catch.

The ball seemed to hang for an extra second in the sky, then dropped back toward Earth, and Shane hurried forward at a perfect pace, easily catching the ball.

Jackie decided the smiles all around were worth so much more than a couple extra runs would have been.

Pratt blew his whistle yet again. "Let's wrap this thing up, folks. Bottom of the fifth. Kaleidoscopes are up by two. Monarchs, you need two runs to tie, three to win. And before anyone asks, there will be no tie-breakers today. I need a beer. Play ball!"

The Kaleidoscopes hustled out to their positions in the field. Owen slapped out a nice hit for a double. Annie followed that up with another double. Owen advanced to third base. Shane batted third, and Dean finally managed to strike someone out, though he looked slightly ashamed to sit Shane down. Shane, however, didn't seem to care. He was still smiling about his amazing catch.

But then Dean struck Kit out, and the Monarchs' chances of pulling off a win dimmed, while also solidifying Dean's spot on the couch for that night.

Annie practically danced on second base, looking like her nerves might get the best of her.

"Hey, Annie," Lynette yelled from behind her in center field. "Weren't you the last runner during that big game we played at camp? You know, the first day we ever met Kit? And if I remember right, you couldn't run fast enough and got tagged out, losing the game for us. Is history going to repeat itself today?"

Annie flipped her off, but laughed. "Not if *I* can help it!"

Renee approached the batter's box. Never one to give up easily, she ignored the potential agony of defeat and stayed focused on the task at hand, tapping out a single that allowed Owen to run home.

The Monarchs were only down one.

Julie, batter number six of the inning for the Monarchs, stepped into the batter's box, and Dean made a show of covering his nose.

"Ha-ha, old man," Julie mocked. "Show me what ya got!"

Dean was tired after some rough innings, and his pitch wasn't hard to hit. Julie lobbed the ball over her brother's head on first and dashed for the base. Robbie, determining that he couldn't beat her back there, threw hard at Jackie on second.

Jackie braced for it, but Robbie had a strong arm, and she bobbled the throw as Renee ran hard toward her. Renee saw her drop the ball and, not even slowing down, she rounded second and raced for third base.

Annie, on the other hand, had slowed, assuming she'd get no farther than third. When she saw Renee barreling toward her, she screeched and turned on the burners, barely able to stay ahead of her longer-legged friend.

Jackie, already flustered by her error, heard the commotion and, instead of throwing to Hailey on third, picked Isaac for her target at home. The throw fell short, and chaos erupted as first Annie and then Renee got tangled up at home plate with poor Isaac, who never got control of the poorly thrown ball.

Once the dust settled, Pratt declared the final score to be Wendy's Monarchs eight and Stella's Kaleidoscopes seven.

Jackie collapsed onto her back near second base.

"Mom!" Hailey screamed at her. "I was wide open on third. I could have got either one of them!"

Someone skidded to a stop above her, and Jackie opened one eye far enough to see it was Owen. "You okay?"

She rolled to her side and sat up with her knees in the air and her mitt dangling between her legs.

"Because if you're pouting, I'll just leave you to it. But if you're hurt, I'll help you up," he said, crouching next to her.

Holding up her right hand, she grinned at the man who still looked a little like that young boy she used to call her best friend. "I'm neither. I probably won't be able to get out of bed in the morning, but wasn't that fun? This game was the perfect celebration, wasn't it? We found out Annie is going to be a grandma again. Shane caught that ball and everyone loved it. What more could we ask for?"

Owen grabbed her hand and yanked her easily to her tired feet. He dropped a hard kiss on her mouth, then playfully smacked the brim of her cap down. "And here I worried you were about to play the 'sore loser' card."

She pulled her cap off and kissed him back.

"Julie said there's beer and wine, along with snacks, for everyone back in your old mess hall," he said, holding an arm out for her. "Shall we? It looks like people are heading that way."

Jackie looped her arm through his and walked off the field where she'd spent so many happy hours as a young girl.

She smiled when she noticed Hailey talking with Colton up ahead. They laughed about something, and Jackie welcomed the sound after the awful pain of her daughter's first heartbreak. Maybe Julie had been right about Colton's interest in Hailey, but Jackie vowed to give them the space to figure things out on their own.

When Jackie and Owen reached the path leading back to the main heart of the development, she squeezed his arm. "Are you happy with how this all turned out?"

He grinned down at her as they walked. "It was fun to be part of the winning team. I just wish Logan could have made it back for the game. My youngest was a hell of a baseball player when he was a kid. He'd have loved this, and you could have used him on your team."

"We sure could have used him," she agreed. She knew that while Owen enjoyed having Adam around, he missed his youngest when work kept the young man away for months on end.

But her initial question about his happiness encompassed more than today's game, and she suspected he understood that. When she waited for him to say more, he stopped and pulled her into his arms.

"I couldn't be happier, Jackie. I've probably never told you this, but I used to be jealous when you'd leave each summer to come here—to camp—and I couldn't come with you."

She nodded. "Boys didn't come to the camp until the second half of the summer."

He laughed. "But now I get to hang out with you here, every day, and help you water the ridiculous number of bulbs and peony bushes you dragged over here from your folks' place."

Jackie let her gaze roam over toward Cabin 7, where her mother's prized flowers were flourishing. Charlotte would love to see how they were thriving when she and Mack came for their visit next month.

"I'm so thankful to have a piece of home here. Maybe I won't chance replanting them again. I could start some new cuttings to use over at the cottage instead."

Owen shrugged. "I'll leave that up to you. But we've each replanted *ourselves* a few times, and I feel like we're both still thriving."

"I agree," she laughed.

"Now, if we want to get a beer or any of the food before it's gone, we better get over there. I don't know how much Julie ordered."

Jackie stepped out of Owen's arms, but grabbed his hand, and together they walked toward the mess hall and all of their family and friends.

"Speaking of Julie, Renee let it slip today that her daughter actually thinks Adam is pretty great, too."

Owen swung their joined hands, laughing as they walked. "I picked up on that today when she rushed to his aid. And I stand corrected.

Maybe Adam will be smarter than his old man and not wait so long for the woman of his dreams."

Jackie pulled their hands up so she could twirl beneath them, laughing. "Owen, I think we should just accept that things work out when they're supposed to. I started out life with you as my very best friend in the entire world, and now we get the chance to be something even better than friends."

He gave her a second spin. "But what about the Kaleidoscope Girls? I thought *they* were your best friends. And aren't the five of you supposed to take a trip together every year? What do you have planned for this year?"

"We talked about Alaska, but since Renee's Robbie didn't end up going back there this summer, that's out. But we don't really mind."

"Oh, yeah? Why's that?"

Jackie released his hand, held both of hers high, and executed one last spin, as if capturing the essence of everything around them. "Because, Owen, you silly goose, we're back at summer camp."

Author's Notes

I hope you enjoyed **Life with Friends**, the final book (for now) in my **The Kaleidoscope Girls** series! Parasailing in Fiji is on my personal bucket list (minus the broken wrist). My fascination with the islands began with a bottle of Fiji branded water as inspiration. When Renee visited Fiji after losing her job in **Whispering Pines** (Book 1 in my **Gift of Whispering Pines** series), it was a bold, almost reckless choice, but sometimes life demands we follow our hearts over our heads.

My decision to have Annie lose Henry in this book wasn't one I made lightly. As a couple, they'd overcome challenges and were in a stronger place than ever. But Annie's journey has always been about her search for fairness in a world that doesn't always deliver it. I've heard from many widows who find strength in their female friendships, and that's exactly what I wanted for Annie. If this story reminds even one reader to lean on friends during life's hardest moments, I'll have done my job.

Including more romance in this book was fun for me. I loved exploring how Lynette and Storm, as well as Jackie and Owen, could build deep, fulfilling relationships as romantic couples later in life. Lynette found her second chance with her first love, while Jackie found new love with her best friend from junior high. While tempted to allow the exes, Annie and Michael, to find their way back to each other following

Henry's death, I didn't feel the timing was right. Both need time to heal. All five women are in different places in their romantic relationships, yet their friendship remains the steady anchor that helps guide them through.

Life with Friends brings **The Kaleidoscope Girls** series full circle. While I might return with a novella at some point, right now I'm excited to dive into a new series that I've named **Seasons on Silvermist Lake**. Set in Minnesota lake country, this series will bring together many things I love: seasoned characters facing real-life challenges, a close-knit family with complex ties, hidden secrets, and fresh starts.

Lakeside living offers me endless inspiration for setting and story ideas. A lake can be as simple as a place for fun filled, sun-drenched days. But on a dark and misty night, one might wonder what lurks in the lake's mysterious depths. **Seasons on Silvermist Lake** will explore the changing seasons of life, from rebirth to rest, and celebration to renewal. Silvermist speaks of timelessness, nostalgia, and legacy—all things I love to explore with you.

This series will celebrate the ebb and flow of the seasons and the people who embrace them, beginning in 2025 with ***Echoes of Summertime*** and ***When Leaves Fall***. I can't wait to introduce you to this new family, with all their dreams and heartaches, set against a backdrop of peaceful, lakeside beauty. But first, I need to get to know them myself. Stay tuned!

You can find more about my books and upcoming releases on my website at www.kimberlydiedeauthor.com, where you can also sign up for my newsletter. It's the best way to stay updated on new books, behind-the-scenes glimpses, and more.

Thank you for being part of this journey. Writing for you and with you in mind makes every story worthwhile.

THANK YOU!

Dear Reader,

I would like to thank you for taking the time to read *Life with Friends*. I am so grateful you selected it and I hope you enjoyed this fifth book in my **The Kaleidoscope Girls** series.

If you don't mind taking a few more minutes with this book, I'd appreciate it if you would leave a review. Reviews are extremely helpful and much appreciated.

For links to all of my books and to sign up for my newsletter, please visit my website at www.kimberlydiedeauthor.com.

Wishing you my very best,
Kimberly

PREVIEW ECHOES OF SUMMERTIME

BOOK ONE

On the shores of Silvermist Lake, each change of season reveals secrets and old wounds, but the enduring strength of family offers the promise of healing and new beginnings.

It's been thirty years since Gigi last experienced the tranquil beauty of Silvermist Lake. Now, she's back for the summer, hoping the peaceful shores will ease the burdens she's grown too weary to carry alone. Her feisty Aunt Pearl, who has always called Silvermist home, welcomes her with open arms. Pearl knows the lake offers more than just healing—it holds the power to rekindle the vibrant spirit Gigi lost to past heartbreak.

As Gigi and Pearl grow closer, they rediscover cherished memories and embrace new joys. Together, they'll confront dark family secrets, release lingering sorrows, and let go of unspoken regrets. Against a backdrop of misty mornings and sunlit afternoons, they'll find laughter and resilience in each other's company. And perhaps, with Pearl's gentle encouragement, Gigi will find the courage to open her heart to love again.

Join Kimberly Diede in *Echoes of Summertime*, her first book in the **Seasons on Silvermist Lake** series, for a heartfelt journey through Minnesota lake country—a story of renewal, forgiveness, and the profound strength we find in family.

Watch Kimberly Diede's website for updates on this 2025 release and more!

https://www.kimberlydiedeauthor.com

ALSO BY KIMBERLY DIEDE

THE KALEIDOSCOPE GIRLS SERIES
BETTER WITH FRIENDS (BOOK 1)
SUNSHINE AND FRIENDS (BOOK 2)
FIVE GOLDEN FRIENDS (BOOK 3)
GIFT OF FRIENDS (BOOK 4)
LIFE WITH FRIENDS (BOOK 5)

GIFT OF WHISPERING PINES SERIES
WHISPERING PINES (BOOK 1)
TANGLED BEGINNINGS (BOOK 2)
REBUILDING HOME (BOOK 3)
CAPTURING WISHES (BOOK 4)
CHOOSING AGAIN (BOOK 5)
CELIA'S GIFTS (BOOK 6)
CELIA'S LEGACY (BOOK 7)

About Kimberly Diede

 Kimberly Diede writes contemporary novels that weave together family, friends, hope, and romance. She writes family sagas, suspense, and women's fiction that you'll find hard to put down. She truly believes we are never too old for second chances in life.

Kimberly enjoys spending the short months of her Midwest summers on the lakeshores of Minnesota and North Dakota. Nothing beats writing and hanging out with family and friends at their cabin. Her love of tradition and all things vintage comes through in her decorating and her stories.

Be sure to follow Kimberly on social media to catch glimpses of the junk she drags home to repurpose and to get updates on her latest books.

Website: https://www.kimberlydiedeauthor.com/

Facebook: https://www.facebook.com/KimberlyDiedeAuthor/

Instagram: https://www.instagram.com/kimberlydiedeauthor/

BookBub: https://www.bookbub.com/authors/kimberly-diede

www.ingramcontent.com/pod-product-compliance
Lightning Source LLC
Chambersburg PA
CBHW061105310726
48974CB00002B/402